HOUSE OF ROUGH DIAMONDS

HOUSE OF ROUGH DIAMONDS

Book 3 of Over Where

JANE LINDSKOLD

BAEN

A Baen Books Original

Baen Publishing Enterprises
P.O. Box 1403
Riverdale, NY 10471
www.baen.com

ISBN: 978-1-9821-9289-1

Cover art by Tom Kidd

First printing, September 2023

Distributed by Simon & Schuster
1230 Avenue of the Americas
New York, NY 10020

Library of Congress Cataloging-in-Publication Data

Names: Lindskold, Jane M., author.
Title: House of rough diamonds / Jane Lindskold.
Description: Riverdale, NY : Baen Publishing Enterprises, [2023] | Series:
    Over where ; 3
Identifiers: LCCN 2023020384 (print) | LCCN 2023020385 (ebook) | ISBN
    9781982192891 (trade paperback) | ISBN 9781625799326 (ebook)
Subjects: LCGFT: Fantasy fiction. | Novels.
Classification: LCC PS3562.I51248 H68 2023 (print) | LCC PS3562.I51248
    (ebook) | DDC 813/.54—dc23/eng/20230508
LC record available at https://lccn.loc.gov/2023020384
LC ebook record available at https://lccn.loc.gov/2023020385

Printed in the United States of America

10 9 8 7 6 5 4 3 2 1

❦ DEDICATION ❧

For Jim, who knows what makes a house a home.

❧ACKNOWLEDGMENTS❧

House of Rough Diamonds was going to be a very different book, with a very different title. Then several upheavals disrupted my personal landscape and I realized that there was another story that I wanted to tell instead.

I'd like to thank Paul Dellinger, Julie Bartel, and Jim Moore, who not only served as first readers for the manuscript, but also encouraged me as I changed my focus.

Once the book was completed, Toni Weisskopf at Baen gave it a home, assuring that the story of Over Where begun in *Library of the Sapphire Wind* and *Aurora Borealis Bridge* would continue. Tom Kidd painted the lovely cover, as well as indulging me with some fun discussions of how he evokes movement.

I am also grateful to Scott Pearson for his thoughtful copyediting, and to Joy Freeman for helping me as I worked my way through the production process.

Finally, thanks to all of you who have joined me Over Where.

HOUSE OF ROUGH DIAMONDS

❧[CHAPTER ONE]❧

Three humans sat around the table in the sky sailer *Slicewind*'s lounge, sipping poffee and waiting to go into action.

"Do you think Grace'll recognize us?" Peg asked anxiously, pausing to check her knitting pattern before setting a marker and continuing.

"It's a little late to wonder about that," Meg replied with deceptive mildness. "We'll be to Grace's Mesa fairly soon. I suspect our companions would not take lightly being asked to turn around at this point. After all, you were extremely eloquent when you explained why we needed to rescue a monster—and sooner, rather than later."

"I suppose I was," Peg admitted, "and I still believe we're doing the right thing. But what if she doesn't recognize us?"

Meg opened her journal, tapping with the end of her pen as she counted off the days. "It's been a bit over a week since we were last there. Vereez assures us that oothynn are quite intelligent."

"I'm sure they are, I guess," Peg said. She lowered her voice. "I'll admit, I wasn't just eloquent on Grace's behalf. We hadn't been back at the Library very long before, even with all the remodeling work to keep people busy, tensions started rising. I thought we'd better get some of the group away from there and let things simmer down."

Teg smiled to herself, thinking how much better she understood each of her friends than she had when she, Meg, and Peg first met. That had been when their local bookstore, Pagearean Books, had announced that it was founding a book club. All three women had shown up for the organizational meeting and had continued to attend thereafter. Before long, they often went out for lunch after to continue the discussion.

Initially, Teg had been a little intimidated by Meg, for Margaret Blake, a recently retired librarian in her seventies, was the sort of person who could hush a noisy group of preschoolers with a glance. Very fair, neither tall nor short, slender, quietly elegant, even in casual clothing, Ms. Blake had immediately demonstrated a vast familiarity with a wide range of written works and, through them, with history, science, and even with Teg's own field of anthropology. Meg was a widow, with a grown son and daughter. Her blue eyes, fading now to a pale sky hue, rarely missed anything that went on around her, but Meg often kept her observations to herself, as if the habit of library quiet had become ingrained, even outside of work.

Ebullient Peg Gallegos—who had immediately asked if she could call Margaret "Meg," and had been very happy to be told that Ms. Blake preferred this form of address—was in many ways Meg's opposite. Of Spanish and Irish descent, Peg looked as if she had magically kept the summer tan common to southern California, where she had lived until moving to Taima, Pennsylvania, to be nearer to her son, Diego, and several grandkids. Peg's eyes were a green-brown hazel. Her dark brown hair was artistically streaked, not so much to hide the grey as to turn it into a statement.

Thrice married, thrice divorced, Peg hadn't so much chosen not to have a career, as she had taken on marriage and child-rearing with an almost terrifying enthusiasm. Raising her kids, stepkids, and various friends of her kids had been an excuse to learn something new or take on a new hobby, so that, although in her sixties, Peg seemed not very different from the enthusiastic, idealistic young hippy who had run off to "find herself" in Haight-Ashbury in her early teens.

Teg—as Tessa Brown had been dubbed by her book club friends—was the only one of the trio who was still working, although this year she was on sabbatical from her position as an archeology professor at Taima University. She was also the only one of the three never to have married—or even to have been in a serious relationship. Teg had always felt she had good reason for this, having been the child of a marriage that had ended in an acrimonious divorce, leaving as its only legacy a quiet, self-contained child who, finding she fit in nowhere, gave up trying and focused instead on her career.

Teg was the shortest of the three, and the stockiest, this last a legacy of having done a lot of hard physical labor from her childhood on. Her skin was brown, her features reflecting a heritage that blended pretty much all the races of the world. Trying to discover where she "fit" had been what had drawn young Tessa Brown to anthropology; fascination with what she had learned made her truly happy in her career.

And yet now, Teg thought, *I've come to suspect that I'm as much of a "holdback" as the three young people who summoned us Over Where to help resolve their issues. Well, now, at least I have people who will be willing—heck, eager—to help me figure out what I want to do with the personal side of my life.*

She was sure of this, for the adventures she, Meg, and Peg had shared in the past few weeks—well, whether you said "weeks" or "months" had a lot to do with which world you were in—had bonded them as closely as family.

Closer, Teg thought, *since I'm not in the least close to my bio family, nor is Meg. But if I could have chosen sisters, these two would be at the top of my list.*

A melodious baritone voice broke into their discussion, just as Meg seemed on the verge of speaking.

"If I can interrupt your no doubt brilliant speculations," said Grunwold, poking his head down the hatch from the main deck, "we're coming up on Grace's Mesa."

Slicewind's captain was a tall young man in his early twenties. It said something about how accustomed to Over Where Teg had become that she no longer saw his stag's head as any more notable than she did physical characteristics that set her two human friends apart from each other.

In this, Teg realized she'd come to embrace the way people Over Where viewed each other. Although the head was the most immediately visible of the animal traits, and the tail the second, the natural coloration of the animal extended to the human-style body that began somewhere in the vicinity of the neck, as a gradual transition rather than a line. Hands clearly showed this blending of traits, with those types that were "hoof stock," like Grunwold, having thicker, heavier nails than the average human, while those whose animal type had claws had sharper, pointier nails that, in some cases, even retracted.

For all his abrupt, often rude manner of speech, Grunwold was probably the kindest of the three young people who had initially summoned Meg, Peg, and Teg to the world Peg had dubbed "Over Where."

Grunwold went on, "Peg, last time we came here, you handled *Slicewind*'s wheel when we went through the vortex. I was wondering if you'd stand by, just in case I have any trouble with the winds."

"Sure," Peg said, tucking her omnipresent knitting away before rising and retrieving a jacket from the pegs on the portside wall, preparatory to following him above decks. "Given your rapport with *Slicewind*, I'm sure you'll be able to read the air currents just fine but . . ."

Her voice trailed away as she clambered onto the upper deck.

"Is it my imagination," Teg said to Meg after the pair were safely out of earshot, "or is Grunwold more careful about *Slicewind* now that he's on the way to owning the ship? Sort of like the kid who's careless about the family car, but hovers over his first junker like it's made from gold and diamonds?"

"Not your imagination," Meg agreed, "although I think that Grunwold's additional care has as much to do with the realization that he and *Slicewind* share a mystic bond, than that he may be its sole owner in the not-too-distant future. Although it's possible that Grunwold could develop a similar rapport with another sky sailer, the process might take him as many years as he's already invested in *Slicewind*. He started working with her when he was hardly tall enough to handle the wheel."

"I was a little surprised when Konnel didn't just give Grunwold the ship," Teg mused, "given that Grunwold basically saved Konnel's life, but this rent-to-own agreement is much better."

"For both of them," Meg agreed, "since Grunwold can appeal to his father for financial aid if *Slicewind* has some unexpected maintenance issue. I suspect that a large part of Grunwold's care for the ship is that he doesn't want to ask for help. Shall we go above and see if we're needed at our posts?"

"Sure," Teg said, dropping her pipe into a pocket of the tunic she was wearing over sturdy trousers of local make. "At the very least, we can cheer the others on. I need to use the head. I'll follow you up."

"Put my book in the cabin?" Meg asked. "I'll rinse and rack the poffee bowls."

"Sure, and thanks."

Teg accepted Meg's much-loved hardcover of *The Wind in the Willows* and headed for the stern cabin she shared with the other two humans. The tidy space had doubtless been intended for Grunwold's parents, Konnel and Sefit, since there was only one bed, about the size of the standard full-sized. Since one of the humans still routinely shared a watch, all three of them were rarely in the cabin at the same time. When they were, it could get a little crowded, but they'd adapted.

After all, both Meg and Peg shared space with husbands and kids. As for me, compared to some of the field camps I've lived in, Slicewind's accommodations are positively roomy—and as a bonus, there's a real toilet and shower.

Teg tucked Meg's book into the appropriate portion of the many-pocketed storage bag that hung on the cabin wall. It was of local manufacture, but Peg's design, an adaptation of the shoe bags back in their own world. Teg could practically hear Peg's perky explanation as she tacked the storage bag onto the cabin wall.

"I got the idea from something my Tabitha came up with for her kids. So much easier for them to stash their smaller things and find them again."

As a self-described "mother-of-many," Peg had somehow retained an infinite capacity to include in-laws, stepkids, stepgrandkids, and other, harder to define relations in her life. Nonetheless, she had been interested, even eager, to continue visiting Over Where after they'd finished assisting their inquisitors to reach solutions to their various inquisitions.

So here we are, getting ready to rescue a monster, mostly because Peg's heart is big enough to take in a walking pipe organ with crab claws. I just hope Grace has gotten over her sinus infection. That was seriously disgusting.

When Teg came on deck, *Slicewind* was sailing above heavy cloud cover through which occasional mountain peaks showed like islands in a sea of cottony white. In the middle distance, the clouds were shaped something like a whirlpool. She leaned against the starboard rail, enjoying the purposeful bustle, which reminded her more than a little of one of her field crews getting ready to leave for a project site.

Grunwold and Peg were consulting by the wheel. Peg's right hand moved in a series of decreasing circles, so she was probably describing the air currents. Apparently eager to take part in the discussion, Grunwold's pet xuxu, Heru, soared down from his perch on the mast to land on the captain's shoulder. Heru somewhat resembled a raven-sized pterodactyl, although Teg devoutly hoped that Heru's eye-searing combination of lime-green upper and violent-orange underbody had not disturbed what she liked to imagine as the tranquil skies of prehistoric Earth.

Over near the port rail, lion-headed Xerak and fox-headed Vereez were admiring the lift harness that Kaj—who had the head of an African painted dog—had designed and sewn. The dynamic between the three of them was peculiar, but not for the reasons that a new arrival from Teg's world might have thought.

A new arrival would be wondering about all these different heads— as well as skin colors, fur, and tails. Wondering if these were different tribes or groupings, whether ostensibly herbivorous Grunwold would be worried at being on the same ship with all these apparent carnivores. I remember trying to figure all of that out. Instead, this dynamic is one of those "tensions" Peg was talking about.

Soft-voiced, Meg said, "The three of them seem to be getting along fairly well. I think Vereez might even be mooning less over Kaj. I'm less sure about Xerak, though. He's rebounding badly from being rejected, yet again, by Uten Kekui. I hope he doesn't set his heart on another unattainable fellow."

"I was having similar thoughts," Teg admitted. "I don't think Uten Kekui so much rejected Xerak 'again,' as that even the heroic measures Xerak went to in order to find his master didn't change Uten Kekui's view of Xerak as much as it should have done. For all he praised Xerak's determination . . ."

She trailed off, partly because she was aware how acute the hearing of their four local companions was, and because she didn't want to risk being overheard criticizing Uten Kekui before his adoring apprentice, as Xerak still seemed to consider himself. Meg, however, apparently either felt they were safely out of hearing or didn't care what Xerak overheard.

"Uten Kekui now, Dmen Qeres then, has/had an inflated view of his own importance. We're going to have trouble with that sense of entitlement before we can settle just who owns the Library of the Sapphire Wind. Perhaps we were unwise to bring Uten Kekui and Cerseru Kham there."

Teg nodded. Only a few days had passed since they had returned from the Roots of the World with the senior wizards, Uten Kekui and Cerseru Kham, augmenting their company. At that time, the Library had seemed the most logical place to go, but now she agreed that Meg had a point.

"But could we have kept them away?" Teg replied. "And, remember, for all its dangers and strangeness, the Library welcomes us as its saviors."

"True. By contrast, I'm not at all certain," Meg said tartly, "that the Library feels anything particularly welcoming toward either Uten Kekui or Dmen Qeres. There is the question of who actually owns the place. Maybe we should have resolved this before retrieving Grace."

Teg was about to reply when her attention was caught by something rising into the cloud-shrouded skies from one of the mountain peak "islands" off to starboard. She reached for her binoculars. Like many archeologists, she had acquired the habit of hanging numerous items from her belt: knife, compass, holster, trowel sheath, and the like, a habit she had adapted for her new life Over Where. In addition to getting rid of her cell phone case, since electronics didn't function here, Teg had substituted a small binocular case for the holster in which she'd carried a .22 loaded with snake shot. As with electronics, even primitive firearms didn't work in Over Where. Now she snapped the case open, extracted the binoculars, and put them to her eyes in one easy motion. What she saw made her adjust the focus, because she couldn't be seeing what she was seeing. However, sharpening the focus only clarified the improbable image.

At first, Teg had thought she was seeing distant hot air balloons. Even in the clarified image, there was definitely some similarity: the large, bulbous shape above, cables hanging down, a basket beneath.

But that was where similarities ended. The bulbous shape wasn't rounded; instead, it was plumply ovoid, closer to that of a zeppelin. Moreover, there was something very weird about the basket.

The others had noticed Teg's action and were now looking in the same direction. Grunwold had taken out a very nautical telescope. Trusting *Slicewind* to keep her course, he was now studying the approaching flotilla.

"Flight of the *Hindenburg*?" Peg said, groping in her jacket pocket for her own binoculars, and coming to stand next to Teg.

"Take a closer look," Teg replied. "No zeppelin has been flanked at the endpoints by wings. And there's something weird about those wings. They look like huge leaves, the sort of heart-shaped type."

"Are those bean leaves?" Peg said, sounding astonished. "My grandson, Timmy, grew beans for his kindergarten project. And the balloon's cables . . . those aren't cables. Those are vines! The balloon's basket is made from the vines, too."

Grunwold, son of a gentleman farmer, made a noise indicative of agreement. "Right the first time. Those are beti-teneh, which fall into the bean family. Don't you have them in your world?"

"No," responded the three humans in chorus.

"Okay," Grunwold said, using the English word. "Quick briefing then."

Grunwold hadn't lowered the telescope from his eye, and, as he spoke, he continued assessing the increasingly large flotilla. Teg counted at least three of the largest of the winged zeppelins, but there were smaller variations as well.

"And I'd better talk fast," Grunwold continued, "because I'll bet just about anything you want that we're about to be raided."

"Raided?" Vereez said sharply, her voice coming out closer to a fox's bark than to a spoken word.

"Sharp-eared as ever," Grunwold said, managing to sound laconic, though the way his large ears flickered back and forth indicated how nervous he actually was. "First thing you need to know about beti-teneh. They have three basic attacks: the vines are mobile and can entangle; the pods can shoot seeds; the interiors hold a really smelly gas."

Meg had pulled out her own binoculars and was studying the beti-teneh. "They seem to be different sizes. Is this some sort of herd?"

"Not precisely," Grunwold replied. "In nature, beti-teneh are rarely much larger than this." He drew a shape about the size of a golf ball in the air with the hand that wasn't holding the telescope. "But a long while back, some genius wizard got the idea of taking advantage of their natural ability to fly and created larger ones. The largest beti-teneh can actually carry a passenger or two."

"I thought I saw people in the baskets," Teg said, wanting to be wrong.

"You probably did. Good news is that the beti-teneh carrying passengers are going to be slower and less agile," Grunwold went on. "That's the reason they're usually escorted by the smaller version. Those serve as skirmishers. The idea is that while we're distracted dealing with the skirmishers, then the larger members of the fleet will move in, tangle the ship, and well . . . You get the idea."

"I count three of the larger bean balloons," Peg said, renaming the creatures as was her habit. The flexible translation spell that the humans had been gifted as part of their being summoned tended to adapt to these, which Teg's anthropologist's mindset found fascinating. "And then there are the ones about the size of a basketball, then some softball and baseball types, as well as the golf balls. Is it too much to hope that these bean balloons are as stupid as beans?"

"Far too much to hope," Xerak replied, coming to join Peg and Teg at the rail. He was trying for casual confidence, but Teg noticed that his hand remained firmly wrapped around his spear staff. "The wizards who enhanced the beti-teneh—according to my master's teaching, the process took numerous generations and a great deal of refinement of the basic concept—felt the beti-teneh would be useless if they could not understand basic commands. On average, they're about as smart as draft lizards."

"Not smart as xuxu," put in Heru, tooting a triumphant fanfare on his crest. "Not as smart, but many, many more than Heru. Heru cannot fight them all."

"And Heru won't need to," Grunwold assured him, stroking the xuxu along his back. "Those pirates don't know what they've taken on. They see a nice sleek cruising yacht, unarmed . . ."

He paused after the last word. Konnel's refusal to arm *Slicewind* until Grunwold had done enough jobs to offset the expense was a sore point with his son.

". . . and apparently defenseless."

"I doubt they will assume we're completely defenseless," Kaj countered somewhat diffidently, "given our destination. We're heading toward a major mana wellspring, and those are only of use to wizards."

"Point," Grunwold agreed, "but not all wizards are as adept at violence as Scraggly Mane over there, and Vereez has proven herself pretty good at magical fighting, too. With that in mind, Xerak, I'm going to put you in charge of attack. Will you need both Teg and Kaj?"

"Teg can assist Vereez," Xerak replied promptly. "I shouldn't need an assistant. I stored quite a bit of mana in my staff, just in case we needed magic to deal with Grace. If I run through that, and we stay close to the mesa, I might be able to tap one of the channels that feed the mana wellspring."

"Excellent," Grunwold said. "Kaj, I want you to join me in repelling boarders. That's certainly going to involve cutting vines, so let's get some machetes out. Peg, I'll turn the wheel over to you. Meg, it's a lot to ask given that we're dealing with aerial attackers, but can you take the crow's nest? I'll assign Heru to guard you."

"If I might borrow one of your lighter spears," Meg said, "and some pruning shears, if we have any such aboard, I would be delighted."

Each one of us, Teg thought, as she moved starboard with Vereez, *learned a great deal during our travels first to the Library of the Sapphire Wind, then to the Creator's Visage Isles, and finally to the Roots of the World. The most important lesson was how to trust each other. Not even two weeks ago, if you'd told Grunwold he'd be asking Kaj to fight alongside him, he would have scoffed.*

"Do those beti-teneh have any vulnerable points?" Vereez asked, only the flicking back of her sharp fox ears showing that she was at all nervous. "I've never had close contact with the magically enhanced type, only the natural seeds. How about those wings? They look fragile. I could target them."

Xerak coughed a very leonine laugh. "The wings do look fragile. By all rights they should be, since the originals were leaves, but the wizards who created the larger beti-teneh didn't overlook that vulnerability. The wings are more like leather than leaf and, sadly, fire resistant."

"*Sadly,*" Teg thought, *because your favorite fire spells are going to be of more limited use.* She touched the sun spider amulet which now rested in a neat little pocket on her belt. *I wonder if I can generate Spidey silk fast enough to catch something in the air?*

"Tough leaves," Vereez repeated. "Got it. Any suggestions, teacher?"

"We've been practicing with your summoning wind," Xerak replied. "See what you can do with that, but keep your channels tight or the overdraft could mess with Peg's ability to steer *Slicewind*. If you can push back the beti-teneh, even just slow them, I just had what might be a brilliant idea. However, it's going to mean borrowing Kaj from you, Grun."

"And I get to deal with any boarders all by my lonesome," Grunwold retorted dryly, not quite refusing to hand over his assistant. "Not that I don't appreciate your faith in me, but can you explain?"

"No time," Xerak said, his gaze getting that distant look that meant he was quite probably inventing a spell on the fly, "but if this works, you should be fine."

"Well, I did ask you to handle counterattack," Grunwold grumbled. "Take Kaj."

"Is it countering," Peg asked worriedly, "if we start before they do? I mean, will this make us the attackers, the pirates?"

"Don't worry about that," Xerak said, motioning for Kaj to join him. "I know that you've said that in your culture something happening 'like magic' usually means instantly, but both Vereez and I are going to need time to prepare. I think it's very likely that any doubts we have as to the intentions of the beti-teneh fleet will be resolved before then."

He turned his back and began to speak to Kaj in a low voice.

From where they stood looking at the advancing flotilla, Vereez spoke, pitching her voice so only Teg would hear. "Teg, promise me that you'll keep an eye on the beti-teneh while I focus. I don't think I could concentrate if I was worrying that something might start spitting seeds at me or flinging vines or whatever."

Teg nodded her understanding and patted Vereez on one shoulder. She'd spent many hours practicing both how to focus her mana and to feed it to others, but she still felt very vulnerable in the half-dream state she had to put herself into in order to do so. In Teg's more recent lessons, Xerak had insisted that she practice storing mana against emergencies.

"Face it," he'd quipped. "I don't look very good if you keep collapsing on me."

Xerak had said Teg was doing well, but as she watched the beiteneh rhythmically flap closer, she felt less confident than she had the first time she'd used the sun spider amulet.

Because then, she thought to herself, *I thought of the amulet more as a tool, like a cell phone or even a handgun. Now I realize that getting the best out of the amulet depends as much—maybe more—on me as on it.*

But Teg didn't mention her uncertainties to Vereez, only pulled the amulet out of its pouch, draped the cord on which she'd strung it around her wrist, and nestled the amulet into the palm of her left hand, saying as she did so, "You can count on me, Vereez. Get ready to blow up a storm."

In response, Vereez unsheathed one of the two magically enhanced, copper-bladed curved swords that served her much as Gandalf relied on his staff: not only as weapons, but as a focus for her magical ability, as well. "With those things flying at us," she explained, "I feel a lot better having a sword in hand. I'd like to have two, but I'll need a free hand for my fan."

In her left hand, Vereez held up a folding fan, the fabric of which was a deep golden brown that contrasted well with her fur. It was painted with images related to that most invisible element: ships with sails belled out, windmills turning, trees bending before the force of a gale, waves rising to crests.

"Xerak's had me use this to direct wind in our lessons," Vereez continued. "Much as I'd like to have both swords, I think this isn't the time to experiment."

"Good thinking," Xerak called from the other side of the deck, where he had apparently concluded his conference with Kaj. Next, he turned to Peg. "Peg, we're going to need you to keep *Slicewind* not only away from the raiders, but out of the vortex of winds that protects Grace's Mesa, without taking us too far away, in case I need to tap the mana. Can you do that?"

"Aye, aye," Peg replied perkily. "I wish we could lure the raiders into the vortex, but I guess that if they've staked out this area, they know it's there."

"Right," Xerak agreed, "and we can't rule out that they have a wizard or wizards among their number who have more practice than I do tapping the mana wellspring."

"Oh, joy," muttered Grunwold, pacing restlessly back and forth. "It's my ship at risk, and I feel completely useless."

"Take the helm for now," Peg suggested. "We can trade if close fighting is necessary."

Grunwold accepted her offer gratefully.

"I wonder," Peg mused aloud, "if I have time to go get a bandana to tie over my head, pirate style."

"If you're serious about doing that," Meg called down from the crow's nest, "you probably do. The flotilla is closing slowly, probably assessing us, just as we are them."

But when Peg came back from below, she wasn't just wearing a bandana tied pirate style. She was also wearing the light sword she'd used to good effect in a few prior battles. She had brought up Grunwold's long sword and took the wheel while he belted it on. Then, her hand lightly resting on the hilt of her sword, Peg moved to the starboard railing and joined the increasingly tense group watching the various-sized beti-teneh as they flapped closer.

"Good tactics on their side," Meg commented from above. "The beti-teneh aren't staying on one plane, but are moving in at various levels."

Heru gave a derisive honk. "Not worry, Meg. I watch you, so you watch them."

"Lots of the smaller bean balloons seem to be aiming for higher up," Teg added. "When they hit *Slicewind*, I think the attack's going to be from the top of the mast on down."

The raiders have done this before, Teg thought, *and since no one has reported them, I guess that means they left no survivors. Maybe they count on the rumors of the dreadful monster that guards the mana wellspring to take the blame for vanishing ships. Poor Grace.*

After what seemed like an interminable period of time, but was only about ten minutes by the mechanical watch Teg wore clipped to her belt, she became aware of a stirring in the air from where Vereez stood.

"Tighten your angle down," Teg suggested. "Remember, you don't want to interfere with the wind *Slicewind* is using."

"Right," Vereez said, adjusting the fan so that the wind she created went upward, as well as toward the approaching fleet. Since she was used to fighting two-handed, she was, if not precisely ambidextrous, more accustomed to working with her off-hand than many.

"Good," Teg said, checking through her binoculars. "I can see some of the lighter tendrils being blown around. You might be pushing back the smaller beti-teneh. If you can increase the wind's intensity?"

"I'll try," Vereez said. "It's harder to direct it then, but . . ."

She trailed off, sinking into concentration.

Teg tightened her fingers enough that the sun spider amulet bit into the skin of her palm. *Xerak said that if this amulet hadn't been damaged in the destruction of the Library, it might be able turn into an actual sun spider. I wonder what it would take to fix it? I'd love to be able to send a spider, or a herd of spiders, running up the sails right now.*

Out in the sea of clouds, Vereez's increasingly powerful gusts of wind were definitely making it harder for the smaller beti-teneh to approach, which was good, since these were the fastest moving. However, the gusts barely fluttered the leaf-wings of the basketball-sized bean balloons, and had no effect at all on the three large ones that carried the passengers. These had chosen to lose a bit of altitude, thereby avoiding the wind that targeted their smaller associates.

I hope that whatever Xerak has in mind will work against those big ones. If there are wizards among the raiders, that's where they're riding.

Teg turned to see what the boys were up to. They'd moved to the starboard rail, closer to the stern. Kaj was kneeling on one of the benches, which let him look over the side while bringing him down low enough that Xerak could stand behind him with his hands on his shoulders. Xerak held his spear staff in the crook of his right arm. Teg noted that the obsidian point at its head was glowing a deep grey. A matching deep grey thunderhead was growing with unnatural rapidity, rising from the puffy white clouds like some sort of demon castle.

I don't think it's just luck that a storm seems to be building right where it will be most inconvenient for the attackers, Teg thought gleefully. *Kaj has an affinity for water, sure, but I don't think he'd be able to do this without Xerak's direction.*

Her musings ended suddenly when a group of basketball-sized beti-teneh began flapping their leaf wings harder and raced toward *Slicewind.*

"Incoming!" Meg yelled from the crow's nest. "Five of the basketball-sized beti-teneh. I think they're using some sort of jet for additional speed."

Peg trotted across the deck to take the wheel from Grunwold, who relinquished control without hesitation. He glanced with concern over to where Xerak and Kaj remained nearly motionless.

"Teg, we've got to cover those two until they get their spell launched."

"Aye, aye, Captain," Teg replied.

She let the sun spider amulet drop to dangle at her wrist, removed one of the smaller boathooks from its clamps, then moved to take up a position to the right of the pair. Grunwold drew his longsword and positioned himself to the left.

Whoever was directing the beti-teneh had chosen their targets well. Three of the basketball-sized creatures headed toward Kaj and Xerak. Another began to rise, aiming for Meg in the crow's nest. The final one moved toward the gap between Vereez and Teg, possibly heading toward Peg at the wheel, or maybe intending to go after Vereez.

Usually, *Slicewind* seemed a little crowded with seven aboard but, at that moment, Teg would have been glad for twice the crew, no matter if they had to sleep in hammocks ranked into the British Navy regulation fourteen inches accorded to crew, something she'd learned from reading the rest of the Patrick O'Brian novels, after they'd read *Master and Commander* for the book club.

What would Jack Aubrey do? she asked herself inanely. *Say something about going right at them. Okay then.*

Teg swung the boathook, baseball bat style, at the nearest of the beti-teneh. The hardwood shaft impacted with a satisfying thump against the creature's somewhat rubbery body. If the bean balloon wasn't hit out of the park, at least it rocked back. Its left wing looked crumpled, too.

Teg couldn't stop to enjoy her little victory, because while she'd been walloping her target, another of the beti-teneh had flapped over the side. Turning somewhat awkwardly, she jogged off to intercept it. She wasn't certain if its target was Vereez or Peg, but she could put herself between it and Vereez, and give it fewer options. Peg, at least, had the wheelhouse for some cover.

Overhead, she heard Heru tooting and whistling. A green tentacle thumped to the deck on one side of her. Refusing to be distracted, Meg continued calling updates as calmly as she might have explained to someone about overdue book fees.

"Vereez, you're definitely keeping the smaller ones back. Keep the wind good and steady. Peg, start taking *Slicewind* up. The boys are building a storm, and we'll want to be above it when it breaks. Grunwold, the basketball you sliced in half is definitely out of action, but the one Teg hit is heading back."

Another tentacle, then a wing hit the deck, indicating that Heru and Meg were doing their part. At that point, Teg lost any sense of the larger conflict, because she had to focus on her own problems. The beti-teneh that had gotten over the rail was poking a few pod-laden tendrils in her direction. When she shoved at them with her boathook, the pods twisted, firing a small fusillade of beans. Most of these bounced off Teg's jacket, but a couple caught her in the face, hard enough to sting.

Teg said something very impolite she'd learned from a Tewa colleague, and swung again at the beti-teneh, this time aiming for the body. She missed all but a few leaves, but her near hit made it decide to go after Peg.

Peg might have her tidy little sword belted at her waist, but she needed both hands to handle *Slicewind*: one for the wheel, the other to handle the lever that controlled elevation. If Peg was distracted, the consequences might only mean wind dropped from the sails, but with the vortex so close by they could find themselves running on rough seas.

Teg swung again, this time trying to tangle her boathook into some of the sturdier tendrils. She succeeded, but rather than trying to pull away, the beti-teneh took advantage of this to grip Teg's boathook and begin methodically wrapping it in green. Teg started to wrest the boathook free, then had an inspiration. She waited until the beti-teneh had firmly anchored itself, then hauled back with both arms. She might be past her first youth, sure, but she'd done as much archeology in the field as she had in the classroom, and there was a lot of strength in her broad shoulders and stocky frame.

For its part, the beti-teneh was certainly stronger than one would expect from a bean with wings, but it had to be relatively light in order to fly. Teg jerked it back, hard, then swung her boathook to the side and slammed the bean balloon into the mast. The impact broke the central bean body, releasing an unpleasant-smelling gas that made her cough, but otherwise didn't seem to have any negative effect.

Teg had to hope that this beti-teneh wouldn't be up to much more, at least for a while, and moved as quickly as she could toward the starboard rail. En route, she encountered another of the basketball-sized beti-teneh crawling on the deck. Its wings had been shredded, and several major tendrils cut clean off. Using its remaining tendrils, it was creeping feebly along the deck toward Vereez, oozing guts and gas. Teg paused long enough to whomp the central bean with her boathook, heard it pop, and kept moving starboard.

Over near the stern, Xerak was now chanting something unintelligible, which Teg took as an indication that whatever spell he was working was nearing completion. Assisted by Heru, Grunwold was slicing into smaller, softball-sized beti-teneh. There were none larger in sight, which was a good sign, but victory was far from certain. The three largest beti-teneh were now close enough that Teg could make out that each basket carried a crew of two, one wizard-robed, and one aiming something like a crossbow, apparently waiting to get into range.

Worse, from the increasingly labored strokes of her fan, and the way she had let her curve-bladed sword drop to the deck, Vereez was clearly getting tired. If she had to let her wind abate, then they would be swarmed by the smaller beti-teneh, targets that Grunwold's sword would be much less effective against.

Dropping her boathook without a second thought, Teg flipped the sun spider amulet into her hand as she ran over to Vereez.

Okay, thingy, she said to it, *I've got you charged up. This time I need you to help me get hooks into Vereez, not into any enemy. Got it?*

She thought it did, because moments later, Teg felt a sharp prickling at the exposed skin of her wrist. She fought her first impulse, which was to slap at it, and instead wrapped both hands onto Vereez's neck, feeling how the silky fox fur of the younger woman's head grew less dense as the head merged into the more human torso.

"We're here with mana for you." Teg kept her voice soft, so as to not startle Vereez. "You should feel it in just a moment." As she finished speaking, Teg felt Vereez wince as the amulet dug some of its hook-ended legs into her skin.

Teg forced herself to relax and concentrate on directing the mana to Vereez. Closing her eyes was almost impossible to do, knowing that the most dangerous of their enemies was approaching, but Teg knew she had to shut out any distractions. Behind the darkness of her eyelids, she saw something not unlike the floaters that had started showing up in her twenties, but these drifting shapes were less random and had a slight glow to them, warm and somehow, although colorless, seeming silvery-goldy, shiny bright. She recognized this as the mana she had stored in the sun spider.

Pretty stuff, Teg thought. Then she tried not to think, just to reach out, to merge with Vereez, to make sure that some of the mana was directed where it would restore the reserves Vereez had drained, not just to fuel the spell. After all, fuel would do no good if Vereez collapsed and couldn't transform it. Teg sensed when the wind from Vereez's fan rose in intensity, and heard Meg's cheer.

"That pushed them back!"

The sound of the wind was muffled as Xerak's chanting rose toward a crescendo, deep and sonorous, just a little rough at the edges. As was usual when the young wizard vocalized a spell, the syllables were not translated. Nonetheless, the sounds were no less powerful, maybe even more so, like listening to someone singing in a foreign language. The air grew damp and slightly chilly. Then there was the rumble of not-so-distant thunder.

Teg couldn't help it. She had to peek, even if just for a moment. Out where the largest beti-teneh hung, rain mixed with hail pelted down in a silvery-grey curtain. Almost immediately, there came the odor of bruised vegetation, made slightly sickening by being mingled with whatever gas it was that the beti-teneh kept inside. Deeply satisfied, Teg let her eyelids drop.

Grunwold was calling Heru to him, then Xerak shouted

something holding the rasping gruffness of a lion's roar. The hail increased in force, and Teg felt Vereez letting her wind drop.

But stay with me, came the unspoken request. *If there is thunder, there are lightning shadows, and I want to make certain they are not turned against us.*

Teg understood. They'd encountered lightning shadows—oehen-serit—guarding the floating mountain that held the Roots of the World. The creatures weren't very smart, but they could be very dangerous. Worse, any that manifested in this storm would not be restricted by the wards as had the lightning shadows they'd encountered before.

Teg decided to sneak another look at what was happening. The storm that Xerak and Kaj had created was hovering over the three largest, and now seriously battered, beti-teneh. These were sinking down into the cloud field below, trailed by the remnants of their skirmisher flotilla. Rain was falling down in dark, almost solid sheets, reminding Teg of the virgas she'd seen when working in New Mexico: isolated rainstorms that dropped rain with incredible vigor over one small area.

The rumble of thunder was fading. Soon after, Vereez opened her eyes and sagged against the rail, almost dropping her fan over the side before she remembered to tuck it back into the sheath on her belt. Teg maintained the contact between them until she was certain Vereez wouldn't faint, then with wordless thanks she let the sun spider amulet know that they were done.

For now. We're going to need to recharge all you held. She felt her own knees sag, and she sank down onto the deck. *We're going to need to recharge me, too.*

She didn't faint that time, though, and felt proud of herself.

CHAPTER TWO

Despite what Xerak kept assuring them had been an amazing job of combined attack and defense—especially since of the four who had been using magic, only Vereez could even be considered a novice; Teg and Kaj weren't even that—the *Slicewind*'s crew had not escaped without injury.

Kaj and Xerak were the least injured, having been protected by Grunwold. Grunwold, however, had numerous shiny marks in the sleek hair of his stag's head where bean seeds had hit. Additionally, he had a nasty welt across the bridge of his nose where a tendril had wrapped around his muzzle before he'd chopped through its softball-sized source.

Although Teg had kept the basketball-sized beti-teneh from reaching Peg, several baseball-sized ones had jetted through the defenses when Teg had been diverted to help Vereez. Fortunately, most of these had seemed unable to tell the difference between the ship's pilot and the wheel. Nonetheless, a few had hit Peg hard enough that she'd been bruised even through her jacket. Vereez's injuries were mostly due to her having—as was typical for her—overdone, but Teg's intervention had kept her from collapsing.

In the aftermath of the battle, Teg was surprised to discover several nicks and cuts, including one at the edge of her right eyebrow that was trickling blood. When she saw Heru, though, she counted herself lucky. The xuxu's leathery green wings were scored with countless small nicks, and his tough hide showed evidence of numerous lashes and cuts. Based on his behavior, though, Heru felt that whatever injuries he had taken were balanced by his pride in having defended his companions.

After Heru, Meg was the most spectacularly battered of the lot, for despite Heru's gallant defense, and her own able use of pruning shears and spear, her delicate skin had been badly bruised by bean seeds released by the smallest beti-teneh.

"At least I was wearing a hat," Meg said, examining her bruises ruefully in her pocket mirror. "Even so, I look a horror. I hope Vereez has something in her box of ointments that will help these to fade more quickly. Otherwise, I may need to duck home and refill my supply of arnica gel."

As Vereez moved promptly to get a first-aid kit out of one of the stern bench lockers, her pointed ears flickered back. Much of what she knew about medications and ointments she had learned from her mother, Inehem. To say the two were "estranged" was an understatement. But for all that she could be very emotional, Vereez also had inherited a solid streak of practicality from her parents. Now she popped open the kit and pulled out a ceramic jar.

"Try this, Meg-toh. Just a little at first, to make certain you don't have a reaction."

"Thank you, dear," Meg said, dabbing ointment on a bruise on one side of her neck. "Your ointments often work so much better than mine, and I really don't think this is a good time for me to go home."

Xerak, who had been bolstering himself with a few pulls from his flask, made a grunt of agreement. "The mana wellspring might cause eddies that would interfere with your gate. If you can wait, that would be better."

"How long until we can continue our approach?" Peg asked.

"Let's make sure everyone is patched up, and has something in the way of refreshments," Grunwold said. "Xerak, are you too drunk to tell if those raiders will be back anytime soon?"

Xerak ignored the jibe, flicking his long tail in feline satisfaction as he looked to where the storm that he and Kaj had created was fading.

"They won't be back unless they have a reserve fleet, and that's unlikely," Xerak replied. "The damage we took from their bean seeds was nothing to what they took from our hail. The disadvantage to breeding the beti-teneh for intelligence is that they can have pretty firm opinions about going into danger. Oddly, or maybe not so oddly, they're more likely to be afraid of storms than they would be of a flight of arrows."

"Maybe," Kaj ventured, "because the fear of storm and wind would be instinctive, while the other would need to be learned. I get that."

"Will they be likely to come after us when we leave with Grace?" Peg asked.

"We certainly can't dismiss that as an option," Xerak said, "but I don't think they will. Remember, they'll know that all of us who can use magic will have been in an ideal location to recharge whatever mana we used—and that we're prepared for their style of attack. The beti-teneh have many advantages, but all of them work best if they can be combined with an element of surprise."

"I wonder," Teg said, "how long they've had this place staked out? This mountain range seemed deserted when we came through before."

"Because of Grace," Xerak reminded her, "and, more precisely because of sick Grace. My guess is that the pirates were accustomed to coming into this area to recharge at a distance. When they did the last time, they realized that the odor of the 'horrific monster' was reduced, and they took advantage."

Peg froze in the act of putting away one of the first-aid kits. "I hope they didn't hurt Grace!"

Xerak looked uneasy. "Me, too. Seems to me we'll all be able to relax better once we're through the vortex of winds and have assured ourselves that Grace is unharmed. When we get back to civilization, I'll contact Zisurru University and make sure someone knows what we encountered."

Teg wanted to keep speculating—not only about these raiders, but about how the mesa and its mana wellspring might be defended in the future. After all, the heart of archeology was speculations, but she understood this was not the time or place. She made a mental note to ask someone, Grunwold, maybe, about how such valuable resources were administered, then set herself to helping Meg apply her remaining arnica gel to injuries she couldn't quite reach.

Grunwold had turned the wheel over to Peg, and was checking over the lines and sails, making chuffing noises as he noted the dings to his paint, as well as the slimy sap on his decks and rails. Nonetheless, he seemed pleased.

"Since none of the larger beti-teneh got off a barrage, the sail is in good shape. Rigging looks sound, too. Let's go in after Grace."

A short while later, Peg blew a sharp whistle on her fingers, drawing everyone's attention.

"We're approaching the vortex," she called. "Everyone to their stations!"

"Excuse me," Meg said politely. She tucked her journal into a pocket of her coat, then climbed, albeit a bit stiffly, back to the crow's nest. Teg thought about offering to take her place, then kept her peace.

Meg would have asked for someone to take her place if she didn't think she could do it. She's old enough to know when to ask for help.

As Grunwold guided *Slicewind* along the increasingly tight spirals of the whirlwind that protected the mesa, the twists and turns became rollercoaster exciting. This time *Slicewind*'s crew was spared the increasingly nauseating odors, as well as the shrill shrieks akin to a bagpipe in which every pipe was out of tune with every other. As before, since they were riding with the wind, there was almost no sound that wasn't generated by the ship herself or the muttered comments of Grunwold at the wheel.

I wonder if he's talking to himself or to Slicewind? Teg thought. During their journey to the Roots of the World, they had learned that what Vereez's swords were to her or, even, maybe, possibly, the sun spider amulet to Teg, *Slicewind* was to Grunwold: a means of channeling and focusing a newly discovered, as yet barely examined, magical ability.

"All right, all right, all right, you can do it!" Grunwold was chanting when *Slicewind* burst out of the enshrouding clouds, over the sandy top of the mesa. Overhead, the sky was blue, with no trace of the whirlwind without. A burst of incongruously familiar music burst forth as the mesa's one resident recognized *Slicewind*.

Running to lean over the side, Peg gave words to the music, "Amazing Grace . . . How sweet the sound . . ."

She turned to face them, beaming in pure delight. "She remembers us!"

Vereez gave a shrill, yipping bark of laughter. "I thought she would. Oothynn are very smart. I'm glad Grace remembers us, and fondly so it seems. That's going to make getting her into the harness a lot easier."

Peg's smile dimmed. "I hope she cooperates. I've had my share of pets, and even a crate-trained dog can be a pain if it doesn't want to be locked up. In fact, the smarter the pets, the more loopholes they seem to find in the rules."

"Vereez and I have been making plans for getting Grace into the harness," Xerak assured Peg, "as well as contingency plans for however Grace decides to express her unwillingness to go for a ride. It's a good thing that Vereez had a pet oothynn when she was small."

"Mine," Vereez reminded him, "was about this big"—she made an oval about the size of a golf ball with her fingers—"and the worst its claws could do was pinch. Grace could probably cut me in half."

After Grunwold brought *Slicewind* to anchor about twelve feet over the sandy mesa top, Teg let loose the line she'd been holding. Stripping off her gloves, she moved over to the port rail to get a look at the creature they had come to rescue.

At the moment, the oothynn didn't look like much more than an array of large pipes and four eyes on stalks poking out of the sand. Then, with a motion somewhere between a scuttle and a heave, Grace shoved her entire body above the sand. This revealed an ovoid, silvery-grey carapace about five meters from end to end, and three meters at its widest point. At each end, one to either side, positioned where the backfin would be on a blue crab, were two impressively large pinchers, not unlike those of a lobster. The eyestalks were anchored closer to the center of the shell, a pair at each end, so the oothynn had a wide range of vision.

Teg had seen for herself that Grace could use those eyes independently, for example employing a couple of eyes to keep track of what the claws were doing, while leaving the other two free to direct locomotion and keep watch for other dangers. Underneath the carapace were her legs, too numerous to count, like those of a centipede, and apparently capable of moving the oothynn any direction with ease.

And in addition to the claws, Grace has the pipes, with which she can make an alarming array of sounds, loud enough to cripple attackers, even those at a distance.

Teg sighed and Kaj looked over at her, his pointed ears flicking back in concern.

"What's wrong, Teg?"

She laughed. "In my world, just about every human culture prides itself that the human form is the pinnacle of creation. In many legends, humans are made in the image of the divine itself. Looking at Grace, I find myself wondering. Especially when you get to be my age, you start feeling the consequences of making your way around the world as a biped—with consequent damage to feet and knees and hips. We can only see in front of us, have minimal ability to defend ourselves, and, frankly, given the trouble our various inventions have gotten our world into, well, even our much-vaunted intellect seems questionable."

From her perch on the mast, Meg called down, "Ah...The assumption of human superiority is not all *that* universal, Teg. Remember all those legends about how kind deities like Prometheus stole fire and gave it to humanity to make up for the design flaws?"

Kaj wrinkled his nose and brow in canine confusion. "Fire as compensation? That most unpredictable of elements?"

"On our world," Teg explained, "the general belief is that all animals, except humans, are afraid of fire."

"Then," Kaj said with finality, "to me that seems proof that all the animals are smarter than humans."

"You may have a point," Teg admitted.

Vereez interrupted, "Not that this isn't fascinating, Teg, but Peg is eager to head down to see Grace. We suggested that she wait until Xerak and I were in better shape to provide magical backup, but she's impatient. Can you—and Kaj, if he is up to it—go with her?"

"I'm fully recovered from the spell we did," Kaj assured her. "Xerak did all the heavy lifting. I was basically his shortcut to tapping the water and building the storm clouds."

Although he spoke dismissively of his own role, his tone overflowed with admiration for Xerak. Vereez's ears flickered back for a moment, before resuming their upright posture. Teg couldn't tell what this meant.

Is Vereez jealous? Or worried that Kaj is going to play Xerak as he played her? Some of the above? All of the above? None of the above?

Teg swallowed another sigh and walked over to where Peg was

waiting by the rail. Kaj inserted himself between Peg and the ladder to the ground.

"I'm going down first," Kaj said firmly. "That way I can brace the ladder for you two ladies."

And you'll also be far faster climbing back aboard if Grace is just pretending to be happy to see us, Teg added silently. *Ah, well, at least Kaj is used to looking after crazy ladies. Compared to his mom, we're positively rock solid.*

Despite Teg's apprehension, Grace not only remembered them, she was delighted to see them. One of the first songs Peg had taught her was the "doe a deer" song from *The Sound of Music*, and as Kaj clambered down the ladder, the oothynn fluted away, showing off her scales. They sounded much clearer now, so the damage Grace had taken to her pipes seemed to be healing.

Even with Kaj steadying it, the long rope-sided ladder bounced as Teg climbed down to the sound of Peg, who had gone down first, joining Grace in midphrase.

Peg could have waited for Grunwold to bring Slicewind *down,* Teg thought, feeling a twinge in one of her archeologically abused knees as she felt for the next rung, *and then we could have put the steps over the side. But, Tessa my dear,* she mock scolded herself as she had done much of her life, *that's thinking like an old lady. If Peg can make the climb, so can you.*

When Teg reached the ground, Grace fluted a short motif, but otherwise seemed completely absorbed with the treats Peg had set out for her. These were disks about the size of a three-layer cake and smelled like deep-fried shrimp, green chile, onion, and vanilla, as much as they smelled like anything from Earth. Peg had made them by crushing commercial oothynn kibbles, mixing them with water, and reshaping them into thick patties so their enormous friend could grip them in her claws.

"All seems well here," Kaj called up to the hovering ship. "You can bring *Slicewind* on down."

Grunwold did so, hovering with the hull just over the sandy mesa top, then extending the legs that could serve as a short-term docking cradle. (They could also be fitted with skis or wheels, although Teg had never seen this done.) When the ship was down, the steps were put over the side, and the remaining crew debarked. Grace fluted a different short phrase for each one, so Teg decided that she was either counting or had given them names or descriptive phrases.

Since the translation spell isn't translating them, maybe they're not words as such. Or maybe the spell is limited to what languages it can handle. It managed whatever language it is that our inquisitors speak, as well as the language used in the Creator's Visage Isles on the other side of the world. But while it lets us humans read, there are limits. The fancier the script, the less likely we can manage it.

Teg put her questions about languages aside until some future date when she was on night watch with one of the inquisitors. Xerak and Vereez were motioning everyone over, and they probably wouldn't appreciate the meeting being hijacked by a discussion of magic and linguistics.

"I know our initial plan was to see about getting Grace loaded up and heading back to the Library right away," Xerak began, "but that was before we had to deal with pirates. Grunwold would like a chance to go over *Slicewind* and make certain her damage really is superficial. I wouldn't mind a chance to rest, just in case the pirates are dumber than I think they are and come back for another engagement. It occurred to me that I could also use this as an opportunity to teach my three apprentices"—he said this last with a mixture of pride and defensiveness, as if he expected to be teased—"how to tap a mana wellspring."

Since neither Vereez nor Grunwold cut into this little speech, they evidently agreed. Meg was already fishing her journal out and moving to the shade cast by *Slicewind's* hull. Peg nodded happily.

"I think that's an excellent idea. Grace may remember us, and even fondly, but this will give me a chance to work with her. I thought I'd teach her some more music, and use that to distract her from my looking her over and making sure she doesn't have any sore spots before we take her up."

"I'll help if you want," Meg said, "or assist Grunwold."

"I help Grun," Heru said importantly, hooting a series of notes that Grace imitated, to the xuxu's mingled consternation and delight.

"Lunch first?" Kaj suggested. "I'm not certain I can concentrate on an empty stomach. And some of us are still battered. A rest and maybe more ointment wouldn't do any harm."

"Good idea," Vereez said. "Let's picnic down here. Heru, if you come over here, I'll put more ointment on your wings."

"Stinky goop," Heru protested, but at a stern look from Grunwold, he went.

Peg bolted her food, then went over to distract Grace, who was showing too much interest in the picnic. After bribing the oothynn with another kibble patty, Peg started her music lesson, choosing selections from the best of the works of the band *Jefferson Airplane*.

"White Rabbit," with its strong reliance on drums and bass, worked better than expected, with the deeper pipes taking up the bass line. "Somebody to Love" went over even better, at least as far as Grace was concerned. For Teg, who worried about the impact of the unresolved romances—Grunwold's crush on Vereez; Vereez's mixture of resentment and attraction toward Kaj; Xerak's frankly sexual gazes at Kaj; Kaj's quiet and deliberate detachment from it all—on their little group, the song seemed a poor choice, especially when Peg bellowed out the lyrics as if she was still the early teenaged runaway who'd left some undefined part of her heart in Haight-Ashbury.

Nevertheless, it was to the backdrop of some of Grace Slick's greatest hits that Xerak set out to teach his three students how to tap a mana wellspring.

"Once you have the hang of it," Xerak said, "it should be a lot faster and easier than using ambient mana. Can you locate the source of the mana? Close your eyes if that helps." He did so. "To me it looks a bit like a fountain coming out of the center of the mesa."

Teg closed her eyes and tried to see, but all she saw was the darkness inside her eyelids, where a few floaters drifted. She let her hand fall to the sun spider amulet and imagined that she was seeing not with her senses, but with its. This worked better, and she felt rather than saw the rich upwelling, as well as the sun spider's desire to suck it in.

"Got it?" Xerak continued, his voice causing Teg to jump and open her eyes. He went on, "Now, after all the mana we used, all of you should have an empty space that needs filling. I want you to do that, but slowly. If you aren't careful, you'll overflow and lose mana."

"Would we lose it all, or just the extra?" Kaj asked.

"All," Xerak clarified. "Think of your internal mana reservoir as a balloon..."

Vereez quipped, "After the beti-teneh, I'd rather not."

"Hush up, Sharp Nose," Xerak said. "I chose that image for a reason. Like a balloon, your internal mana reserve can stretch, but stretch it too far or too fast, and it will burst."

"How about like a soap bubble, then?" Vereez said. "I think that's the image my tutor used."

"Maybe, although I think a balloon is a better image," Xerak replied, something in the cant of his ears showing what he thought of Vereez's previous teacher. "It's sturdier for one, but if you can work with a soap bubble, then use that."

"Sorry," Vereez said. "I'm getting in the way of your answering Kaj's question."

And I wonder if that was deliberate, Teg thought, *a little showing off to remind Kaj that for all she tends to go to extremes, she has studied magic.*

Xerak continued, "So, too much, too fast, you lose everything. Overfill too often, and you'll risk damaging your mana reserve, possibly permanently. Now that I think about it, maybe that's why Vereez's tutor chose the soap bubble for his image. He wanted to restrict the chance that his students would injure themselves."

Where his painted dog head met his neck, Kaj's short hackles rose. "I'm glad that when I tapped Qes Wen, I was letting the mana out as fast as I could take it in. I had no idea how dangerous that was."

"The risk you took was necessary," Xerak said. "I certainly didn't have leisure to tell you then just how big of a one you were taking."

"Well," Kaj said, "we all took risks then. We'd be dead if we hadn't. I'm just saying that, now that I know, I want this lesson even more. How do we start?"

"Focus on however you see the wellspring," Xerak said. "Then create a mental image of yourself tapping it."

"Like using a bucket?" Kaj asked. "Or a hose?"

"Whatever best enables you to control the flow and bring it into yourself," Xerak said.

Teg closed her eyes, but no matter how hard she tried, she couldn't find a way to bring that rich upwelling into herself. There was a period of silence, then Vereez said quietly: "I'm full. I don't want to push further."

Xerak must have done something to check, because he said,

"Looks good. Let the mana sit there. Get used to feeling that 'full.' Right now, it's like you've had a bit too much for dinner and need to keep it down."

"Right."

Okay. Don't feel so bad. Vereez has the most formal training of us three apprentices.

However, when Kaj also announced he had filled his reserves, Teg felt distinctly frustrated. She wasn't used to being at the bottom of any class she took.

She kept trying, even after she heard Vereez, then Kaj move away to join the others.

Eventually, Xerak said with supreme gentleness, "Tell me what's happening, Teg."

"I'm not finding gathering mana this way easier," she said. "This is harder."

"Open your eyes," Xerak said. "Relax and tell me about it."

Confirming that the two of them were alone, except for Meg who was sitting some distance away, absorbed in writing in her journal, Teg groped in her pocket for her pipe and started fussing with it. Xerak nodded permission for her to smoke, shifted upwind, then looked at her from his golden lion's eyes while she sought the right words.

"Tapping mana from the font isn't easier," Teg said slowly. "Gathering ambient mana, well, that's like hanging out in a hot tub after a hard day's digging. You feel yourself soaking in both moisture and heat through every pore and aching muscle fiber but this, whether I think of a bucket or a hose or even cupping my hands and drinking, it just doesn't work."

"Did you try using the sun spider amulet as a focus?" Xerak asked.

"I did, but it didn't work any better. The mana just dropped through the webbing."

Xerak tapped his chin with one finger, but as the claw tip wasn't extended, Teg knew he wasn't annoyed, just thinking.

"You have a very literal mind in some ways," he said.

"Despite what many people think," Teg retorted, "archeology *is* a scientific discipline."

"But I don't think it's that literal mind that's getting in your way this time," Xerak said. "Remember what you told me about being commitment shy? About how you're too careful about letting anyone inside your 'space'? I wonder if this is part of that. You haven't had any trouble when you've been channeling mana to someone else. You give, but you're really scared of taking." Xerak twitched his whiskers. "Think about it."

Teg did for a long time, staring at the smoke wreathing up from her pipe.

He's, what, maybe twenty-four? Who is he to lecture me about what I'm scared of? On the other hand . . . He's right at the age when thinking about how you fit in with other people is almost always on your mind. Maybe he has a point.

She looked at the pipe, which was beginning to gutter out. Thought about how the smoke kept people just that little bit away.

Okay, maybe he's right.

She took out the sun spider amulet. *All right, thingie,* she thought, then interrupted herself.

"That," she said aloud, "is incredibly rude."

"Pardon?" Meg said, looking up from her journal.

"I realized I've been really rude to this amulet." She had both Meg and Xerak's attention now. "I don't know if it's a person or not, but when I use it, I talk to it as if it is. And I haven't even been polite enough to give it a name."

"You aren't required to . . ." Xerak began . . . but Teg waved him down.

"I want to. I've even thought of a good name: Petros. In one of the languages from our world, that means 'rock,' and this amulet has a bit of meteorite as a center." She turned her gaze on the sun spider amulet, looking at the tiny jewels that were its eyes. "Would you like to be called Petros?"

The delighted giggle wasn't her imagination. At least she didn't think so. And Xerak's pleased expression wasn't either.

Yeah, kid. Maybe you're right.

Later that afternoon, when they put Operation Airlift Grace into action, Grace proved to be remarkably cooperative. Indeed, the gigantic oothynn was so pathetically happy when she realized she wasn't going to be left behind, that Teg felt glad all over again that they'd come for her. The only adaptation they had to make in their initial plans was to create a stretcher-style platform from sail cloth and some spare spars for her many legs to rest on, once it became obvious that there was no comfortable gap between her many, many legs for the harness straps to fit. The lift harness straps went under the stretcher. When Peg stood on the platform and started to sing "Come Together," Grace scuttled to join her.

"That's a good girl," Peg crooned as she tossed the straps of a sort of "seatbelt" over Grace's shell, then scurried to the other side to knot these to the edge of the platform. "Now, I'm going back up"—she pointed to the hull of the hovering sky sailer, and broke into song— "an' donchu you worry 'bout a thing."

Grace tootled an echo of the line as she folded her legs under her.

We'd have more trouble getting Grace off there than keeping her in place, Teg thought. She stood by on the ground with the wizards as Grunwold brought *Slicewind* slowly aloft, just in case Grace panicked. However, instead of getting nervous, the oothynn settled down and piped a drowsy melody that for some reason reminded Teg of a cat purring.

"All aboard," Peg called, hanging over the side rail. "Next stop, Library of the Sapphire Wind!"

During runs for water and to discharge sewage, Grunwold had discovered that it was far easier to sail out of the whirlwind than in. However, since Grace's platform hung below *Slicewind*, some of Grunwold's visibility was blocked. Over the day they had rested and prepared, Heru had grown fond of Grace, and so was very willing to fly down and ride with the oothynn. This both kept her company and made the xuxu available as a backup navigation aid. Heru even offered to carry down a basket containing various goodies for Grace.

Following a course calculated to keep them from passing over any major population center, *Slicewind* set sail for the Library of the Sapphire Wind. Late one night, Teg woke, needing to pee, and decided to go up on deck for a rare cigarette. Most of the time, she smoked the pipe Xerak had given her, because the rest found it less offensive.

As she was climbing up the ladder from the lounge to the upper deck, she heard Vereez say, "Peg-toh, you've been married a lot, right?"

"Three times married. Three times divorced," came the laconic reply.

"My parents only married the once. Same with most of the people I knew well. I guess that's why I thought, with Kaj and all, when you fell in love, it was for real and for always."

Teg debated going back to bed, but her curiosity had the better of her. She continued her climb up the ladder. Vereez was in the wheelhouse, where she could keep an eye on *Slicewind*'s headings. The sky sailer had the equivalent of autopilot and could send out alerts, but with Grace riding below, there was always the chance the ship wouldn't "see" something until they were right on top of it.

Peg was sitting on one of the stern benches, knitting what looked like a hat. She smiled as Teg emerged onto the deck.

"Sounded like a serious chat," Teg said. "I can take my cigarette to the bow and cover my ears. But, I admit, I'm interested."

"It's okay, Teg-toh," Vereez said.

Peg smiled. "You can even smoke one of your cigarettes. Just go where we don't need to inhale with you." She knitted a few stitches, then paused. "I've thought about 'for real and for always' a lot. Not just for me, but as my kids and stepkids get old enough to get into serious relationships. I think the problem with 'for real and for always' is that for that to work, either there has to be a lot of willingness to accept change . . ." She paused and waggled a finger. "Or no change at all."

Vereez flicked her ears sideways and wrinkled her nose. "That doesn't make sense."

Teg laughed. "It does, actually, at least to me. Peg, you're the expert, go on."

Peg started knitting again. "My first husband, Don, and I met when I was still a minor. We fell in love with . . . being in love and love, especially sex, being forbidden. It was hot, it was heady, and when I turned eighteen and we could get married without anybody getting in our way, we couldn't get it done fast enough. And then it turned out that Don, and maybe me, too, was more in love with the forbidden. Once I was just his 'old lady,' his 'ball and chain,' all those 'affectionate' terms for a wife, he started getting his thrills elsewhere. And there I was, pregnant, dealing with morning sickness and . . ."

Vereez's ears were drooping, as if this was all too familiar, and Peg was looking uncharacteristically depressed. Teg rushed to the rescue.

"We get it. You broke up. So, was this changing or not changing?"

Peg bit into her lower lip, then said, "He didn't change. I did, especially since I was the one with the baby bump, not wanting to get stoned or drunk or stay up all night. He wouldn't change with me. Done."

Teg decided to save Peg from relating more marital failures. Besides, she had thought of an example of a relationship that hadn't changed, and so was successful, that would reach Vereez better than any examples Peg could come up with.

"Your parents," Teg said, "Inehem and Zarrq, they're a great example of a relationship that has survived because it never changed. They started out with Zarrq protecting Inehem, being the thug, so she could do the magic. That hasn't changed. We saw it when they came after Brunni. They've changed their arena from 'extractions' to high finance, but it's the same."

Vereez nodded. "As a kid, I never felt I meant as much to them as they did to each other. They didn't change to be parents. They just added an element in *their* relationship."

Peg had recovered some of her usual pluck. "I don't know if people do this here, but in our world, 'liking' someone often starts with the superficial: I like blond hair and blue eyes, or I like big breasts or no body hair or whatever."

"It's like that here," Vereez said, "different in some ways, but sure . . . Physical attraction."

"Well, I always tell my kids, and some of the grands, now," Peg went on, "to remember those physical attributes will change with time. Mister Tall, Dark, and Handsome, will probably become stooped, greying, and, if you're lucky, 'distinguished.' What I'm trying to get them to think about is what else might change. If you're in love with the star of the college football team, what's he going to be like when he can't play ball? What else does he base his sense of self-worth on? Is he going to be forever caught in the past or can he move into the future?"

Her gaze unfocused as she looked at something that they couldn't see. "That's what happened with Nash, my second husband. He was a pretty good musician, even belonged to a couple of bands that got gigs as opening acts. But after a while, Nash realized that bar band was about the best he'd ever be. I tried to get him to use his music in other ways, but once his dream broke, so did he. I got steps Samantha and Wilson out of it, as well as our Esmerelda, so no regrets, but Nash..."

She shook her head. "We split. He pretty much vanished, even from his kids' lives, a few years later. Not good. Really not good. By then I was starting to see I was attracted to the 'wild type,' the 'free spirit.' So next time, I decided I'd go for stable, solid, dependable. Did Irving change? I thought so, but maybe now, after a lot of thinking... Maybe he just kept going in the direction he'd been all along, a direction that called for me to be Corporate Wife."

"You?" Teg laughed.

Vereez said, "You mean, like married to the business? My parents have friends like that. I guess it's in my parents' favor that I always felt that if it was the business or each other, they'd choose each other."

"That's about it," Peg agreed. "I tried a lot longer than I should have, probably, but in the end, I couldn't take the expectations that I dress a certain way, do only certain things. The kids were growing up by then, and I was never meant to be one of the 'ladies who lunch.' Irving did me the favor of falling for a secretary and wanting a divorce, so I got out with a really nice financial package, and the sympathy of all the kids."

Silence fell, long enough that Teg finished her cigarette and was beginning to feel sleepy. Peg continued knitting. Teg was about to make her excuses and go below, when Vereez cleared her throat.

"Peg, was there ever anyone you thought would change with you?"

Peg sighed. "Oh, honey, I always did, except when I thought we'd never change." She looked suddenly vulnerable, and oddly, somehow, much, much younger. "There was one. I met him post-Don, pre-Nash. I was still hanging out with the more or less hippy set. They were a lot of help with Diego and Tabitha, even before I gave up on Don. I met Jackal that way."

"Jackal?" Teg said. "Was that his real name?"

"Probably not," Peg said, but she didn't laugh. "A lot of us didn't use our given names then. I went by Pesky for a while. One of the older hippies—probably all of nineteen—called me that and it stuck.

I liked it. Peg was so 'last generation.' Jackal was probably John or Jack, but he insisted everyone call him Jackal, so we did. Funny, I was thinking about him just the other day. He always claimed that he was two people in one head, that he could do magic. But he was sweet, loved to talk about existential things, the nature of the real, all that. He'd hold Diego while I nursed Tabitha, and we'd talk about what was real and how did we know. A stoner, I guess, but I really liked him, and, unlike Don, he seemed to like the kids and, well, the square, routine stuff, that having kids was making me do more and more of."

"What happened?" Vereez asked.

"He died," Peg said, not bothering to hide her tears. "That two people in one head thing . . . It sounds cool, but there were times he was all over the place. They found him dead one morning, down under a bridge near a river. I'm not sure if it was suicide or an overdose. I have always hoped it was an overdose, a dumb mistake, because I'd have hated to fail a friend."

"Peg," Teg said, sliding onto the bench next to her and putting an arm around her shoulders. "You can't save everyone. Really, you can't save anyone. Best you can manage is saving yourself, and you've done that, and even managed to keep smiling."

Vereez sniffled back her own tears. "I'm sorry, bringing up old pain. I'm so selfish. You ladies, you all seem so cool, so together. I forget."

Peg forced a wobbly grin. "Well, maybe we are cool and together now, but it's been a hard road getting here."

"Don't fool yourself," Teg put in. "I'll settle for cool. I know I'm not in the least 'together.'"

❈CHAPTER THREE❈

A couple days later, they arrived at the plaza that still fronted on the Library of the Sapphire Wind, although the entry to the Library was now well below surface level, when once it had been right on the plaza.

Grunwold brought *Slicewind* down slowly, until excited honks from Heru, accompanied by trills from Grace, confirmed oothynn touchdown. Next Peg and Kaj went over the side to release Grace from the straps that had secured her to the stretcher for the duration of the flight. Once Grace had scuttled out from under the ship, and the stretcher had been removed, Grunwold brought *Slicewind* down to rest in the simple cradle they'd built during their last layover. *Slicewind* could float like a normal boat, but they'd seen things in the nearby lake that made them feel docking the sky sailer on land was wiser. There was the added benefit that those who had berths aboard *Slicewind* could still use them if they so wished.

"I hope Grace will be safe here," Peg said worriedly, watching the oothynn—eyestalks extended, claws raised—examine her surroundings, starting with the open areas they'd created on the plaza, moving from there to the tangle of second-growth, almost junglelike, forest that had grown over and around the ruins of what had once been a complex that contained, according to brochures, not only the Library, but an elite hotel, and a separate building that had held labs, a scriptorium, and lecture halls.

These other buildings had been added after the death of the Library of the Sapphire Wind's founder, Dmen Qeres. Knowing what they did about him now, including his purpose for founding the Library, Teg wondered what Dmen Qeres would have thought of the additional structures. For that matter, she wondered what Uten Kekui, Dmen Qeres's reincarnation and Xerak's master, thought.

"Grace will be at least as safe here as on that isolated mesa," Xerak reassured Peg. "Probably safer, now that we know that pirates are hanging about. She'll certainly be healthier."

Vereez nodded agreement. "We've discussed this, Peg. Oothynn are tropical originally. That sandy mesa top gave Grace a surface she could burrow into, but otherwise wasn't an ideal environment. The Library's surroundings are more temperate than tropical, but there's ample water, food, and, probably most important, company for her."

"I was worrying about the land squids, and the piranha toads, and the spike wolves, and the lizard parrots," Peg said, "and whatever lives in the lake. And—"

"Grace is larger than some apartments I've lived in," Meg chided, "and, as we learned, can defend herself very well. Save your fussing for your children and your grandchildren."

Teg chuckled to herself. They had been over this before, and Peg would come around again, especially when Grunwold reminded her, as Teg suspected he would any minute, that Peg had been the one to suggest they relocate Grace from the mesa.

I wonder if we'll ever learn how Grace came to be stranded on that mesa for so long? Teg thought, taking her pipe and pipe weed from one of the pouches on her belt. *Probably not, since our best guess is that whoever left her there long enough for her to go through several molts and be damaged because the decorative bands constricted her pipes as she grew, is probably not going to come forth.*

After checking to make sure the light breeze would blow her smoke away from the sensitive noses of her companions, Teg strolled over to where she could hoist herself onto the pedestal that held the impressive statue of Dmen Qeres. Leaning back against the raven-headed figure's wizard-robed lower body, she began to pack the pipe's bowl.

From her elevated position, she saw a small, white-furred head poke over the upper edge of the ravine, at the bottom of which was the Library's front façade. The head was followed by the rest of four-year-old Brunni. Teg noted how Vereez stiffened slightly, obviously hoping that Brunni would come to her, but reluctant to put pressure on the child. However, Vereez's hopes were foredoomed to be disappointed. Brunni had no idea that Vereez was her biological mother, nor that Kaj was her biological father. As far as someone as young as her could understand relationships, her mother was Vereez's aunt, Ranpeti, since Brunni had been taken from Vereez moments after her birth, and Vereez hadn't met with her again until several weeks ago.

Of those who had rescued Brunni from a fate worse than death, Brunni's favorite by far was Grunwold, and it was toward him she ran.

"Grunwold! Grunwold! I've been a good girl. Did you bring me anything?"

Grunwold laughed and scooped the little girl up, spinning her up over his head, before settling her into the crook of his arm.

"How about that?" he said, pointing to Grace, who was staring with three of her four eyestalks at the noisy new arrival.

It was hard to imagine that someone the size of Grace could be overlooked, but Brunni had the gift of tight focus found naturally in small children. Now her eyes, very dark against her white fur, widened, and her small ears flickered back and forth.

"Is that for me?" she said, not at all certain if she was pleased by the idea.

"Actually," Grunwold relented, "Grace—that's her name—is her own person, but she's come to live here, and we hope she'll be a friend for all of us."

"Oh," Brunni said, relief evident. "So, she's not my present?"

Grunwold chuckled. "I might just have something for you. Let me put you down so I can check my pockets."

By the time Grunwold had gone through an elaborate show of checking of each pocket, then coming out with a small, brightly wrapped package, two others had climbed up from the Library to join the group on the plaza. One was Ranpeti. Ranpeti had the large brown eyes, small ears, and rich brown fur of a sea lion. She was taller than her older sister, Inehem, and had none of the other's silver-fox elegance and grace.

The other was Nefnet, a specialist in magical healing who had been in residence at the Library at the time of its destruction, and, thus far, the only one of those archived by Sapphire Wind to be awakened. To this point, Nefnet had chosen to reside at the Library, adjusting to the idea that after what had been to her a sleep filled with not unpleasant dreams, she had awakened to find that something like twenty-five years had gone by. Superficially, Nefnet was not unlike Ranpeti, but her characteristics were those of an otter, rather than a sea lion. Her build was less curvaceous, although definitely female.

Grunwold looked over at Ranpeti. "If I promise you that this won't ruin Brunni's appetite for dinner, may I give it to her?"

Ranpeti smiled, an expression of curled whiskers and a slight curve to her lipless mouth. Teg knew that Grunwold had actually checked in advance what might be a suitable present, so his question was clearly to support her maternal authority.

"Brunni has been remarkably good," Ranpeti replied, in a rich, alto voice. "I think so."

Only then did Grunwold hand over the package.

"Thank you, Grunwold!" Brunni piped, then plopped butt-down on the elaborate pavement, swept clean now of the vegetative debris that had all but obscured it when they had first come to the Library ruins. Growling in concentration, the little girl undid the knots that tied closed a bandana-sized piece of fabric commonly used instead of paper for wrapping, revealing a bundle of what were, essentially, crayons. There was also a small pad of drawing paper. By way of thanks, Brunni immediately started drawing what was evidently, based on the spikes coming up from the head, meant to be a portrait of Grunwold.

Meanwhile, Nefnet had been looking at Grace with evident interest. "She's magnificent! I can see where her pipes were damaged. Although I'm no expert, I think a few molts should take care of the remaining indentations."

Peg had been over by Grace, gently crooning to her, and now she patted the oothynn next to one eyestalk. "Isn't that lovely, my dear? Nefnet says soon you'll be back in full voice."

Teg doubted Grace actually understood but, then again, who knew what the translation spell might be capable of? Whether coincidentally or not, Grace fluted the "doe a deer" scale song that Peg had taught her as a means of testing her musical range. In definite imitation of Peg's habit of waving her hands to mark time, Grace moved one pair of enormous claws.

This caught Brunni's attention, and she stopped drawing to stare in fascination, then started bouncing to the beat and waving her crayon. Teg had been enjoying the scene so much that she'd missed seeing the arrival of Ohent, mother of Kaj and, through no direct fault of her own, one of those who had contributed to destruction of the Library.

Teg was delighted to see that Ohent's snow leopard's head, although topped with a sort of cap out of which her rounded ears poked, was not shrouded within veils. The veils were there, attached to the cap, but pulled back. That Ohent did not feel she must cover those brilliant blue eyes said a great deal about the efficacy of the course of treatment she had been following under Nefnet's direction.

It probably also helps that Ohent is no longer being sent nightmares by Ba Djed of the Weaver. Still, that she could begin to recover so quickly says a great deal, not only about Nefnet's skills, but about Ohent's own strength of character.

Ohent had gone over to Kaj and was leaning against her son. Kaj might be a playboy who had left a string of broken hearts and fond memories behind him—and quite possibly more by-blows than Brunni—but he had been a devoted son to his borderline insane mother. Now, without even seeming aware of doing so, he put an arm about her shoulders and gave her a little squeeze.

Teg's childhood had been pretty much without affection, although she'd been spared outright physical abuse. Now, watching Kaj and Ohent's quiet reunion, she felt more than a little wistful. Remembering her pipe, she pulled out a book of matches bearing the logo of Taima University and struck a light.

She barely had the pipe drawing nicely before Brunni looked up from her coloring with a yelp of disgust. "Teg's doing the stinky thing again!"

"That I am," Teg agreed, "and if you don't like it, go inside. You can color there just as well."

Ranpeti looked at her daughter in mild reproof. "Remember what we've discussed, about how if we're going to live here with other people, we need to learn to compromise?"

Brunni stiffened. "I don't want to go back to the Isles. Here's more fun. I'll remember." Pushing off from the ground with her hands, she got to her feet, then bent to collect her crayons and drawing pad. "But it's still stinky."

Teg had to laugh. "You're in the majority on that, Brunni, but I'm not quite ready to quit."

Meg and Xerak went inside with Brunni and Ranpeti, followed by Grunwold, partly dragged by Brunni, who had stuffed her crayons into a tunic pocket so she could grab his hand. Vereez trailed after.

Ohent and Nefnet stayed out long enough for Peg, assisted by Kaj, to introduce Grace to these new friends. Eventually, however, they also went in, leaving Teg to finish her pipe with Heru and Grace for company. Heru seemed to have taken charge of Grace's orientation, the two of them communicating with a series of hoots and whistled notes. They were venturing off into the tangled growth when Teg finished her smoke.

"Be careful, you two," Teg called after them. "Heru, remember that Grace can't fly away if some spike wolves or piranha toads decide to find out what she tastes like. And remember the lizard parrots do seem to find you tasty."

Heru squawked in indignation. "As if thems trouble forz us! Grace would cut them up: snip, snip! We go to the lake, by the trail. She misses water so much."

"Remind her to stay in the shallows," Teg cautioned. "There are supposed to be some nasty creatures out in the depths."

"Will do!" Heru assured her. "Will do!"

Teg thought about trailing them, then shrugged. If Grace was going to live within the Library grounds, it was better to find out if anything would be a threat to her while they were here to help. She scraped the dottle from her pipe bowl and decided to leave the pipe on the statue's pedestal to cool—which should also spare her more of Brunni's criticism.

I really should give up smoking, Teg thought. *At least I've cut back a lot on the cigarettes, partly because they're impossible to get Over Where.*

When Teg walked through the doorways into the Library of the Sapphire Wind, she found that just about everyone had gathered in the large reception hall. Back in the Library's heyday, the reception hall had included information desks, sage stations, waiting areas, and long tables where those who wished to work in groups could meet.

When Sapphire Wind had first admitted them through the towering doors, the reception area had been littered with rubble, the walls blackened with smoke, and most of the furniture overturned. Today, while the reception hall was not exactly restored to its former glory and there was still rubble heaped around the edges, it looked a whole lot better. The floors and tables were cleaned and polished. Broken stone had been removed to reveal what remained of the sage stations. Above, the lovely constellation mural set into the domed ceiling was now as richly colored as if it had been freshly created that very day.

From the amount of work that had been done even since their last visit, Teg guessed that Sapphire Wind had regained control of more of the various weird and wonderful creatures that enabled it to protect and maintain the Library. Some of these creatures, like the abau—round, flat creatures that Peg had dubbed "flying pancakes"—handled routine dusting and polishing far better than even a large janitorial staff could have done.

Today, Teg hardly registered the changes, because the first thing she saw was a barrel-chested man with the head of a bison in the midst of a vigorous argument with a tornado delineated by dense blue sparkles. She froze in midstep, unwilling to draw attention to herself, but determined to stay and watch—she couldn't resist the image—the sparks fly.

Confrontation between Sapphire Wind, the *genius loci* of the Library, and the wizard Uten Kekui had been brewing for a while. Teg felt deeply relieved that the altercation had broken out while they were present to witness it, rather than otherwise.

Or maybe, she thought, *it broke out precisely because we are here. Sapphire Wind knows who its allies—even its friends—are.*

Uten Kekui was the reincarnation of Dmen Qeres, the founder of the Library of the Sapphire Wind. He was also the custodian, in both lives, of Ba Djed of the Weaver, one of the three great artifacts that maintained the Bridge of Lives. Possibly, most importantly, given this situation, Uten Kekui was the long-sought, much-admired, much-desired teacher and apprentice master of Xerak.

Teg had apparently walked into the middle of a tirade, for Uten Kekui was building up to his peroration.

"And I am fed up with your balking at even my most simple request!" he bellowed.

"It is the policy of this facility," replied Sapphire Wind, its words coming from the beak of Friba, the purple-and-green lizard parrot Sapphire Wind had been training so that Meg would not need to be available for it to speak, "that appropriate request forms be filled out before materials are released or facilities activated."

Only the increased rapidity of the sparkling tornado's spinning showed that the *genius loci* was other than perfectly calm. Uten Kekui did not appear to notice.

"I don't see you bothering Nefnet with forms," he countered.

"Nefnet is on the Library staff," came the prim reply, "a position she agreed to resume when she was taken from among the Archived."

"Ohent? Cerseru Kham? Ranpeti?" Uten Kekui turned each name into an accusation.

"None of these have objected to filling out document control forms. Ohent-lial even found the forms where they had been protected from destruction within a drawer in a sage station."

From where she sat at one of the long tables, Ohent chuckled, the narrowing of her blue snow leopard eyes making clear she was anything but amused.

"I did find them, that I did. I've always had a gift for finding lost things."

Uten Kekui bunched his shoulders and looked as if he might butt the spinning tornado with his horns. "I only asked for the book I was reading yesterday!"

"And duly returned," said Sapphire Wind. "Thus, a new requisition form is required."

"But you know exactly where it is! You could send Emsehu or one of your creatures to fetch it and have it back to me in less time than it would take me to fill out the form."

The tornado only twisted in the air.

Uten Kekui bellowed. "There are fewer than a dozen adults in residence here! Such procedures are unnecessary!"

"Thirteen, if we count Emsehu," Sapphire Wind corrected, "which I most certainly do."

"Thirteen, then. Fourteen with the kid. Fifteen with the xuxu, I suppose."

"If we're counting Heru," Peg said to Grunwold, not quite *sotto voce*, "then what about Grace?"

Grunwold hushed her.

Meg interjected herself into the conversation, acid dripping from every syllable. "And what about Sapphire Wind? Since the Library was not created for the use of their sort of creature, I suppose I can see discounting the xuxu or the oothynn. Even Emsehu falls into an odd category as a unique monstrosity. But how would you classify Sapphire Wind? Surely not as a juvenile."

Uten Kekui must have been a superlative teacher, or else Xerak would not have sacrificed so much to find him. However, clearly, he was not accustomed to being questioned, at least not on a subject on which he felt himself an authority. He wheeled on Meg and snapped out his reply.

"An artifact! One I, or rather my prior self, created to serve this library."

"Which is precisely what Sapphire Wind is doing," Meg retorted tartly. "Serving this library."

"But it seems to have forgotten that this is *my* library!" Uten Kekui bellowed.

And this "forgetting" is really the point, Teg thought, *isn't it?*

Through the cross currents of argument, Sapphire Wind had continued to swirl silently in place. Now Nefnet spoke quickly, before Meg, whose pale cheeks were each accented with a bright pink anger spot, could get out a coherent retort.

"Actually, Uten Kekui," Nefnet said, flashing her teeth in a manner that reminded that "cute" otters were top-end predators, "there is some question to that claim. Dmen Qeres did not leave the Library of the Sapphire Wind to you."

"How could he?" Uten Kekui replied pedantically. "We may come to recall our past lives, but we cannot know who our future selves will be."

"Precisely," Nefnet said. "At best, you would have needed to—after you had remembered your life as Dmen Qeres—visit the Library and reclaim Ba Djed of the Weaver from where your earlier self had hidden it in the repository to await his future self. Despite this future need, he did not leave you the Library."

"Fine. True enough," Uten Kekui said with such careful patience that Teg knew he regretted his outburst, if for no other reason than it showed him at his worst. "However, Ba Djed is what Sapphire Wind draws upon to function at its fullest capacity. Correct?"

Vari-shaped heads dipped in acknowledgement. Even Sapphire Wind's funnel inclined.

Uten Kekui continued. "If one accepts that, one might go on to say that since Sapphire Wind cannot function as intended without Ba Djed, and, in turn, that the Library cannot function at its best without Sapphire Wind, therefore, if Ba Djed is my inheritance, then, by extension, so is Sapphire Wind, and so is the Library. I am certain that is what my past self intended."

Teg felt uneasy. *I hadn't really thought about all the different sorts of people there are in this world. It's been enough of an adjustment that "people" don't even have the same sort of heads or tails or markings. Could it be that no matter how intelligent, determined, and adaptable Sapphire Wind has proven to be, especially since the destruction of the Library, that it will always be considered property of a sort? How are unique monstrosities like Emsehu rated? Heck, Meg has a point. What about xuxu and oothynn?*

"Does anyone know who owns the Library now?" Peg asked. "It must have been left to someone. I guess those are the ones with whom Uten Kekui-va is going to need to argue."

When Uten Kekui swiveled to look at Peg, it occurred to Teg that the bison-headed wizard was not necessarily being bull-headed. It was only a week or so since Uten Kekui had formally accepted the custodianship of Ba Djed and, with that, the fact that he was the reincarnation of the somewhat problematic Dmen Qeres. It was completely possible that, with all of this hitting him at once, especially if any memories of the entitled egoist that he had been were finally mixing into his own, Uten Kekui might have overlooked just how much time had passed since Dmen Qeres's death and his own new awareness.

It's been something over twenty-five years since the Library was destroyed, and Dmen Qeres had been dead for many years before that.

"Good question," Teg put in, doing her best to infuse her response with warmth and curiosity rather than challenge. She moved from the arch of the doorway where she had been standing and drifted to join the rest over by the long tables. "Any poffee? What's on *Slicewind* had gone cold."

"Here's some," Ranpeti replied, indicating a carafe on the table. "As for Peg's question, I asked Konnel if he'd look into the question of ownership the last time that he was here for a treatment from Nefnet. I'd been worrying about ways that Inehem and Zarrq"—her sister and brother-in-law, Vereez's parents—"might try to get leverage on us. We wrote a pretty tidy contract, and I'm sure Xerak's curse would restrain them from direct action, but it occurred to me that if they could get a hold of the real estate—or even some of the surrounding land or water rights, we could have trouble."

"Brilliant!" Xerak said, the relief in his voice as much, Teg suspected, for how Ranpeti had helped defuse the tension as for the information. "We did put in a clause about interfering with the Library 'directly or indirectly,' but would that be enforceable for the associated lands?"

"Has Dad found anything?" Grunwold asked. "Or hasn't there been time for him to get back you?"

"He sent a note via messenger xuxu," Ranpeti said. "It came while you were away. Ohent, where did we stash it?"

Ohent rose and went to one of the lower sage stations where, in the Library's heyday, experts on many subjects had made themselves available for consultation while carrying on their own research.

"I put it in here," she replied, removing a small bone tube from a drawer.

Teg noticed Kaj was gazing at his mother with pride. *And not only because she's staying rooted in reality. I'd bet my last pack of cigarettes that Ohent suggested having Konnel check into land ownership. And that Ohent also suggested that Ranpeti do the asking. Sefit might not know that long ago Ohent and her husband were lovers, but she's the jealous type, and best not to take chances.*

Ohent handed the tube to Ranpeti, who unscrolled the document and started skimming. Teg glanced over at Uten Kekui. The bison head didn't have the expressive ears of many of the others, but from how his nostrils flared, he was annoyed.

I bet they didn't tell him about their queries, Teg thought, *but I'd bet anything that they told Sapphire Wind.*

Ranpeti glanced at Grunwold. "The first bit is medical stuff, for Nefnet. You can read it later, but the short version is that Konnel is walking again, and he hopes that he'll be able to stop using a cane soon."

Grunwold's ears melted flat in relief, but he only said gruffly, "Good. If the old man gets well, that'll keep me outta the brickworks. What does he say about the Library?"

"Apparently, Dmen Qeres left the Library in the care of a trust. More details on that will be coming. Anyhow, when the Library was destroyed, the trustees were in a bind. They had taken out insurance..."

"As they should have," Uten Kekui muttered.

"...but the level of destruction was so unprecedented..."

Ohent actually looks a little proud of that, Teg thought, bemused. *Well, I guess if you're going to be part of creating a disaster, it shouldn't be trivial—and she already knows that, thanks to Sapphire Wind's intervention, the death toll was minimal.*

"...that, although the insurance paid out, the entire area was deemed an attractive nuisance and, therefore, uninsurable. This didn't release the insurance company from paying out, mind you. In fact, Konnel says that there's still a reserve for any who can prove themselves survivors of the incident."

Everyone looked at Nefnet.

"I have considered contacting the insurance company," she said, "but I thought I might wait until other of the Archived, even a few, could join me. Ohent said a deposition from those of you who relocated the Library and could testify as to the situation would be useful."

"Count us in," Vereez said. "Anything else, Aunt Ranpeti?"

"The next part is complicated," Ranpeti admitted. "I don't quite get the legalities, but they should be spelled out in the longer document Konnel has promised. However, the basics are that the insurance paying out didn't change the fact that the trustees were still responsible for what was now a dangerous and uninsurable area. In return for being indemnified against suits postdating the catastrophe itself, the trustees disbanded the trust on the grounds that the Library and related facilities no longer existed."

"So, who owns it now?" Peg asked again. She was doing something complicated with her knitting involving a crochet hook.

Until Teg had met her, she hadn't realized the two skills overlapped.

"Konnel is still researching that," Ranpeti said, "but not the House of Fortune. I'd bet my ears on that." She wiggled her little sea lion ears for emphasis. "Even at her meanest, Inehem wouldn't take on that level of liability."

"And even if she felt mean enough to risk it, Zarrq wouldn't let her," Ohent added firmly. "He was always very protective of her."

"I agree," Vereez said stiffly. "My parents aren't stupid. Between liability and the curse, if the House of Fortune decides to get involved, it will be at several removes."

"I wonder," Meg spoke dreamily, clearly thinking aloud, "if there is anything like squatters' rights in the legal code here. Or could we file to homestead the area? There would still be the liability issue, but it would give us a semilegal status."

"What's the difference?" Grunwold asked, looking up from reading Konnel's letter, which Ranpeti had handed him as soon as she was done giving her report.

"In our homeland, at least," Meg said, "a squatter claims the right to a property owned by someone else by living on it and maintaining the property as much as possible."

"Hmm... If that's the case," Nefnet said, speaking a little too brightly, and glancing at Uten Kekui from the corners of her eyes, "then Sapphire Wind might well qualify."

Meg made a seesaw gesture with one hand. "In our country, things like paying property taxes apply, but it's possible that wouldn't be an issue here. Homesteading is similar to squatting, but it's more or less official. Land that belongs to a public body, a state, or a national government is 'bought' by virtue of the homesteaders living on it for a predetermined period of time and improving it in some fashion. That last might be our best chance."

"I'll ask Dad to look into all of this," Grunwold said, pulling out the journal in which he more usually drafted poetry. "Thanks to Peg going fierce, we all walked away with some money in our settlement with Inehem and Zarrq. I'd absolutely invest some if that secures ownership of the Library for our group."

"Me, too!" Vereez said.

Looking at how the young woman's eyes glittered darkly, Teg

thought, *She wants to secure the Library for us. That's true enough, but Inehem isn't the only member of her family with a mean streak. Vereez likes the idea of using the hush money we screwed out of her parents against them.*

❦ CHAPTER FOUR ❦

Grunwold didn't get a chance to finish composing his letter. The very next morning, Konnel himself arrived on the sky sailer *Cloud Cleaver*. Heru, who had been out visiting with Grace, came streaking in to alert them. Teg went out with Peg, Meg, and the inquisitors to welcome the new arrivals.

Grunwold's mother, Sefit, was at the wheel. Sefit had the head of a camel, one of the shorter-haired, desert varieties. Since she lacked antlers, she looked much shorter than did her husband and son, but was actually nearly as tall as either one. Like Grunwold, Konnel had the head of a stag. The first time they'd seen him, he'd been ill and in bed, his antlers seeming too heavy for him. Now he was strong enough to lean over the side and wave greeting as *Cloud Cleaver* made her descent.

Sefit glided *Cloud Cleaver* down, skillfully spilling the wind from the sails so that the ship hovered a few feet over the plaza. While Tenneh, a fellow with the head of a wildebeest, opened a section of the side rail and put into place a short set of stairs, Konnel started talking.

"Turns out we're not the only ones who've been recently asking questions about who owns the Library and its environs," Konnel said, walking stiffly toward the stairs to debark. "The situation is complicated enough that we decided to come directly here."

Sefit slung something over the side that looked like what Teg had always imagined a bosun's chair would be, back when she'd read about Maturin using one in the Patrick O'Brian novels. It looked a bit like a kid's swing, but instead of the ropes going straight up, they met at a triangle.

"Grunwold, take this," Sefit said. "These days, your dad can handle the steps to get off the ship, but he still has trouble with those ladders down into the Library."

Grunwold, who had been visibly twitching as he watched his father make his halting descent, hurried over to take the apparatus.

Sefit seems tactless, Teg thought, *but that was actually considerate of her. She protected Konnel's fragile independence and gave Grunwold something useful to do. Once again, I am unsurprised that she managed to run KonSef Estate while hiding just how ill Konnel had become.*

When Sefit and Konnel were both down, Tenneh took the helm, while the other crew member, beaver-headed Abeh, readied the sails.

Grunwold waved at them. "You know where the berth is in the meadow over near the lake?"

"Absolutely!"

"Do you need anything?"

"We're fine. Send Heru over to tell us when Konnel-lial and Sefit-lial are ready to sail."

"Will do! Oh, and don't worry if you see the biggest oothynn ever splashing around. That's Grace. I'll get Heru to tell her you're friends."

During this short exchange, Konnel had been making his careful way over to the first of the two drop-offs that led down to the main doors of the Library. Sefit took the bosun's chair from Grunwold and started attaching it to previously prepared hooks. She paused in her work long enough to give a careful once over to both *Slicewind* and Grunwold, whose hide still showed up close the marks left by the beti-teneh seeds.

"What did you do to *Slicewind* this time?"

"I kept her from getting taken over by pirates equipped with a flotilla of beti-teneh," Grunwold snapped back. "It was an epic battle, and we're lucky that most of our damage was to paint and sails. I still think we need to equip the ship with weapons. If I hadn't had four wizards, Peg, and Meg as crew, we might well have lost her."

Sefit glanced at the others, checking to see if Grunwold was exaggerating—something she knew neither Xerak nor Vereez would ever let him get away with—and seeing only nods made a gentle "harrumph" of approval.

"Weapons, maybe," she said, "but we'll definitely okay paint and extra sailcloth. Now, come help lower your father."

Inside, they found that Nefnet had already set up a comfortable recliner-type chair near one of the long tables. Emsehu had probably helped, given how the crocodilian-canine creature was squatting nearby, looking smug. From how automatically Konnel took his seat in the recliner, Teg guessed that the chair was where he sat when he came for his treatments.

Nefnet said, "I know you have news for us, Konnel-toh, but why not let me assess how you're responding to my latest ointment while you're here?"

Konnel gave her an unmistakable look of gratitude. "You have done so much already, but if I would not be imposing . . ."

"I think you'll be helping me with the news you've brought," Nefnet said. "Think of it as imposing on each other." She motioned for Sefit to come sit next to her. "If you don't mind, you're better than I am at telling when Konnel is being 'brave.'"

"Stupid, more like it," Sefit grumbled, but she joined Nefnet readily enough, and took Konnel's hand in her own.

While Konnel was being settled, Peg and Ranpeti had vanished into the Library's newly set-up kitchen. Now they emerged, wheeling a multitiered cart. The top tray held carafes of zinz tea and poffee, while the lower held drinking bowls and plates of fresh fruit and sweet pickles.

To the gentle background clatter of drinking bowls being filled, Konnel began his increasingly alarming report.

"After Ranpeti and Nefnet asked us to look into who currently owns the Library of the Sapphire Wind and the land associated with it, I contacted some business associates in Rivers Meet and asked then to look into it—but discreetly. They got us an initial report pretty quickly, and we sent it via xuxu. Did you get it?"

"It came yesterday," Ranpeti said, deftly moving a jar of sweetening syrup out of Brunni's reach before the little girl could add more to her bowl of zinz tea. "So, we know about the trust, and how the trustees closed the trust, in part because of the insurance liabilities. What wasn't clear was who owned the land after that."

"That was harder to find out," Konnel said, "probably deliberately—to make future claims more difficult. Our agents finally confirmed that the Library—and for now, take it as given that when I say 'Library' I mean not just this building, but the associated lands that were owned originally by the founder, Dmen Qeres—is now administered by the regional government. The Library's designation is complex but, when you strip off the legalese, it comes down to this: no one owns the Library, in the sense of assuming liability for anything unpleasant that happens to anyone who decides to come exploring. However, it is open for exploration."

Sefit put in, "We checked that because we wanted to make certain you people couldn't be charged with trespassing or theft or something."

"Letting people explore seems rather generous," Peg put in. "I mean, there is a fair amount of potential wealth here—especially down in the repository."

Sefit spat, neatly hitting a small spittoon she'd set on the floor to one side of her. "So it seems, until you realize that permitting exploration—even treasure hunting—frees the administrative body from even having to post No Trespassing signs, much less rescue anyone who is stupid enough to take the risk."

Her wording just skirted accusing any of those present of actually being stupid, but Grunwold's ears flapped, and he might have said something, if Vereez hadn't reached out and poked him in the ribs with one black-nailed finger.

And were we really stupid? Teg thought. *After all, we did come here in response to a summons, a prophetic verse, whatever you want to call that stuff I babbled after we came through into Hettua Shrine. And if we hadn't come here, Konnel wouldn't be doing as well as he is, and Grunwold would likely be doing much worse. And, as we learned, we were, after a fashion, expected.*

Meg had been taking notes, and now she looked up, ballpoint pen in hand. "What you've told us so far could be considered good news, Konnel-lial, Sefit-lial. But neither your unheralded arrival, nor your body language, give me the sense that you expect us to be in the least happy. May I hazard a guess?"

Teg admired Meg's adroit way of sparing Konnel from having to be the bearer of bad tiding, as well as giving him a little more time to catch his breath. "Stronger" did not mean that Grunwold's father was anything like "strong."

"Please do," Konnel said, lapping from the poffee bowl Sefit held up for him.

"We had already been wondering if the Library might be available for purchase, or for homesteading. Has someone else already put in a claim?"

Sounds of dismay, including a whooshing sound, almost like a scream from Sapphire Wind, filled the air.

Teg thought, *We already think of the Library as "ours"—all of us do, not just Uten Kekui. Could we turn it over to someone else without protest, just because they have the right paperwork?*

"Not yet, Meg-toh," Konnel replied, lowering his antlers in salute. "Sefit, you have the paperwork. Would you take over?"

Sefit nodded. Setting the poffee bowl where Konnel could reach it, she pulled from deep within a square pocket of her caftanlike robe a folded sheaf of papers tied closed with a wide band of fabric. Setting the packet on her lap, she cleared her throat. When she spoke all her cantankerousness had vanished.

"As Meg-lial has already deduced, when our agents began researching what it might take to secure private ownership of the Library, they learned that we were not the only people inquiring about the Library of the Sapphire Wind and associated properties. Nor was this something that happened routinely. The Bureau of Land Management official they spoke with commented that he knew exactly where the appropriate documents were, because he had had to dig them out of the inactive files a short while before."

"My parents," Vereez snarled.

"Indirectly, perhaps," Sefit agreed. "However, not directly."

"They wouldn't dare," Xerak reminded. "The agreement they signed with us barred them from direct or indirect interference."

"But," Vereez snapped, "what if someone came to the House of Fortune for funding for an expedition, and they suspected, but didn't actually *know*?"

"That might avoid invoking the curse," Xerak admitted.

"If I might continue," Sefit said, with just a trace of her usual acid, "while I am not ruling out Zarrq and Inehem, what is interesting is that, for some reason, there seems to be a new awareness of the Library. More than one group has queried."

"But has anyone made any sort of offer?" Meg asked levelly.

"Yes," Sefit nodded, lowering her long eyelashes as she consulted her papers. She raised her voice to be heard over the panicked bedlam that had arisen at her single word. "Konnel and I have—with full intent of transferring the rights to officially homestead the Library of the Sapphire Wind and associated property over to those of you who might be interested."

The babble hushed, and Sefit went on. "The paperwork we have brought with us would initially put you in place as our agents. However, you have our word of honor that we would immediately put into motion the necessary process to have us transfer the homesteading claim over to you. Or, if you are not interested, we would relinquish the claim in a year. This should give you ample time to clear out."

Sefit looked as apologetic as her haughty camel features would permit. "We are sorry, but we could not afford an outright purchase, nor could we afford the associated liability insurance, even if we could have done so."

"Can we afford the insurance?" asked Vereez, daughter of bankers.

"You cannot," Sefit said firmly. "I'm not certain that even Inehem and Zarrq could without undergoing severe financial hardship. The Library has been rated as an incalculably high-risk area for insurance purposes. The good news is that as homesteaders you are not required to have insurance. If you keep and improve the property, by the time you have earned ownership via tenancy—or, I suppose, by finding sufficient financial resources to both purchase and insure the land—you should be able to get an insurance company to recalculate the premium."

Konnel had been lapping poffee. Now he very carefully set down his empty bowl. "We took out the homesteading license immediately upon learning that there were others inquiring about the status of the Library. It's possible that these inquiries were nothing more than another rash of treasure hunters—but if it's something more serious, we weren't taking chances."

"Treasure hunters," Xerak moaned, as if not long before their group hadn't been little better than that themselves. "Sefit-toh, may we see those homesteading documents?"

"I transcribed several copies on the flight over," Sefit said, handing him one set of documents, then offering similar stacks around.

Teg scooted over to where she could read the stack Meg had claimed. Peg joined them.

"Oh, good," Peg said. "Sefit's handwriting is tidy enough that the translation spell can handle it. I wasn't looking forward to having someone dictate it, so we could make a clean copy in English."

Except for Brunni talking to Emsehu as she built something out of small blocks of rubble that had been repurposed as toys, silence reigned while everyone reviewed the homesteading agreement.

Teg broke it by saying, "The agreement looks reasonable. I see we'd be expected to reclaim and improve the land in order to qualify as owners. We can't just squat and pay the property taxes. What about taxes anyhow? Someone mentioned a government. Where there's a government, there are taxes."

"Covered in the fifth section below," Meg said. Not surprisingly, the librarian read the fastest of any of them. "Currently, the taxes are quite low, which is perfectly consistent with the present classification of the Library as a hazardous wilderness area."

Peg nodded. "And since the government isn't collecting any tax revenue now, not even rent, even what little we have to come up with will be a win for them."

A certain amount of further discussion and clarification followed, but Teg didn't expect anyone to refuse to sign, and no one did. In fact, it took them longer to decide on a name for their new company than anything else.

When Teg suggested the accurately descriptive name "Library of the Sapphire Wind Improvement Charter Company," Peg snorted.

"Who would be inspired by that?"

"At least it makes us sound professional," Teg protested. "It's not as if we have any idea what we're doing."

"Nonsense!" Peg said, waving a knitting needle in the air. "We have lots of ideas, and a host of very interesting talents. It's just a matter of figuring out how we combine them."

"It's going to be a hard job," Vereez said. "What about something to do with diamonds? Aren't they supposed to be the hardest thing in the natural world?"

"Rough diamonds!" Peg crowed. "That's it. We're all diamonds in the rough, but we're hard enough that even dealing with this won't crush us."

"I like it," Xerak said. "The Rough Diamond Charter Company, maybe?"

"People will mistake us for jewelers," Grunwold said. "Let's go for something more poetic . . . How about 'House of Rough Diamonds'?"

"I like it," Meg said. "It sounds like a noble house of some sort. It has dignity, as well as humor."

"Show of hands," Teg said, putting her own up first so there would be no doubt that she liked this choice better than her own suggestion. A vari-hued, vari-sized array went up, including Brunni's little hand, which was just beginning to show proper claws. "We're unanimous. Let's fill in the blanks and get started with the signing."

Meg got out a fresh ballpoint pen, while Xerak readied ink and brush for those more accustomed to that manner of writing. Uten Kekui, Cerseru Kham, and Ranpeti all had personal seals: rounded cylinders after the manner of those that had been used throughout Mesopotamia, although these had handles, and were designed either to be heated, then rolled to emboss the paper, or to leave an impression in sealing wax.

"I think it is obvious who the first signatory to both agreements should be," Meg said, a challenging note underlying her pronouncement.

Uten Kekui started to step forward, halted, then looked up at the sparkling blue whirlwind. He made a little bow.

"There would not be a Library for us to improve," he said grandly, "nor open lands for us to claim without the ongoing efforts of Sapphire Wind. Moreover, our including Sapphire Wind as a signatory on these documents will further establish it as an independent entity. As I see it, the only real question is whether Sapphire Wind prefers a pen or a brush."

Sapphire Wind spoke through Friba, the purple-and-green lizard parrot.

"I can do without either," Sapphire Wind said, very formally. With that, it dipped the pointed tip of its funnel cloud into the pool of ink Xerak had prepared.

When her turn came to sign, Teg hesitated as to which form of her name to use, but only for a moment.

I'm "Teg" here. Professor Tessa Brown belongs to another world.

The humans had all learned to write their names in a simple form of the local script, although Grunwold grumbled that their lettering looked "as if we've included a couple of kids Brunni's age in our charter." Teg, looking down at the unfamiliar characters, thought that they hadn't done all that badly.

Shortly after the documents were signed, Konnel and Sefit departed, leaving a selection of odds and ends that Sefit had found in storage at KonSef Estate, and bearing away not only the documents, but a fresh jar of the ointment that Nefnet had compounded. Most of the group went outside to see them off, Brunni sitting up on Grunwold's shoulders, grasping his antlers with one hand, and waving vigorously with the other.

By the time *Cloud Cleaver* had vanished into the distance, darkness was gathering. Everyone went inside to help prepare and then share a celebratory meal. When they had settled in over after-dinner poffee and tea, paired with selections from a box of candy not unlike pralines, Uten Kekui cleared his throat and spoke almost sheepishly.

"Those documents we signed have made it necessary for me to officially return from my unplanned absence. Since the role of custodian of one of the great artifacts is not one that is generally known, I cannot precisely explain why I was absent without warning for over a year. However, wizards are often mysterious, and I shall fall back on that. Nonetheless, I do have loose ends to tie up—my school to officially close, and such."

"I can fly you to Rivers Meet," Grunwold replied promptly. "My parents have agreed to let me use their credit line to make repairs to *Slicewind*. Dad did suggest that I wait a few days, though, so he could set things up."

"A delay of several days will not be an issue," Uten Kekui said, "since until that paperwork is filed, any rumors about my return will not begin to spread. Indeed, if it were not that I feel certain that it will be rumor worthy that there is a group officially homesteading the Library, I suspect my signature would go unnoticed."

"What about the transport portal we used to get to the Creator's Visage Isles?" Peg asked. "That was super cool, and I recall that Xerak said the instructions included a setting for Zisurru University."

Uten Kekui looked uneasy. "At the time I vanished, my lessons with Xerak hadn't progressed to in-depth study of various types of magical items. Transport items, in particular, can malfunction after repeated use—and this one, as I recall, encountered interference the last time you used it."

"When Inehem and Zarrq attempted to hijack Brunni," Peg agreed. "We had to keep the portal open a lot longer than we'd planned."

Cerseru Kham added, "There are reasons that transport artifacts have not replaced more traditional forms of getting from one place to another."

Like flying ships, Teg thought, suppressing a giggle, *or carriages pulled by frilled lizards.*

"I noticed," Meg said thoughtfully, "a certain similarity between the Bridge of Lives and the pathway that was created when Inehem intercepted our use of the transport spell. The transport spell works quickly, so I'm guessing the user doesn't see the bridge, but there is one, isn't there?"

"Precisely," Cerseru Kham said, looking at Meg with admiration. "Too many such bridges would wreak havoc on the fabric of space and time. There are reports, millennia old now, so hardly more than legends, that provide warning."

Uten Kekui said, "I will inspect the transport artifact that we have, as well as any others we may find in the repository, to make certain they are safe to use. I could never create such a device, but I can do that much."

"I will help," Cerseru Kham said, "and perhaps Xerak can sit in and treat this as a lesson."

Xerak nodded. "Absolutely. Better a partial lesson than not at all, and I don't think I'm going to be enrolling at Zisurru University any time soon."

Left unsaid was, *If at all.* Xerak's formal magical education had taken a strange turn when he had devoted himself to his search for Uten Kekui. Although he had qualified for the equivalent of his undergraduate degree, someone with his raw talent would certainly benefit from more training, but Xerak had a self-admitted "itchy foot," a fondness for roaming, that a year of travel had fed rather than sated.

Kaj, who was sitting over to one side, carving a spinning top for Brunni, said, "I was planning to go the Isles, both to make certain that Qes Wen was still safely hidden, and to let the acolytes of the Grantor know that they can keep up their cult of miracles all they want, but as long as I live, they're not going to be linking up to Qes Wen for extra juice."

"We"—Cerseru Kham gestured to Uten Kekui—"can help you to check on Qes Wen from here. As for the cult of miracles, perhaps it is best if they don't realize precisely how and where the power behind many of their miracles came. I believe the cult existed before the Grantor and the custodian of Qes Wen became associated. It simply rose to greater prominence then."

Kaj looked relieved. "I don't really mind not having to tell them off, but I was worried that someone would get a line on Qes Wen anyhow. After all, the Library draws on Ba Djed."

Ohent patted her son on one muscular arm. "I'm sure you'd do a brilliant job of telling them off, but maybe it would be enough if your new associates showed you how to protect your charge."

Her pride was evident, and no wonder.

Ohent did the least well of the extraction agents. Now, not only is she something of a hero for how she protected the Bird, her son is raised to prominence. And, best of all, her own long nightmare is ended.

Uten Kekui and Cerseru Kham were quick to reassure Kaj that they would help him learn to protect Qes Wen.

Cerseru Kham added with a throaty chuckle, "After all, Kaj, you're certainly much easier to convince to take your responsibilities seriously than my other colleague."

Uten Kekui made an ambiguous gesture, indicating something between annoyance and resignation, and she laughed again.

In an obvious attempt to change the subject, Uten Kekui said, "It's actually a good thing that we will have a few more days before we set sail for Rivers Meet. When we arrived here at the Library, I was not precisely in the best of health. I've been rather limited in my ability to explore the Library, and I just realized, I have no real idea of what we have undertaken to improve and defend in our role as homesteaders. Would it be possible to have some sort of tour?"

Peg looked up from her knitting and gave a brisk nod of approval. "A tour would be a good idea. Even those of us who have seen the surrounding area numerous times from the air should look it over with our new duties in mind."

Vereez, who had been playing catch with Brunni, tossed the soft fabric ball right over Brunni's ears in her sudden enthusiasm. Ahmax, one of the dobergoats who had assigned themselves the role of serving as Brunni's guards and playmates, fetched the ball back, wriggling its bronze-and-gold-striped, snake-scaled haunches with pleasure when Brunni patted it as a reward.

Who would ever have thought that a creature that we first encountered because it was trying to kill us could actually look so darn cute? Teg thought. *But I think we'll be grateful for the fiercer side of the dobergoats and some of the other creatures—up to and including some we humans haven't seen yet—before this is over.*

Vereez apologized to Brunni, then continued, "Up to now, we've been looking at the area from above, and that's good in its way, but we're going to need to remember that most of the treasure hunters and land grabbers and whatever else who will try to get in here will sneak in on the ground. We're going to need to arrange defenses."

Meg put in, "I wonder if Kuvekt-lial has had a sudden run on his archives, and, if so, if he'd tell us what he's sold?"

"Good thoughts, both of you," Xerak said. "Kuvekt has a reputation for collecting information on the Library and its surroundings following the destruction. I don't think he'd be averse to letting us know, especially since we're on the way to being the new owners."

"Tomorrow then, early," Grunwold said, shifting from one booted foot to the other, as if he could hurry the dawn along, "we'll take *Slicewind* up and do an aerial survey to familiarize Uten Kekui, and anyone else who wants to come along, with what our surroundings are like. Then we can do as Vereez suggested and inspect where we'll need ground defenses."

He scooped up Brunni and handed her to Ranpeti, all in one smooth motion. "We're going sailing tomorrow, kiddo. If you want to come along, you'd better go sleepy-bye."

"I think that applies to the rest of us as well," Teg said. "I'm off for a final smoke and then bed. Catch you all in the morning."

❦⟨CHAPTER FIVE⟩❧

Slicewind rose into the skies the next morning with a fair-sized group, all bundled against the chill they would find at higher elevations, gathered on the upper deck. In addition to the wizards, there was Ranpeti, who had admitted that she had felt so safe within the Library's walls that she hadn't thought much about their surroundings. "But now I want a look."

After the promise of the night before, nothing short of physical restraint was going to keep Brunni from coming along. That meant that Vereez was set on being part of the expedition. Teg went because her specialized skills in aerial survey would be useful. Surprisingly, Emsehu asked if he could go along.

"It has been a very long time since I have seen the Library's grounds," he said, "and never from above. Even what I remember from my attempts at ground level will be useless by now. Each time, aspects of the terrain had changed. Among the treasure hunters—of which I did not consider myself, I assure you—there was much speculation as to whether these changes were indications of active defenses or merely the result of seismic activity, latent vulcanism, and the increasing territory claimed by the lake."

"Certainly, the latter would be sufficient reason for changes," Teg said, "but we know that even in its diminished state Sapphire Wind was defending the Library until what it had decided were the 'right' people arrived."

Not everyone joined the expedition. Meg and Peg stayed behind, as did Ohent and Kaj.

"I want to work up a basic map," Meg said, "so we have something ready to add details to."

Peg said, "And I'm going to put together a pot of chowder. Grace caught a whole basket of lobsaws, which is great, but they'll spoil if they're not cooked."

"Kaj and I can start working on plans for tricks and traps," Ohent said, rubbing her hands together in anticipation. "I was always good at that—and I didn't lose it all during my 'problems.' Sometimes I think that seeing the world inside out and sideways was actually an advantage. Kaj picked up a surprising amount about passive safeguards and defenses while working at various necropolises."

At setting them or dismantling them? Teg wondered, for there had been some hints that Kaj and Ohent had augmented their earnings by robbing mausoleums. *And it's also likely that Xerak's mother, Fardowsi, bought some of the take for her antiquities shop. No . . . Better not to ask.*

Grunwold brought *Slicewind* slowly aloft, then circled the ship around, so that they could study the ground closest to the central plaza. Teg let her gaze skim over the terrain below, not so much looking for anything in particular as searching for anomalies that should be inspected later.

I wonder if Sapphire Wind has some sort of internalized map of the terrain. Somehow, I doubt it. Maybe an awareness, but not anything as precise as a map, and I bet that awareness is more detailed closer to the Library itself. It's tempting to think of Sapphire Wind as having a sort of GPS but, from what I can gather, I think what it feels is more like the entire area is its residence, and it has an "ear" for what sort of sounds are normal and which are "off." This will certainly be helpful, but it's not going to make our job simple.

Since Grunwold was fully occupied between handling *Slicewind's* wheel and answering Brunni's questions ("No, you can't steer the ship today." "Thank you for the cookie, but I need to give some attention to the sail settings."), Xerak and Vereez were nominated tour guides. Xerak took up a post in the bow, and Vereez climbed up into the crow's nest.

"Our tour is going to be not only of what is here now," Xerak began, "but of what was here before. We're basing this on old maps, and also what Nefnet was kind enough to tell us."

Nefnet had also stayed behind. She'd seen the surrounding landscape already, shortly after she had been unarchived to treat Konnel's illness. Xerak had tried to get her to come along on this trip, but she'd refused.

"For you, Xerak, what happened here occurred before you were born. Even for those like Cerseru Kham, who had visited the Library, twenty-five years have gone by. For me, it has only been a few months. For most of you, this is a historical site, while for me it was— if not precisely my home, then where I worked and had my current residence. I still don't know how many of the people I knew here survived to go on living their lives or if, like me, they ended up among the Archived.

Teg thought that Nefnet's reaction was more than reasonable.

And a reminder, even if Nefnet didn't mean for it to be, that we have more to deal with than the possibility of treasure hunters or claim jumpers. Sooner or later, we're going to need to deal with people who have no idea that the world they knew is gone.

Compared to contemplating problems like that, viewing the overgrown landscape below and trying to pinpoint landmarks was positively welcoming.

When *Slicewind* had achieved sufficient altitude, Grunwold called out, "Xerak, Teg, I'm going to shift our heading so we can drop the wind from the sail. When I do, you two furl it."

He turned so that he could address all the passengers. "We'll more or less hover, so you can get an overview. Then we'll set sail and take a closer look at various features—assuming that's what you want."

After assisting Teg with the sail, Xerak returned to his place on the slightly raised bow platform, folded his hands around his spear staff, and assumed a slightly artificial "lecturer" tone.

"Dmen Qeres built his original library in the foothills of what was then a gentle upthrust mountain range within easy reach of a moderate-sized lake. The climate of the area he chose was temperate verging into subtropical and, due to the influence of the lake, was protected from more extreme temperature shifts.

"Originally, there was only one building, the Library of the Sapphire Wind itself. Dmen Qeres chose not to place the Library precisely in the center of his property, but on higher ground, somewhat to the west, nearer to the mountains. The lake was to the northeast of the Library. Forested land filled in most of the rest of his property. When the Library began to expand, several more buildings were built on the hill, near the Library, around a central plaza. A village was established in a meadow near the lake for the increased number of support staff required to permit the scholars to focus on their intellectual pursuits.

"The disastrous events of some twenty-five years ago changed the terrain to a considerable extent. When the Library was pulled—or dropped, we really don't know which—beneath ground level, the shape of the original hill was altered, and the general nature of the forested landscape became less gently rolling, more interrupted by fissures and the other artifacts of seismic activity. The lake expanded, becoming the northern border of the property. Something—we suspect one or more warding spells gone wrong—actually transformed the mountains to the west. From a gently eroded upthrust range, they became what you now can see: a spiky, craggy range. According to the numerous travelers' journals that Meg has read, the mountains are nearly impassable."

Xerak made a sweeping gesture with the tip of his spear staff. "Dramatic as the changes to the lake, the mountains, the forested terrain, all are, the most startling alteration to the terrain was to the south. Remember what I said about how originally the area was mostly forests? When you look south, you'll notice an interruption in the forest—a brownish, blackened area."

Ranpeti asked, "Was there a forest fire? There seem to be stands of dead trees, although not nearly enough to account for a forest."

Xerak coughed a lion's laugh. "You're both wrong and right, Ranpeti-toh. There was a forest fire but—and again, this is mostly speculation, based largely on the journals we got from Kuvekt-lial— the conflagration was lit from beneath. From the mountains in the west, all the way along the southern edge, down to where the lake overflowed in the east, the land became volcanically active."

Cerseru Kham raised a hand, and when Xerak gave her a little bow of acknowledgement, said, "I visited the Library of the Sapphire Wind several times before the destruction. I was somewhat older than you are now, doing advanced study. Some of us who were staying at the hotel took advantage of a nearby hot springs. I recall making our way through the woods, not toward the village, nor toward the lake, nor the mountains, so probably to the south."

"One of the memoirs," Xerak said, "this one from a scribe who lived in Meadow Village, and was one of the survivors of the catastrophe, also mentions hot springs. Our guess"—he looked at the two senior wizards, clearly inviting comment or speculation—"is that, as with the mountains, warding spells went out of control."

Uten Kekui had been listening with half-closed eyes, something in the tilt of his bison head, and the slowness of his breathing, making Teg wonder if he was trying not only to listen, but also to remember.

"Given that Dmen Qeres established the library and repository," said the man who had been Dmen Qeres, "to mask and protect the magic in Ba Djed of the Weaver, I am certain that powerful wards would have been placed on all the boundaries. Meg-lial was kind enough to permit me to borrow some of the journals Kuvekt-lial entrusted to her. If even half of what is described as happening during the catastrophe—including the critical magical overload—actually occurred, then not only would the wards have been activated, they would quite likely have tapped into the rampant free mana. Having wards drain magic not recognizable as belonging to what the ward is meant to protect is a common precaution."

Vereez spoke from the crow's nest. "I did something like that, when I used the power of the lightning shadows against them. Wouldn't the wards have recognized that all the mana was coming from inside their own boundaries?"

Uten Kekui replied, "A reasonable question. Yes, if the mana had been more or less normal—and what 'normal' means is too complex for discussion—this would have been the case. However, the critical magical overload would have mutated the mana, as well as destroying any, oh, call them 'stamps' or 'seals'—although they would have not been merely physical—put onto items that belonged to the collection. Then the mana would have blended, and what that blending created would have been nothing the wards would recognize."

"Thank you, Uten Kekui-va," Vereez said formally. "Your mention of lessons reminds me. My question has definitely taken us from our original purpose for this tour. Let's get back on focus. Have you seen enough, or would you like to continue on a more detailed tour? We do need to figure out where any intruders might try to get through, especially since we don't have the wards the original Library did."

Everyone agreed that they wanted to see more, so the sails were reset, and Grunwold took *Slicewind* out in a slow spiral, heading first to the north.

Vereez took up the role of tour guide. "The lake is the obvious 'easy point,' for entry. It's also the border over which it will be the easiest to see anyone approaching. We've glimpsed creatures that seem to support the rumors and stories of monsters in the depths. Even the more 'normal' ones, like the lobsaws Peg is cooking for us, are larger than usual."

Teg added, "And we have our own monster to help. Grace seems to have decided that she likes the area where Meadow Village was, and where we have the backup landing cradle for sky sailers. If we could work out a way for her to get messages to us, especially when Heru is away with Grunwold, we have a start there."

Having seen the lake repeatedly, she didn't crowd over to the rail, but pulled out her little notebook and started a list. After they had skimmed over the lake, Grunwold turned *Slicewind* to the east and south, over the area that looked like a burned forest.

"In daylight," he said, "especially from up here, the lava field doesn't look nearly as bad as it is. At night, you can see the hot blood of the earth is still there, under the rock. It's very dramatic, and actually very creepy."

Teg put in, "Volcanic rock—basalt and obsidian both—are sharp and rough. I've ruined a lot of good boot soles hiking in the *malpais*." She trusted that the translation spell would handle the Spanish for "badlands," as easily as it seemed to handle English. "So, even if there are cooler areas down there that could serve as trails, the area won't automatically provide easy access for invaders. In fact, where the obsidian is broken up, those areas would be like a field of razor blades."

"That's a thought," Grunwold said. "I bet we could create a more defensible border by dropping some rocks onto the glassy areas from the ship."

"Not a bad idea at all," Xerak agreed.

Teg said, "I'll make a note of it. Let's finish the tour first."

Vereez said, "I'd like us to take a closer look at the mountains.

Now that we know both the lake and the fiery plain aren't open and easy, the mountains become the obvious entry point. From above, we'll be in a better position to see where there are any passes."

No one disagreed, so they spent a productive time surveying the sharp-peaked mountain range. Gusts of wind and thermal updrafts provided anything but smooth sailing, and several of the passengers got airsick. Nonetheless, before they turned back, Teg had sketched a rough map with several potential passes marked.

As they sailed back toward the Library building, the tour group's mood was decidedly mixed. On the one hand, the area they had signed on to homestead did have defensible borders. However, there were plenty of areas where a determined or creative group could sneak in.

Ranpeti, who was sitting on one of the side benches, a drowsy Brunni in her lap, voiced what Teg felt certain was a concern they all felt.

"There simply aren't enough of us," she said, "to hold this large an area, particularly if we face some sort of coordinated invasion.

"You're thinking of my parents, aren't you, Aunt Ranpeti?" Vereez said.

"Actually," Ranpeti replied, "I wasn't. I think Inehem and Zarrq are going to be very careful. The agreement we signed with them did say 'direct' or 'indirect' inference would invoke the mange curse. However, there may well be others who will be interested in keeping us from proving our claim. While you were away, I had some very interesting talks with both Cerseru Kham and Nefnet. They have very different points of view and, between them, they have several theories as to who might decide that it's worthwhile to come poking around—especially once the rumors spread that the Library building itself has been located."

Cerseru Kham leaned forward. "I don't think that there has been a single year at Zisurru University that hasn't had at least one club form with the goal of finding the Library. Most of these don't make it beyond the initial research and dreaming stage, but treasure is a powerful lure. Once rumor leaks out that someone has actually found the place, well, I don't think our having filed for homesteading rights will dim the shine."

"Brighten it, more likely," Uten Kekui said. "When the impossible becomes possible, then the dangers are minimized, in favor of grabbing while the grabbing is good."

Teg added, "My profession contains numerous examples of thieves who view ability to commit theft as permission to do so. Whether you call them tomb robbers, pot hunters, or treasure hunters, it doesn't matter. I guess it's no different here than where I come from. People think that if they're smart enough to figure out a way to steal, then that gives them the right."

She noticed that Xerak was swishing his tail and forth in an agitated manner. She wondered if he was thinking about the antiquities business his parents owned, and the recent revelations that it was likely that not all of what they sold had been legitimately acquired.

"But we don't want," Uten Kekui asked, "to take on more partners in our venture, do we?"

Various vocalizations, combined with pinning back of ears or curling of whiskers, where appropriate, made clear that this, at least, was universally agreed upon.

"Which seems to indicate," Cerseru Kham said, "that we will need to hire help. I have some savings and so, I gather, do most of you. However, these would be exhausted fairly quickly if we needed to hire the equivalent of a mercenary force."

"And," Vereez said from above, her voice tight, "the problem with mercenaries is that they can be bought by whichever side pays a higher rate. We need reliable help."

Emsehu made a deep grumbly noise in his throat. "There are guardian creatures, but most are neither as powerful nor as intelligent as I am. Assets, yes, but not solutions."

"Even if I asked my parents for a loan of people from KonSef Estate," Grunwold said, "they would still need to be paid. I think that, unless Teg-toh has a major objection, we're going to need to turn treasure hunter ourselves." He gave one of his eloquent shrugs. "Then maybe we could hire some of my parents' labor, or something."

"Or something," Ranpeti said thoughtfully. "I have the beginnings of an idea. We're almost back to the Library. Once we're docked and I've put snookums here down for an n-a-p, I'll see if I can explain it. It's a bit dicey, but it might be a start."

✳✳✳

While Ranpeti went to put a still slightly airsick Brunni to bed, the rest assembled in the reception hall. Over bowls of Peg's excellent lobsaw chowder, they briefed those who had stayed behind, including showing off Teg's rough map of the mountains. From the expressions on various faces, it was clear that no one was going to argue that they were short-staffed.

Soon after Teg had settled herself at one end of the table and begun to help Meg add details to her map, Ranpeti returned, accepted a bowl of poffee from Peg, then slumped into a chair.

"Ranpeti-toh," Xerak prompted, "you said you had a suggestion?"

Ranpeti sucked in about half the bowl of poffee, then sighed.

"I'd like to start with a question for Sapphire Wind," she said, raising her face to look at Friba the lizard parrot, who was perched on one of the sage stations overlooking the long tables. "You cared for these lands—for all of Dmen Qeres's property—for many years, even after Dmen Qeres had died, even after the breaking of Ba Djed left you weak. Can you continue to do so now? My understanding is that you are more powerful now than you were for many of those years."

Friba shifted from foot to foot. "I could, but only if you did not care if anyone died, and only if you did little more to make this area habitable."

"I was afraid of that," Ranpeti said.

Peg patted her on the shoulder and refilled her poffee bowl. "I know, making the property habitable is one of the conditions for fulfilling the homesteading charter." She shifted her voice to mimic a sort of Monty Python and the Holy Grail accent. "So, leaving it filled with peril is right out."

"We were discussing just this point while you were out," Meg added. "Anything we do to prove we are sincere about homesteading this property will make it easier for someone else to take it away from us."

"It's an old problem," Teg said, "at least where we come from. There's a fairly convincing argument that one reason the more aggressive of the indigenous peoples in the American Southwest did not wipe out the less-aggressive farming peoples is that if they did so, they would need to take over the tedious work of farming. So much easier to raid every few harvests, and so much more exciting than trade."

Ohent nodded. "As a reformed thief—which is what I was, no matter how much prettier 'extraction agent' sounds—part of the reason we took it up was the adrenaline buzz. Part was feeling clever. And a good many times, the reason someone hired us was because hiring us to get whatever it was that they wanted was cheaper than buying the goods outright."

Ranpeti turned her attention to Nefnet, her large, brown seal eyes sorrowful and apologetic.

Although how I can tell that, Teg thought, *given that she lacks the mobile ears that makes it comparatively easy to read so many of the others' moods, I don't know. Maybe it has to do with the curl of her whiskers, or maybe it's her body language. That's human enough.*

"There is one group," Ranpeti said, "who might be willing to work with us, a group that has, or could have, an attachment to preserving the Library, and yet no more sense of ownership than do tenants of a rental apartment for their home."

She paused, and Meg spoke into the uneasy silence.

"The Archived. Nefnet, do you think that would work? Could we possibly recruit some of the Archived?"

Nefnet frowned. "There could be difficulties. For example, I was permitted to sign the homesteading charter. Others might feel they should have the same option, especially since I was hardly the most powerful or important person in residence at the time. On the other hand, if someone else took over the Library, and somehow gained authority over Sapphire Wind, they might never be unarchived. That should count for something."

Grunwold said gruffly, "We could argue that you were asked to sign the charter because your skills were what we needed to help my dad—and me—which in turn led to us being able to do what we needed to do to win Sapphire Wind's cooperation."

Uten Kekui cut in, "I'd prefer that we didn't mention precisely what that was. The less general knowledge there is about Ba Djed of the Weaver—of any of the three artifacts that maintain the Bridge of Lives—the better."

Cerseru Kham nodded so hard her large ears flapped. "I agree. We need to keep knowledge of the great artifacts and what they can do close, not only because that has been traditional since the Bridge was established, but . . ." She looked uneasy. "My teacher hinted that if the knowledge became too general, bad things could happen. She never said precisely what, but given what we've already seen, let's just say that I don't want to find out."

"I think we can manage," Ohent said. "It helps that, in one way or another, all the lives of those present here have been touched—corrupted even—by one of those things. We already know what one third of Ba Djed did to me. I don't think we want to risk any other such life lessons."

A general murmur of agreement followed this, then Ranpeti returned her attention back to Nefnet. "Would you have any idea who among the Archived might be more inclined to be hired on?"

"I might," Nefnet said hesitantly. "The problem is, I didn't know even all of the staff, much less all of the support personnel, nor do I know who was here at the time of the catastrophe and who was away. The extraction agents chose the Hebs Henu holiday, when many of those who lived at the Library were away."

"Sapphire Wind," Xerak said, addressing Friba as Ranpeti had done, "when we first came here, you told us just how many you had archived. I seem to recall a rather large number."

"Four hundred and twenty-three," replied Sapphire Wind immediately.

"Oh, no," Nefnet said, "that's not possible. I don't think that even when the Library was in full session there could have been more than nine hundred, and that would have included every researcher, scribe, cook, bottle washer, laundry worker, and well . . . everyone! Some of the support staff had their families with them, although most of those would have been away for the Hebs Henu. I recall hearing that most of the children were gone."

"Four hundred and twenty-three," repeated Friba on behalf of Sapphire Wind.

"I can't believe that," Nefnet insisted. "I remember feeling as if we were rattling around liked dried seeds in a pod."

"Four hundred and twenty-three," repeated Sapphire Wind stubbornly, and as a sort of punctuation, the stars in the astronomical mural overhead glittered. Teg recalled how Sapphire Wind had claimed to have archived those who would have otherwise been killed in those stars.

"That's the size of a village," Vereez said, sounding a bit faint. "I don't think I really considered what that number meant at the time—we had so many other things to think about."

Including that your parents, your mother most specifically, had been responsible for setting off a critical magical overload, Teg thought.

Ohent, who had been listening with focused intensity, spoke, "Sapphire Wind, Nefnet is right—your numbers are too high." She made an apologetic noise deep in her throat. "As one of the extraction agents, as you have been kind enough to term us, we did careful research before choosing our target date. We estimated no more than two hundred residents would be present, and that included some generous padding to allow for people sneaking in guests. We learned later that some of those who were in Meadow Village did escape. They were lucky that there were several vessels waiting at the lake to take off the last of those who would be leaving on holiday."

"Four hundred twenty-three," repeated Friba.

Meg cut in, "Do you have an inventory? You must, I feel certain. How else could you have found Nefnet for us when we needed someone capable of treating Konnel and Grunwold?"

Friba the lizard parrot nibbled up one wing, then flexed its crest, before speaking for Sapphire Wind. "I do. It is not written and would take a great deal of time for me to dictate. However, I could design a facsimile that could be displayed in the Font of Sight."

Meg gave a short, crisp nod of approval. "That would be perfect. How long would you need to prepare?"

"Transforming my information into something like a readable text will be a complex process," Sapphire Wind replied. "Many of you are already weary from your voyage. Perhaps we could convene tomorrow morning?"

"That would be great," Grunwold said. He shoved himself to his feet and ran his fingers over his antlers, something he only did when very anxious. "Meanwhile, I'll admit, I'm feeling edgy. Unless anyone has any objections, I'm going to take *Slicewind* on a perimeter patrol."

Kaj rose and stretched. "I missed the tour, especially the part over the mountains. Now I'm thinking that was a mistake. Can I crew for you?"

At this, the rest of the prior stay-behinds opted to join Grunwold. Although she wanted to work on the map, Teg joined those who were putting together the evening meal, taking a turn washing the bowls from which they'd eaten their chowder.

We do need help, Teg thought. *Even keeping the dozen or so of us fed, and doing the routine cleaning up, takes too much time and resources. I'm beginning to understand why the Library of the Sapphire Wind had such a large support staff.*

Uten Kekui proved to have a tidy hand with a cleaver, and was chopping up the vegetables that would be the basis for the stir-fry-style dish Cerseru Kham had offered to make for dinner. He paused in the midst of chopping up ysiyenes, a long root vegetable, white as a daikon radish on the outside, but with a bright violet core.

"I wish I could remember more of what Dmen Qeres might have hidden in the Library or grounds," he said, "but I don't have the faintest idea."

"It's likely," Cerseru Kham reminded him, "that whatever wealth he had he signed over to the trust for the maintenance of the Library."

"True," Uten Kekui said, "but surely, he would have wanted himself—me—to have funds. On the other hand, he sounds arrogant enough to assume that in whatever station he was reborn, he would be able to achieve wealth and status by the time he remembered who he was."

Teg smiled to herself, wondering what Xerak would think if he could hear his revered "Master" talking this way.

And how much of Uten Kekui's initial attempt to claim the Library as his own was showing off for Xerak? He may not want Xerak's love, but there's no way he doesn't want his admiration.

The next morning after breakfast, they all headed into the room off the main reception hall that was devoted to the Font of Sight. The dust and sense of disuse that had shrouded the chamber the first time they had entered it were abau-polished away. More than ever Teg felt as if she was taking her seat within the interior of a pearl. The only flat part of the room was where the base of the Font itself—an elegant nacreous-white marble chalice—rested, with just room enough that a lecturer could stand alongside.

The first times they had used the Font, they had carefully grouped so that they were all on one side, so no one would need to look at the images upside down or from the side. Today, as they filed in, Meg said, "Sit wherever you would like. Sapphire Wind has just informed me that 'like magic' the images will appear correctly aligned from any seat."

Grunwold chuckled, "But I bet my antlers will still get in the way, so I'll sit toward the back. Want to join me, Vereez?"

Brunni cut in before Vereez could reply. "Me! Me! I wanna sit with Grunwold!"

Teg wondered if Grunwold had counted on that because, if there was bait to lure Vereez, it was the little girl. If so, his ploy worked, and Vereez, Brunni, and Grunwold took seats in one of the back rows. If Grunwold was disappointed that Brunni inserted herself between Vereez and himself, he was too smart to show it. Ranpeti seated herself one row in front of the trio, a visible reminder of maternal authority.

"C'mon," Peg said, grabbing Teg's wrist. "Let's grab seats in the first row." She lowered her voice. "If we need to read text, I'm going to need to dig out my cheaters."

Friba flew to perch on one of the vacant seats, and announced, "Behold, the Roster of the Archived."

A list unfurled within the Font's chalice in a fashion that rather reminded Teg of the opening credits of the movie *Star Wars*. The information it offered was simple enough: a name, a professional designation, and whether the person in question was staff, support, or a visitor. Visitors were subdesignated as researchers or guests. A short description of the person's primary role was also included. From these, Teg could see how what she persisted in thinking of as a Library could have needed so many people. Librarians were listed, but so were sages, scribes, lab technicians, archivists, catalogers, bookbinders, pages, herbalists, illustrators, and cartographers. A little pink diamond indicated those who possessed magical skills.

And these were just the staff. The "support" included cooks, gardeners, livestock handlers, cleaners, laundry and tailoring, drivers (who doubled as stable hands), dishwashers, quartermasters, security guards, bartenders, doctors, and even a small team who ran a general store. The same little pink diamond marked those with magical abilities, which sometimes came up where Teg would never have expected it.

"It's one thing to be told that this was a complex community," Peg whispered, "but this really brings it home."

"I've been thinking the same thing," Teg whispered back. "This wasn't just a library and repository. It was a research center without the impedimenta of unenthusiastic undergrads."

By the time the unfurling list reached several people the translation spell designated as "jack-of-all-trades," Teg had lost count. Nonetheless, she didn't think there had been anything like four hundred people.

Then the character of the list changed. Instead of name and profession, there was name followed by what Teg thought must be species, because the first dozen or so were "xuxu." There were also several oothynn, the same type of creature of which Grace was apparently an over-sized representative.

Vereez, her voice choked up, as if she was barely holding back tears, said, "Sapphire Wind saved *everyone* it could, not just the sennutep and variuvar, *everyone*."

"Sennutep? Variuvar?" Peg asked in a tone that said she'd already half guessed the answer.

"Sennutep are people like us," Xerak said, "what you called 'people with animal heads,' when you first got here. Variuvar are other types of people—like oothynn or xuxu—language users, but not necessarily tool users or city builders, although they can be. It's a pretty loose category, to be honest."

Teg noticed how Grunwold had reached to touch Heru, where the xuxu had nestled down on his shoulder.

"The flyers might have escaped," he said gruffly, "but xuxu, especially the imprinted ones, are very loyal. Or, if these were housed inside this building, they might not have been able to get away."

Nefnet was actually smiling, her posture signaling relief. "We had a roost of xuxu right here. They carried messages both inside the Library and between buildings. I had wondered..."

Her voice trailed off and Teg, thinking how happy she'd been when her cats, Thought and Memory, had found their way Over Where, understood that Nefnet had not so much "wondered" as dreaded that the doubtless engaging flock of mini pterodactyl-like flyers had died—perhaps trapped, doubtless terrified—in the conflagration.

"You are pleased," Sapphire Wind said. "I had wondered if you would be, since there often seemed to be a division between types of living creatures. I am relieved that I expended my resources correctly."

"You did absolutely correct," Peg said firmly. "Now that we've seen the list, I wonder if our first area of recruitment should be the xuxu. Our guarding the borders would be a lot easier if we could get messages to each other more quickly. Nefnet, you did say they took messages outside of the building, right?"

"They did," Nefnet assured her. "Many times, messages needed to be carried to other buildings up here on the plaza. They also went to the lakeside docks and Meadow Village. They knew the entire area—as it was then, of course—very well."

Grunwold spoke to Heru, "Maybe you can explain to these other xuxu what happened, buddy."

"Can! Will!" Heru trumpeted. "Xuxu are very smart, not like those silly efindon."

Sapphire Wind's spokes-creature did not rise to the taunt, and Heru seemed vaguely disappointed.

Meg said, "What do you think of our idea, Sapphire Wind? Can you unarchive the messenger xuxu?"

"I can," Sapphire Wind replied, "but they will cope better if we have their roost prepared for them. I can show you where it was on the original library map, but it was in an area where no one has gone since the catastrophe. I cannot say how safe it will be."

"Only one way to find out," Xerak said. "Shall we take a look?"

Meg begged off joining the roost search party.

"There's something I want to investigate further regarding Sapphire Wind's list. And"—she smiled gently—"although I have shown myself to be an excellent watcher, I am not the best fighter in our band."

"We'll be fine, Meg-toh," Grunwold assured her. "All the better for knowing that you'll organize a rescue if we don't make it back."

❦ CHAPTER SIX ❦

The need for a rescue party was not as ridiculous a statement as it might seem to someone viewing the calm, strangely domestic gathering. During their earlier explorations into the Library's stacks, they had been attacked by acid bats, book worms, and dobergoats. Even if Sapphire Wind now had better control over some of the Library's denizens—especially those like the abau which were not very intelligent, or those which had been designed for nonaggressive tasks—the *genius loci* was the first to admit that it did not know what lurked in the rubble-filled corridors amid burned tomes.

Planning their expedition didn't take a great deal of time, since by now they had a firm idea of each other's strong and weak points. Teg might not have had Peg's training with a sword, nor done much actual fighting before her arrival Over Where (playground brawls excepted; as a mixed-race outcast, she'd had more than her share of these), but there was no way she was going to back out.

Although their practical needs meant that Teg could not submit the Library to the sort of systematic excavation she would have liked, being on the spot meant that she might still be able to make some discoveries—not so much about what the Library had been like; the Archived would be able to tell them that—but about what might have happened in the days, weeks, months, even years, when the Library was in flux, as the forces of fire and magic reshaped the structure, and quite possibly created something entirely new.

In the several months since their earliest explorations, they'd had indications that the Library had changed to a far greater extent than they'd anticipated. Those initial explorations had been tightly focused, first on finding the artifacts repository, then on retrieving the fragment of Ba Djed of the Weaver. However, later, when Nefnet, then Ohent, then Ranpeti and Brunni, had taken up residence in the structure, Grunwold had spearheaded a project to create a more habitable environment—a dwelling place, rather than an indoor camping spot.

Their first goal had been opening up the staff bathroom. That had gone more or less as expected. Encouraged by this, first Ohent and Nefnet, later assisted by Ranpeti, had decided to create individual bedrooms off the reception hall. Sapphire Wind had been in favor of this, and suggested they use the area through the eastern arch, where the reference room had been. The *genius loci* had assigned Emsehu and other guardian creatures to help with clearing away debris—as well as to protect them against whatever menaces lurked amid the ash, the result of the release of so much magical energy in an enclosed space.

When they'd taken on opening up the public restroom, they'd been in for a surprise.

Although the staff break room had been comparatively well appointed, with two toilets, a double sink, as well as a combination shower/tub unit—and everyone had appreciated the improvement over the porta-potty arrangement Konnel and Sefit had donated from *Cloud Cleaver*—as the resident community had grown, both restroom facilities and tempers (since most of those living there had been accustomed to more luxurious accommodations) had been increasingly strained.

For this reason, after *Slicewind* had returned with Uten Kekui and Cerseru Kham, both of whom intended to become long-term residents, Sapphire Wind had suggested that they open up the public bathroom off the reception hall. Not only did this have more toilets and sinks, but the plumbing could provide water for additional bathing facilities. By then, they'd been prepared for spontaneously generated monsters or former guardians gone feral. What they hadn't counted on was discovering that several of the toilets—stalls and all—had vanished. Where these had been was now a small pond, complete with resident fish and flowers.

The "fish" actually looked closer to very small plesiosaurs, with minutely scaled skins in shades of copper and gold, and long fluttery veils trailing off their swim fins. Vereez identified them as ketjibetu, and commented that they were not uncommon in more high-end ornamental ponds. Peg, of course, promptly dubbed them "nessies." The "water lily" grew in a similar fashion to the Earthside version, although the pads had four lobes, more like those of a shamrock, and the pale blue flowers had many small, spikey petals, closer to those of a lotus.

When Ohent's reconstruction crew—augmented by *Slicewind's* crew—had recovered from the shock, and confirmed that neither nessies nor water lilies were dangerous varieties, they'd adapted their plans. A makeshift wall had been erected to one side of the pond, creating a separate room, mostly to keep Brunni from having easy access to the water feature. This had the added benefit of providing a private area where an adult or two could get away from the rambunctious four-year-old. The remaining part of the public bathroom (which still had toilets and sinks) was a vast improvement over the previous arrangements, so everyone was happy.

In part to keep anyone from jockeying for a suite with a private bath, in part because it already had sinks with running water, the staff break room was then converted into the kitchen. They'd set up another interior wall, so that the sink was isolated from the toilet and shower, leaving those available for continued use.

Cerseru Kham and Uten Kekui could offer no explanation why the pond had manifested in the public restroom, but the puzzle had given them all many enjoyable hours of speculation. Currently, the favored theory was that someone had left a text on aquaculture in the bathroom, and it had provided the impetus for the transformation. Xerak held out for some creature that had been lurking in the pipes.

None of this scholarly chatter left Teg feeling particularly secure about what they might find when they once again headed into the Library's interior.

"So, the good news is that the route up to the old xuxu roost is pretty direct," said Peg, and paused, very much a performer awaiting a cue.

Teg obediently provided it. "And the bad news?

"Is that the stairwell starts over there," Peg said, pointing to where a heap of rubble was just visible behind one of the sage stations.

Grunwold looked at the other four young people. "Let's get on it. At least we have wheelbarrows and shovels, picks, and all the rest."

Teg said, "Let me supervise. It's too easy to pull out the wrong bit of rubble and start everything going every which way."

Xerak laughed. "You don't fool me one bit, Teg-toh. You want to be close by in case we uncover something interesting."

She grinned at him. "I refuse to incriminate myself. Let me grab some work gloves from *Slicewind*. Can I get anything for anyone else?"

"My gloves," Vereez said. "They're in the righthand drawer under the bottom bunk."

As Teg was hurrying out, she heard Uten Kekui say, "How about I stand by to provide magical support if needed? I'd haul stuff, but Nefnet has promised to cut off my right horn if I get anything into my injuries."

Xerak cleared his throat, but it was Vereez who spoke. "Remember, we use magic as a last resort until we figure out just how volatile the Library is. Spells only if we can't deal with problems by using more normal methods."

By the time Teg returned with gloves and her dig kit, the work was already in process.

"It makes sense that there's a stairway up to the roost right from the foyer," Teg said, taking her place in the line relaying buckets full of smaller detritus to one of the wheelbarrows. "Even the grandest structures need service access that isn't obvious."

"*Especially* the grandest structures," Peg put in. "When I was still working the nightclub circuit—wow!—did I ever get an eyeful. You'd have these utterly glamorous places—velvet and gilding on the chairs, incredible carvings ornamenting the walls, intricately tiled or parquet floors—then behind a little door, a door that sometimes had been built into the paneling, so unless you knew it was there it just vanished, there'd be raw concrete walls, carpet underfoot, sure, but only because they needed to deaden the sound of footsteps, dim lights. Only the big stars had cool dressing rooms, because sometimes they did interviews or received big shots there. The rest of us? Honestly, cattle live better."

"Vereez," Grunwold said, speaking with the same steady authority he showed when at *Slicewind*'s helm, "when Kaj and I get this large slab of marble far enough up"—he gestured with a crowbar to a slab that had probably once ornamented the wall above—"I want you to get a rope under it. You're the smallest of us, and the most nimble. Xerak, you grab the rope when it pokes around the side and knot it off."

Teg half expected either Vereez or Xerak to remind Grunwold that this wasn't the *Slicewind*, and he wasn't in charge, but they only nodded and moved to where he'd indicated.

Kaj shoved his crowbar into position and, at Grunwold's count of three, joined him in levering up the slab. The bulge of his magnificent muscles showed that this was an effort, but it didn't touch his voice when he responded to Peg's comment.

"It's the same with the necropolises I've worked in. Tunnels underneath so the austere tranquility or whatever vibe they were going for wouldn't be interrupted by incidentals like plumbing or whatever it was they were using to create the ambiance." He flashed his fangs in a canine grin. "Made some of my jobs a whole lot easier, though."

And by that, Teg thought with resignation, *Kaj doesn't mean groundskeeping. Question is, did he do more than tomb robbing? From how both Vereez and Xerak are giving him the unkind side-eye, I bet he's giving off a scent that adds the subtext that Kaj enjoyed those isolated tunnels for a very different sort of plumbing project. Well, best that neither of our smitten youngsters forget too quickly that while Kaj may have shown a great many admirable qualities, he's no less the seductive bad boy, breaker of hearts—nor that he hasn't made any promises to give up that role, no matter how much he wants to learn the magical arts and improve his situation, both socially and economically.*

Once they had hauled the large marble slab back and away, managing not to break it any further, they discovered it was the last major obstacle. An ornately carved, two-paneled wooden door stood revealed, dusty but otherwise not unduly marred.

Three abau flapped their way closer overhead and circled nervously.

"Let the flying pancakes have a go at that door," Peg suggested. "It will be a lot easier to work with if it's clean."

The doorway measured about a meter and half wide overall, but the panels were not evenly split. The one on the right was about a meter wide; the other took up the remaining width. Each panel had a separate keyhole, but neither were locked when Peg—who had gotten into picking locks, ostensibly at the prompting of one of her grandkids, and had been practicing lately—checked.

"Makes sense," Peg said, getting up and absently dusting the knees of her heavy-weight blue jeans—when they didn't need to worry about being seen by locals who didn't know them, the humans tended to wear Earthside clothes. "The Library was still open for business when the catastrophe hit."

With a flourish, Peg flung open the wider, then the narrower of the double doors, revealing a staircase on the wider side, and a smoothed ramp on the narrower. Both rose one story before angling to the right, after the fashion of interior staircases in most large buildings back home. The ramp was positioned on the inside, where it made a more gentle curve.

"Bet that ramp's for moving heavier items," Teg speculated.

"And providing a flyway for xuxu, abau, and other small flyers who worked here," Grunwold added. "I hadn't thought about it, but you wouldn't have such flyways in your world. Oh, no you don't," he interrupted himself, reaching up to stop Heru when the xuxu flapped his leathery wings as if preparing to demonstrate. "Who knows what's living up there? You stay close for now."

"Best we go up single file," Xerak said. "Vereez, you first, since you're shorter and need room to use your swords. Then me. That'll give us blades and magic, right up front—and I can use my spear around or over you. Grunwold, how about you take the back, so those antlers of yours don't block anyone's view?"

Teg glanced up. As she'd begun to take for granted, the clearance was somewhat more than she was used to, probably because sennutep with horns and antlers were not uncommon. Although Grunwold's antlers were scaled down compared to those of an Earthside stag, it was rather as if he was always wearing a tallish hat.

I wonder if anyone ever gets deliberately dehorned, Teg wondered. *And if when an antler tine or horn tip breaks, does it grow back? Not the time to ask.*

Usually, those with elaborate head gear automatically adapted:

turning slightly sideways to go through a narrow door, or stooping where the clearance was low.

Although, from what I've glimpsed in our journeys, architectural design also differs. I've seen numerous examples of doorways that are somewhat wider at the top. Really, the way Over Where takes people with different shapes for granted is incredibly cool.

After Grunwold had agreed to bring up the rear, Xerak continued. "Given that we may face another dead end after the right turn ahead, let Vereez and me do a preliminary scout. If it looks like we can go further, then you follow."

"What if something attacks you?" Grunwold protested.

"This part of the Library was only three stories," Xerak said. "Even if there's a separate stair to the roof, we're not going to be beyond rescue."

Unspoken was that if anything could take him and Vereez out that quickly, it was best the others weren't too close behind or they'd be goners, too. Vereez drew one of her copper-bladed swords and began to slowly ascend the stone stairs. As she did so, built-in lights glowed to life in both the treads and the walls. They shed enough light to prevent a misstep, but not enough to be glaring.

I bet when we first came to the Library of the Sapphire Wind, Teg thought, *those lights would have taken Sapphire Wind's personal attention to work. Now the Library building is beginning to work as it was designed to do.*

Vereez paused at the top of the first flight of stairs and looked around. "There's a door up here, probably into the second-floor stacks. The stairwell is clear to the next bend. Sapphire Wind said that the roost would be on the roof. Shall we keep going? Or do we check out what's behind the door?"

Grunwold inspected the map Sapphire Wind had given them. "It looks as if—before at least—that door led directly into some of the more commonly used parts of the Library."

Xerak looked at the door, his long tail twitching as if he expected something to spring out and pounce. "For now, let's head for the roost. It doesn't look as if anything has opened that door since the catastrophe. It's completely possible that we'll find it blocked."

"Maybe," Kaj said, turning to Grunwold, "we should make our next construction project putting up brackets to hold a sturdy bar.

From the look of the hinges, these doors opened into the stairwell. Now that we've opened the door at the bottom, I hate the idea of something creeping out of the stacks and into the reception hall."

Peg shivered theatrically. "Like a haunted house."

Xerak's response was more pragmatic. "I'm beginning to realize how big a project we've taken on. Not only do we need to guard the homestead's borders, we need to be careful what might be lurking within."

"We're definitely going to need more people," Vereez said, then sneezed. "Another advantage to waiting before we open the door. We can have Sapphire Wind send some abau up here to dust."

"Okay, so we should continue up," Xerak said.

Vereez started up the stairs, Xerak at her heels. "If we don't mind picking our way around some junk, we can get to the third-floor landing. There's another door there."

"Skip it," Grunwold said. "Does the stairway go to the roof, or do we need to deal with a trapdoor?"

There was a pause as booted feet mounted further up.

"The stair goes up," Xerak said, adding a moment later, "Even from here, I can see that the door is heavier duty, an exterior door."

"Sounds like the roof," Teg said. She'd been bouncing on her toes, wondering what the "junk" Xerak and Vereez were working around might be. *Probably just bits of ceiling plaster, but I want to see!*

"Is there room for us to join you?" she asked, trying not to sound too eager.

"Sure," Xerak said, and she could hear the laughter in his voice.

Vereez added, "I hate to make you wait, Teg-toh, but we need Peg first, since she's the one who's good with locks."

"Right-o," Peg said. "On my way. The rest of you, come along, so Teg doesn't bust a blood vessel."

At the top, Peg knelt and shone a small flashlight—of local manufacture; the ones from home didn't work Over Where—around the edges of the door. "This one has a small deadbolt. Sadly, it was shut and turned down when the catastrophe struck. It's pretty much corroded in place."

"I could use a spell," Xerak began uncertainly.

"Give me a moment to get some tools," Kaj said, and trotted down the stairs. A short time later, he returned with a small chisel and a mallet. "Room please. I think I can strike this whole plate off. We may need to take the latch off, too. It's in bad shape."

When he finished, he said, "I had to take the latch off, but I was able to leave the handle in place. It seems solid. We can pull on that."

Xerak gave a considering nod. "Teg-toh, since you can use the sun spider amulet one-handed, you come and open the door, then squash back to let Vereez and me through."

Kaj stepped away, edging down the stairs to make room.

"Right!" Heart-pounding, Teg took the Petros amulet in her left hand. In her mind, she spoke to it: *Will you work with me?*

She felt the warm expectancy that she'd come to think of as meaning, *"You bet!"*

"Everyone ready?" Xerak said.

Vari-shaped heads nodded. Teg put on a pair of gloves, then gripped the handle, feeling the slight crumbling of the corroded surface even through the fabric. She glanced over at Xerak, noting that the head of his spear staff was glowing with a soft, greenish light.

"Do it!" he said.

Teg gave the door a gentle pull, felt the hinges grating as they gave up their burden of rust. Teg pulled harder and heard the rust pattering down. The third time she pulled, she felt the door moving more easily. Vereez and Xerak tensed, poised for action. Xerak gave a small nod of his head, mutely urging Teg on.

She hauled back, half fearing the handle would come loose in her grip, but the door moved first. She hardly had time to be aware of the change of temperature or the scent of the air—bitter and musky, causing Kaj and Grunwold both to sneeze—because Vereez was moving, twin swords poised, Xerak close behind. Teg peered around the door, careful not to get in the way, and froze, astonished.

Their guess that this door might lead out onto a roof had been correct, although the surface in front of them was liberally covered with leaves and other vegetative detritus. Teg recalled that by the time they'd finished clearing the way to the stairwell door, it had been early afternoon, but her first confused impression was that it was night. Then she realized that what she'd taken for nighttime darkness was instead something large looming overhead, blocking out the sky.

Why does that seem somehow familiar? And why am I suddenly scared? she thought, before she remembered and froze, aghast.

From behind her, she heard Grunwold say, "That's a cargo hauler! Get back!"

Vereez and Xerak leapt, and Teg slammed the door.

"I remember those," Peg said, "from when we stole *Slicewind* from your parents. The flying shag rugs, right?"

"That's it," Grunwold agreed. "The domesticated ones aren't that bad, but this one is either feral or descended from some left behind here. Either way, it could be rough to deal with."

"Not part of the original livestock?" Peg asked. "Like the messenger xuxu?"

"Probably not," Grunwold said. "At least I wouldn't count on that. I think it's more likely that this one is feral."

Vereez nodded. "Feral seems like a good bet. Surely some ambitious treasure hunter thought a cargo hauler would be a good idea. And I feel sure that any cargo haulers that were here during the catastrophe would have been used to get valuables away."

Teg tried to remember what she'd learned about cargo haulers the last time they'd encountered one. The problem was separating knowledge from fear. Stealing *Slicewind* had provided their first up-close and personal introduction to just how weird Over Where could be. Before that, what they'd seen—people with the heads of Earth animals, creatures like xuxu or kubran or the domestic fowl on the riverboat they'd taken down from Hettua Shrine—had slotted into categories her brain was more or less ready for. Flying shag carpets that gaped open to engulf their prey, not so much.

And then there were the tranquilizer darters, she thought. *I hope we won't meet up with any of those here.*

"Grunwold, the last time we ran up against one of these, you were able to divert it by using commands on a sort of slide whistle," Teg said. "Any chance that will work this time?"

Grunwold shook his head. "Probably not. Do you remember the trouble I had with the one at KonSef Estate?"

"Oh, right." Teg slumped back against the wall, wishing she could light up a cigarette, but knowing everyone would protest. "The first commands you tried didn't work. If the one for 'stand by,' I think it was, hadn't, we might not have gotten away in time. Damn! I was hoping they were standardized, like the hand signals shepherds use with sheep dogs or something."

"Some animals are trained with hand signals," Vereez put in, "but cargo haulers are often used in shipping facilities or the like, where several different owners might be working in the same area. If they all responded to the same commands, it would be chaos."

"Makes sense," Teg admitted. "So, what do we do?"

Peg put up a hand and extended a finger. "One: give up and have Grunwold and Kaj build us a new xuxu roost. Problem with that, we'd still have the cargo hauler up there. We're lucky it hasn't attacked us so far."

"It probably was dormant," Grunwold said. "They're closer to plants than animals, and soak up energy from sunlight."

"Maybe it will just go back to sleep, then," Teg suggested.

"I have nothing against optimism," Peg said, "but as we saw with the bean balloons, plants here can be more aggressive than most at home."

Xerak pointed to Peg's raised hand. "Any other suggestions?"

Peg put up a second finger. "We figure out how to chase it off. Three"—another finger went up—"we kill it. I really don't like that last. After all, we're the trespassers, not it."

"I agree with Peg on that last," Vereez said. "It's completely possible the cargo hauler was posted there by some group of treasure hunters who didn't come back. If so, that probably is why it hasn't attacked us before. It was told to wait and it's waiting."

"Commands to wait, especially in potentially dangerous areas," Grunwold said, "often include permission to defend if the cargo hauler feels threatened. The more active we become, the more chance there is of that happening. I don't think we can afford 'wait and see' as a fourth option."

"Wait and see," Peg teased, "is actually part of option one. Option four is that we try to capture and tame it."

Kaj said, "Cargo haulers can be really useful, but I've never dealt with wild or feral ones."

"If we chase it off," Xerak added, "it's going to just relocate somewhere else, probably within this territory we've agreed to homestead."

Peg smiled. "So, we either kill it or catch it? Which will it be?"

"I guess," Vereez said slowly, "we try to catch it."

No one disagreed. At that moment, Ranpeti's voice floated up the stairway.

"We can hear you all talking. What's this about killing someone?"

Xerak called back. "We'll come down and tell you. I think we need to do some research."

"I wonder," Peg said to Teg a while later, as they turned the pages on the battered books Emsehu had brought from some deeper reaches of the stacks, "if Sapphire Wind knew that cargo hauler was up there all along."

"Hmm," Teg said. "It did suggest we look at the xuxu roost."

Meg, who was seated a short way down the table, looked up from her own tome. "I don't think it knew, but I think it may have suspected something was up there, even that the something might eventually become a threat. I don't think Sapphire Wind can 'see' what's outside the Library building or even inside, but I think it can sort of feel/hear."

"Feel/hear?" Teg asked.

Meg tapped the eraser end of her pencil on the table. "Feel, like you can feel an itch on your back, but when someone else looks, there's no bug bite or anything to account for it. Hear...Like a distant sound, kids playing a couple houses away in a neighbor's yard, or the person in another apartment moving around. Nothing so distinct as a sound, but an awareness."

"You've been thinking a lot about Sapphire Wind," Peg said. "Haven't you?"

"I have." Meg smiled. "If I am able to eventually move Over Where, I want to live here at this library. Sapphire Wind will, in some senses, be my roommate, even my boss. There's a temptation to think of it as a sort of computer AI, but while it's definitely artificial, and definitely intelligent, it isn't a computer."

"What is it then?" Peg asked.

"I don't know," Meg replied, "and speculating won't help us. Teg, when you looked out there, other than the cargo hauler, what did you see?"

Teg squinched her eyes shut, forcing herself to envision the scene. She gave a soft chuckle.

"What's so funny?" Peg asked.

"I couldn't see much," Teg said, "because there was an overhang built over the door, the sort meant to keep outside weather from coming in. There was a door to my right, I think."

"To the xuxu roost, maybe," Peg put in.

Teg shrugged in a "Yeah, maybe" sort of way and went on. "And then right in front was the cargo hauler, blocking most of what was in front, but I did get a glimpse around the edges, and, y'know, I think I saw trees, or at least shrubs and like that."

Peg made a puzzled sound, but Meg nodded briskly.

"The staircase took you up three stories, then to the roof," she explained, "and the ravine that fronts the Library is about thirty-plus feet deep. So, that would mean the Library dropped enough to put all of the building except for the belltower at about ground level."

She took a pencil and made a quick sketch of the Library building. "The original main building was three stories, plus bell tower. Eventually, two-story wings were built along the sides and back, but more of the expansion went down."

"Like to the artifacts' repository," Peg put in. "Makes sense. Better security for valuables."

Meg nodded. "All the accounts of the disaster include the bell tower crashing down. However, it's likely the adjacent wings dropped along with the main building, so the backs and sides of the library would be flanked by a gully. Twenty-five or so years is plenty of time for the surrounding forest to colonize the area—especially in this ecosystem which seems to have its share of fast-growing plants and vines—concealing everything."

"Wow," Peg said. "It's a wonder the roof has held up."

"We don't know if it has," Teg reminded her. "We haven't been into any of the rooms that would be under the roof."

"Later," Meg said firmly. "One problem at a time."

❧ CHAPTER SEVEN ❧

A few hours later, they settled around a table in the reception hall to finalize their plans.

Grunwold began. "I may have the most experience with cargo haulers, but I'm also the best at getting *Slicewind* to do impossible things..."

He paused, but no one disagreed. On their journey to the Roots of the World, they'd discovered that Grunwold's skill at handling the sky sailer wasn't just a matter of experience. His rapport with the vessel was, quite literally, uncanny.

"...so the next best person to put in charge of the roof-side team would be Kaj—or Ohent."

Ohent shook her head, making the sparkling metal disks on her headscarf ring together. "I've loaded cargo haulers, sure, but that's it. Kaj has actually directed one."

"Sure," Kaj said, "an elderly one, that I knew, that knew me."

"That beats the rest of us," Xerak said. His comment was followed by nods from the assembled company.

At a gesture from Grunwold, Meg took over the briefing. "Our team's research into the fapa—that is, the cargo haulers—gave us a few interesting ideas. As was noted earlier, cargo haulers are actually plants, not animals. They're either descended from, or magically manipulated from, a small creature about the size of a potholder." She gestured to one on the table, left from their earlier meal. "The cilia on the exterior are sensory organs, sensitive to wind currents and vibrations, as well as to a certain degree of light, and possibly even color."

"After the beti-teneh," Peg said, "another flying plant is not a surprise. Did you find out how to catch one?"

"Sadly, none of the books we could locate," Meg replied, "talked about how to capture a wild cargo hauler, I suspect because there are sufficient domestic ones that the need rarely arises. We could look further, but . . ."

"We don't have the leisure to do so," Vereez put in, sounding a little regretful. "We are in a crunch. We need to get that thing off the roof so we can check out the xuxu roost, so we can unarchive the messenger xuxu. Any suggestions?"

Meg nodded. "Since our goal is to capture the fapa, we need to restrain it. Happily, we had purchased a fairly large net, in case we needed it when we went to reclaim Grace. The cargo hauler is too large for us to net from below, but if we can get it to take off from the roof, a team aboard *Slicewind* could drop the net over it. The net is not unlike those used for trawling, so we should be able to bag the cargo hauler, then drag it down into the plaza. After that . . ."

Nefnet took over. "I think I can put together a sufficient quantity of a sedative to calm it down. I've been harvesting soporifics from the herb garden here for weeks now. Unfortunately, the concoction I can put together from available supplies would have a deleterious effect on anyone who breathed it in, which is why I don't think it's wise to, say, sprinkle it on the cargo hauler from above."

"Not to mention," Grunwold added, "that the cargo hauler would be a lot harder to bag if it was flat on the roof. They aren't very heavy, but they are bulky."

"So," Peg summed up, "prod it into flight. Bag it. Dope it. Then what?"

"You sing to it and charm it, of course," Teg teased.

"Actually," Uten Kekui interjected, "perhaps I can put a short-term charm on it. The process will take time, however, which is why I can't just go up on the roof and work the spell. The cargo hauler would likely either leave or attack, neither of which would serve our purposes."

"Next point," Meg said, "who serves where? I'd like to stay here in the Library in case we need to coordinate between teams." Unspoken was that she was the most likely to get Sapphire Wind to help, if help was needed.

Further discussion followed. Muscle would definitely be needed to work the trawling net, and with Kaj on the roof crew, that meant Grunwold and Xerak would definitely be aloft. Uten Kekui offered to join them. Peg also would be aboard *Slicewind* as backup pilot.

Teg thought about offering to join the shipboard team—she wasn't as strong as any of the males, but even during the off-season, she kept herself in shape for the field season. The days when she could take it easy, then get into shape fast, were at least a decade behind her.

More, if you're honest about how much you hurt back in your forties when you went from the classroom directly to field work.

"I could—" she began, but Kaj cut her off.

"Teg-toh, I was hoping you'd be part of my crew. You have a real gift for quickly assessing the lay of the land. We're going to need that, since we beat feet pretty much as soon as we stepped out onto the roof last time."

Teg nodded, feeling obscurely flattered. "Okay. Just remember, I'm not much of a wizard."

"Magic should be a last resort, anyhow," Kaj said, "especially for those of us who will be standing on the Library's roof." He looked over at Vereez. "If Grunwold can spare you, I'd like you on my team."

Grunwold cut in. "Actually, I do want her. If we're going to be using Scraggly Mane's dubious muscles, then he won't be able to do that spell—y'know the one he used when training Vereez to toss around lightning? I was thinking that could be useful if we needed to steer the cargo hauler from a distance."

"That makes sense," Vereez said. Teg couldn't tell if she was disappointed not to be able to find out if Kaj was interested in having her on his team for reasons other than her definite usefulness. "And I'm not too wimpy myself."

Ohent said, "How about me for your team, Kaj? I'm good with a sword, and not all that slow on my feet."

Kaj looked indecisive. "But you don't react well to stress, Mom. We've got to face that."

"We're running out of options," Ohent reminded him. "There's me, or maybe Cerseru Kham. Nefnet is too valuable a resource to risk. Ranpeti has a kid. I suppose Emsehu..."

The heavy-headed crocodilian creature shook his head back and forth in a slow arc. "I am good for fighting, but this is not fighting."

Cerseru Kham said, "We're putting two of the three custodians of the great artifacts at risk as it is. I think I'd better stay in reserve."

"Compromise, then," Kaj said. "You come, Mom, and keep watch, especially for anything on the roof—or maybe we should be thinking of it as a hilltop."

After the inevitable last-minute refining of plans—*Whatever we are, we aren't a crack military unit,* Teg thought—Grunwold's group went out to *Slicewind*. Teg, Kaj, and Ohent headed up the stairs. Kaj and Teg each carried one of *Slicewind*'s spare boathooks. If by any chance this cargo hauler was feral, it might be familiar with being steered by such. Even if it wasn't, the hope was the boathooks would serve as prods if the cargo hauler was reluctant to fly up into *Slicewind*'s range.

They waited at the door out onto the roof until Meg called up the stairs.

"Okay, Heru says *Slicewind* is in position, staying to one side of the tree line."

As had been agreed, Ohent pulled open the door and first Kaj, then Teg stepped out. Nothing loomed overhead, and Teg felt a surge of guilty relief as she looked around the lightly forested glade.

"Maybe it's left," she was beginning, when she realized that the mossy green she'd originally assumed was plants growing from the roof decking was actually the cargo hauler, lying flat on the roof.

The first time Teg had seen one of these creatures, it had been rising from the wooded land that bordered the fields of KonSef Estate. In the light cast by *Slicewind*'s running lights, it had looked, as much as it looked like anything familiar, like an enormous, rather ugly version of the shag-carpet-style bathroom rugs that had been popular in her youth. Now, lying there on the roof, gently pulsing or vibrating or something, it looked rather more horrific. Each strand of "shag" was about the diameter and length of one of Teg's fingers. As she watched, some of them shifted, as if to get a better "read" on what had just entered its territory.

Kaj said calmly, "We were ready for the possibility that the cargo hauler would sense that *Slicewind* is in the vicinity, and wouldn't automatically take off just because we opened the door and walked out here. Looks as if we're going to need to coax it to launch."

"I'm ready," Teg said, trying to sound a lot braver than she felt. The cargo hauler blended into its surroundings, so it was hard to tell just how large it was, especially as the sunlight was filtered by tree limbs. What she remembered was how large it had seemed when it had loomed over them earlier. She also kept remembering how the cargo hauler at KonSef Estate had opened all along one edge, looking quite capable of swallowing *Slicewind*'s bow.

I thought of that as a mouth, then, but the research texts we were looking at spoke of it as a "cargo pod." Either way, the cargo hauler can open up and engulf a whole lot more than one short and stocky archeologist, that's for sure.

"Do we know," she asked Kaj, "what side it opens on? I mean, will we be walking right at its open side?"

Kaj shrugged. "It's hard to tell which is the pod edge. Domestic cargo haulers are often marked on that side, so we should look for those. Marks would also give us a clue as to whether this one is feral or truly wild."

Teg wanted to ask what sort of marking—a tattoo? Or something more like a nose ring on a bull? Or maybe paint? Dye?—but Kaj was stepping out, and she had to hurry to keep up.

One reason the cargo hauler blended so well into its surroundings was that the roof decking was covered with many years of leaf matter and blown debris, certainly far more than the roof had been originally meant to hold.

Sheesh! Peg's right. I wonder if we're going to have to deal with roof leaks or other problems, as well as monsters? Teg thought. *Water wouldn't be good for what remains of the library collection. And I wonder what the plumbing is like after decades of not being used?*

She bounced just a little on her toes, trying to get a feeling for how strong the roof was. Kaj mistook this for eagerness to get into action and chuckled.

"All right, Teg-toh. Let's do this." He shifted the boathook so that the hook end was down. "On my count of three. One ... two ... three!"

They matched steps, Kaj remembering to pull in his stride out of respect for Teg's shorter legs. Placing the tips of their boathooks about two meters apart, they slid them through the rooftop detritus, with the intention of going under the edge of the cargo hauler and prompting it into flight. Teg worried that the boat hook would snag on bits of branch or maybe rubble from the fallen bell tower, but it moved with relative smoothness through the damp vegetative mat.

I wonder if the cargo hauler has been eating the leaves and branches and stuff that falls down here? Plants do eat other plants. I wonder if this stuff is part cargo hauler poop? Do plants even poop?

Teg's frantic train of thought bounced completely off its rails when her boathook suddenly slid unimpeded, causing her to rush closer to the cargo hauler than she had intended. At her side, Kaj also sped up, his greater strength causing him to actually run a few paces. When he tried to pull himself up, his foot slipped on some of the damp duff and he knocked into Teg, losing his grip on his boathook in the process. Teg fell forward, tried to roll, failed completely, and pitched onto the cargo hauler's upper surface.

It felt like hitting a rubbery hedgehog. Or what Teg imagined hitting such would be: lumpy, bumpy, but bouncy and prickly, too. It certainly could have been a lot worse.

The cargo holder, which had been silent, as if hoping silence would enhance its camouflage, let loose a horrific scream, a shrill sound that made Teg drop her boathook to clap her hands over her ears. Kaj, blessed—or, in this case, cursed—with the much sharper hearing of his kind, wrapped his arms around his head.

Still screaming, the cargo holder rippled its surface, launching into the air with Teg sprawled on its upper surface. Her boathook rolled to the edge and plummeted off.

A different scream rose from below, competing with the cargo hauler's if not in shrillness, then definitely in intensity. Trying not to grab any of the rubbery fingers on the cargo hauler's surface, Teg wormed her way over the cargo hauler's surface so she could look down over the edge. Ohent was running over the roof toward the cargo hauler. Scooping up Teg's boathook, Ohent tried to hook one edge of the cargo hauler, as if she could drag it down by sheer willpower. Given that cargo haulers were routinely used to move quantities of grain and other commodities, Teg had her doubts that one woman, no matter how ferocious and determined, could pull it down.

However, the cargo hauler had risen too high for Ohent and Kaj—who, ears plastered flat to his skull, had joined his mother in her efforts—to get their hooks over an edge. The creature rippled further up into the air, while scooting sideways to avoid *Slicewind*, which was now sailing toward them. Although the cargo hauler didn't move quickly, its peculiar form of locomotion was effective.

Last time we had to deal with one of these, I was too strung out to think about it, but the cargo haulers move a lot like flying carpets are always depicted as doing in storybooks. Did the stories get the idea from someone bringing a cargo hauler over into our world or did it work the other way around? Or maybe it's just parallel evolution. Different cultures come up with similar ideas all the time.

Teg knew her mental chatter was her way of distracting herself from the reality that she was in serious trouble. She glanced over her shoulder and saw that *Slicewind* was gaining, the trawling net hanging over one side. However, the cargo hauler had not gone far enough up to be in reach of the net. Although what she wanted to do was contribute to the general chorus of screams, Teg forced herself to assess her situation.

Treetop level, and even if none of those trees are particularly tall by majestic forest standards, still, that's a lot more than I want to try jumping. It sure is easy to see why we never really thought about that hilltop being the building's roof. Even the shelter over the door we came out of is covered over with greenery. Some rubble—I wonder if from the bell tower?—is visible, but even that has its share of vines and moss and all.

Teg made a mental note that this natural camouflage would be to the homesteader's advantage, then glanced up. *Slicewind* was getting closer, and she could see Xerak and Uten Kekui's heads peering over the railing, looking down. She waved, and Xerak waved back.

An idea hit her. Before she could think about just how crazy it was, Teg carefully rolled onto her back, then sat up. Next, she dug Petros out of her pocket. Touching the embryonic awareness that she had felt at other times was easier than she'd thought it would be. *Maybe this entire situation is so bizarre that talking to a bit of meteorite and metal seems almost normal.* She raised her right arm and held the amulet toward the ship above.

"What do you think? Can we get a line on the hull? Pull ourselves up to where the others can get us aboard?"

She sensed that the amulet liked the idea, but doubted that it could produce enough of the web goo to make a long enough cord of sufficient strength.

"Got that," Teg thought. *"Then let's get them to come in range. Tell me when you think we can do it."*

She didn't know if real sun spiders giggled, but this one definitely did when it thought they were going to do something clever. Holding the amulet so that the sun spider's many eyes could see—something she wasn't certain if Petros needed to do or not, but helped her to keep her focus—Teg used her left arm to make a "come on" gesture toward the sky sailer. She wanted to try shouting, but didn't think she could out-compete the still protesting cargo hauler.

At least Ohent stopped screeching . . . Teg thought. There was a seemingly interminable interval before she was certain that *Slicewind* was definitely dropping lower, as well as coming closer. Was it her imagination that she could feel the amulet's long spider legs twitching as they counted off the interval? What she wasn't imagining was that the cargo hauler was also aware that *Slicewind* was closing, and that it didn't like this one bit. It stopped screaming, as if it needed all its breath. The surface under her rolled, then tilted.

Oh, holy hell, Teg thought. *It's gonna spill me off. Spidey silk time now!*

She felt Petros's doubt, but also a wild exhilaration as it tapped into her core of stored mana to supplement what it already contained. Teg's vision blurred and her chest tightened, but she managed to grab hold of the rubbery fingers under her and keep her seat on the cargo hauler. Now that the cargo hauler had stopped making so much noise, she could hear Xerak's voice, raised nearly to a roar.

"Teg! This is absolutely *not* the time to pass out! Grab hold of the line!"

The command in his voice brought her around, and she saw that Petros had succeeded in getting a line onto the hull, somewhere amidships, to one side of the keel. It was a slender rope on which to trust her life. In fact, it looked far too much like a wad of chewing gum that had stuck to someone's shoe and was stretching out. Nonetheless, she grabbed hold with her left hand. Dropping Petros to hang around her wrist, she grabbed on with her right hand as well.

The ship's motion pulled her to her feet. At the same moment, with a rippling, wavelike motion that reminded Teg of her failed attempts at water skiing, the cargo hauler pitched her off its surface. Teg felt the jolt right up both arms, into her shoulder joints. Forced to bear all her weight, the Spidey silk cord started stretching. She thought it might snap, envisioned how taffy hardened when pulled, felt Petros giggling at the image. Then the cord hardened. Teg felt her feet tearing through branches, then *Slicewind* was rising.

However, so was the cargo hauler. Teg felt herself swinging in the breeze caused as the creature swirled around. She glanced down and saw it was coming back for her, cargo pod gaping wide.

Does it want to eat me? Or does it feel some sort of weird responsibility to pick up anything it's carried?

Not feeling much like testing just how benign the creature's motivation was, Teg pulled her legs up until her heels were closing on her butt. She still felt far too much like a fishing lure being dangled above a surfacing manta ray.

There came a sharp, electrical crack. From the lightning-strike ozone odor in the air, Teg guessed that Vereez had fired off a shot of ball lighting. The cargo hauler gave an indignant shriek. When Teg dared another glance down, she saw that it was undulating away over the trees at a fairly respectable pace, carrying her speculations with it.

"Teg-lial, can you climb that rope?" Uten Kekui called. "If you could get higher, we might be able to catch you in the net."

"Fuck that nonsense," Teg called back. "I can hold on. That's about all."

"Hold on really tight, then." Peg's face peered over the rail. "Grunwold's steering for the meadow, where there will be plenty of room to set you down. The plaza is just too full of junk."

Teg agreed with the decision but, since Grunwold had also pulled in *Slicewind*'s speed, so that Teg's sun spider cord would not be overly stressed, the relatively short distance to the river meadow seemed to take forever.

Vereez's pointed fox muzzle poked over the side next. "Update. Since we don't want to risk your breaking a leg or ankle, we're going to bring you in over the water and let that cushion you. Peg's getting dry clothes from your cabin."

Teg was too tired to reply. She could feel Petros drawing on her mana reserves to maintain the cord. Although she wanted to vomit, some vague sense of how that would look managed to keep the bile down. Teg smelled the bright freshness of the lake water, heard Grace fluting something that sounded like concern, then there was water around her ankles, rising up her calves, to her knees. She felt the sandy bottom touch the soles of her shoes.

Let it go, she told Petros. *We're down. You did great. Wish we could have gotten that cargo hauler, though. Oh well . . .*

She spilled down onto her hands and knees in the shallow water and then, even as Xerak and Vereez vaulted over *Slicewind*'s side and came splashing toward her, Teg passed out.

"More than ever, we have to face it," Peg said, pouring sweet syrup into her after-dinner poffee, "if we're to have any chance of pulling off this homesteading, we need help."

Some hours had passed since the failed attempt to capture the cargo hauler. Once Teg had been put aboard, Grunwold had apparently taken *Slicewind* out in a search pattern, but they'd failed to see any sign of the creature. By the time Teg had come around, head pounding from mana depletion, *Slicewind* was back in her docking cradle near the statue of Dmen Qeres, and she'd been tucked into bed in the stern cabin.

After crawling from bed, she'd read the note Peg had left for her, showered, eaten some medicinal dark chocolate bridge mix from the stash she'd brought from home, and joined the others over in the Library in time for dinner. Apparently, they'd been waiting to have a serious discussion until she came over, but it was also clear that matters had moved ahead while Teg had slept. For one, Kaj, Grunwold, and Vereez had descended via the stairway to the roof when the dinner bell had been rung, while Uten Kekui, Xerak, and Cerseru Kham had come out from the chamber that held the Font of Sight.

"I agree," Meg said. "Even if we don't need to deal with claim jumpers—and I strongly suspect we will—there simply aren't enough of us to handle keeping people fed, living areas clean, and all the rest, not if at least half our number will be needed to make any substantial improvements."

"I'd love to be able to disagree," Ranpeti said, her hands busy combing out Brunni's fur pre-bedtime, "but I can't. I've been sorely neglecting Brunni since we've been here. Ahmax and Ufatti, the dobergoats, are fine for keeping her out of trouble—well, from hurting herself—but she's starting to act out."

Brunni looked mildly offended, but something about the cant of her ears said she knew perfectly well that her mother was right.

"So, we're back to the same problem," Xerak said somberly, sipping from his wine glass, "who to recruit and how to compensate them."

Meg nodded. "And I think the answer is the same: the Archived. We can still start with the xuxu, but we're going to need more sennutep: bipedal tool users. While you were out dealing with the cargo hauler, Nefnet and I put our heads together over Sapphire Wind's list."

She glanced at Nefnet and the otter-headed woman took over.

"I could make a few recommendations as to some who might accept an offer to work with us, but most of those aren't going to have the sort of skills we need. Frankly, most of the scholars would only add to our difficulties at this point. They're going to expect to be waited on, and would be horrified about being asked to camp. I suspect most would insist on being taken back to civilization."

"And some," Cerseru Kham put in, "would be likely to attempt to take legal action as soon as they were able."

"What about the support staff?" Grunwold asked. "I seem to recall a fair number of those on Sapphire Wind's list. They're more likely to have the skills we need right off in any case."

Meg nodded. "Nefnet and I reached the same conclusion. However, this is where we reach another difficulty."

"Why," Grunwold muttered, "am I not surprised?"

Meg waggled a gently reprimanding finger at him, and went on. "Do you all remember the journals that Kuvekt-lial loaned us? In the course of our journeys, I read all of them. Since Sapphire Wind showed us the list, I've been dipping into those written by the survivors, rather than the treasure hunter journals. I found one particularly interesting possible source of information."

She pulled out a volume, beautifully bound in leather than had been dyed a rich violet. Stamped in gold onto the cover, in a script so ornate that Teg almost couldn't read it, was the title: *Fire-Bright Rain:*

An Account of the Destruction of the Library of the Sapphire Wind, as Written by One Who Was There. In much smaller type was the author's name: Septi Scribe.

"This is a later edition of an earlier volume," Meg continued, "and the publication date is, so Nefnet tells me, quite current. The About the Author note lists this Septi Scribe as living in someplace called Hidden Horizon with his wife, Leeya, who was also a resident of Meadow Village."

"Not just a 'resident,'" Nefnet noted. "Leeya was the chief cook for the entire Library community. She worked out of a large facility down in Meadow Village and was given tremendous respect by the permanent residents. Leeya would definitely know a great deal about the Archived."

"It's likely this Septi would as well," Meg put in. "His book is quite gossipy in a gently caustic fashion. As a scribe, his role was somewhere between staff and support. Although he chose to live in Meadow Village, my impression is that he could have claimed quarters closer to the Library if he had wished."

"Leeya and Septi sound ideal," Peg agreed. "How far is this Hidden Horizon where they are listed as living?"

Grunwold pulled out a battered atlas and turned pages until he found what he was looking for. "About a day out from Rivers Meet, as the sky sailer goes. Uten Kekui-va and Cerseru Kham-va have said they want to go to Rivers Meet. How about we bundle the trips together? I hate leaving you all without *Slicewind*, but this seems too good an opportunity to miss."

"Just what I was going to suggest," Meg said. "My thought is that Peg and Grunwold take with them at least a partial list of those of the Archived who are listed as support."

Peg nodded. "I'd like to try and recruit this Leeya and Septi, if possible, but they may be happily settled. If we have a list, we can try to get suggestions as to who might be most amenable to working with us."

Teg cut in, sensing a decision reached while she was asleep, and not quite getting the logic. "Why are you going at all, Peg? Are you certain that confronting them with humans is a good idea?"

Surprisingly, it was Grunwold who replied. "I do. I absolutely don't want to steer anyone astray, and you humans are too big a part of how we found the Library, not to mention how we mean to keep it, to leave out. Even if we can't recruit them, they need full disclosure if they're going to help us figure out who might work with us."

Teg saluted him with her poffee bowl. "If you want me to go with you and Peg, I will, but I think one 'monster' would probably be enough. I'd like to stay here. If we're going to have additional residents—whether these survivors or the Unarchived—we're going to need more rooms, and that means delving further into the Library."

Peg laughed. "And you'd want to be a part of that, absolutely. So, I'll go with Grunwold. You and Meg stay here."

"Are you sure you three can stay over here?" Vereez asked, concern evident in the cant of her ears. "I mean, in our world. I know that Peg and Meg have families back there, where you came from. Teg has someone who comes to her house every day to feed her cats. You three came up with some sort of excuse for being away, so that you would be the ones checking in with your people, and they wouldn't worry, but how long will that excuse last?"

"We were, if I dare say so myself," Peg said, buffing her fingernails on the front of her tunic, "very clever, and because of that, we still have a fair amount of time here covered by our original excuse."

Xerak looked embarrassed. "I was seriously distracted on that first day we met you, and I can't say I remember the details of that excuse."

You were, my dear young man, Teg thought affectionately, *more than a little drunk that day, and no wonder. Not only was Hawtoor blaming you for leading a summons without waiting for him, your faith in the knowledge of your—at least as you saw him then—all-wise apprentice master had been seriously shaken, since it seemed that the ritual you'd swiped from his library had gone awry.*

Peg brightened at the memory. "When you three summoned us, we were at a Valentine's Day book club meeting. When we decided to become your mentors, we needed a reason that we would be away and out of contact. Since Teg is an archeologist, we decided we would tell our families that we were going away on a trip with her, and that the trip would involve going to places where we couldn't count on being able to link to e-mail or phone service."

By now, all the residents of Over Where understood at least the idea of both e-mail and phones, although most of them thought that being expected to be in touch with all people at pretty much all times was more inconvenient than not.

Meg picked up the thread. "What I told Charles and Judy—and I assume Peg told her family—was that at the book club meeting, Teg had mentioned there was space for a few people on an informal field school and tour of sites in the southwestern United Sates that she was associated with."

"Cancellations," Peg said, "that's what I told the kids. Cancellations. That explained why this had come up all of a sudden, and we had to pretty much jump on it."

Meg nodded. "In my case, leaving was not a great difficulty. Neither of my children live near me, and I could easily excuse myself from the few volunteer activities I was involved with in Taima."

"It was a little harder for me," Peg admitted. "My son, Diego, and his family live in Taima. I'd actually moved there to be closer to them, and because I wanted a change from where I was living. When we decided to spend time Over Where, my good luck was that Diego and his family were away on a trip of their own. There had been a death in his wife's family, and they'd decided to take the kids and stay a little extra time. When I phoned Diego, I apologized that I wouldn't be there when they got back, but promised I'd stay in touch."

She motioned to Teg, and Teg took over.

"Since we had several days before Diego would be back in Taima, we decided to delay the departure of our 'tour,' until right before then. It was only four days, our time, but with the time difference, that gave us nearly an extra month here. It has worked very well."

"You've been here—except for when you've slipped back to your own world to 'phone' or 'e-mail'"—Xerak very carefully used the English words—"for closing on a hundred days, our time. So, you do have quite a lot of time left from your original month and four days. That's great, but we don't want to waste any of that precious time. Grunwold, can you be ready to leave tomorrow?"

Kaj cut in. "Wait! Before we settle that, there's something else to report. Grunwold, Vereez, and I located the xuxu roost. While Vereez stood guard, Grunwold and I did what Heru assures us is an acceptable job of refurbishing it. We were figuring on having the xuxu unarchived tomorrow but, if Grunwold is leaving with Heru, then maybe unarchiving should wait."

"It doesn't need to," Grunwold said. "Heru is a great help, but it's not as if he has to go everywhere with me. How about it, fellow? Will you stay here and help the new xuxu get acclimated?"

Heru hooted something complex and thoughtful on his crest, then hopped onto Grunwold's shoulder and nuzzled his neck. "I could do. If you stay 'til I meets 'em. Wanna makes sure they's civilized and'll listen to me."

Grunwold turned to Xerak, and Teg realized what must have been being discussed in the Font chamber. "How long will unarchiving the xuxu take?"

"Not too long," Xerak said. "We were preparing while you were getting the roost ready. If we got up early tomorrow, and we started right after breakfast, you could head off before noon, maybe sooner."

Grunwold nodded. "I'll take *Slicewind* over to the lake to top off the water, then."

"Don't be gone too long," Peg cautioned him. "I'll need to put supplies aboard for our voyage, and we all will need to get to bed early. It sounds as if tomorrow is going to be a very busy day."

﷽CHAPTER EIGHT﷽

With three trained wizards available, Teg and Vereez weren't needed to help with the unarchiving process—even though it was more complex than when Sapphire Wind had unarchived Nefnet, because so many creatures were involved, and there was a degree of uncertainty as to how the xuxu would react to not having their usual handlers.

Teg and Vereez were on *Slicewind*'s main deck when a chorus of honks and whistles came from the vicinity of the Library roof. A few moments later, the entire flock of xuxu burst forth and did some sort of elaborate aerial dance over their heads.

Teg set down her daypack, into which she had loaded several changes of clothing, and tried to figure out what the diving, circling mob reminded her of.

"Fruit Loops," she said aloud. Vereez turned to stare at her. Teg laughed. "Sorry. I'll bring some back next time I go shopping at home, then you'll get it. It's a brightly colored breakfast cereal that was really popular when I was a kid. That flock of xuxu is colored just like them: wildly improbable reds, oranges, yellows, and greens."

She studied them happily. "They're all like Heru in that the upper side of the wings is green, but the underside is a contrasting color—and boy-oh-boy, what a contrast. I wonder if the green is to help them blend into the tree cover, and that lower is 'Watch out, I taste bad!' We have creatures in our world like that."

"Sounds possible to me," Vereez replied. "You're always thinking that way, all three of you, aren't you? And I bet not just about things here, but back in your own world, too."

"Yeah," Teg said, "I'd say that's true. Meg's a librarian, and you've got to have a solid curiosity bump to be good at that, because making connections between types of ideas is a big part of being good at that job. Peg... Well, she was a real rebel when she was young, and to be a proper rebel, you've got to ask questions. She took that active curiosity into being a mom and grandmom. You've heard how many things she's learned from keeping up with their hobbies and school subjects. She might not have finished college, but she's seriously educated."

Vereez sighed deeply. "You all make me feel I need to rethink everything about how I plan for the future. In a good way. I want to be like you when I'm your age."

Teg chuckled. "Thanks. Just remember, 'like' doesn't mean 'the same.' It means finding your own way to keep feeling good about being alive."

The xuxu were coming to roost on the trees in the plaza. A loud thump from the direction of the Library made most of them flap up into the air, but Heru—who had taken his perch on the head of the statue of Dmen Qeres—trumpeted something and they fluttered obediently down.

"That's promising," Teg said.

"And so's that," Vereez said, pointing.

Teg looked and saw Kaj making his way across a narrow plank bridge that extended from the top of the Library, across the ravine, and came to rest on the edge of the plaza pavement.

"Where did they get the lumber?" she asked.

"Scavenged it from some of the shelving units," Vereez replied. "Lots of those were badly enough damaged that they weren't going to ever hold books again, but the timber is solid, well-seasoned, and meant to hold a lot of weight. Peg suggested that we rig it as a drawbridge, and Grunwold's going to stop for some heavy ropes and hinges."

"Good thinking," Teg said. "When I was dangling from the underside of *Slicewind*, I noticed how well concealed the upper doorway was. We don't want to have a permanent bridge that would serve as a pointer to it."

"We noticed that, too," Vereez said. "One of the things we talked over while you were sleeping off mana depletion was how we could maintain the cover while using the roof."

"I should take naps more often," Teg quipped. "I like waking up to all problems solved."

Once Grunwold was assured that Heru not only felt comfortable with the newly released xuxu, but that he was likely to be lording over them before long, *Slicewind*'s captain made certain he had everyone's requests on his shopping list, got his crew aboard the sky sailer, and set off for Rivers Meet. Heru led the xuxu flock off to tour their greatly changed territory. The remainder of the residents went in to have a midday meal.

"Only four people gone," Ranpeti said, dishing out a helping of umm-umm cobbler for Brunni. The little girl had been only moderately mollified for the loss of her hero by Grunwold's promise to bring her back a present. "But the table seems a lot emptier."

"Enjoy it while you can," Teg advised. "We're going to be a lot more crowded soon. Next, we need to figure out where we can make a bunch more living space."

Meg nodded, opened a folder, and removed a drawing she'd made of the Library's layout. It was based on the maps in the Library's brochure, but larger, and with the notations meant for library patrons removed.

"There are two main doors off the reception hall," Meg said, tracing her finger along the map. "We've been making most of our adaptations in the east wing, because that's what Sapphire Wind suggested. It's also closer to the bathrooms. I suggest we continue in the east wing, focusing on the former offices, since they should be less cluttered. According to the maps, there's also a conference room."

Teg leaned forward to inspect the map. "Looks as if we'll have open stacks to the left, with offices and the conference room to the right. What's shelved in the open stacks?"

"That area's problematic," Meg said. "It was organized by need."

"By need or *at* need?" Teg asked, baffled.

"*By* need," Meg replied, stressing the first word. "As I understand it, in that particular area, the Library of the Sapphire Wind took 'open shelving' to a new level of sophistication. Patrons would be assigned a starter shelf on a topic of interest. After they'd done some research, related books would start showing up, based on what the patron was most interested in among the starter material."

"Damn!" Teg said. "I was hoping we might guess what we could be up against based on what was in the area to begin with, like the nessie pond showing up in the bathroom."

Meg shook her head. "We may be able to guess elsewhere in the Library. But in this open shelving area, what will be there—if anything—will be related to what had been on those shelves when the disaster struck. That will be related to what the Library itself felt was needed by the patrons. The reason these particular stacks were situated across from administrative offices was so that help would be available if the Library became—shall we say 'overenthusiastic'?—and needed to be redirected."

"Well," Teg replied, her eagerness to get started overwhelming any apprehension she felt about possible monsters, "we'll just need to be prepared for anything. Now, as for teams, I can work on deconstruction with Kaj, Xerak, and Vereez."

"I want to help, too," Ohent said, just as Nefnet said, "Don't leave me out."

They grinned at each other, then Nefnet said, "Seriously. All of you have done your very best to make me feel welcome. Let me be part of preparing the way for the next group."

"And we'll need as many hands as possible," Ohent added, "especially since someone is going to need to do some patrolling outside, or we might get sneaked up on."

Vereez nodded, her ears flickering back in a fox's frown. "There is that, but without *Slicewind*, what we can see is going to be limited."

"I've been thinking about how best to make sure we spot possible invaders," Xerak said, "preferably before they see us. Heru understands very clearly that anyone who is a stranger isn't welcome, and he can teach the other xuxu that. Grace should be perfect for keeping an eye on anyone who tries to get in via the lake."

Emsehu's gravelly voice spoke from where he was having his lunch down on the floor, where his messy eating wouldn't disturb anyone.

"I will help with defending the Library from outside. While I am not very fast compared to those who fly, I can move as fast as any of you bipeds. If the xuxu see any strangers, I will go and inspect them. I can even snarl at them if the need arises. This will mean you will not need to waste time waiting for invaders who may not arrive, and will provide a delay if any do."

Meg nodded approval. "That should work. We could assign Grace a couple of xuxu to relay messages from her. I was up on the roof when the xuxu flew up to inspect the roost. As is to be expected, given they were employed to carry messages, all of them can speak the local language. Their vocabularies are not as large as Heru's, but most lack his strong accent."

"Can we enlist the piranha toads and spike wolves," Vereez asked, "and the lizard parrots and other creatures that attacked us when we first arrived? It seemed as if Sapphire Wind had a certain amount of control over them. I mean, Sapphire Wind pretty much admitted that the spike wolf that knocked Teg into the ravine did so because Sapphire Wind told it to."

Sapphire Wind spoke through Friba. "Near this building, I can do some things with the creatures. Farther away, I cannot. The predators were already watching you, stalking you. I only encouraged that one to knock into Teg."

Teg suspected there was more to what had happened that memorable day. *But why pick a fight with Sapphire Wind? It is the first to admit that it was frantic, not fully right in its mind. And I didn't get worse than bruised, and we found the door. Let's move ahead.*

She cleared her throat. "We've probably got at least a week until Grunwold gets back, but that may be barely enough time. Shall we get started right after lunch? If people have other things to do, I won't need a full crew right off. We need to look at what's there before we can start work."

Xerak laughed, "But, Teg-toh, you're going to be supervised, whether you want to be or not. Your people may say that curiosity killed the cat, but from what I've seen of your Thought and Memory, they are immensely more sensible than a certain archeologist."

Belt heavy with trowel, crystal flashlight, canteen, knife, and sundry other tools, her hand wrapped around the polished wooden handle of her favorite shovel, Teg waited impatiently by the large arched doorway that led into the east wing.

This doorway had first opened into a general reference room. The books, to Meg's unmitigated disappointment, had been reduced to ash. Even the shelf units and tables had been ruined beyond saving. Although the loss of the reference materials was to be regretted, it had left a relatively large area that had already been converted into sleeping rooms.

Xerak and Vereez had assigned themselves to accompany Teg, leaving Kaj and Ohent to put their very practical skills to work on creating cot frames—Grunwold and Peg's shopping list included mattresses and pillows.

Sapphire Wind had reactivated much of the lighting built into the ceilings, so Teg moved at a brisk pace along the corridor, until it ended at a closed door.

"Remember, we're going to be dealing with open stacks," Vereez said, "so this could be like the sections we went through on the other side of the reception hall, back when we were looking for the way to the artifacts repository." Her hand drifted to touch her leg where a bookworm had burrowed straight through her trousers and into the muscle.

"I hope it's like that," Xerak retorted. "We'd know what to expect. Can we get this door open?"

"Cover me," Teg said, "and I'll try the handle."

She twisted the knob, slightly at first, then further. "I don't think it's locked, and there's no reason for it to be trapped, right, Sapphire Wind?"

A minute sparkling whirlwind appeared, then bounced up and down in what Teg thought was the equivalent of a nod.

"Okay, then," Teg said, and she slowly pulled open the door.

She'd been ready for monsters. She'd been ready for rubble. Or burned shelves or collapsed ceilings. She wasn't ready for a room filled with words: floor to ceiling transparent curtains of neatly ranked characters hanging in place, layer upon layer of them. It was like looking into a book in which all that remained was the print.

From the soft gasps from behind her, Xerak and Vereez were equally astonished.

"Is it my imagination," Vereez asked, her voice hushed, "or are those letters moving?"

"Not your imagination," Xerak replied. "They're watching us."

"Waiting and watching," Teg agreed. Her head was pounding. She could feel the translation spell working behind her eyes, trying to make sense of the characters in front of her. Its effort was confused, not only by the variety of fonts, but by the characters from the curtains behind bleeding into the "page" in front. She swung her head away so she wouldn't need to look. "Do those actually say anything?"

"It *is* difficult to read," Vereez admitted. "There are several languages all mixed up. From what I can make out, there is a mixture of things: warnings, pleas, threats. Could the books be trying to talk to us?"

"Meg said something about the Library being categorized by need," Teg said, daring another peep. The alphabet she was most familiar with Over Where was completely different from the Latin alphabet. However, like the good old ABCs, the Over Where alphabet had evolved from pictographs that had come to represent sounds. It seemed to Teg that, as she watched, some of those symbols were reverting back to their original pictographs and that not all of those images were precisely friendly.

In the Latin alphabet, the letter "A" had evolved from a pictograph for "ox." Oxen could certainly be dangerous, but some of these letters were looking positively ferocious. Impulsively, Teg spoke, hoping that the translation spell with which Hettua Shrine had gifted the three mentors would change her words into something that the linguistic chaos that confronted them might understand.

"We're not interested in hurting you, not one bit. We'd actually like to fix things, as best we can. Can you at least talk in one language?"

"That did something, Teg-toh," Xerak said a moment later, his tail twitching back and forth in excitement. "But I'm not sure . . . The characters are changing. I thought I was pretty well educated, but this doesn't make any sense now."

"Do you mean it's a completely different language?" Teg asked. "One you don't read?"

"More than that," Xerak said. "I can only read about three languages, and I prefer to have a dictionary at hand for anything but my native tongue. But I recognize a bunch more, even if I can't read them."

Teg understood. She couldn't read Japanese or Chinese or Korean, but if the words were transliterated into the Latin alphabet, she could usually guess which language was which. She did even better with languages she knew a little about, like Spanish, French, and Latin.

"So, the characters have shifted into an unfamiliar language?" she prompted.

"It's more complicated," Xerak said. "Some of the characters are sort of familiar, but overall—I've never seen this sort of writing."

Vereez cut in, her ears pricked forward with enthusiasm. "But I have! I have! Meg and Peg and Teg have brought over books from their own world. I've glanced through them, especially the ones with pictures. Those characters are the ones in those books. Take a look, Teg-toh. See if I'm right!"

Teg was already steeling herself to look. If her vertigo had been caused by all those different languages mixing up, if this had solidified into one language, she shouldn't be hit so hard. She looked and found herself seeing not only the familiar Latin alphabet, but text written out in English in a very basic font—Courier, she thought. Even the bleed-through from the back pages was no longer as confusing, because she knew what the words were supposed to be.

"You're right, Vereez," she said. "It's 'my' alphabet. Better, what's there is either written in English—that's my natal tongue—or the translation spell is doing something. I can read this."

"What's it saying?" Xerak asked. His tail twitching had slowed, no longer agitated, more like that of a cat hoping to pounce, but not sure that was a good idea.

Teg read aloud, "Do not hurt me/us. We are unhappy/afraid. We will not be idle."

She then addressed the roomful of words. "We don't want to hurt you. Can you shift to the language my friends are speaking? I can read that."

"Yes. Wait," came the reply.

The words started shifting, the curtains moving like scarves in the wind, twining around each other, sculpting a bipedal shape out of words.

The shape was flat, like a paper doll, and with some of the same stiffness of posture: arms held out from the sides, legs close together. The head, Teg noted with interest, was a generic therianthropic shape: ears higher set than those of a human, a suggestion of a longer face, but no mane or ruff or anything that made it feline or canine or any other creature in particular. The only facial feature the doll possessed were two eyes that sparkled when the light caught them. With a flash of insight, Teg realized that the eyes had coalesced from fragments of the data crystals that the library had among its collections, most often used to store graphic representations, particularly when two dimensions were not adequate.

A representation of a sennutep, Teg thought. *Not any particular person or type of sennutep. I wonder, will it be represented as naked or clothed?*

But it was represented as neither. Instead, once the figure was outlined, a line of words shaped in the general vicinity of its mouth, then traced down the neck, across the breadth of the shoulders, and down the torso. Words were not hyphenated, but changed in size to fit the space, making reading a challenge, but the simple Courier font was maintained, which made it easier.

"Talking to you, this way. Can you understand what is being said?"

"Yes," Teg said, then glanced at the other two, both of whom were nodding, wide-eyed.

"Speak to it," Teg suggested. "I think words are very important to this person."

"Oh! Of course!" Vereez said. "Where did I leave my manners? Yes. I can understand you when you talk this way. Thank you for making the effort."

Xerak gave a brief bow. "Yes. I understand, thank you. May I ask, who are you?"

"We are some of us," the letters spelled. "Those who were not destroyed, eaten or burned or made sodden or given over to rot. We are parts of some of us."

"We guessed right, then," Vereez said. "This is the Library trying to talk to us."

"But not Sapphire Wind," Xerak clarified. "This person is somehow speaking for the tomes, the scrolls, perhaps even for the data crystals. I wonder, did Sapphire Wind know that the collection had acquired some sort of agency?"

"I don't think Sapphire Wind did," Meg said from behind them. She made as if to ease by so she could see through the open doorway, but was stopped by the surprised expression on their faces. "Your voices *do* carry. I was going to my room for a nail file when I heard you talking. I couldn't tell to whom you were talking, so I came to check."

Meg leaned around Xerak and got her first look at the book person. "That isn't a sculpture, is it? It somewhat reminds me of works by an artist named Melissa Zink. Her book people had writing on them, but the writing didn't move."

The text on the book person was again moving, not shaping words as much as shaping agitation. Once again, Teg had the sensation that some of the characters were reverting, for lack of a better term, to their original forms.

"It seems to be an expression of the identity of some of the library collection," she said.

Meg patted her palms together in excitement.

"You are The Librarian," the book person spelled. "We are books. Will you defend us?"

Teg bit down on her lower lip, but let Meg take charge.

"Of course, I will defend you," Meg responded without pause.

Xerak swallowed a groan, but Teg didn't think he disagreed with Meg, just wished she'd employed some of her more usual caution before answering.

Meg didn't appear to have heard him, but went on, "If you fear those of us who have newly arrived within the Library of the Sapphire Wind, you need not. We came to this place seeking knowledge; having found what we sought, we are not ungrateful."

"We do not fear you newcomers," the book person spelled, "at least not more so than we fear any creature who uses water and fire, thus could do us harm. Some have felt the hands of a healer. For this reason, we thought to look at you."

"Nefnet," Vereez said softly. "When she got bored, she started repairing books. Looks as if we owe her."

Meg nodded. "If not us, then do you fear Sapphire Wind?"

"Only a little," the book person spelled. "It has an agenda that is not quite the same as that of a librarian, but we do not think..."

The translation spell had trouble with that word, so Teg suspected that however a collection of damaged library books—magical library books at that—cogitated, it was not quite the same as the thinking of organic creatures.

"...think it will do us harm unless we come in the way of its mission to keep this building and its collection at its best."

"Would you feel reassured," Meg said, "if I told you that I believe Sapphire Wind intends to preserve the collection as much as possible, even to keeping portions of otherwise damaged books?"

"Yes." The single word was repeated many times. Teg's eyes swam, so she suspected that the translation spell was struggling with a wide variety of languages and fonts, as if all the books were now speaking, rather than just the book person. When the letters settled down, Meg continued.

"Is that all you need from me?"

"No," the book person spelled. "Please! Keep the book wraiths from eating us."

"What is a book wraith?" Meg asked.

"They eat us so that they can live large," the book person replied. "They care not if we die if they can thrive."

Meg glanced over at Vereez and Xerak. "Do you have any idea what the book person is talking about?"

"None," Xerak answered. Vereez shook her head in agreement.

Further questions about the book wraith only made the book person more agitated, to the point that the bipedal shape began disintegrating.

"Whoa!" Teg said. "Let's back off before some of those letters come disconnected." She addressed the book person. "We will help you. All we ask is that you try to help us understand what these book wraiths are, so we can figure out how to get rid of them."

The book person did not reply, but the shifting characters slowed down. Teg took that as a win. She took a deep breath, redolent of ash and damp, and continued.

"We were hoping to use some of this space to make sleeping areas for those who are coming to help us repair the Library of the Sapphire Wind. The land outside the walls is also filled with dangers."

Meg put in. "No books will be harmed in the process of making these sleeping areas. Any partial texts, even pages, will be set aside for future assessment. Knowing that, will you let us continue with our remodeling plans without interference?"

"This is reasonable," the book person spelled. "Many hands make light work. We would see this ruin a library once more, and feel appreciated and needed as more than fodder. I will assist."

"Very good," Meg said. "Do you have a name by which we may address you?"

This led to a confusion of characters that resolved in what Teg could tell was "No," in a variety of languages, followed by: "It would be very long if all of us were to be included."

Meg seemed to have anticipated this, because she went on without pause, "Since you understand the value of words, you may understand why I would find it more convenient and more polite if I had a name by which I could call you. May I suggest one?"

"Yes!"

"I would like to call you 'Zink,' after a person from my world who would have been delighted to know that some of her sculptures were so like you."

"Zink..." The characters swirled and shifted in what Teg was coming to feel certain was a reflection of an internal discussion from the numerous texts and fragments of texts that made up the book person. "We would accept this, and some say to express gratitude for your courtesy in seeing us as more than an edible resource."

The book wraiths again, Teg thought. *I'd better remember not to use phrases like "devouring a good book." That could get seriously misinterpreted.*

"Glad to have the extra help," Teg said. "Let's get to it. Time's a-wastin.'"

By the time they'd done their initial investigation, Teg felt certain that the offices could be adapted into living quarters. Each of the office doors had been closed and locked, probably when the librarians had quit work on the fateful day. This had spared the areas the worst of the smoke and fire damage, although it was evident from patterns emblazoned on just about every surface area that the critical magical overload had extended into these areas as well.

When they reported over the evening meal, Ranpeti put in a request for one of the offices for her and Brunni.

"I think she'll sleep more soundly if we're further from the reception area," Ranpeti explained. "She has good hearing, and an even better imagination, so even if there isn't much noise, if she can convince herself she's missing out, she gets restless. From what you've said, those rooms are large enough that we can divide them, front to back, into a sleeping area and a sitting room, so I can still use the room if she's napping."

"You aren't worried about being further back in the stacks?" Vereez asked. "With books forming people-shaped things, and who knows what else going on?"

"Not really," Ranpeti said. "After all, we're neither books nor book wraiths. We should be as safe as we are anywhere, maybe safer. I have the impression the books want us to fix things, as well as protect them from the book wraiths."

"Does anyone have any idea what a book wraith might be?" Meg asked. "Sapphire Wind admits to having no idea, and none of the references I've looked at are at all helpful."

Xerak shook his head. "Uten Kekui-va never taught us about book wraiths, but he did touch on how magical energy does attract various sorts of creatures. I'm guessing that the book wraiths might be something like the book worms, creatures that prey on books, especially old or damaged books. It may sound weird but, just as in the natural world predators often benefit their prey species by culling the injured and weak, so supernatural predators often leave vital magical resources alone, but destroy those that are no longer functioning at their best. It's one reason the world isn't littered with the magical creations of generations past."

"So magic is alive?" Teg asked.

"Of course, it is!" Xerak had been about to drain his wine goblet, but he was so surprised he put it down, untasted. "Surely you've felt that."

"I've felt something," Teg admitted, "but I guess I thought it was, I don't know, like electricity."

"But lightning is alive, too," Vereez said, her reply giving some hint of how the translation spell had coped with the term "electricity." "Surely you haven't forgotten the oehen-serit, the lightning shadows."

"Never!" Teg said. She stretched, feeling abused muscles complaining. "I'm going to take a hot bath, then. Vereez, do you have any more of that muscle rub?"

"Absolutely," Vereez said. "Call when you're out of the tub, and I'll rub some into the places you can't reach."

"Thanks," Teg said. "We've got a lot to accomplish in the next week, if we're to have rooms ready when *Slicewind* returns, hopefully with some help."

❦CHAPTER NINE❧

When they opened the door into the stacks the next morning, Teg ignored the burnt and broken shelving units. These were mostly heaped with ash cemented into rough semblances of the heavy tomes that had once occupied the shelves. Those could wait until the offices had been cleared.

Meg had joined the team, and insisted on taking charge of triaging texts. Zink immediately partnered with her.

"I/we will assist you," Zink spelled. "Not all tomes/texts are as magical/valuable/enhanced as the rest. Some..."

Teg had the distinct impression the book person sniffed in disdain, although there was no noise, just an alteration of posture.

"...are merely records and administrative paperwork, lightly saturated from the critical magical overload, as a book left outdoors..."

This time Zink definitely shuddered.

"...would be imbued with water."

"That would be very helpful," Meg said, speaking with considerable poise, especially given how she had not always reacted so well to the weird and strange. "Can you possibly also help me to find out if the books contain something that would do damage either to the tome itself, or to one of our organic type who was attempting to inspect it?"

"I can definitely try."

The next week was—as far as Teg and Meg were concerned, at least—a joyful immersion in discovery. There were four offices, situated with a conference room in the middle, and all five rooms had escaped transformative magics. Teg first gave the conference room a once-over, deemed it without interest, and let Kaj and Ohent take over converting it into a simplified studio apartment. She and Meg decided to deal with the offices in order of clutter, starting with one that seemed to have belonged to a new hire, who had barely gotten situated.

"This makes me think," Teg said to Vereez, who had chosen to assist her, probably to keep from seeming to make excuses to hang around Kaj. "Whenever possible, we should box up anything in these offices. Especially if the person using the space is among the Archived, we'll have an easier time with them if we haven't messed with their stuff."

Vereez, who had been making an inventory on the Earthside clipboard Teg had loaned her, nodded. "Good idea. We can ask Sapphire Wind to check. Even if the occupants were among those who were off at Hebs Henu, maybe we can buy the Rough Diamonds some goodwill by offering to return any obviously personal items we found. The less greedy we seem, the better."

Meg paused from where she was going through a shelf of books. "I'll sort books according to whether or not they are marked as belonging to the Library of the Sapphire Wind. Dmen Qeres set up a very nice system, where books were marked, not only inside the cover, but with an imprint along the page edges. I wish we'd had the budget to do something like that at the libraries where I worked. It really would have cut down on stolen books or parts of books—especially color plates."

Although Meg and Teg mostly remained inside the Library, the young people took turns going outside. Heru had done a good job explaining to the unarchived xuxu and Grace what their new duties would be, but no one was taking any chances. Now that the stairwell up to the roof was open, Xerak used the rooftop as a classroom for his three students, usually one at a time, since Vereez, Kaj, and Teg each needed different sorts of instruction. Vereez had the most formal training. Kaj had the general background that Teg lacked, but almost no formal training. Teg in turn, often had questions about things that the other two took for granted.

Vereez was continuing her study of manipulating air currents, which was definitely best done outdoors. She was also the only one using spells, chanting strings of words in Hekametet, the only spoken language the translation spell refused to translate, and being corrected when she got the pronunciation wrong. To their relief, Kaj and Teg would be spared such until they were much further along in their studies.

The rooftop was also used by Ranpeti and Brunni as a relatively safe place for the little girl to run around. Nefnet was setting up a container garden with transplants from the overgrown herb garden off the plaza. And the xuxu were in and out, back and forth, filling the air with friendly chatter and bright colors.

Seven days passed, and there was no sign of *Slicewind*.

"It's probably too soon," Nefnet said, in the tone of someone who was reassuring herself. "I wish we had a better way to find out when to expect them. It's hard to know how much we need to prepare for meals."

"I wouldn't worry about that," Meg reassured her. "Remember, Peg is with them, and they'll be the ones bringing supplies to us. I bet she'll have food for us, not expect us to feed them."

But when eight days went by, then nine, Teg drew Meg aside. "I was thinking, one of us could possibly contact Peg by going to her house and using her door. It wouldn't be a definite thing, because the portals aren't reliable in some areas, but . . ."

Meg nodded. "I'd had similar thoughts, but then I realized that if Peg felt we needed to be briefed, she could come to us in the same way—and it would be easier for her."

"But what if something has happened to her?" Teg said.

"Let's not borrow trouble," Meg said. "Or at least not quite yet."

On the tenth day, Teg was on the roof having a smoke when a loud fanfare from Heru, echoed faintly by Grace down on the lake, heralded the arrival of *Slicewind*. Teg thumped down the stairs to the reception hall.

"*Slicewind* is coming in!" she yelled at the top of her lungs, then, without waiting for the rest, headed out the main doors to get the ladders set in place. She was up on the plaza as *Slicewind* settled lightly into her landing cradle. Teg grinned up at the hull, and would have sworn the eye painted below the bow winked at her.

"Ahoy, there Teg, me lass," Peg called down. "We're back and with treasure beyond our wildest dreams. Hope you've gotten the extra bedrooms set up."

"We do," Teg replied, laughing. She hadn't realized just how much she'd missed Peg's warmth and exuberance until that moment. When Peg picked her way down the deboarding steps, she gave her a tight hug. "Welcome home!"

Peg beamed and squeezed Teg back. Then she turned to assist the new arrivals. The first, a portly figure with the characteristics of a racoon, wasn't a stranger. They'd first met the scholar and historian, Kuvekt, when they had been attempting to locate the Library of the Sapphire Wind. Without his generously sharing access to his extensive collection of maps, brochures, and journals, their search would have been greatly prolonged.

Teg came to relieve Kuvekt of one of his obviously heavy satchels.

"Kuvekt-lial," she said. "It has been a while! Delighted to see you."

Kuvekt stepped to one side to let others debark, edging over to where he could look down into the ravine for a glimpse at the legendary doors. "Uten Kekui-va suggested that my resources might be of further use to your group in your homesteading attempts, and I concurred—but I made part of my fee being permitted to come along."

Teg didn't need to ask why. Kuvekt had long been obsessed with the fate of the Library. The chance to actually see it, no matter how dangerous the area might be, would have overridden any apprehension he might feel.

"We will be very glad to have you here," she said, and meant it. "Meg's been working on the account she promised you, but she won't share it with any of us. Maybe you'll have better luck."

Others were debarking, but enough of the Library's residents had emerged that Teg didn't think she should join the crowd. Instead, she stood back and watched as several strangers made their way down the steps. First came a small, wiry older male with the characteristics of a tricolor goat.

"That is Septi Scribe," Kuvekt said, *sotto voce*. "A fascinating fellow, and one of the most communicative eyewitnesses of the catastrophe. We had some fascinating talks about the event during the voyage. He and his wife were able to provide a great deal of information about which accounts were based on truth, and which were flat-out falsehoods."

"Is that his wife?" Teg asked, indicating a robustly built, but obviously not young—even maybe elderly, given how carefully she was moving down the stairs—woman with the head of a brown bear.

"Yes, that's Leeya. She was one of the key members of the Meadow Village settlement. Their daughter wanted to come with them, but they convinced her to stay back with her husband and kids. Pippea was quite young, an apprentice chef, at the time of the disaster. Afterward, Leeya and Septi adopted her—she'd been an orphan, without family of her own. I think Pippea plans to visit eventually, even if just to put bad memories from her past to rest."

"If Uten Kekui-va and Cerseru Kham-va both returned, *Slicewind* must have been rather crowded," Teg commented. "Anyone else come with you?"

Kuvekt shook his head. "No. Peg turned over the stern cabin to Leeya and Septi. Peg and Cerseru Kham had the cabin near the mast that is apparently usually Vereez's. Grunwold insisted I have the bow cabin, but I insisted on sharing it with Uten Kekui. Grunwold took the small cabin during the shift that he turned the wheel over to Peg. The rest of the time, he pretty much stayed on deck."

"Grunwold's protective of *Slicewind*," Teg said fondly, "as I obviously don't need to tell you. But I also am certain he wanted to make a good impression on you four who were kind enough to come here. Grunwold can come across as a temperamental goof, but really, he's a sweet young man."

"Speaking of making a good impression," Kuvekt said, "you'd better go over and get introduced. We'll have plenty of time to catch up."

The next several hours sped by as introductions were made, rooms were assigned, cargo unloaded, tours were given, and, finally, a meal was served. As predicted, Peg—it turned out with Leeya's help—had used *Slicewind*'s galley to make several casserole-style dishes, as well as a fruit-filled dessert, so that not only was there more than enough for everyone, there would be leftovers for anyone who desired a late-night snack.

Clean-up was handled communally. Then, after filling her bowl with poffee, and taking a seat at one of the long tables out in the reception area, Leeya addressed the group.

"Thank you for this fine welcome. I am sure I can speak for Septi,

and perhaps even for Kuvekt-lial, when I say that we are all grateful."
Pausing to acknowledge the general murmur of agreement that
followed this statement, Leeya continued, "Let's skip the part where
all of you worry that we're too tired from travelling to get down to
business—and get down to business. I'm no idiot, and compared to
those of you who stayed behind, those of us aboard *Slicewind*, with
definite exceptions of Peg and Grunwold, have had an easy time of it."

This last roused general laughter. Then Meg rose from her
accustomed seat.

"Thank you, Leeya. I'm sure Peg has briefed you as to what we're
trying to do, and how we need extra help if we're to succeed. We're
very grateful that you three came to assist, but I think that before we
accept that aid, we need to clarify what your expectations may be."

Leeya nodded. "Peg and Grunwold both made clear that while
you were willing to pay for our aid, you did not think it would be
wise to further amend your homesteading agreement. That is
reasonable. Uten Kekui-va has already paid us an advance on our
services, enough to cover the next six months."

This was apparently news even to Peg and Grunwold, and a
general murmur of surprise went around the table.

Uten Kekui looked into his tea bowl, then raised his head and said
in a voice that carried, "When Grunwold dropped us off in River's
Meet, I had the opportunity to check my bank account. Even with
refunding tuitions to those of my students for whom I did not fulfill
my obligations, I had a healthy balance. After all that was done for
me during my time of need, it seemed this was the least I could do.
Please, say no more. I do not expect future compensation, rather I am
offering compensation."

Xerak gripped his wine goblet and absolutely beamed.

*At last, his beloved master is living up to Xerak's high opinion of
him. That's terrific.*

Kuvekt spoke quickly. "Uten Kekui also offered me compensation,
but I refused, since I more or less thrust myself upon your
hospitality. If you will give me room and board, and accept that I
am completely enchanted to finally be here, that would be enough.
Well . . . Later, I might like to write an account of events, to augment
whatever Meg is doing. It would not be offered to the public without
your approval, of course, but even if my chronicle only became the

newest volume in the Library of the Sapphire Wind's collection, I would be thrilled."

There were a few protests, but Kuvekt held firm. Finally, Teg spoke up.

"In my world, in my profession, academics and scholars write a considerable amount of material and receive little if any compensation beyond the recognition of their peers. Kuvekt-lial's enthusiasm is one I recognize. Why not accept his offer? If we pull this off, then we can reward him in some more tangible way."

There was some brief discussion, but once Kuvekt had assured them that he was in no danger of failing on his mortgage or being unable to pay his own small staff—"Who are doubtless delighted to be able to get ahead on their own projects, without having me distract them"—the discussion moved on to when Septi and Leeya could take a look in the Font at the list of the Archived.

"As soon as we can," Septi said. "We're selfish enough that we would like to know as soon as possible which of our lost associates are still alive, even in this peculiar fashion."

Peg clapped a hand over her mouth. "You'd mentioned this before, and it's selfish of me not to have remembered."

"There was not enough time," Septi assured her. "Other matters needed to be settled. However, we would sleep more easily on our newly prepared beds if we could see the list."

Friba said, "The list is ready and can be displayed to you. Meg, would you be their guide?"

"Happily," Meg said, rising a little stiffly to her feet. "Right this way. Nefnet, why don't you come along as well, since you're the other contemporary of the Archived?"

Teg opted to help with grating ysisora, a tuberous vegetable that Grunwold had identified where it had gone feral in the lakeside meadow. This batch would be used to make a sort of hashbrown casserole that would be the foundation of tomorrow's breakfast. The others dispersed to handle more chores, including filling water pitchers for each of the bedrooms and making up the last of the beds.

When the small group who had gone to view the list returned, Peg rang a metal rod around the angles of a triangle they used to call folks to meals. Soon everyone was settled in. Unsurprisingly, Septi and Leeya looked both relieved and tense.

Because, Teg thought *now that the initial relief of seeing who survived is over, it's coming home to them that they're going to be the ones to decide who gets to wake up, and who keeps on dreaming. I certainly wouldn't want that choice.*

Vereez hurried over with fresh cups of tea for them, from the aroma, a soothing blend Nefnet had concocted from tuatnehem and zinz. The couple nodded with quiet appreciation. Then, with a glance at his notebook, Septi spoke.

"We've made some notes here as to who might be good candidates for unarchiving, but before we go into that, we want to explain a little about the sort of people who were part of the Library's more or less permanent staff. I think Nefnet has explained that these fell into two general categories: those like myself who worked more directly with the Library collection, as well as assisting those who came here to use it. Then there were those who made life comfortable for everyone."

Leeya spoke next, not interrupting so much as one expert taking over from another. "Septi belonged to the first group. I, obviously, belonged to the second. What you need to know about those of us who were recruited to work at the Library full time is that, in addition to our job qualifications, a willingness to live and work in a relatively isolated community was part of the job requirements. I accepted the job as the head of the Library's kitchens because I really had no ties, and I liked the challenge. At the time of the catastrophe, I don't think I'd been away from the Meadow Village for at least three years. The trustees also recruited from orphanages, seeking people without families and promising, in addition to salary, room and board and on-the-job training. Pippea—our adopted daughter—was one of the orphans, but there were many others."

"Three years?" Grunwold asked with obvious astonishment.

"She didn't trust anyone else to get the job done right," Septi replied before Leeya could.

Leeya bopped her husband between the horns and kept talking. "What I'm saying is that we can suggest people who don't have families waiting for them somewhere, and who never thought that working at the Library of the Sapphire Wind gave them a claim to ownership. True, the situation will be somewhat different since the Library's ownership is up for grabs, but if you were able to pay well, and maybe even offer something like a bonus if you manage to keep the homestead, then that should be enough."

Septi ran a hand along the curve of one of his horns. "However, the situation would be different for many—although not all—of the Library staff. Many of the librarians agreed to work here because they would have access to the collection for their own research projects. Others because it was, frankly, a prestigious post. If we reach the point of needing librarians, I can make a few suggestions, but for now, I'd hold off unarchiving them."

"What about kids?" Peg asked. "Were there children here?"

Leeya nodded. "There were, quite a few, actually. However, when the catastrophe hit, many of the children were away. Hebs Henu is associated with reincarnation, with an emphasis on children who may be one of the family returned. The trustees encouraged those with children to go. They even provided transportation to a couple of areas known for their elaborate festivities."

Ranpeti looked wistful. "I can't say I liked the idea of having kids archived away, but I was hoping for playmates for Brunni."

"Keep that thought." Septi looked up from the list. "Before we make our recommendations, we'd like to know what sort of skills you need the most."

Xerak spoke out. "We need people to cook, build, help clear both the interior areas and the plaza. I'm a wizard, and while I don't mind helping with these sort of tasks, I feel that I could be doing more useful things. I'd assign myself to work outside, where I can use my magic without needing to worry about setting off some reaction."

Grunwold nodded. "Scraggly Mane is right. I'm willing to take my turn washing up or whatever, but I really should be patrolling the borders on *Slicewind*, or helping with the work on the grounds. I never thought the courses in agronomy my parents insisted I take would help here, but..." He gave an eloquent, very Grunwold, shrug.

"Also, we need people who won't mind sharing space," Teg put in. "We can't keep using resources creating more and more living quarters."

Meg added, "If we're going to prove that we're homesteading properly, we will need to deal with whatever might still be lurking in the stacks—including the book wraiths Zink warned us about—then get the damaged materials triaged and cleared away. Eventually, we'll need to build new stacks. So carpenters would be helpful."

"Since both indoor and outdoor work is going to be potentially hazardous," Peg added, "we need people who are levelheaded enough to behave intelligently if they come across something dicey—not just hit it or run screaming. Zink is a great example of a Library entity who has become an asset. Handled wrong though..."

Peg waved her hands in the air, as if outlining an image. "I keep seeing the Library as sort of our castle on the hill, but it's also our treasure, the place that any treasure hunters are going to want to get inside of. We need people who can share that vision."

"We understand," Leeya said, "and I believe we have a suggestion. On the day of the catastrophe, the Peraunter family was up here on the hill, taking advantage of almost everyone being away to do maintenance. Septi and I were delighted to see they are among the Archived. I'd suggest some or all of them for starters."

"Family?" Meg asked. "As in all related? Forgive me, but sometimes the translation spell can be peculiar."

Leeya wrinkled her nose in a bear smile. "All related, although sometimes by marriage, but very close. I never got the details, but I think the Peraunters were political exiles from somewhere to the east. They rarely left the Library grounds for that reason, but traded their vacation time to others in exchange for other services. That's another reason they'd be terrific for the Library's needs. They don't have a lot of outside ties."

Ranpeti asked, "When you said 'family,' I thought again about children. Any chance there were any Brunni's age?"

Leeya leaned forward to review her notes before replying. Teg didn't need to ask why. If the children hadn't made it, or had been evacuated and were now grown, that would be a major complication.

"Yes! And they're here. I remember! The Peraunters were staying at the hotel for the holiday, as a treat for the kids, with the added bonus that it kept the little ones close while their parents were working. There are three, two quite close to Brunni's age, one an infant."

"As long as you don't think having little ones here would be a problem"—Ranpeti addressed the group—"I'd really like the children, as well as the adults. I know it's an added complication, but so is raising Brunni without any other children."

No one disagreed, although several of the younger Rough Diamonds looked a bit overwhelmed at the idea of more little kids.

"I'd also suggest unarchiving Tamildah," Septi said. "She was one of the orphans, in charge of the xuxu roost, but she also tended the herb garden, as well as helping with the landscaping. She'd be a terrific resource."

Nefnet raised a hand. "I have a request. While I deeply appreciate that all of you have trusted me to serve as your doctor, I need to remind you once again that I am more of a medical researcher. My skills are closer to those of a pharmacist, although I do have some advanced emergency treatment skills."

"Very advanced," Vereez put in. "I mean, you saved my arm."

Nefnet smiled, otter fashion. "I was scared out of my mind. However, with a larger resident population, and with everyone taking on jobs where injuries are pretty much guaranteed, I'd like someone else to be in charge."

To the evident surprise of most of those present, Kuvekt cleared his throat. "Actually, one of the reasons Uten Kekui-va supported my desire to come along is that I was a practicing physician for many years, and still keep my hand in within my local community. I had planned on suggesting I assist you, Nefnet, but if you would prefer the reverse..."

Nefnet interrupted him. "I do. I absolutely do. I've been having nightmares about being unable to deal with some medical emergency."

"Then if there isn't a physician among the Archived..." Kuvekt said, and paused to let Septi and Leeya reply.

"There isn't," Septi said. "Doc Hrutu was among those evacuated after the catastrophe."

"Then I would be very willing to make myself more useful, although I still would like to help with the exploration of the Library."

There was a general murmur of agreement and appreciation.

"All right," Peg said. "Leeya and Septi, we have your recommendations, and they look sound to me. One last question: Are you sure all of those people got along at least relatively well? Families don't always."

Leeya considered. "I'd say we should be fine. The trustees were pretty good about getting rid of troublemakers."

Septi nodded. "Life here wasn't perfect, sure, but this was an artificial community, created and maintained for a specific purpose."

Peg nodded, then addressed the general group. "If Sapphire Wind can handle doing so, I suggest we unarchive all these people at the same time. There's no way to make what we need to tell them any easier, so why should we repeat the orientation over and over?"

"Another advantage," Meg put in, "is that if anyone does want to leave, we can send them off in one trip."

No one objected.

Sapphire Wind said, "With some hours to prepare, I can unarchive these."

Peg nodded crisply. "Then, how about tomorrow, right after breakfast? We're all tired now, best we start off on this newest challenge well rested and properly fed."

That night, Teg slept aboard *Slicewind*, but in the morning, she packed all her belongings, preparatory to carrying them over to the Library. She and Meg had been assigned one of the new suites to share, while Peg planned to continue bunking on *Slicewind*.

"Feels odd," Teg said to Peg, when she came out, wearing her pack, a tote bag with various odds and ends dangling from one hand. "For most of the time we've been in this world, *Slicewind* has been, well, home. I feel more wistful about leaving that overcrowded cabin than I have about leaving my house back in Taima."

Peg chuckled. "That's because you haven't really left your house. You know you can go back any time, and other than random hairballs and a diminishing supply of cat food in the pantry, it's more or less the same. This time, though, until and unless we take off on another grand voyage of explanation, *Slicewind* is no longer our base. The Library is, and the Library is far from what we're used to."

Teg nodded. "You're right. Still, I'll manage fine rooming with Meg. And I've lived in a lot less comfortable field camps."

"Come on," Peg said, glancing at the mechanical wristwatch she was wearing. "It should be about time for the unarchiving, and we're all supposed to be present."

"Especially us," Teg quipped, "so we can do our big monster reveal, yet again."

⅊CHAPTER TEN⅊

The magical side of the unarchiving went with the lack of hitches that Teg realized she was coming to take for granted when the new, improved Sapphire Wind was in charge.

I must remember to offer appropriate compliments, she thought. *I certainly would for a more usual sort of person.*

The newly unarchived people were first met by Nefnet, Leeya, and Septi, accompanied by Cerseru Kham. The relatively unchanged appearance of Nefnet and the newly unarchived, as compared to the evident aging of Leeya and Septi, gave immediate credence to the initial explanation.

The orientation had been designed primarily by Cerseru Kham, who had quite a gift for such things. She explained that for something like a decade her role as custodian-in-waiting for Maat Pexer had included running the affairs of her aging predecessor. She suggested that Grunwold, Vereez, Xerak, and Kaj's being the offspring of those responsible for the catastrophe, and that certainly Ohent's role as one of the extraction agents, should certainly be kept for a later—although not too much later—time.

"Let them get to know you as people who are trying to fix what was broken first," Cerseru Kham explained, slowly flapping her large, deerlike ears. "However, if we wait too long, then they may resent being given half-truths."

"I'm fine with telling them right off," Vereez insisted. She'd developed an almost fanatical aversion to half-truths. "Let Nefnet tell them and explain. If they don't like it, they can choose to leave."

"I agree with Vereez," Grunwold said. "We have enough hanging over our heads without wondering if the people we need to be our allies will suddenly turn against us."

"A show of hands, then?" Peg said. "All in favor of revealing the full backstory, raise your hands." Then, when everyone's hands went up, even Ohent's, "Cerseru Kham, are you sure you're fine with changing your presentation?"

"I am," the wizard said. "Let me cross a few things out, and add a sentence, then I'm ready to get this started."

After the first shock of learning what had happened was over, the newcomers came out to meet the rest. There were eight adults and three children. Since many of the group were related, several head types were repeated, including those of prairie dog, raven, and wolverine. There was also a tall, slender young woman with the head of a white tiger. From how she stood a little apart from the rest, Teg guessed that this must be Tamildah, the xuxu keeper and gardener.

Teg thought that the fact that the Library's company was so eclectic in race and age—ranging from four-year-old Brunni, to Leeya, who had admitted she was closing on eighty—and so obviously nonmilitary, kept their group from being threatening.

The exuberant reaction of the unarchived xuxu upon being reunited with Tamildah definitely lightened the mood. And then, of course, there were the three humans, testimony by their very existence that strange things had been going on—and would likely continue to do so. Thought and Memory, Teg's cats, had joined them, and drew nearly as much attention as did the humans.

We do, rather, seem like people who need help, Teg thought in amusement.

The leader of the Peraunter family was Qwahua, a sturdy woman with the head of a wolverine. She proved to be married to Wagh, one of the prairie-dog types. Two of the children were theirs: six-year-old Sweks, who shared his mother's appearance, although as a young wolverine, he was much cuter; and four-year-old Mwetor, who looked more like her father.

Huy, the other of the prairie dogs, was Wagh's younger brother. He was unmarried. The other married couple were Throog, who had a raven head, and Peynte, who resembled some sort of pig, possibly a peccary. The youngest child, Oino, was theirs. Someday, the baby might resemble her mother, but right now, she lacked the heavy adult beak. With her feathers sticking out every which way, she was impossibly adorable.

Rudbarr and Morwe were, like Huy, unmarried, and somehow related to the others, but Teg, her mind whirling with names, professional specializations, and all the rest, was beginning to lose track of who did what and how they were related to whom.

Despite all the Rough Diamond's careful planning, there was ample shock, many tears, and a certain amount of anger at what had happened to the place that had been these peoples' home and refuge. Eventually, however, everyone settled around the long tables for an early lunch of lobsaw chowder, flat bread, and fruit.

After that, there were necessary tours, indoors and out, assignment of living quarters, and dispensing of basic clothing and sundries.

It's a good thing that loose smocks and drawstring trousers are considered basic work clothes here, Teg thought. *Peg and Grunwold did a good job with their selection, and all of the newly unarchived at least had the shoes they were archived in.*

As she helped hand out clothes, and did her part as tour guide, Teg kept waiting for someone to take up the offer to be flown to Rivers Meet, from which point, transportation would be paid for to any location within reason—which, as far as the Rough Diamonds were concerned, was anywhere they could afford. However, no one took them up on this offer. Apparently, Leeya and Septi had been correct in thinking that the Peraunters had had very few ties to the world beyond the Library. Tamildah, fussed over by her flock, was clearly also "at home."

In time, like it was for Nefnet, I guess the shock will wear off, and some will want to find out what the world looks like beyond these borders, but for now, they need to adjust.

By evening, led by Qwahua, who seemed to take the damage to the Library and its campus as a personal affront, the Peraunters were already making plans as to how best to start improving the grounds and the Library, while staying alert to what Qwahua stated was "the inevitable arrival of trespassers." The complexity of these shared goals pulled the newly augmented community together as nothing else could have done. After a great deal of discussion and brainstorming had taken place in groups of various sizes and specializations, Peg convened a general discussion.

"We all seem to agree that one of our priorities should be making sure our borders are secure. Tamildah, you have some thoughts on that."

The young woman rose more shyly than Teg would have expected from someone with her impressive white tiger's head.

"I'll put the xuxu on regular watches along the borders. I'll assign pairs, so one can relay a message, while the other keeps an eye on any intruders. I'll keep at least one xuxu with me, probably Uah. That way I can quickly relay anything brought to me. Those who are off duty can stay at the roost or around the plaza, so they can be called on in a pinch."

"We have only a dozen xuxu, plus Heru, who I'd like to keep with me, especially when I'm out on *Slicewind*," Grunwold said. "Won't that stretch the flock pretty thin?"

Tamildah shook her head. "I don't think so. We don't expect daily attacks or anything, do we? Most of the time, they're going to be taking it easy."

She quickly resumed her seat, as Peg turned to Grunwold.

"What about using *Slicewind* to patrol the borders?"

"Actually," Grunwold said. "I've been thinking about how often *Slicewind* should patrol. Since Tamildah can set things up so the xuxu should be able to get relatively quick alerts to us, I don't think we need to do regular aerial surveys. An irregular survey would have an advantage, too."

Ohent cackled. "Any trespassers won't be able to slip through gaps in the routine. Good thinking, boy. You take after your dad in more than looks."

Peg next recognized Kuvekt, who rose, clearing his throat and shuffling his notes.

"Based on my research into explorations of this area since the cataclysm, there will be two main ways people will try to get in: the western border, where mountains cover the approach, and the lake. If there are still creatures in the depths of the lake, as reported in some of those journals, that may help dissuade any who hope to just sail in."

"There are definitely creatures," Grunwold said grimly. "We've glimpsed some very big things."

"And I've noticed," Vereez added, "that Grace is very careful not to leave the shoreline. Given that wild oothynn don't confine themselves to shallow waters, I think she's avoiding coming in reach of something."

Peg nodded acknowledgement. "With Grace assisting in the shallows and on the shoreline, the lake is unlikely to be a popular option for entry once the word gets out. The one thing we must all remember is that any trespassers we release are going to report what they've learned." She continued, "The other two priorities are closely related: the interior and exterior of the Library. Qwahua?"

Qwahua, who had been seated next to Meg, deep in conference, shoved herself to her feet. Unlike Tamildah, Qwahua's aggressive confidence went perfectly with her wolverine traits.

"Meg-lial has briefed me on what you people have already done, and we've worked out what to do next inside the Library. However, especially to impress any review boards that might drop in, as well as to aid in securing the campus, I think we need to get the plaza cleaned up. I'll make up a crew with the specialties I need for indoor work, but will leave at least three with Wagh for the outdoor work. Tamildah can work with the outside crew as well."

Peg smiled her satisfaction. "Ranpeti and I have discussed having Ranpeti take charge of the kids. Then there are going to be routine chores. We'll work out a rotation for those, based on who is needed where at any given time."

There was more discussion of specifics, then the gathering broke into smaller groups. Teg, feeling a bit overwhelmed by all the new people, went up on the roof to smoke a pipe, a habit that guaranteed her a certain amount of privacy.

Teg hadn't been surprised that the newly unarchived were eager to get immediately to work. She'd seen the same thing during numerous field seasons. The project was the reason for being together; without it, people tended to feel awkward and out of place. Given that the Unarchived had more reason than any archeological team to feel out of place, she wasn't surprised that they settled to work as if this was just a continuation of their previous job.

Teg requested a place on Wagh's outside team and was made welcome. Meg worked with the indoor team, especially when they were in the stacks. Peg managed to be everywhere. The inquisitors often opted to work outside, where they'd be available in case of an incursion on the borders.

By the third day of work, Teg was feeling quite attached to Wagh's group, and threw herself into her own labors with vigor, eager to show that the monster was not a slacker.

Or too old to be useful.

"What a terrific location for a dig," Teg said, leaning on her shovel and scrubbing at her forehead with a bandana. As she gulped cool zinz tea from her water bottle, she surveyed the tangle of green and brown and blue that was the forest surrounding and overgrowing the plaza, and the sky above the central campus of the Library of the Sapphire Wind. A few flowers lit colors among the greenery, but apparently the season was closer to midsummer, so most of the plants were producing seed and fruit rather than flowers. "I'm actually glad that they don't need me inside."

Xerak, stripped to the waist, his mane tied out of his face by a red paisley-printed bandana Teg had given him, paused in the process of chopping away a mat of vines.

"Teg-toh, aren't you afraid you're going to miss some great discovery as they clear away debris in the stacks?"

"Not really. Meg promised she'd let me know before the next section is opened up so I can be there. Right now, they're mostly seeing what shelving can be rescued, as well as doing some construction to adapt our living situation to so many more people. I'd only be an annoyance."

Teg chuckled softly to herself and resumed rhythmically shoveling away the ashy dirt that had accumulated on the intricate mosaic of pavers that had originally been the central plaza's surface.

Grunwold echoed her laughter. "You're thinking about Meg, aren't you? She's already pushing the inside crew's patience with her insistence that every little bit of printable material be saved, but with Zink backing her up, no one wants to complain. Zink's cool, sure, and really helpful, but still kinda creepy. Having you working inside, Teg, deciding you had to look at every little scrap of metal or bit of glass they uncovered, would probably have the crew all begging to be archived again."

"Hardly that," put in Tamildah, from over where she was getting a combination herb and flower bed into shape. "Being archived wasn't terrible, but the dreams, visions, whatever it was that Sapphire Wind created to occupy our dormant minds, now that I'm awake again, I don't think I could go back. Sapphire Wind did the best it could, but being caught in a waking dream only sounds good." She wrinkled her nose. "And I suspect that if one realized—or even suspected—that one was dreaming, the visions couldn't take, and that would be terrible."

Wagh had been pleased to see how, during their original search for the Library, a good deal of vegetative material on the rise leading up to the Library had already been cleared away. He made his crew's first goal determining precisely where the ruins of the other buildings on the plaza had been—especially the hotel and the research facility—so they could be cordoned off to keep anyone from pitching into a basement. Although the lower levels would have been partly filled by the debris from the burning buildings, they still were major hazards.

"Are there any lesser structures we should be looking out for?" Teg asked on the first day. "Ones that wouldn't be on Kuvekt's maps, because they were too utilitarian: storage sheds or water tanks? Like that."

Wagh shook his prairie-dog head. "Not that I recall. Dmen Qeres wanted to set a rarified, elegant atmosphere for the Library campus. The trustees, when they expanded the facility, remained faithful to his vision. Storage, plumbing, and all that practical stuff were concealed, which is one reason for the original builders going to the trouble of lower levels, when there was really more than enough room for above-ground storage and conduits. Down the hill slope to the south there was a stable for the vikrew who pulled the commuter coach. We'll need to remember to watch out for those foundations when we move that way."

Wagh was on the older side, although still younger than Teg. His build was what Teg would have called "beefy," except the word seemed weird when applied to someone with the head and little tail of a prairie dog. Though he definitely carried extra weight around his middle, Wagh had the sort of stocky build that comes from hard work, rather than working out. His brother, Huy, resembled him, but was a little less fit.

Conversation faded as the crews concentrated on their tasks, the sounds a symphony that Teg knew well from so many other projects: the rhythmic scrape of her shovel, then expertly lifting neatly measured quantities of soil; the swish as she tossed it into a screen; the gentle *crumpfh* as it landed. It was a while since the inquisitors had been surprised by how accurately she could hit her target, even without turning to look, but the newly unarchived were a fresh audience to show off for, and Teg was enjoying that, too.

The sounds of Teg's clearing away soil blended with the sharp "clip-clip" of shears as Tamildah trimmed the herbs in the nearby garden into shape, carefully saving her cuttings in different baskets for Nefnet to turn into infusions and tinctures, with plenty left over for seasoning of meals.

Xerak hacked at the invading mat of vines with a machete, while Grunwold assisted Wagh's crew in moving heavier blocks of masonry and chunks of timber. Vereez stood on the pedestal that held the statue of Dmen Qeres, perk-eared and alert. None of the original discovery team had forgotten being attacked by piranha toads and spike wolves on that very hill, so keeping watch had been deemed as vital as any other bit of labor. In time, Vereez would trade with one of the others, since a fresh set of eyes was the best way to make certain nothing would be missed, especially when, as to this point, nothing had been seen.

Over the days, the plaza had begun to reveal itself. Much of what had overgrown the paved central area had been vines and shallow-rooted plants that could establish in the accumulated duff. While these did not clear away easily, when they were hacked loose from their supporting matrix and heaped to one side, the results were so dramatic that Wagh had ropes tied to mark the general vicinity of the foundations of the hotel and scriptorium, then put his crew to work clearing away the vegetation.

"It will be a lot easier to get around if we don't need to keep tripping over this stuff," he said. "Just stay clear of the area behind the ropes for now."

An informal competition started up, with Grunwold, Vereez, and Xerak pitting themselves against Wagh's crew. Teg took her turn up on the pedestal. Since Sen, a scarlet-and-green xuxu was keeping her company, its jewel-bright eyes watchful, its head swiveling to scan the compass round, Teg figured she could light up her pipe. She had just nursed it into drawing well when Peg came up the ladder from the Library.

She tsked at Teg. "Slacking off?"

"I'm keeping watch," Teg replied, making a sweeping motion with her free hand to indicate the surrounding forest. "I mean, even Gandalf let himself pause for a pipe down in Moria, right?"

"I think he did," Peg admitted. "These days, I get the book and the movies confused. Where's Wagh? I have a message for him from Qwahua. She needs to borrow Throog, something about a drain."

"Wagh's over on the other side of the heap of greenery, I think," Teg replied, casting her gaze side to side, and realizing she didn't see the man's prairie-dog head. She saw Throog's raven head, but no sign of Wagh.

It rapidly became clear that Wagh was nowhere on the plaza, not with his crew, not with the inquisitors.

"I think he went off to have a pee," said Xerak. "We were working together on that matt of vine, and he made a joke about watering a tree, then wandered off."

"That was dumb," Teg said, all her years as a crew chief coming to the fore. She leapt down from the pedestal, lit pipe in hand, and strode over toward Wagh's crew. "Where's your boss? We've said over and over that this place is dangerous. What part of dangerous didn't he get?"

She was swinging toward Tamildah to ask if the younger woman could organize the xuxu into an aerial search squad when a ropey tendril of vines shot out of the heap of vegetative detritus. It grabbed Teg's pipe from her hand, then slammed it into the nearest of the buckets of water set around the plaza so people could wash their hands or tools as needed.

"Hey!" Teg protested.

More vines came shooting out of the mass, wrapping around Teg, pinning her arms to her sides, and her legs tightly together. Faster than she could have imagined, Teg found herself being dragged toward the mass of cut and oozing greenery. Even as it hauled her toward itself, the heap was somehow managing to move itself in fits and starts toward the cover of the forest. Teg's head rocked with each strong tug. She would have shouted again, but a broad leaf—prickly, soft, and flexible, rather like that of a mullein—wrapped itself around the lower portion of her head, covering nose, mouth, and ears. There was something in the prickles that made Teg's skin itch horribly, even as the leaf itself was cutting off her air.

I am really getting tired of everything complaining about my smoking! she thought, fighting down terror with irrational anger.

Although the prickly leaf muffled her hearing, Teg could hear various reactions to the compost heap's new agency: Xerak's almost roar of rage; Vereez's voice, sharp and shrill, saying something about swords. Something else about Wagh's feet. That definitely didn't sound good. Teg hoped she wouldn't hear anyone talking about *her* by body-part references.

She started kicking, but it didn't do any good. Her arms and legs were both firmly wrapped in vines. Panic rose in her throat, choking her with the screams she couldn't get beyond her sealed lips. Her vision was veiled in green as leaves and vines wrapped her head. About the only motion she could manage was a sort of undulation that reminded her of inchworms or dolphins. It wasn't at all useful, and exhausted her limited supply of air all too quickly, so that she found herself breathing the wet, humid air she'd gasped out a moment before.

Teg knew her wisest course of action would be to lie still and await rescue, but something in her rebelled. She'd grown up knowing she couldn't count on anyone. Not even her parents and grandparents—especially her parents and grandparents—would come to her rescue. As she'd grown older, she'd been the one doing the rescuing: socially, later financially. She didn't know how to trust that anyone would care enough to bother.

I wonder how they'll explain the cause of death back home, was her last coherent thought as she faded out.

Teg came to, vaguely surprised—and definitely relieved—to find herself doing so. She was lying on her back, and someone was gently washing her face, which felt hot and puffy, with something with a not unpleasant astringent odor.

I will not say "What happened?" or something else stupid and cliché.

Teg opened her eyes just enough to see that her attendant was

Vereez, then fluttered her lids open the rest of the way and managed a hoarse, "Did you save Wagh, too?"

Vereez's ears melted down in pure relief, while her jaws gaped in a smile. "We did. Kuvekt-lial is with him. Wagh's battered and is going to lose some hair, but Kuvekt said he's going to be fine."

Now that her eyes were fully open, Teg could see she was on a blanket that had been spread on a cleared portion of the plaza pavement. She struggled to sit upright, and Vereez put an arm around her to help.

"You can lean back against Dmen Qeres's pedestal," Vereez said. "Want some water?"

Teg nodded. Her tongue felt spongy and slightly swollen. She reached up with her free hand to touch her face, and Vereez pushed it down.

"The leaves that wrapped around your face had little spines in them. Usually, even someone furless like you could brush against them and not even feel it, but the way they were pressed down was a problem. Nefnet says this ointment will soften the prickles, and you should feel better by bedtime tonight."

"I really want a shower," Teg said, after taking another drink from her water bottle. "Can I do that?"

"Absolutely," Vereez assured her. "Let me get this on your exposed skin. Then, when you feel steady on your feet, we'll take you aboard *Slicewind.*"

Teg nodded and dropped her hands into her lap so Vereez could go back to applying the ointment. After her shower, most of the puffiness had left her face, though her tongue still felt thick. Nefnet prescribed a hot tea with lots of the sweet syrup that was used in place of sugar or honey in drinks.

"Take a nap," she advised. "We'll call you in time for dinner."

When Teg joined the rest for dinner, the mood was subdued. Wagh's face and arms were a patchwork crazy quilt of golden-brown fur and a thick pea-green ointment. His right ear was carefully bandaged, and had apparently been badly blistered by some sort of sap.

"Do you think we can do this?" Teg asked without preamble once everyone was seated. "We were just clearing brush and we nearly lost two people. If even the plant life is fighting us, what can we do when the real trouble starts?"

Kaj half raised a hand. "Teg-toh, I've noticed that you three humans all seem to underestimate plant life. Why is this?"

Teg frowned. "Well, in our world, it's not as—"

Peg cut in. "It doesn't walk like we've seen the tetzet do. It doesn't fly like the beti-teneh. It certainly doesn't punch and grab like Septilial tells us the uaftet did. Compost heaps usually just sit there."

Septi passed a tray of fish filets to Leeya. "That uaftet was an unusual circumstance. But is it true in your world that plants don't move of their own accord?"

"They certainly don't," Peg said, just as Meg said, "They do but . . ."

They looked at each other, then Peg inclined her head, encouraging Meg to go on. Meg gave a short summary of the ways plants did, in fact, move, fly, and even engulf or strangle their prey.

She concluded, "But I cannot think of any plants with as much volition as many we've encountered here, and certainly I have never heard of a compost heap attacking."

Uten Kekui and Xerak exchanged glances, then Xerak said, "It's probably happened, I'll admit, but what happened out there today was definitely unusual. At least we hope it was."

Cerseru Kham, mutely appealed to, nodded agreement. "Sadly, none of us are specialists in botanical magic. However, we do know something about latent magic, and I think we're all in danger of forgetting just how much raw magic was released in this area at the time of the Library's destruction. Plants are much more infused by ambient life energy than are mammals, reptiles, or insects. What non-vegetative creature could go from something the size of these"— she held up a roll that had been sprinkled with orange specks about the size of poppy seeds—"to a shrub as large as an end table in a few months? With plants such transformations are the rule, not the exception."

"We should have been warned," Tamildah added, "by how well the herb garden had survived, as well as how even delicate ornamental plantings are still thriving. It's likely the plants soaked up a lot of magic, and it only makes sense that they'd use it to survive."

As the discussion continued, Teg thought about how, in almost every mythology she knew, plants were considered lesser. Even those mythic traditions that gave them some sort of intelligence or indwelling spirit, like Greek dryads or those huge cedar trees the Japanese enshrined, were usually trees, not just routine plants. Respect for plants was usually given to some deity assigned to agriculture, not to the plants themselves. The classic "Western" ranking of importance put plants at the bottom, animals next, then humans. Humans were ranked below various supernatural creatures, although which ones depended on the culture.

I think what Cerseru Kham and Kaj said actually makes more sense. Even in our world, plants are amazing.

"Triffids," Peg was saying. "I get it. We need to think of any plant we're dealing with as if it's a potential triffid."

She went on to summarize *Day of the Triffids*, which, like so many of Peg's tales, ended up a hybrid of the book and the movie, but she got her point across. What was interesting was how the locals took this not as a horror tale, but as completely reasonable. By the time dessert was finished, and the plates were being cleared away, Teg, Peg, and Meg had a great deal more of an education as to what to expect from baseline vegetation.

"I wonder," Vereez said, "if we can use the latent magic in these plants we're cutting back in our favor? What if, instead of just heaping up the greenery for some future compost heap, we haul it down to the Qubhaneb River and use it to make getting into the forest a little less easy? I'd been wondering if we could do something similar with some of the more dangerous wildlife, too. What if, instead of trying to hunt it down and kill it, we encourage it to move out to the fringes of our homestead? Let any trespassers deal with spike wolves and piranha toads. We had to."

Cerseru Kham said. "I like that. Most wild creatures prefer to stay away from domesticated lands unless they think they can get an easy meal. Let's see if Tamildah or Huy have any suggestions. I think Uten Kekui and I could offer magical aid as well."

Grunwold put in. "I could haul the greenery on that platform we built for Grace. You'll notice, the heap didn't attack until Teg brought her wand of stink and fire over near it."

"Not true!" Teg protested. "It got Wagh first."

Wagh shifted uncomfortably. "Actually, I may have provoked it, too, or maybe tempted it. I went around back of the heap for a piss, and..."

He trailed off. Prairie-dog faces couldn't blush, but something in the cant of his one unbandaged ear gave the same impression.

"You encouraged it to think of you as edible or tasty," Tamildah said, failing to suppress her laughter. "Vereez has a good idea. I'm not an expert in botanical magic, but I think this could work—as could convincing our more dangerous co-residents to relocate."

"And even if these precautions don't keep intruders out," Cerseru Kham added, "we'll be making it harder to penetrate our borders, which makes it more likely we'll get warning when trespassers do arrive."

❦CHAPTER ELEVEN❧

Teg's unpleasant encounter with the compost heap was all it took to toss her into full project-director mode.

"We may not have OSHA looking over our shoulders, but I want coordinated goals and safety methods. I'm as guilty as the next person about getting all excited over new discoveries, but we're going to curb enthusiasm in favor of safety. That includes knowing where everyone is at any given time. Just the other day, I heard two different people insisting they'd seen Throog—one inside, one out. We were lucky that Peg came looking for Wagh soon after the compost heap grabbed him, or he might have been killed."

If Meg had eased into the role of Head Librarian, and Teg was Chief Archeologist, Peg had become Commander-in-Chief, a job no one else really wanted, but which was crucial since they had so many projects going on at the same time.

Peg bounced the eraser end of her pencil on the table and frowned at her To Do list. "Vereez's idea of convincing the piranha toads and spike wolves to join our newly trimmed vegetation in providing obstacles against invaders needs to be a priority, since that could serve as both attack and defense. Huy, I want you to take point on that."

Huy didn't object. "I'll start with relocating the piranha toads to where the Qubhaneb feeds into the lake. Most are there already. There should be good hunting for the spike wolves across the stream, in the mountains. They're already venturing over that way, since the area's a lot more peaceful than near the Library and lakeshore. It's more a matter of making them decide not to cross back."

Peg toasted him with her poffee bowl. "Next item. Tamildah, I think our xuxu-enabled early warning system needs refinement. Put your head together with Grunwold and see how we can better use our resources. We need xuxu at the borders, but at least one assigned to each outdoor crew."

"I'd be very happy to work with Grunwold on this," Tamildah said.

Peg gave Teg the faintest of winks, then continued. "I'm also worried that we'll be too easily trapped inside the Library. Right now, we have one way in, one way out. It's time we got that upper drawbridge fully in place."

Kaj raised a hand. "Now that Grunwold's brought back the hardware, I could handle that, with one assistant, I think. Let me ask Qwahua who can be spared."

Xerak looked as if he wanted to volunteer, but only sighed. "I'll do what I can to design lessons for my apprentices that will contribute to our outdoor work. You inspired me, Peg, since I heard you suggesting to Ranpeti that the kids' lessons could be useful, as well as educational. Maybe we can help Huy convince the critters to move in the right directions."

Peg smiled serenely at Xerak's compliment. "I don't see why our littlest residents should practice their numbers counting beads or blocks, when there are plenty of other things that need counting. It's amazing how much can be learned while assisting in the kitchen or in the garden or even making beds. Never forget, even little kids like to feel useful."

When the first invasion came three days later, it was nothing like what anyone had expected. The alert came late one afternoon, shortly before the crew working on the plaza was going to knock off for the day. Sefex, one of the xuxu, came soaring into the plaza, honking an alert on her crest. She landed on the head of Dmen Qeres's statue and announced with a precision very unlike Heru's heavily accented speech:

"We have an incursion by the Qubhaneb. Difficulties are being experienced. Assistance is needed."

"At last," Xerak breathed, dropping his shovel. "The waiting has been so hard. Sefex, please report to those in the Library. We'll head down immediately." Without further comment, he loped toward the trail heading west. Wagh's crew, including Teg and Vereez, immediately followed.

The trail they took toward the Qubhaneb had been sculpted to look like a game trail. This sculpting, along with a couple of not too obvious fords in the stream, had been another of Vereez and Peg's tactical brainstorms. Even with the xuxu, the stream's course was a lot of area to keep watch over.

"But people and animals alike tend to take the course of least resistance," Vereez had explained, "so we can steer them where we want them to go."

Creation of the trails had been eased by the fact that people and animals *did* tend to take the path of least resistance. Therefore, there had already been game trails that only needed to be adapted to look a little more inviting. The fords would have been more difficult to construct but for the joint cooperation of Grace and *Slicewind*. Between oothynn and flying ship, boulders were moved to where they provided a couple of crossing points that were inviting without seeming planned.

"Even if anyone does suspect they're constructed, not natural," Peg had said, hands on hips, as she surveyed their work with satisfaction, "they're not going to immediately assume we're the ones who did it. People have been trying to find the Library of the Sapphire Wind since the worst of the critical magical overload died down."

It was only when Teg had joined the group pounding down the trail toward the Qubhaneb that she wondered what sort of danger they were heading into. Her first impulse had definitely been, in the best tradition of Kipling's Rikki-Tikki-Tavi, to "run and find out."

If I ever turned into an Over Where sort of person, sennutep variety, Teg thought ruefully, *I think I'd be a mongoose.*

She was far from the fastest runner, and so came up at the tail end of the group when it paused at the forest's edge. Aftu, another of the xuxu assigned to the western border, was perched on Xerak's shoulder, and had probably been briefing him. Trying not to breathe too hard, Teg peered around the people in front of her, wondering why no one was moving forward.

Today's incursion had been at the more northern ford, which in itself was no surprise, as the overflights of the mountains had shown a moderately decent pass in that vicinity. What did surprise Teg, when she managed to get a better look, was realizing that rather than fighting off invaders, they were likely going to need to rescue them.

A group of six people, three with robes girded up so that their hems hung at midcalf, were arrayed along the series of large rocks that made up the ford. The three without girded robes wore serviceable armor and were notably older than the others. None of the six trespassers appeared to have noticed the people hanging back at the edge of the forest tangle, but this made perfect sense, because their attention was fixed on the pack of spike wolves that had them trapped from both sides of the ford.

Teg's throat tightened with remembered fear. She'd had her own too-close encounter with a spike wolf back when their group had been seeking the Library. Even her later excitement, when that encounter had contributed to them finding the doors far more quickly than they would have otherwise, hadn't eradicated the fear.

The spike wolf had a dry odor, acrid and sour, and when it slammed into me, its body felt hard and spongy at the same time, like a baseball bat covered in foam rubber. Then I was falling.

Teg shook her head and forced herself to focus on the current problem. Spike wolves—or "qwesemu," to give them their non-Peg name—were long and lean bodied, with extended muzzles, more or less like wolves, or rather what people who've never seen wolves imagine wolves are like. The "spike" part came from a liberal overlay of porcupinelike quills that covered the qwesemu's body and served as both offense and defense. Qwesemu also shared general coloration with wolves, although Teg was sure that no wolf from her world had a coat that extended into the darker, more "piney" greens.

The shadow cast by the mountains meant that the apparent time of day had shifted into evening from late afternoon. This was doubtless one reason the qwesemu, whose habits were crepuscular into nocturnal, were active. Another reason was that it was highly likely that the six trespassers had crossed into territory the spike wolves had recently claimed for their own. Finally, the spike wolves had them outnumbered.

"Pretty smart of the spike wolves," Xerak commented, "waiting until the invaders were committed to fording the stream to come in from either end."

"So," Vereez said, shifting uneasily from foot to foot. "What do we do? I'm the one who suggested we convince the spike wolves to relocate, but I can't say I feel comfortable just standing here and watching those people get eaten."

Xerak was thoughtfully studying the group out on the ford. "The spike wolves might find eating the trespassers harder than they imagine, but I think the qwesemu would win in the end—but they'd also get hurt, and that doesn't seem fair either, given that the spike wolves live here, not those people."

Wagh said softly, "Several of us brought the tools we were using when Sefex sounded the alert. We have a couple machetes, and a shovel. I'm not really sure the pruning shears would be of much use, but..."

Teg did a quick head count: Wagh and his crew made four; then there were herself, Vereez, and Xerak. Xerak had his spear staff, but neither she nor Vereez were carrying even a pair of pruning shears.

I do have Petros, though, she thought, touching her pocket and feeling some of her earlier panic ebb, *and Vereez can do magic, even without her swords to act as foci.*

Grunwold and *Slicewind* were off on a supply run, taking with them Peg, Cerseru Kham, Ranpeti, Brunni, and her new best friend, Mwetor. Uten Kekui had escorted Nefnet, Tamildah, and Kuvekt down to the eastern lakeshore to forage for a variety of plants, medicinal and otherwise.

"Air support would be nice," Teg thought aloud, "as would more magic, but I think we should be able to manage. Can we drive the spike wolves off on this side of the Qubhaneb, get the trespassers across to this side, then retreat?"

"That's tantamount to an invitation," Vereez said dubiously. "Shouldn't we be driving the trespassers off?"

"There are more spike wolves on the other side," Teg said. "Five there, four here." Teg felt her lips moving in a ferocious grin. "And don't worry. We can make it clear we're not inviting them. Xerak, are those ones wearing robes wizards?"

"Probably," Xerak said, "though with the robes all bunched up like that, I can't get a good look at whatever iconography they're presenting." He paused, hand drifting toward his wine flask. "Actually, I think I recognize at least one of them. It's been more than a year, but I think the sennutep with the raptor's head is Leelee, who was one of Uten Kekui-va's other apprentices."

"Do you think she's looking for him?" Teg asked.

Xerak shrugged. "I really don't know, and I could be wrong about it being her. That raptor look isn't exactly uncommon, but those pale feathers are less usual. Yeah, could be her."

"So, the not-robed three are probably muscle," Teg said, "since we all know that wizards are pretty useless if they need to work a lot of magic."

Wagh interjected uneasily, "The spike wolves on this side have noticed us. They're poking out their prickles."

When Wagh finished speaking, Teg realized that everyone was looking at her for orders. *I'm an archeologist, Jim, not a battle commander*, but with Peg and Grunwold both away, she guessed she'd have to do.

"Xerak, can you target a fireball to drive the spike wolves back from this side of the ford?"

The young man gave his head a speculative tilt. "I can try. It would be more effective if I get to the north side of them first. That way I'll drive them south, away from us."

"Go. Take Aftu with you. Send him back when you're in position." Teg turned to Vereez. "Vereez, you're going to have to be spokesperson." When Vereez pinned back her ears in a "why me?" look, Teg said, "Remember, the trespassers aren't going to be used to humans. We don't need the whole 'what sort of monster are you?' thing right now."

"Oh, right..." Vereez gave a fox's grin. "You're just one of the family now. We don't care how weird you look. What do you want me to say?"

Teg, who had never in her life felt she was part of anyone's family, not even—or maybe especially not even—the one she'd been born into, felt inordinately happy.

"Tell them they can either go back or come over here. Make it clear we're offering to protect them, not welcoming them to a party. Also, make it clear that if they hurt the spike wolves, we won't be thrilled."

Teg turned to Wagh. "Your crew's job is going to make sure the spike wolves don't come toward us."

"No problem," Wagh said. "We'd do that anyhow." He hefted his shovel and went to brief his crew.

Teg patted Vereez on the shoulder. "Okay, do your bit. I'll wake up Petros, just in case someone decides to do something 'clever.'"

Vereez nodded, then stepped out to where she would be clearly visible to the group on the ford. She raised her voice to carry over the sound of water over rocks, as well as the increasingly loud growls and grumbles of the spike wolves.

"Attention! We're going to clear a way for you to get across the stream to this side. If you do anything except cross, we're going to be even less friendly than we feel right now. Got it? And don't think about trying to turn the spike wolves against us or hurting them. If we have to deal with them, we're going to forget about pulling your tails out of trouble."

No exactly diplomatic, Teg thought, *but Vereez is the daughter of Inehem and Zarrq. Diplomacy is for when you're not doing someone a favor, I guess.*

At the sound of Vereez's voice, vari-shaped heads moved to see who had spoken. These included the heads of the spike wolves on their own side of the Qubhaneb.

"We don't need . . ." began one of the robed ones, male from the voice, his head some sort of canine.

A dingo? Teg thought.

He didn't get to finish whatever defiant statement he'd been about to make, because one of the not-robed ones, a towering fellow with the head of a panda, clamped shut the dingo's muzzle with a big hand and called back, "Got you. Standing by."

Aftu swept down from the forest fringe, landed on Vereez's shoulder, and said something in her ear. Vereez took a few steps back, right before a series of fireballs, large and dark orange, burst from the northern forest edge. From studying with Xerak, Teg knew that the large size of the projectiles and dark hue of the fire meant that Xerak was attempting to scare the spike wolves. If he'd been trying to hurt them, the balls would have been more compact, and the flames would have been a brighter orange, with the core showing yellow, or even a hint of white.

The spike wolves were definitely startled. The smaller two of the four bolted south along the riverbank. The other two seemed inclined to follow when one of the robed figures—the one with a raptor's head—tried to push past Panda and bolt for the riverbank. Panda was still holding the Ding-dong Dingo, and so was knocked off balance. He flailed with his free hand and managed to keep his footing, although the Ding-dong struggled free.

The raptor-headed wizard (who just might be Leelee), pulled up short because the two remaining spike wolves on the eastern bank had rounded to face the flailing sennutep. Glancing south, Teg saw that the two spike wolves that had bolted were slowing, peering back to see what was going on.

Wondering if they need to come to the rescue? Maybe they just figure dinner is finally being served.

On the far bank, the five spike wolves which had been, to that point, content to wait and keep the prey from fleeing, began picking their way out onto the ford. Their quills rose, much as the hackles might on a dog, but looking a whole lot more dangerous.

As the spike wolves stalked forward, the six sennutep trapped on the ford started edging away, ending up crowded together in the middle, shoving as they tried to put some distance between themselves and the prickly canines. Limbs flailed. Teg was pretty sure she saw the dingo wizard shove at Panda, who didn't budge from where he was holding the line against the two spike wolves at the eastern end of the ford. It was only a matter of time until someone ended up in the stream.

All that flailing is making the situation worse, Teg thought. *The spike wolves may be smart enough to set a simple trap, but they're still predators. To them all that motion means is panic, and panic is all to their advantage.*

Forsaking the cover of the trees, Teg stepped forward and bellowed, "Stop thrashing about, you idiots. Are you trying to get eaten? Xerak, a bit more convincing, please!"

"Right, Teg-toh!"

Xerak must have had the spell prepped, because the fireball burst forth almost immediately after. This one was brighter and tighter. It whomped into the ground to one side of the spike wolves nearest to the eastern edge of the ford, and should have set them running. However, Ding-dong Dingo screamed and kicked, looking way too tasty, Teg guessed.

Rather than running away, the foremost of the eastern spike wolves sprang out onto the ford. When it landed it bashed into the raptor-headed wizard "who just might be Leelee" knocking her into the water. One of the three quite-probably-guards reached to grab her and instead tumbled in after. The removal of these two created an opening on the ford that was instantly filled with snarling spike wolves coming from opposite directions.

Screams and shouts mingled with growls and barks, as well as a few low-pitched howls from the two spike wolves that had fled south and who were running in an agitated fashion back and forth, clearly trying to decide how best they could rejoin the rest of the pack.

"Wagh," Teg yelled, "send a couple of your people to see if they can help those who fell in. Do the retrieval from downriver, away from the ford. Have the rest of your crew form a barrier so those other two spike wolves can't come back."

"Right!"

Out on the ford, Panda had lifted up Ding-dong. Using him as a makeshift ram, he pushed them both past the spike wolves and onto the east riverbank. The remaining guard type, a woman with a rhino's head, was protecting the remaining wizard, a rabbit, who was now wailing at the top of her lungs. After a moment, Teg realized that these wails were not of panic, but were a spell of some sort. When one of the spike wolves lunged for the rabbit wizard and her protector, then bounced back, Teg guessed that the rabbit had put up a shield. How long the shield would last, especially since it had to protect two, was anyone's guess, but those two, at least, had the sense to stay still.

Once Panda was safely on the bank, he got his first good look at Teg's face. Teg knew that to the sennutep, humans with their naked skin and relatively flat features were startling although not precisely horrific, since the sennutep had skin, not fur, on their bodies below the neck.

It said a lot about Panda that he didn't react except to say, "You seem to be in charge. Truce? While we get people to land?"

"Truce, but only that," Teg replied. "We're not granting sanctuary or anything like that."

"Fair." Panda set Ding-dong on the shore, then nudged him with the toe of his boot. "You heard that, right?"

Mumble.

"Right?"

"All right!"

Panda looked to where Huy and Peynte, assisted by Vereez, were helping maybe Leelee and her sopping guard (another rhino) to shore. Then he picked his way out onto the ford.

The spike wolves were now a pack of seven, and soon they'd be nine, since the two who had bolted south were using the more southern ford to rejoin them. Teg looked at where Ding-dong, a sulky slump to his shoulders, was watching as Panda, sword now drawn, bravely confronted the spike wolf pack, so that the remaining rhino and the rabbit could pick their way to shore. The rabbit was leaning hard on her escort, confirming Teg's suspicion that the shield hadn't been easy for her to create and maintain.

Ding-dong was moving his fingers and Teg didn't trust his judgement enough to wait and see what sort of spell he was working. Petros had been almost fidgeting in her palm. Now she let it shoot a blob of Spidey silk onto those suspiciously moving digits.

Sparks went up. Ding-dong swung his head around in surprise, got his first good look at Teg, and suddenly was sitting very still.

"Sit," Teg said. "Stay. Or else."

Now that the last two were nearly to shore, Panda started walking backward along the ford, keeping his steps measured. When there was an opening between him and the spike wolves—who were reconsidering their options now that they realized the number of sennutep had more than doubled—Xerak shot a fireball across the water and hit the lead qwesemu soundly in the chest.

The fireball was one of the large, reddish ones, more for show than to cause injury, but it tilted the balance. Xerak didn't waste more mana following up his spell, but looked over to where Vereez was treating a freshly bleeding wound on the presumptive Leelee's leg.

"She okay, Vereez?" Xerak called.

"Pretty bad cut," Vereez said. "Sliced it on some rocks. Looks superficial, though we'll want Kuvekt-lial and Nefnet to take a look at it."

"Leelee?" Xerak said. "That you?"

"Senehem," came the reply. "Or rather Xerafu Akeru. I am now called Mennu Behes."

The wizard name was spoken with haughty pride. Xerak grinned.

"Good name, and easier for us, since we already have a Leeya. Less confusing."

Leelee, or rather Mennu Behes, was darting glances side to side. "Is Uten Kekui-va here?"

"Not here, precisely," Xerak replied, leaning on his spear staff. "Did you come looking for him? I'm going to take some convincing, just to warn you. Now that he is officially found again, his mailbox at Zisurru University does get checked. It's hard for me to imagine that you made this difficult journey without writing first."

"Maybe," the former Leelee said, "I wanted to prove myself devoted, if not as fanatically devoted as you, then at least devoted enough to make the trip."

Teg admired the brash response, but she also knew a bluff when she saw one. She cut in before Xerak could reply.

"Make sure, Mennu Behes," Teg said, "that your story will match what everyone else will say when we interview them privately. Especially that young person"—she indicated the rabbit, who had passed out in her rhino's arms—"who you're not going to have a chance to brief."

Panda stood to attention. "It may be possible that Mennu Behes was looking for her former master. However, if so, I did not hear him mentioned in a fashion that indicated a reunion was anticipated. Rather, there was a degree of concern, since he is apparently considered a very versatile, if not unduly combat-oriented, practitioner of the magical arts."

Mennu Behes shot Panda a look of pure venom. "Have you forgotten who hired you, Nuzt?"

"No. Absolutely not." Something in how Nuzt said the words made Mennu Behes look a lot less fierce.

Teg sighed. She didn't like the idea of taking these six any closer to the Library, but she liked even less the idea of staying near the Qubhaneb as dusk shifted into night.

"Can you walk?" she asked Mennu Behes, who was being helped to her feet by Huy, while Vereez stood by, one of the machetes held in a practiced grip.

Mennu Behes tested her injured leg, looked at Vereez with astonishment, then nodded.

"I can carry Kitet Un," said the rhino-headed guard who had been protected by the young wizard's shield, "if Nuzt will help get her on my back. I've carried her before, and she's light as a feather."

"Do it," Teg said. She turned to Ding-dong. "You've shown yourself foolish and impulsive several times. This is not the time to try your luck again. Several of our company will recognize magic being prepared."

"Are you taking us prisoner?" Ding-dong retorted, trying to sound defiant, but only managing to sound nervous.

"Not at all." Teg pointed to the ford where, even in the gathering darkness, the pack of spike wolves could be seen moving restlessly. "You are welcome to retreat there, away from our homestead. The other side of the stream is not in our grant. However, it does seem that the spike wolves are even less kind to trespassers than I intend to be. You can take your chances with them if you wish."

He didn't.

‡CHAPTER TWELVE‡

They were only partway back when reinforcements showed up, summoned by Sefex, who had reported to Tamildah, who had taken the time to gather appropriate members of the community. These included Uten Kekui, who did not greet Mennu Behes with glad cries, merely a stiff nod. Remembering that Uten Kekui had been back to Zisurru University, and therefore would have spoken with former colleagues, Teg wondered what he might have heard about his former apprentice's reaction to his perceived abandonment of his responsibilities.

"We're not letting these treasure hunters into the Library," Teg stated firmly. "And I meant what I said about interviewing them each separately. I only wish Peg were here. She's good at getting people to say more than they ever intended."

Vereez laughed. "Oh, so are you, Teg-toh. So are you."

Teg, remembering how both Vereez and Xerak had confided in her what they felt were their deepest, darkest secrets, decided not to argue.

When the much-augmented group arrived at the main campus, Teg called a conference of the available Rough Diamonds, while Wagh and crew kept watch on the six trespassers. These had been cautioned not to talk or else. The "else" was left vague, but since Teg was issuing the warning, and the trespassers were far from comfortable with her alien appearance, even Ding-dong took her seriously.

"Since we want to keep general goodwill for our homesteading efforts," Teg began, "we need to make sure no one can accuse us of attempting to murder these people by leaving them vulnerable. Therefore, I suggest we have them camp up on the roof of the Library. Kaj and Peynte have finished the drawbridge, and we'll post guards. Next, I suggest we interview them. Nuzt"—she pointed with her chin—"seems eager to talk. I suspect he's a professional mercenary who has hit his limit with covering for young idiots."

"Why don't you talk to him, then?" Vereez suggested. "He's already decided you're in charge."

"Let me interview Mennu Behes," Uten Kekui said. "I know her well enough that I think I can catch if she's leaving details out."

Xerak said, "I'll take the most idiot of the three young idiots, then, the dingo-headed fellow. He's spoiling for a fight, and I have a feeling Mennu Behes has been talking down my achievements. I can use that."

The other three were assigned to Vereez (guard who had fallen in stream), Nefnet (rabbit mage), and Ohent (rabbit's guard). They spread out around the plaza, with the Unarchived volunteering for guard duty around the perimeter. After the interviews had been completed, the six trespassers were permitted to set up their tents on top of the Library. Guards were assigned, then anyone who was available met indoors for dinner and to compare notes.

There were a certain number of contradictions, but their basic story agreed. The group that had set out from Zisurru University had been much larger: ten young wizards or wizards-in-training, and an escort of hired help, not so much mercenaries, as the sort who handled rough-camping trips.

Nuzt had been getting fed up with his employers well before the spike wolves had attacked. He and the rest of the travel company had been assured that there wouldn't be anything too dangerous until they actually reached the Rough Diamonds' territory. This had not been the case. After several very nasty encounters with the creatures who lived in the mountains, all but these three wizards had dropped out. Nuzt and the two rhinos had accepted a promise of a bonus if they'd continue on to their destination.

"Which was?" Meg asked, tapping the eraser of a yellow number-two pencil on the table.

"The Library," Teg said. "Nuzt said that he and his buddies

took the job because they figured that otherwise the three young idiots wouldn't be coming back, and they didn't want that on their consciences."

"Probably," Kaj said, "wouldn't do their business any good either."

"Cynically put," Teg said, "but probably true."

Vereez turned to Xerak. "So, basically, these trespassers belonged to one of those 'Find the Library of the Sapphire Wind' clubs that you told us about."

"Most were recruited from one of those," Xerak confirmed. "Mennu Behes wasn't part of the club though. She was a pretty serious student."

"What you're too polite to say," Meg said, "is that her motivation was hearing a rumor that you—a student junior to her, something of a laughingstock for chasing around after Uten Kekui, when most had dismissed him as a flake—not only found Uten Kekui, but found the Library as well ... and were one of those on the homesteading charter. Envy is a powerful motivator, and she had drunk deep from its poisoned cup."

Teg glanced sideways at Meg, wondering if she'd been spending too much time among old books. That last bit didn't sound like how she usually talked.

"So," Vereez said, "do we just let them go?"

Teg shook her head. "That's not going to discourage anyone, and since we're not going to kill them or jail them, then we need to use them to send a message that we're pretty harsh with those who waste our time and energy."

"Go on ..."

Teg raised a finger. "First, we put them to work, outside of course. We tell them that they need to earn back the work hours we lost because of their interference. Since seven of us were pulled off working on the plaza, we make a base estimate and multiply it by seven."

Kaj's ears flickered. "That's seriously wicked. Do we divide the number by six, since there are six of them?"

"Nope. Each one is responsible for the full amount, because even if there had just been one of them, we would have still had the whole crew pulled off duty. If they fuss, I'll point out with infinite kindness that I'm being generous and not including the second group that Tamildah assembled because it turned out we didn't need them."

"Wicked," Kaj repeated to a background of appreciative murmurs from several others.

"When they've worked off their time," Teg continued, "and a bit extra because we're going to need to assign guards to them twenty-four/seven, since we can't trust them—they'll be free to leave. Under their own power, of course, and only with the equivalent of the supplies they brought in with them. We'll escort them back to the western border. If they whine, I'll threaten to make sure they leave at dusk, just as when they arrived."

Xerak looked startled. "I'm glad you weren't my apprentice master."

Teg laughed. "I'll admit, I was inspired by memories of one of my early crew chiefs who assigned KP and other chores to anyone he caught slacking, on the grounds that the slackers still owed work."

"What if they ask us to transport them out?" Meg asked.

Teg grinned. "Then they need to work off their passage in sweat equity—no cash. And we base the hours not only on what they'd pay a professional transport company with a sky sailer, but on the hours we'll be deprived of *Slicewind*."

"I'm not sure I like the idea of having them stay that long," Ranpeti said. "They could become dangerous."

"All right," Teg said. "Compromise. If they want to offer us cash for transport, we'll take it—but for the whole group. We'll make clear we're doing them a favor, and we won't drop everything to ship them off, no matter how much we want them gone. Personally, though, I'm in favor of sweat equity. Wizard types seem especially accustomed to being treated as if they're in a class above everyone else. I'd like to send the message that they're not. When the word gets out how we treat trespassers, that should discourage most of the lightweights."

Xerak tugged the edge of his mane. "But what if the word doesn't get out? Mennu Behes isn't the type to tell a tale that shows her in a less than admirable light."

"Oh, we make sure it gets out," Teg said. "I'll put a word in Nuzt's ear that repeat incursions on the part of companies like his will be viewed severely. Return visits of any sort will score extra penalties."

Leeya had been listening from one end of the table, sipping fyari tea and holding hands with Septi. "I heard you say something about kitchen work. I have suggestions that should keep these people busy. When Septi and I went down to where Meadow Village used to be, I saw you'd been digging ysisora. I think the tubers may be descended from some of what we left behind. Harvesting all we can find would put us a long way toward supplies for the cold season. Ysisora can get boring, but you can live on it."

"Elven waybread," Meg whispered to Teg, who grinned.

Septi added, "And what Leeya isn't saying is that she knows enough ways to cook ysisora that it will never be boring, not with the variety of herbs we're finding in the gardens here."

"Another job our trespassers can be put to," Ranpeti said, getting into the spirit of things, "is laundry. Even with Grace showing unexpected enthusiasm for swishing around net bags of clothing in the lake, there's still an awful lot of dirty clothes and linens to be wrung out, hung to dry, and folded."

Uten Kekui raised a hand. "I'd like to supervise our new workers, if we assign them to outdoor chores. Someone skilled in magic should be near given that three of our trespassers have earned wizard names. I'd also like a chance to spend some time with Mennu Behes, ask her about her studies, things like that."

"Fine with me," Teg said. "You won't be sent alone, though. There's plenty of work to be done in the meadow, certainly enough to keep a few of our people busy."

After the meeting had concluded, a delegation of Rough Diamonds went up to the roof. There they found the six trespassers had devoured the meal Leeya had sent up, and were more or less collapsed on their bedrolls. They woke up fast enough when Teg announced that she was there to tell them how they were going to atone for the inconvenience they had caused.

When the treasure hunters were informed of Teg's terms, there were the expected protests, but Teg had anticipated most of them. The assigned "sentence" was three hours of labor, multiplied by eight, so a minimum twenty-four hours, more if the treasure hunters chose to request transport back to the nearest town where they could get safe transport to Zisurru University.

Ding-dong (whose wizard name was Ha Uher) and Mennu Behes had protested that three hours was extreme, that at most they owed an hour. Ohent, who had insisted on being part of the delegation, "because I'm mean," pointed out that she'd argued for six hours per person, given the amount of extra work the trespassers had caused by the need to make places for them to stay, the labor that would be lost by the need to assign guards, not to mention the extra food and the medical care for Mennu Behes's injured leg.

"We'll give you a pass on the various scratches and dents we treated for the rest of you," she concluded.

Ohent was no longer as crazy as she'd been when Teg had first met her, but she could do a very good facsimile when she wanted, and she clearly enjoyed her role as "bad cop." Protests ended, although rebellion simmered in Mennu Behes's and Ha Uher's eyes. The three guards and the rabbit wizard, Kitet Un, seemed, if not happy, at least resigned.

When the trespassers had signed the contract, Uten Kekui made it clear that if they wanted to work twelve-hour days, he'd be happy to supervise.

"We can break the workday into four-hour shifts, if you'd like, with an hour between for rest, meals, bathroom breaks, like that. That would burn fifteen hours each day. Add on eight hours for sleep, and an hour for your personal needs, and we've allocated a full day."

"That'll be simple," Ha Uher said. "You've obviously forgotten how demanding Zisurru University can be."

However, the next morning, after four hours of digging ysisora, Ha Uher admitted that longer breaks would be a good idea.

"But only because we're not at our best after battling our way through those horrible mountains."

"I would have loved to be here to watch Teg lay down the law," Peg said, when they returned that evening.

Slicewind had glided down into her cradle with enough time before dinner that new supplies had been unloaded and the travelers had been brought up to date.

Teg was about to protest that Peg would have probably done better, when Uah, the xuxu, landed on the closest of the several perches Tamildah had set up around the reception room, and tootled the fanfare that meant she had a message to deliver.

"For Teg-lial, from Nuzt. He begs a moment of your time."

"Sure," Teg said. She made an apologetic dip of her head. "They've decided I'm in charge."

"The price of decisiveness," Peg said. "Can I come along? I mean, this isn't a tryst, is it?"

Teg drained her poffee bowl. "Absolutely not. I mean, absolutely not a tryst, and sure, you can come along."

They mounted the stairs, and found Nuzt waiting near the xuxu roost, under the watchful gaze of Heru and several others of the flock. The other five trespassers were over by their tents, either resting or, in the case of Ha Uher, trying to pretend he hadn't been resting. Teg made a quiet bet with herself that tomorrow the wizards, at least, would make maybe eight hours.

I'd better put a word in with Uten Kekui that the more robust types are not to be permitted to make up for their bosses slacking. That would defeat the purpose.

Nuzt gave a brief bow. "Thank you, Teg-lial."

"No problem. This is Peg. She just got in on the *Slicewind* a few hours ago."

Nuzt offered Peg a bow. "I am honored she would take the trouble to meet with me. *Slicewind* is the sky sailer, I believe. It is her return that has initiated my request."

Teg made a mental note that he was clearly speaking for himself, not the entire group.

"Go on."

"I realize I am in no position to ask for favors, and I would be happy to provide compensation for what I request, but I was wondering if tomorrow, when daylight has returned, if it would be possible for *Slicewind* to make a pass over the western mountains."

Teg didn't mention that Grunwold intended to check all the borderlands tomorrow in any case. "May I ask why?"

"I have been concerned about those who turned back," Nuzt explained. "It was the best option we had at the time, but still, I have been worried. There were a few injured people in that group, and the young wizards..."

Carefully hidden from his companions by the angle of his body, he made a wobbly gesture with one of his hands, indicating his lack of faith in something.

Probably their good judgement.

His next words confirmed this. "They were less prepared for the arduous elements of the journey, as well as how doing magic would weaken them for travel. I'm not asking you to mount a rescue . . ."

His tone said he hoped they would.

". . . and hopefully such would not be needed, but I would be greatly reassured if I knew they had at least gotten out of the mountains. There is a farmstead not too far west that they intended to head for, owned by a family called Yemgar."

Teg looked at Peg, but she had no doubt what the answer would be. Peg inclined her head in the slightest of nods, indicating both her agreement and that she knew Grunwold would agree.

"We'll talk to *Slicewind*'s captain, but your request seems entirely reasonable, even admirable."

Teg now raised her voice, just to make certain that the five other trespassers, as well as those guarding them, would be certain to hear. "However, if this turns out to be some not-so-clever plan to get *Slicewind* away so someone can attempt to undermine the terms of your group's remaining here, we will put the lot of you on a leaking raft and have Grace tow you out into the lake and leave you to fend for yourselves. Got it!"

"Got that!" Nuzt said, and to Teg's amusement, most of the trespassers echoed him a beat after.

"You all have enough to eat?" Teg asked. "Drink? Blankets?"

"Yes, Teg-lial. As detention areas go, this is very comfortable."

Teg was about to bid Nuzt good night when Peg suddenly spoke.

"What do you think we are? Me and Teg, I mean? Surely you and your companions have speculated."

Nuzt blinked. "There has been conjecture, but the general opinion is that you are like Emsehu, guardian creatures of the Library of the Sapphire Wind."

Peg smiled. "I like that. Like Emsehu, huh? Sleep well. You've got a lot to do come morning."

The following day, Teg, Peg, Ranpeti, and Grunwold took *Slicewind* to look for the missing "Let's Rob the Library" band. When they found no sign of them in the mountains. Grunwold took the *Slicewind* over to the Yemgar Farmstead, where they learned that Nuzt's comrades and their charges had indeed reached there, battered but intact, and had been able to arrange for passage back to Rivers Meet.

The residents of the settlement were also homesteaders, although their charter was much less complicated. Initially, they were wary of their new neighbors, but it was hard to see much threat when the spokesperson was Ranpeti, with Brunni and Mwetor in tow. Ranpeti had the good sense to realize that potential customers were a lot less threatening than mystic warriors over the mountains, and made arrangements for the purchase of some of the farm's surplus come harvest. She also arranged to have their mail dropped at the farm.

To sweeten the deal, Ranpeti immediately bought a variety of fresh foods, including a small flock of the local equivalent of chickens, since Leeya had been complaining that she didn't have enough eggs to make many of her recipes.

Later, when Teg and Peg went down to the meadow to let their prisoners know the news, Nuzt and his associates were clearly relieved. Teg noticed that Mennu Behes and Ha Uher looked wistful, as if they wished they'd chosen to retreat as well, but little Kitet Un just dug harder.

The trespassers left on the day after they'd completed their three days of labor, earlier than expected. Konnel and Sefit had arrived on *Cloud Cleaver* that evening, bearing with them a letter requesting that they check if Ha Uher was in the vicinity of the Library, and, if so, could they help arrange for him and his surviving associates to be rescued.

"Ha Uher's grandfather is one of our agribiz associates," Sefit explained. "When he learned what his grandson had done, he did not precisely approve, but . . ."

"His grandson," Peg said with an understanding sigh.

Although, Teg thought with amusement she took care to hide, *you were more likely to have been the grandchild in need of redemption than any of your own grandchildren, based on what you've told us about them.*

"When Ha Uher's grandfather learned that the Library was being homesteaded, he checked the charter," Konnel said, his voice strained, since Nefnet was massaging one of her treatments into the muscles of his legs. "He recognized our family name and got in touch. He has promised compensation if we provide transport, and Sefit negotiated for it to be in the form of wholesale supplies, rather than money."

Since the six trespassers had worked off their twenty-four hours by then, Teg was willing to let them go. To their surprise, Kitet Un, the petite young wizard with the features of a rabbit, didn't want to leave. In contrast to Mennu Behes and Ha Uher, Kitet Un had been very quiet. Uten Kekui had reported that the little wizard had worked as hard or harder than any of the others.

"I want to stay!" Kitet Un wailed. "I hoped if I worked very hard, you'd consider letting me stay. I've dreamed about working in this Library since I was small. I think I might have lived here in a past life. Please, please, please!"

Despite her evident sincerity, and that she was as cute as a plush bunny in an Easter basket, no one relented.

Meg did offer a small amount of encouragement. "Finish your education. Get some training, not only in magic, but in how libraries work. Then, after we secure our homestead, perhaps we can hire you as an intern. If you like that, then we'll see."

Kitet Un agreed, but only reluctantly. When *Cloud Cleaver* departed the next morning, she could be seen staring back over the stern rail until the sky sailer vanished in the distance.

The day the trespassers departed also saw a shift in the work around the plaza. The initial removal of rubble and vegetative debris had reached the point where the burned and collapsed structures could be cleared away.

"Excavation," Teg said to Meg that night as they were getting ready for bed, "but not my sort of excavation. So, since Wagh and Qwahua are taking the entire maintenance crew outside, I'm moving in where my desire to focus on details will be considered an asset, not a hindrance."

"I'll be glad to have you." Meg paused in her rhythmic brushing of her shoulder-length silver hair. "The indoor crew removed all the damaged shelving. Not all of it was burned beyond use, and we've set that aside. They took the rest outside. Quite a chore. Wagh and Qwahua asked if we could prioritize locating the freight elevator next. If we can get that working, it will be a lot easier to deal with clearing away the unsalvageable material, if the Library's deeper stacks are as much of a mess as what we've seen."

"Makes sense," Teg agreed. "I'd love to work in the artifacts repository, but that's a lower priority." She grinned. "Well, from the homesteader point of view. My inner Indiana Jones figures that's where we'll find real treasure."

Meg's hand paused in her rhythmic brushing. Teg thought she was going to say something, but after a moment, the brushing resumed.

Probably she was going to remind me that books, even damaged books, are treasures, Teg thought, *and I certainly wouldn't disagree.*

The core of the indoor team was Meg, Zink, and Septi, assisted by Kuvekt when he wasn't treating various minor injuries. Sapphire Wind, via Friba, assisted, when possible, but the *genius loci* was frequently needed elsewhere.

Cerseru Kham and Uten Kekui had both volunteered to help, and Meg often consulted them regarding magical texts, so she could prioritize which ones to refurbish when the time came to attempt to build a new collection.

Vereez was permitted to be an exception to the "avoid using magic in the library as much as possible" rule, because her ability to summon and control a very light breeze—until recently, just about the only magic she had thought she could do—was so useful for removing the ashy portions of partially burned pages that everyone agreed it was worth the risk. When he wasn't needed at *Slicewind's* helm, Grunwold kept finding ways to make himself useful to the indoor crew, and no one, not even Vereez at this point, could overlook that he was most likely to be there when Vereez also was.

Over the next several days, Teg noticed how often Tamildah started showing up when Grunwold was indoors, ostensibly to ask his opinion on something related to xuxu assignment. She really was the expert, since Grunwold's experience was limited to raising Heru from an egg, after he'd found the nest raided by a predator, leaving only the one unbroken egg. Heru was, therefore, more or less imprinted on Grunwold, although, like any intelligent child, once he hit adulthood, he'd made his own decisions about his relationship with "Grun." Nonetheless, Tamildah kept finding excuses to consult

Grunwold as to how often to rotate the xuxu to different posts, or some matter of diet.

Teg swallowed a sigh. *Another love triangle? Or does this make two interlocking triangles, with Vereez in both? Or maybe three, given the whole Xerak/Kaj thing.*

Vereez had said she wanted to give up on Kaj, but "wanting" wasn't working. She'd told Teg that her head knew that Kaj didn't particularly care about her, but as long as he was more or less available, she kept finding herself wanting to avail. Teg wondered how long Kaj would hold out, but for now he was either being extremely discreet or finding experimenting in chastity amusing.

Xerak also hadn't stopped admiring Kaj, but since he was also Kaj's apprentice master, he was working hard at keeping a professional distance. All in all, the tangle of relationships was sometimes awkward and sometimes trying. Although, Teg had to admit, if these hadn't been real people, all of whom she cared about to varying degrees, the intricacies of the romance dance would have been amusing.

Each time Tamildah dragged Grunwold off, Teg saw Septi grinning his slightly wicked goatish grin. Even in his seventies, he hadn't lost the roguish twinkle that had put Leeya off for so long—as she told the tale—until the sweeping storm associated with the critical magical overload had shown her that Septi wasn't nearly as frivolous as he'd made himself out to be. One of the pleasures of working on the indoor team was getting to know both him and Leeya better. Teg looked down at the heap of bits of metal, worked stone, and the like that had been set aside for her inspection, and sighed happily as she went back to separating trash from potential treasure.

After a couple of days, Teg brought some of her finds with her to dinner, so she could consult with Xerak after they'd eaten. Although his major concentration from a very young age had been related to his magical studies, Xerak *had* grown up in his parents' antiquities and curiosities shop (which he had only recently learned had been his mother's base for her work as a high-end fence). Once Teg had cleared away the obvious junk, he was quite happy to help her sort through the remnants.

They were doing this when she heard her name.

"Yes," Peg was saying cheerfully, "that's right. It nearly carried Teg off with it. We never really were certain if it had been domesticated or not."

Grunwold put in, "I'd bet it had been."

Wagh looked wistful. "Our lives would be a lot easier if we had a cargo hauler, even one that's gone feral. We could get the burned timbers moved off the plaza in half the time. *Slicewind* is terrific for hauling the big ones, and we have wheelbarrows for the scraps. It's the medium-sized junk that's ridiculously labor intensive."

Teg, all too aware how much time her field crews spent moving waste material, rather than doing proper archeology, asked, "What are the odds a feral cargo hauler could be caught and retrained? Is there anyone on your crew who knows how to train one?"

"Huy has volunteered for the training part," Wagh said. "Tamildah has a few spare xuxu out scouting to see where the cargo hauler might have moved to. If she finds it, I hope you don't mind reassigning some people to catching it."

Catching the drift of the conversation, Tamildah leaned down the table to answer. "I suggest we make an enclosure for it down by the lake. There's plenty of room there, and it wouldn't be overwhelmed by too many people. I've been working on a basic design, built from saplings lashed together. If we anchor it properly, the cargo hauler shouldn't be able to lift it."

Grunwold joined in. "If you find the cargo hauler, Tamildah, we can use *Slicewind* for the capture."

Tamildah's whiskers curled at that "we," only to droop when Grunwold reached out to poke Vereez, who he was, as usual, sitting as near to as possible at the communal table.

"Hey, Pointy Ears, I think you'd be a terrific help when we go after the cargo hauler."

"Sure," Vereez said. "I watched how Xerak lowered the intensity of his fireballs so he could use them as warnings. I'll practice doing that with my lightning arrows."

She snuck a hopeful glance at Kaj as she said this, obviously hoping she'd impressed him with her new-found prudence. Kaj, however, wasn't paying attention to the conversation. He was immersed in a battered copy of a book on magical techniques for beginners that Uten Kekui had brought back for him at Xerak's request.

If I were into serious emo-drama, Teg thought, *I'd be wondering if Kaj was trying to impress Xerak with what a serious young apprentice he's trying to be, now that his mother is no longer keeping him from learning magic. I think I'll give up while I'm ahead.*

Vereez wilted and Teg, looking away from the on-going drama without words, saw that Septi was watching with the familiar wicked twinkle in his yellow, rectangular-pupiled eyes. She just barely managed to keep from rolling her eyes in agreement, remembering that Xerak was nearby, and noticed a lot more than he let on. Instead, she shoved an oddly shaped piece of metal at Xerak.

"Too small to be a door hinge," she said, "but definitely some sort of hinge. It didn't seem quite right for a box, though."

"Book hinge," Xerak said promptly. "You find them on a lot of magical texts, so they can be locked. Not magical in themselves, usually."

"So, magical books are really dangerous," Teg said.

"Not always." Xerak shifted into lecturer mode.

Completely content, Teg started taking notes.

Teg was still thinking about her finds when she went back to the room she shared with Meg. They'd divided it down the middle, although after several months of sharing the stern cabin on *Slicewind* with its one bed, they didn't waste space on a curtain, especially since a reading light wouldn't keep either of them awake.

Teg was snuggled down under her blanket, letting her mind drift on its way to sleep when she heard Meg click off her magical light (you turned it at the base to disconnect the power from the crystal that was sort of kind of the bulb) then get up. She expected to hear the scuff of Meg stepping into her slippers, then the soft flumph as she put on her robe. Pre-bed bathroom trips were pretty normal.

Instead, she heard Meg opening the chest at the foot of her cot, getting something (presumably clothes) out, and getting dressed. Next came the sound of her soft-soled shoes crossing the floor, then the door opening and closing.

Teg thought about getting up and going after her, just to make sure she was all right, but one of the banes of getting older was restless sleep. Tonight, Teg was comfortably tired, rather than the flat-out exhausted she'd been after a day working outdoors. Why should she embarrass Meg, who had probably just gone out to the reception hall for a cup of tea rather than tossing and turning?

Tomorrow, I'll keep an eye on her, make sure she's not staying out late, working all day...

₴CHAPTER THIRTEEN ₴

Teg found it easy enough to fool Meg into believing she was asleep, since she'd been conking out most nights pretty quickly. When for the third night running, Meg dressed in the dark, then left their shared room, Teg decided to follow. Since she slept in loose pajamas that, except for the lightness of the fabric, weren't much different from a tee shirt and sweatpants, she didn't both changing her clothes. Since she used moccasins for slippers, a habit dating back to field camps, she didn't even need to worry about her footwear.

Meg wasn't in sight, but the logical first place to look was the reception hall, which was not only the common living room/dining room, but was also close to the bathrooms. Nefnet and Morwe were playing a popular board game—something like Chutes and Ladders, but a lot more complex strategically—but otherwise the reception hall was empty. Teg gave a casual wave, then checked the bathrooms. No Meg.

Leeya was in the kitchen, taking out trays of muffins for tomorrow morning's breakfast. No one else was up. Teg took the muffin Leeya offered, a moist, dense creation whose body came from quantities of fresh fruit and eggs, and when Leeya suggested she take one back to Meg, she knew Meg hadn't been this way.

"Meg's looking tired," Leeya commented. "It took me a while to get used to how to read your faces, but I don't think she had those shadows under her eyes when we first met, and I'm sure she's lost weight. Septi thinks she's working too hard. Now that you're on the indoor crew for a while, can you get her to ease off?"

Teg, feeling a bit guilty because she had been so absorbed in her own work that she hadn't noticed, promised that she would. She took the proffered extra muffin because otherwise she'd have had to explain that Meg wasn't quietly in their room (and because it was excellent), and headed off on her search.

First, she trotted back to their room, just in case Meg had returned, but it was still empty. Then she got her crystal-topped flashlight and considered where to check. Their work area was close by, so she went there next, since Meg might be obsessing over some unfinished task. Although the low level of light they left on when they finished for the day was not enough to work by, it was sufficient to show the room was empty. Teg went over to the doors that had not yet been opened and tried the latches. They seemed to be as they had been, not yet worked free of the melting and corrosion that had worked as well as any lock and key—or any spell—to keep them closed.

Any sleepiness Teg had felt was gone now. Fueled by Leeya's muffins, she headed back into the reception hall. The light in the kitchen was dim, so Leeya had gone to bed, but Nefnet and Morwe were still moving pieces around the brightly painted board. Teg considered asking them if they'd seen Meg, but felt reluctant to reveal her concern.

Three ways out of here, she thought. *Outside. Up the staircase to the roof. Through the door on the other side of the reception hall.*

On impulse, Teg chose the last option. She didn't precisely sneak past Nefnet and Morwe, but took the route that led behind the sage stations. Qwahua's team had cleared away much of the remaining rubble to make it easier to access the stair to the roof. Reaching the stair confirmed Teg's suspicion that Meg could have gone through the reception hall this way without being noticed.

Not counting the doors to the outside, the reception hall of Library of the Sapphire Wind had two major exits. When they'd made their first visit to the Library, their exploration had been tightly focused on finding the pieces of Ba Djed of the Weaver. That had led them through the westernmost exit into the stacks, then to the hidden door that went down into the repository where magical items were stored.

Lately, their focus had been on the eastern side, so Teg hadn't been through the western arch recently. Qwahua's crew had done some danger reduction, including installing a simple lashed sapling gate to keep the kids from wandering where they shouldn't, if they managed to escape their watchful guardian dobergoats, Ahmax and Ufatti. Teg opened the gate, wishing she'd see some indication that Meg had been through before her. As elsewhere, a low level of light made it possible to navigate without tripping over one's feet, but Teg flashed her light around.

The burned shelving units had been secured so they were no longer in danger of toppling, although they remained in place until what remained of the texts and data crystals could be salvaged. The walls, floors, and ceiling were much cleaner, revealing lovely bas-relief carvings bordering doorways and the occluded windows. Teg reflected that the cleanliness probably had more to do with Sapphire Wind's diligent crew of abau than with Qwahua's work crew.

Thinking of the abau made Teg wonder where Sapphire Wind might be. The *genius loci* had an uncanny tendency to show up when something was going on, sometimes via Friba, sometimes as a sparkling whirlwind, more or less visible, depending on whether it felt a need to be acknowledged.

Teg glanced around uneasily, but neither the purple-and-green lizard parrot, nor the whirlwind, were apparent. *Does Sapphire Wind sleep? Or is it simply taking advantage of not being constantly asked questions to get some of its own work done? When we first met, it could hardly keep lights on, but now...I wonder what backlog of maintenance it might feel it has to do? I suppose it could be with Meg, wherever Meg is.*

For the first time, Teg found herself wondering if she was being imprudent. Maybe she should go and wake someone up. Peg and Grunwold were bunking on *Slicewind*, but Vereez and Xerak were indoors. Kaj still shared a room with his mother, since Ohent was most likely to relapse when she was asleep. Any or all of them would go with her.

But even as she entertained these thoughts, Teg kept walking deeper into the stacks. With the tables and benches stacked to one side, the rooms seemed emptier. Even her footsteps in her soft-soled shoes seemed to echo, although Teg knew that was merely her overwrought imagination.

Finding her way to the entry to the repository was easy enough. When Teg got to where the door was, it was closed and sealed, very easy to overlook. She'd half expected to find it standing open, but the abau-polished floors gave no hint whether Meg—or anyone else—had been through here.

Teg hesitated. She was already taking too many risks. She knew that. The old books held book worms and acid bats, and who knew what else. Not all of the Library's less intelligent guardian creatures might have gotten the briefing about who to attack and who not to attack. And the repository, with its haze of ambient magic, was not one of the safer locations, even if it was a familiar one.

And I don't know if Meg is down there. I haven't checked outside. She could be aboard Slicewind, *chatting with Peg. I haven't gone up to the roof. I might have missed her when I was going one way and her another. And...*

And Teg had to admit it. She didn't want to go down those stone steps alone. Backtracking, Teg checked the roof, disturbing only sleepy xuxu. When she got back to her room, she hoped to find Meg quietly asleep, but the other bed was still empty. Teg considered trying to stay awake until Meg returned, but gave it up as a bad idea.

What can I say? I can't exactly ask her where she's been this last— Teg checked her mechanical watch—*hour and a half, without seeming nuts. What am I going to say if she says she's somewhere she wasn't? No. Better talk to Peg, make sure Meg wasn't visiting her. That's probably the answer, right?*

But as she drifted off to a restless sleep, Teg remembered the expression on Meg's face when Teg had joked about wanting to search the repository because that was where the treasure would be. Meg had looked as if she wanted to say something, but had stopped herself.

What was it? But Teg's dreams did not offer a convenient answer.

In the morning, Teg sought out Peg, only to find that she was on a routine patrol of the area with *Slicewind*. Teg went back to working with Meg's crew, saying (untruthfully) that she needed a break from looking at the box of hardware, and wanted a crack at the books. Meg seemed pleased. As they sorted pages, Teg tried to decide if Leeya was right about Meg looking more worn out. She couldn't be sure, but certainly Meg was doing serious damage to a bottle of fyari tea, a blend that, unlike zinz, had at least as much kick as Teg's preferred poffee.

At the lunch break, Teg snagged Peg, who was nearly beside herself with excitement since *Slicewind*'s routine patrol had happened on a group out on the lake.

"They were going to get eaten by Cthulhu, I'm pretty sure, but we tossed them a tow line and got them out of the deep parts. Then we took the ship down, and Grunwold told them that there was only one rescue per group, and next time, they'd be sea monster chow."

"Do you think they'll stay away?"

Peg laughed. "I think so. Ranpeti got the idea that we need to post the farther shore with warnings. The kids are helping with the signs. They're coloring in all the details including tentacles, bulging eyes, and dripping blood."

"I'm impressed that kids that young can stay inside the lines," Teg said.

"Oh, they can't, but that just makes the monsters look creepier."

"Listen," Teg said, remembering her mission. "I really need to talk to you, but privately. If you can find time, that is."

Peg nodded. "Grunwold thinks it would be a good idea if *Slicewind* was a bit more visible for the rest of today. Tamildah asked him to help her with something to do with the feral cargo hauler. Want to come aloft?"

"That would be great. I told Meg I'd be a couple of hours late, since I haven't put in my KP time this week. I was going to help Leeya by cutting up some of the ysisora."

"Great! I'll sharpen extra knives. *Slicewind* can handle the patrol route on autopilot."

When they were aloft, to the backdrop of rhythmic chopping, Teg started by asking if Meg had been visiting Peg shipboard, knowing she was going to feel really foolish if Peg said yes. But Peg only frowned and shook her head.

"No, Meg hasn't been visiting me. Why?" Peg listened without interrupting as Teg explained, up to and including her search of the night before. "Are you sure Meg hasn't been going back to our side?"

Teg felt stupid that she hadn't even considered this as an option. "I'm not, but I can't figure why she'd be going what seems like every night."

"Maybe one of her kids is unwell," Peg said. "Or grandkids. Meg being Meg, she wouldn't necessarily tell us."

"True," Teg considered as she reduced a ysisora to cubes. "We certainly need to rule that out. Still, I have this feeling that whatever Meg's doing has to do with here."

"Are you sure you're not projecting?" Peg asked. "You've mentioned wanting to spend more time in the repository, rather than what you've been doing."

"Actually, I am sure. The archeology I've done for most of my life is a lot less thrilling than even a routine day here. About my only regret is that I can't publish papers about our finds."

"Who says you can't? There are universities. Kuvekt and our trespassers aren't the only people interested in the Library of the Sapphire Wind."

"Huh," Teg brightened. "I could collaborate with Kuvekt. He could do the actual writing, since the translation spell doesn't work both ways. Good idea!"

Peg grinned, then sobered. "Whether Meg is sneaking off to our side, or whether she's sneaking off somewhere else, the point remains. She's sneaking. And sneaking means hiding something. Since I don't think she's trysting with someone, which is the most innocent reason for sneaking off, then I think we need to figure out where she's going. It might be something that could offend our local associates, or embarrass Meg in some way, so I think you and I need to be the ones to take this on."

Teg nodded. "Fair. Do we just ask her? Or do we do our own sneaking?"

"Asking would be most sensible," Peg said, "but sneaking would be a lot more fun. Besides, she can't deny she's up to something if we catch her at it."

"Mother's wisdom?" Teg asked.

"Nope, playing to my strengths," Peg replied. "I always found it a lot harder to talk my way out of something when I'd been caught. Here's my plan."

✳✳✳

Since Meg clearly was waiting until she was certain Teg was asleep before leaving their room, the initial stalking would be up to Peg, who knew a hiding place in the reception hall where she could see without being seen.

"Sweks found it when the kids were playing hide and seek. It's up on one of the sage stations. I'll even have room to knit while I wait."

At bedtime, Teg did her very best to seem normal, chatting with Meg, who was sitting up in bed reading a copy of the mystery novel that had been the Pagearean book club's choice for March.

"Even if we're not likely to attend," Meg said, "I'd like to stay current."

Teg sat up in her own bed, clipboard against her knees, making notes for the paper she'd sounded out Kuvekt about collaborating on that night over dinner. Kuvekt had been not only willing but eager, suggesting several other writing projects they might work on. Given that they'd talked so long that Teg had almost missed when it was time for her to turn in for the night, Teg thought it was completely reasonable that she'd be eager to get her own ideas down rather than read.

Her eventual yawn wasn't feigned, though, and she set the clipboard and pen down on the clothes trunk that served as a nightstand.

"Much more, and I'll be mixing in *Indiana Jones and the Temple of Doom*," she commented. "Bathroom then lights out for this girl."

When Teg came back to the room, Meg had her own light out. "I got to the end of a chapter. If I keep reading, I'll be up far too late."

"Sleep well then," Teg said, and proceeded to not do precisely that.

As always, it was much harder not to fall asleep when you were trying to stay awake. Teg was glad that she typically slept on her side, facing the wall, so she could periodically open her eyes without Meg noticing. She found herself wishing she could have a smoke.

Teg thought she'd been solidly awake when the creak of Meg's cot as she sat up pulled Teg out of a dream in which she and Kuvekt were talking about the book they going to write. She should have realized that she was dreaming, since she'd been smoking her pipe. Kuvekt, in his role as staff doctor, was one of the hardest on her about her unhealthy habit.

Forcing herself to keep her breathing steady, Teg listened as Meg followed her now familiar routine. After Meg had left the room, Teg counted slowly to thirty before getting up and shoving her feet into her moccasins. She'd left a flashlight where she could find it without turning on a light, along with Petros's bag. So equipped, she eased the door open and checked the hallway. Finding it empty, she turned and made her way to the section of the stacks where they'd been working. This room was the one place Meg could go that Peg couldn't cover from her chosen watch stand out in the reception hall, so they'd decided Teg should check it first. Finding it empty, Teg hurried out to the reception hall.

When the Library of the Sapphire Wind had been at its peak, the sage stations had been where resident scholars worked while making themselves available for consultation. Built from pink and white marble, with shelves for books and drawers for papers, the mini-offices had been severely damaged by fires that had, ironically, not done as much damage to tables and benches.

"Because," Wagh had explained, "those were treated to resist burning, as was much of the shelving, and many of the books. However, no one thought to protect stone."

"And," Septi had added, his gaze haunted, "when a catastrophic magical overload is causing the damage, there really is no way to protect against it."

There hadn't been much worth salvaging from the sage stations, even by Teg and Meg's exacting standards. What hadn't been reduced to ash and crumbling stone, either by fire or—more likely—the unpredictable effects of the catastrophic magical event, had been boxed up for later examination. Then, in the interests of making the reception hall more or less livable, what remained of the sage stations had been swept and polished. Parts had been repurposed for storage of shared items, like game boards, popular reading material, dishes, and drinking bowls.

Peg's hiding place was in one of the more intact mini-offices.

"No one will even think twice if they see me going up there. I'm always everywhere, my fingers in all the pies. I'll just hunker down and wait."

She'd done just that. When Teg came out into the reception hall after her fruitless inspection of the stacks, Peg was waiting for her at the doorway of the kitchen, quivering like terrier who had a hot scent but was too well trained to go charging after it alone. She handed Teg one of the stoneware bottles that were the preferred alternatives when drinking bowls would be too sloppy.

"Poffee, strong. Figured you might need it."

Teg accepted it, although right now she was wide awake. She glanced around, noting that tonight everyone seemed to have gone to bed.

"Leeya and Huy would probably have been awake still," Peg said, "but I helped them finish off the sausage sandwiches for tomorrow's breakfast. Huy's all excited because Tamildah's xuxu have narrowed down where the cargo hauler's probably roosting."

"Where did Meg go?" Teg asked, refusing to be distracted.

"First, she ducked into the kitchen for a bottle of fyari tea and to fill a wrapper with muffins," Peg said. "I thought she might be heading for the roof, but she only paused at the base of the stairs to listen. She then went through the western arch. I hung back, in case she looked, but she never did, so I was able to see where she ended up."

"The repository?"

"The repository." Peg patted her knitting bag. "I've gotten a set of keys."

"Let's go."

Given that the value of the contents of the repository was literally incalculable, only the signatories of the homesteading charter had access. At full strength, Sapphire Wind was better than the best burglar alarm ever designed, especially since the loophole in the security system that had enabled the extraction agents to hide past closing had been eliminated. However, each of the Rough Diamonds had access to keys that would open the hidden stairway. As in the days when the Library was a going concern, the act of unlocking alerted Sapphire Wind.

"You realize that Sapphire Wind must be in on whatever it is that Meg is doing?" Teg asked. "And that it's going to know we're coming, at least as soon as we open the door into the repository stairway."

Peg nodded. "That doesn't mean it's in collaboration with Meg, because she's one of the Rough Diamonds, so she's allowed to go into the repository."

Unspoken were all the suspicions they had felt back from when

Sapphire Wind had possessed Meg, using her as a speaking device, much as it now used Friba. Meg had never seemed offended, but her friends had been worried.

Is Sapphire Wind using Meg again? Is it even aware of how fragile a living creature can be? Heavens know it can be ruthless, not from any inherent evil, but from not understanding quite what it's taking from those it manipulates. It has to be aware just how fragile our tenancy of the Library is. What might it do to assure it doesn't find itself a genius loci *without a loci or, maybe worse, in service to someone who would view it as Dmen Qeres apparently did, less a person than a very elaborate artifact?*

Teg wondered if she should discuss this with Peg, whether they should go back and get help. But would they have another chance? Sapphire Wind was far from omnipresent or omnipotent, much less omniscient, but who knew how it might react if it felt threatened?

In the end, Teg said nothing. She might not be nearly as impulsive as Peg could be, but she had more than her fair share of curiosity. There was no way she was going meekly back to bed tonight, pretend tomorrow, while she worked alongside Meg, that she didn't have all these crazy suspicions.

Peg was about to unlock the door when it slid noiselessly open. Meg stood there, her expression bemused, but Teg thought, also relieved.

"I hoped if anyone found me out it would be you. Come on down. We need to talk about book wraiths."

The room at the base of the stairs had also been cleaned up since the first time they'd seen it. Some of what had once been banks of safe deposit boxes were still uprooted or toppled over, but the loose rubble through which they'd once tracked Emsehu had been swept up, although not thrown away, since who knew what might be in there.

However, worktables had been set up, along with chairs and good lighting. Friba was perched on the back of one of the chairs. Zink, the book person, was flat against one wall, like a signboard. A stoneware bottle and the cloth wrapper of muffins showed where Meg had been sitting. To one side, carefully set away from the food and drink, was a stack of mutilated books.

"I see you brought your own drinks," Meg said. "There are still plenty of muffins. Make yourselves comfortable."

Teg and Peg took seats down at the muffin end of the table. Teg took a muffin and handed one to Peg. Meg rolled her bottle of tea between her hands. Teg guessed she was trying to figure out where to begin, and decided to help her.

"You said something about book wraiths?"

Meg nodded. "That's right. Do you know what the difference is between a wraith and a ghost?"

Teg shook her head, but Peg piped up, "I do, actually. My granddaughter didn't know what to be for Halloween one year. She left it to the last minute, and finally went as a wraith. She won a prize for 'most creative,' which annoyed some people, but I loved it."

"Huh?" Teg was definitely confused.

"A wraith is different from a ghost," Peg went on, "in that a ghost is the visible spirit of a dead person, while a wraith is the image of a living person. In a lot of traditions, that person is in danger of dying soon."

"A wraith is very similar to a German doppelgänger," Meg added. "A double-goer, sometimes more poetically translated as 'double-walker.' Both are doubles who are indistinguishable from the original. Seeing one's doppelgänger is never a good thing."

"And a book wraith?" Teg asked. "Is it a duplicate book that destroys the original?"

"It is a duplicate of the author," Meg replied. "'Wraith' is a good term because, although a wraith is a double in appearance, it is less substantial. However, while a wraith or doppelgänger can portend ill for the original, a book wraith more than 'portends.' Especially if the original was magically gifted, the book wraith may be able to use that magic as a link, which then leads to the death of the original."

Peg popped the rest of her muffin in her mouth, dusted off her fingers, and pulled out her knitting. "Why didn't either of our senior wizards know about book wraiths? I asked them after Zink pronounced its ominous warning, since Xerak had never heard of one. Neither Uten Kekui nor Cerseru Kham had anything to add beyond what Xerak said about some sort of predator that preyed on books, like the book worms."

Meg's smile was tight. "It may be that the book wraith is unique to the Library of the Sapphire Wind. One of the things we"—her gesture encompassed Friba and Zink—"have been researching is whether book wraiths have manifested elsewhere. So far, we have no evidence other than some very vague mentions in folklore."

"Since book wraiths may not really exist," Teg nodded, catching on, "you can't simply research a cure or solution, and then implement it."

"Precisely." Meg rubbed her face with the heels of her hand. "I did so want to present a possible solution as well as a problem."

"Why," Peg said gently, "didn't you bring this up sooner?"

Meg sighed. "I guess I wanted to show that I am still useful. I've been feeling more like an impediment than an asset since we docked *Slicewind* and began to focus on the Library—and that's the last thing I ever expected, since I'm a librarian, and this is a library. Here though, we have a ruined library, no real collection. Teg's the archeologist. People listen to her because her expertise matters. She's running crews. And, Peg, don't try to hide in your 'grandmotherly' mode, like Miss Marple in her knitting. I haven't overlooked that you're basically commander in chief of the House of Rough Diamonds."

"Well," Peg said, "someone has to be a generalist among all these specialists. I think Ranpeti would do a good job as head of the House of Rough Diamonds, if she didn't have Brunni to worry about, but she does. I don't mind. It gives me an excuse to poke my nose into other people's business. But what you're doing is valuable. The House of Rough Diamonds is going to have a lot of trouble making good its charter if we can't show we made an effort to preserve the library's holdings."

This made sense to Teg, more sense than her own efforts to preserve artifacts for future study into the impact of catastrophic magical events on material culture, but Meg seemed determined to keep denigrating her own contributions.

"I've heard the grumbles that all of this would go faster if all the books were just shoveled up and dumped in the lake."

"Surely not *all*!" Teg exclaimed, horrified.

Meg managed a hoarse chuckle of the sort that sounded dangerously close to a sob. "All right, certainly not all, but I know my desire to preserve parts of books, even intact pages, has annoyed some of our newly unarchived assistants. They want the Library of the Sapphire Wind a going concern again. The fastest way to get there would be to clear the space, then buy new books."

"Now that I think about it," Teg said, "I'm amazed that we haven't had any requests to leave from at least some of the Unarchived."

Peg said, "I've been listening and consulting with Leeya and Nefnet, especially. We did choose people who didn't have a lot waiting for them elsewhere, but it's more. Nefnet admitted that just hearing Rivers Meet described was overwhelming, because there've been so many changes, big and small. Despite monsters and trespassers, construction hazards and all the rest, on some level, she feels safer here."

"I actually get that," Teg said. Then guiltily aware that she'd pulled them away from Meg's confession of insecurity, she turned to the librarian. "I get the same grumbles every time I ask for something to be set aside for future study. I think the reason I get away with it is because I found the key to the doors. I just keep my lips shut on how I wouldn't have found the key anywhere like as soon as I did if Sapphire Wind hadn't slipped a hint onto the book the statue of Dmen Qeres is holding."

Peg's knitting needles clicked more rapidly, strangely creating the impression of her rubbing her hands together. "I strongly suspect that dumping even partial tomes in the lake would do us a world of hurt, so I don't think Meg really needs to worry. Still, I think we can use this whole book wraith thing to raise her stock—which will help remind the people who weren't here when book worms and acid bats were quite literally being a pain—that she's someone they need to listen to."

She stopped knitting and turned the full force of her hazel-green gaze on Meg. "You've told us what a book wraith is. Now tell us what you're not telling us."

"You really are a mother, aren't you, Peg?" Meg's inflection almost made the statement an insult, but her laughter, this time without any hint of a sob, took away the sting. "I've been trying to figure out how to present this next part, because there's no way it's not going to add to our difficulties."

She pushed the mutilated pages over for their inspection. "Zink has been incredibly helpful. These are all pages from books where some or all of the book was 'devoured.' Notice what they have in common?"

Teg skimmed. In some cases, the font used was elaborate enough that the translation spell only managed a partial transcription, but after a few moments, she and Peg spoke almost simultaneously.

"Shit!"

"Dmen Qeres?!"

❧CHAPTER FOURTEEN ❧

"You got it," Meg said. "All of these are from books either written by Dmen Qeres, the esteemed founder of the Library of the Sapphire Wind, or from articles he contributed to works by other scholars. Since, on the one hand, he is probably the most represented author in this library, it may be a coincidence, but I don't think so. I think the book wraith spell was intended to be his . . . Call it life insurance?"

"We know he founded the Library of the Sapphire Wind to hide and protect Ba Djed of the Weaver," Teg said. "And we know that he fully intended to reclaim it, that he believed he was the only one suited to be its guardian."

"But his plan didn't work," Peg protested. "He was reborn, but as Uten Kekui, who to this day has almost no memory of his past self."

"It did work," Meg disagreed. "Uten Kekui doesn't remember much of his life as Dmen Qeres, but he did inherit the guardianship. Take the next step . . . Remember, in Over Where reincarnation isn't a theory or a belief. It's as real as dirt."

Silence, then Teg said slowly, building her conclusion word by word, "Dmen Qeres set up the Library not only to protect Ba Djed but to enable him to take over his successor, if his successor wasn't enough, what? Enough him?"

"We think so," Meg said, indicating Friba and Zink with an inclination of her head. "Sapphire Wind, why don't you explain the next part?"

Friba shifted from one foot to another, then sidled up and down the back of the chair it was using as a perch. It opened its beak a few times, revealing a thick tongue not unlike that of an Earthside parrot, but with a split tip, like a snake's.

"Please," Friba managed at last, then turned its head sideways, twisting it almost upside down. "Hard to talk. Dmen Qeres didn't like talk."

"They need to hear it from you," Meg said firmly.

Peg coaxed, "We can't promise we won't repeat what you tell us, because someone else might need to hear it. However, we can promise we won't rush in blindly."

Friba made a sound between a croak and a hiss, then said, "If Dmen Qeres does form a book wraith, then Uten Kekui will cease to be a wizard, maybe even cease to live. And I, I may not be able to be your friend anymore. Dmen Qeres created me to serve him, and to serve his Library. I may be unable to resist that. Already, I am less certain of myself. I have tried, but I cannot find where the book wraith is assembling itself. If it were not for Zink, we would not have done so well."

"Zink," Meg said, "is ironically protected from quietly accepting dissolution by the spells that protect the books."

"Wouldn't Dmen Qeres have anticipated that?" Teg asked.

Zink, always silent, but still as a poster to this point, shifted so that it could easily be read by Peg and Teg. Words marched across its torso.

"Dmen Qeres did not anticipate the critical magical overload which caused the protective spells to combine and intertwine, else all the Library would have been nothing but ashes and crumbled stone. The event created me to speak for the books. However, if enough books are destroyed, then I will not be able to do so."

"Shit," Peg repeated. "I can see why you didn't know how to present this, Meg. If we start with the risk to Sapphire Wind, we need to mention why. If we start with the risk to Uten Kekui, then we're going to have him and Xerak both stressing out. If we start with the possible return of Dmen Qeres via book wraith, then everyone is going to freak, because it's completely possible him coming back would undermine our homesteading charter, especially if he bribes enough people, because you can be sure that while we don't know where his treasure is hidden, he does."

"Do you really think Dmen Qeres had a treasure?" Teg asked, diverted, because thinking about treasure was a lot more fun than thinking about the problem in front of them.

"Absolutely," Peg said. "There's no way someone so obsessed with coming back to life because he was the only one worthy of being in control of one of the great artifacts that anchors the Bridge of Lives would have chosen to do so as a penniless hermit. There's treasure, and I'm betting literally physical treasure, because he wouldn't have wanted to need to prove he was himself to access a bank account. From what we've seen, metals and gems are valued here just like at home, even if somewhat differently."

"Right," Teg said, nodding. "Their use in magic means that gems, especially, aren't valued just because they're beautiful and rare."

As Meg had listened to the exchange, she had visibly relaxed. Teg thought she even had more color in her cheeks.

"I'm glad," Meg said, "that you think it's as complicated a problem as I did. I've been driving myself crazy, trying to figure out how to deal with this, thinking maybe I'm too old, slowing down."

"It's complicated," Peg said. "It's insanely crazy, but surely we can solve it."

"Do we tell everyone?" Teg said. "I'm not sure that's a good idea."

"I agree," Peg said, all Commander in Chief now. "We can't risk a general panic. I mean, this situation got even Meg twitterpated. My suggestion is that we confide the whole truth to our inquisitors—and I include Kaj. Then we assign ourselves the job of going after the book wraith."

"What do we tell the others?" Meg asked.

"Nothing too detailed," Peg said. "If it seems necessary, a version of the truth. Truth is always best, especially since we just might need to be rescued."

"What version?" Teg pressed.

"We need to get the book wraith while there's only one. To most everyone, we leave out that the book wraith might be able to kill Uten Kekui or suborn Sapphire Wind. We say we're prioritizing this because, if we don't, there might not be an intact collection and that would weaken our homesteading claim."

"Damn! You're good," Teg said. "I can work with that."

"I'm very grateful for you two getting on board with this," Meg said. "I will admit, I wasn't sure even you would believe me. I know you haven't always trusted that Sapphire Wind doesn't have an undue influence on me."

Teg shrugged. "If that was the case, then both you and Sapphire Wind would have withheld that part about how Dmen Qeres could possibly take Sapphire Wind over. I'm afraid we're going to need to give up on putting Sapphire Wind in the role of evil genius."

"After all," Peg added, "we know who to cast as evil genius— Dmen Qeres."

The next morning, shortly after breakfast, they briefed the inquisitors down in the repository. Meg took point, neatly explaining what she, Sapphire Wind, and Zink had been researching. The young people agreed that the book wraith was a problem that their core team was best suited to deal with.

"We're used to trusting each other even when the going gets weird," Vereez stated.

Heads nodded all around, and Teg found herself warmed.

"I'd noticed that my master has seemed oddly incapable and absentminded from time to time," Xerak said, frown lines appearing between his eyes, "especially when we are actually inside the Library. I'd excused it as his needing to remember to use as little magic as possible indoors, but I couldn't help but notice that Cerseru Kham did not seem to have similar problems."

"We're going to need to assign people to cover for us," Grunwold said. "I hate trusting *Slicewind* to anyone else, but I think Ranpeti could handle her, and maybe Tamildah could assist. She's coaxed me to let her handle the wheel a few times."

"If you're really worried," Teg suggested, "we could do without aerial patrols for a few days. We do manage when you're off on a supply run."

"True," Grunwold said. "That might be best. I'll let Ranpeti know she can take *Slicewind* up if there's an emergency, and we'll leave it at that."

Vereez turned to Zink and Friba. "Do you have any thoughts as to where we should start looking for this book wraith?"

The words flowed from Zink's mouth and arrayed on its chest. "With Meg, I/we have thought. There was a special collection room dedicated to Dmen Qeres's works. It has never been open to the public. That would seem an ideal hideout."

Sapphire Wind added through Friba, "If you look at the map, you will see the space the special collection occupies, on the second floor, west-central area. It has a private entry from the west wing."

"That's a plus," Peg said. "However, we haven't taken a look at the second floor at all. Any idea what shape it's in?"

She glanced at Friba, and Sapphire Wind replied, "I have no idea what we may encounter there. I am sorry."

"No need to apologize. Can we count on you for lights?"

"Unless the panels are damaged, I have ample mana to activate them. They may even be currently activated."

"Good, so we don't need to plan to explore by flashlight."

Setting down the bowl from which he'd been drinking fyari tea, Xerak said, "Zink, can you tell us any more about the book wraith? Will it just be an image of Dmen Qeres? Will it be able to work spells? Is it even corporeal?"

Zink's torso text didn't move for long enough that Teg wondered if Xerak needed to limit himself to one question at a time. Then it began slowly writing.

"I don't know. I don't know. I don't know. I don't know. All I know is that it destroys books to create itself."

Xerak got up and put his hand on the agitated book person's shoulder. "People of all sorts learn by asking questions. Your not knowing is information. You didn't fail."

Zink's stiff frame couldn't relax, but it texted, "Thank you. Books are made to supply information. To give information that is lacking information does happen, but usually there is something. I am glad to not have failed."

"You warned us," Xerak said firmly, and patted Zink between the "ears." "If you hadn't, our first awareness of the book wraiths would have been when Uten Kekui became completely addled."

"I did not do what I did for Uten Kekui. I did it for us, for the books."

"And that's fine, too."

With a final pat, Xerak resumed his seat, then rolled his drinking bowl between his palms, clearly contemplating a stronger drink than tea. "Step one, we see if we can get into the special collections room.

Maybe we'll find a book wraith there, waiting for us. Maybe not. When can we start?"

Everyone looked at Peg, whose lips were shaping a count. She put a row marker on her current piece of knitting—a shawl for Ranpeti in a forest green that was going to look great with the woman's brown seal coloring.

"Any objections to starting this morning, as soon as everyone gathers up their gear?"

"Do we brief anyone else yet?" Teg asked.

Peg shook her head. "That can wait until we see if this is a complicated problem. This is just recon."

"Last night you said . . ." Meg began, then paused.

"I know," Peg admitted, "but what if we find out we can't even get through the door? I'd feel a fool for stirring up a ruckus."

"Very well," Meg said. "I'll need to tell Septi we won't be resuming working in the stacks, at least not this morning."

Teg went with Meg, mostly because after their late night she had a serious desire for more poffee. When Meg made her apologies, Teg thought that Septi might try to invite himself along, but he only nodded and said he'd be happy to help Leeya in the kitchen.

"It's a baking day. I can help keep track of when various batches need to come out of the oven, and update our records on the books we're salvaging at the same time." He tilted his head, as if to shove them along with his curling horns. "You'd better be hurrying along. It's about time for Tamildah to come in with a question or two for Grunwold."

"Too true," Meg said, and laughed.

As they hustled off to meet the others in the west wing, Teg said, "What would you bet that Grunwold is as unaware of Tamildah's crush on him as Vereez was of his feelings for her?"

"You won't find me taking that one, even if you gave wonderful odds," Meg replied. "I am so glad not to be twenty again. I'm not sure all the romantic confusion and the rest is worth it, not even to have a sexy young body again."

Zink, armed with what Meg, managing to keep a completely straight face, called a "book club"—a weapon that had been woven of burned and damaged pages—was waiting to guide them to where the others had gotten open a door that went more deeply into the west wing. From there, they had worked their way through a maze of partially collapsed stacks without acquiring injuries other than a few scrapes. Injuries were definitely much easier to avoid now that no one was even remotely tempted to open a seemingly intact tome or get too close to a heap of scrolls.

When Teg, Meg, and Zink arrived, Peg and Vereez were busy checking the next door that they needed to go through for "locks and traps" as Peg (who had played quite a bit of D&D with kids and grandkids) insisted on phrasing it.

"Remember the map?" Xerak explained, reaching up to stroke Friba, who was perched on his shoulder. "The door they're working on leads into that rounded central foyer. The foyer provides a hub into various specialized subject areas. The central pillar in the middle of the foyer conceals the way up to Dmen Qeres's exclusive collection."

"Looks as if the door is safe to open." Peg hefted a ring of keys that had been one of their better finds when they had been clearing the administrative offices. "We're going to try the mundane way to get the lock open and save the magic key, since it's such a pain to recharge."

"Not 'a pain,'" Xerak clarified patiently. "But it does take time."

The fourth key they tried fit the lock, although a liberal application of lubricant was needed to get it to turn. The door itself split down the middle, sliding into pockets in the walls. Kaj prepared to slide one panel, while Xerak took the other. Grunwold and Vereez drew their swords and prepared to intercept anything that might have been attracted by the inevitable noise that had accompanied working on the lock.

The doors grated on their tracks, but could be moved into their assigned recesses. The lighting brightened, whether because of Sapphire Wind's intervention or because it had been set to do so when the doors were opened. When nothing raced forward with mayhem in mind, Vereez and Grunwold picked their way forward, then turned to check in each direction.

"Clear as far as we can see," Vereez called. "Two visible doors closed."

"Heru, check around the loop," Grunwold ordered the green-and-orange xuxu. "Remember, keep to a middle height. Don't touch anything."

"Only th' air, Grun!" Heru launched up, flapped his way around the wide pillar that occupied the middle of the rounded room, then returned, tootling a muted fanfare as he landed on Grunwold's shoulder. "Clear of critters. Far-side doors shut tight."

Teg was bouncing up and down on her toes, wishing that she was a little taller. From what she could see, this area had suffered a lot less destruction than elsewhere, possibly because the doors had been closed. The ceiling was intact, so other than ambient dust and grit, the foyer looked almost as it had done when the Library had been open.

Vereez and Grunwold advanced, trailed by Peg on one side, Kaj on the other. Xerak helped Meg and Teg keep watch behind, assisted by Heru, who had moved to Teg's shoulder.

Teg knew she should be watching behind, but she found herself inching forward, eager to see more. The foyer's walls showed some smoke damage, especially above oddly shaped areas that were shaded a dark brown. After consideration, Teg decided this must have been where something had hung on the wall. She dearly hoped that what had been there had been signage giving directions or reminding visitors of the Library's rules. She made a mental note to ask Sapphire Wind.

The large, rounded central pillar was another matter. It had been embellished with a stunning mosaic depicting what Teg assumed was a representation of scholarship and the pursuit of magical knowledge. Numerous therianthropic figures in ornate wizard's robes consulted books or crystals, wrote with quills or reed pens, painted elaborate dioramas, and otherwise pursued their art.

Teg longed to go closer, to ask Xerak just how idealized this scene was, to buff away some of the grit so she could look at details, but she remembered book worms and acid bats, and dobergoats summoned by taking a step into the wrong area. So, despite her impatience, only after the all clear was given, and Heru had left for a perch from which he could assist Zink in keeping an eye on the stacks behind them, did she cross the threshold.

"The door into the pillar must be concealed in the mosaic," she said, after a quick inspection found no obvious entry.

Before Teg could ask, Friba said for Sapphire Wind, "I will know the door when you find it, but I do not see as you see, so I cannot show it to you."

"Fair enough." Feeling her reputation as solver of puzzles was on the line, Teg started slowly circling the pillar.

The door's not going to be hidden anywhere as obvious as in an image of Dmen Qeres himself, she thought. *Sure, he had ego and to spare, but he wasn't at all stupid.* She paused, considering. *Or should that be "isn't"?*

She continued her inspection. *Doors here aren't all that different from doors at home, except for the ones that flare at the top to allow for head adornments like Grunwold's antlers. So, straight lines at the base. That would rule out most of the sennutep figures as the door itself, although they might be incorporated as elements.*

Teg let herself fall into the same almost trance state she used when walking survey. There was a trick to it, to detaching yourself from extraneous details and seeing what might hardly be there. On her second rounding of the pillar, she noticed a geometric pattern that would be useful for hiding straight lines in plain sight. It was built along interlocking four-pointed stars and hexagrams. The interior of each hexagram was delineated by six lines, and when one ignored all the extraneous details of borders and shading, the centermost line made a nice straight line. Once she had this, finding the door was a matter of finding where this background element either extended far enough or the center line was integrated with another linear element.

She found it in a depiction of a wolf-headed wizard holding a staff in one hand and a book in the other.

"Got it!" she announced, tracing her finger along the border, and confirming that there was no grout, only paint that mimicked the color of the grout. "Sapphire Wind, can you open this?"

Friba flew over and landed on her shoulder. "Yes. I can. I have always been one of the keys to this door."

Everyone had gathered around by the time the curved panel slid into the wall. They now were faced with a small room dominated by a floor to ceiling rectangle along the sides of which were two ladders. Compared to the area outside, with its riot of colorful mosaic, this one was not exactly utilitarian, but the rich green paint and gilded accents were more elegantly restrained.

"An elevator!" Peg said. "I wonder if it still works?"

Sapphire Wind replied by sliding the elevator doors open. The elevator would hold about four people, squished close, or a person and two book carts. It was upholstered with an emerald-hued brocade, quilted over padding by golden upholstery tacks.

"Fancy," Vereez said, "but also a really a great way to get rid of unwelcome guests, at least if the shaft also drops down to the lower areas. I suggest some of us go up via the ladders and make certain there isn't some guardian creature lurking up there."

No one objected. Grunwold and Kaj each took a ladder and started climbing. Xerak turned to Teg.

"Since my usual fire spells and Vereez's lightning would be really bad ideas here, could you get Petros ready, just in case? Vereez and I will look for any magical traps. I'm hoping, though, that since Sapphire Wind admitted us, even if there were any, they won't have been armed."

Teg nodded and readied the amulet. She did not feel the least disappointed when, an hour later, she put it away unused. She thought Petros might be, though, and gave it an affectionate pat, rubbing her thumb against the rough meteorite that formed its middle.

Don't worry, buddy. You can't always be the hero.

She probably imagined the tiny "Why not?" that sounded in her head. At least she hoped so. Petros had been damaged when she'd found it, several months ago, local time. There had never been an opportunity to have it given a detailed analysis. Maybe she should see if Cerseru Kham or Uten Kekui could take a look at it, or, if they didn't have the skills, if they could recommend someone reliable.

During the hour that had gone by, the companions hadn't been idle. The hatches above the two ladders had been opened, revealing a room that seemed to be empty. The elevator had been tested and deemed reliable, so the three mentors would be able to ride up to the next floor. There had been much debate over whether to leave the door from the room within the pillar open or closed. Eventually, they'd decided on open, with Heru given permission to squawk his loudest if anyone or anything came investigating.

When the elevator doors slid back to reveal the room that housed Dmen Qeres's special collection, Teg gave a low whistle. The room was a vision of polished wood, plush carpeting, and glass-fronted bookcases, each holding tomes bound in unblemished leather, the titles stamped in gold. The cases also held data crystals: long, slender, faceted rods, not unlike those formed naturally by many quartz-family gemstones. These rested not in practical racks, but on tiered shelves, lined in velvet. The scrolls were also in racks made for display, not merely storage, and their cases were of precious woods or ivory, intricately carved.

Probably so as to not distract from the glass-fronted cases, the room's other furnishings were minimal. There was a table about the size of a standard card table, although made from something like ebony, with the legs carved as stylized sennutep wizard ravens. Three chairs with low backs and cushioned seats were tucked under it.

The room was also remarkable because, alone of all the places they'd seen in the Library so far, it was spotless. The entry foyer below had been undamaged, but it had at least shown some dust. This room was pristine.

Peg laughed. "Well, this place takes corner office with a view or penthouse suite seriously, doesn't it?"

"What?" Grunwold said. "This room doesn't have a single window and it's in the middle of the building."

"Sorry, dear," Peg said, stepping out of the elevator and patting him on his arm. "I bet Vereez knows exactly what I meant."

The young woman dipped her fox nose in agreement. "A room meant to impress, to overawe. This isn't just a secure storage area for valuable, even irreplaceable, books. It's a brag. No wonder so many wizards donated their collections to the Library of the Sapphire Wind. They probably imagined them being displayed like this."

Meg stepped forward, turning slowly, a look of pure bliss on her fine-boned face. "It really is something." Then she frowned. "But after what Zink told us, I expected more visible damage. Remember those mutilated pages I showed you?"

Kaj nodded. "The ones that Zink said had come from devoured articles. You're right. Nothing here has been treated that way. Maybe we came to the wrong place."

Xerak was tugging at the lower edge of his mane, the part Teg always thought of as his "beard." "I don't think we did. There's a feeling..."

He trailed off. After an anxious minute or two, Grunwold said, "I'm sorry to interrupt your brooding silence, Wizard Boy, but are you talking about a good feeling or a bad feeling or just some sort of feeling feeling, like when the wind's shifting?"

Xerak jerked up his head and shook out his mane. "Sorry. More a 'feeling feeling.' There's something here. Not good or bad, but like how you can sometimes feel static electricity before you get shocked. There's a mana build up, and I'll bet it's to do with the book wraith."

"Maybe," Kaj said, hesitatingly, all too aware he was the most junior apprentice, "there's something in one of the cases, something that's serving as a focus for the spell Dmen Qeres left behind."

"Good thinking," Xerak said briskly. "If we can find it, then maybe we can disrupt the spell. It's possible there isn't even a book wraith currently manifesting, just the potential for one."

Vereez put her hands on her hips and looked around with a certain amount of dismay. "But where do we start? There are a lot of books here, as well as journals, as well as the data crystals. Compared to the entire Library collection, I agree, this is a small sample, but if we need to look at every page of every book, unroll every scroll, view every crystal, then we're going to be at this for months, or at least for weeks."

Meg had been walking up and down, scanning the contents of the cases. Now she turned to Xerak. "We're basically looking for a stored spell that was made to create the book wraith of Dmen Qeres when the circumstances were appropriate, correct?"

"Correct."

Meg continued, "Very well, we can begin by eliminating those texts that aren't suitable. From what Septi told me when I asked him about his work as a scribe, a stored spell cannot be printed. It must be handwritten."

Xerak inclined his leonine head in a nod.

"Can a spell be stored on a data crystal?"

"Under specialized circumstances, yes," Xerak said, "but it's much more difficult and much more likely to go wrong."

Meg rubbed her hands briskly together. "Then we'll start with handwritten texts."

When Grunwold took an eager step toward the case closest to him, Meg held up one hand. "Wait! I have an idea that may save us a great deal of difficulty. I'm sure I saw..."

She bent and removed a tome from where it was tucked almost out of sight to one side of a shelving unit. Teg leaned so she could read the spine. After a moment, the translation spell resolved the characters stamped into the leather to read *Bibliography of the Complete Works of the Wizard Dmen Qeres.*

The bibliography was only about an inch thick, quite thin compared to the majority of the set. The soft leather cover was embossed front and back with an elaborate design, embellished on the front with an assortment of cabochon cut gems. The book cover lacked a stiff spine, but was instead folded around heavy paper that had been loosely stitched into the binding. Elegant bronze latches shaped like some exotic long-necked creature held the book closed.

After giving everyone a chance to look at the book, Meg carried the bibliography over to the table and unclasped the bronze latches. Almost reverently, she opened the soft leather cover to the title page. This was typeset, the lettering embellished with elaborate illuminations. The next several pages were also in type. Then the entries switched to handwritten bibliographic notations, only a few items per page.

"I thought so," Meg said triumphantly. "Keeping an up-to-date bibliography is a chore, even in our world, where all that needs to be done is updating a computer file. After all, there's always something better to do. Here, when each print edition would need to be typeset, it would be so much easier to write in each new publication."

"And," Vereez said, bouncing a little on her toes, her fox tail swishing in enthusiasm, "since the book wraith spell is associated with the wraith drawing on copies of Dmen Qeres's body of published work, why not put the spell somewhere in the bibliography, then link the two texts? Meg, you are brilliant!"

Meg blushed, her very fair skin turning a bright pink. "Thank you, Vereez. I've talked with Septi a great deal over the last several weeks. Whenever we've needed to decide which of the damaged books we should save, he always prioritizes anything handwritten, because it's likely to be rarer. One of the jobs that kept the scriptorium here busy was copying portions of unique works for visiting scholars."

She returned her attention to the bibliography, but after a moment stepped away from the table. "The handwriting here is beyond the ability of the translation spell. Xerak, why don't you take over?"

He stepped over eagerly, bending over the pages, flipping them back and forth, clearly checking for something specific. When he looked up, his expression was disappointed.

"You're right, Meg. This bibliography is definitely keyed to a spell." He pointed to a handwritten glyph that followed each entry. "Superficially, this looks like Dmen Qeres's personal seal, and could indicate that he has reviewed the entry and confirmed its accuracy. Thing is, as we've poked around the Library, I've had a lot of opportunities to look at his seal, and this is slightly different. I'm willing to bet that if I did what Peg calls a 'detect magic' spell, I'd find an aura. But nowhere on these pages is anything that could be the book wraith spell."

Peg chuckled softly.

"What?" Xerak said, ears flattening in annoyance.

"Oh," Peg said, "I was just thinking that although you're the son of a highly successful 'extraction agent' who is currently operating as a fence, you don't have a sneaky bone in your body."

Xerak's ears perked back up. "I don't, really. I didn't even suspect my parents' side business until a few months ago. You're sneaky, though. If only half the stories I've heard you tell are true, you could probably teach my mom a few tricks. So, wise mentor sent from beyond the world, what next?"

Peg reached for the bibliography, then pulled her hands back and looked at Meg. "Is it okay if I handle this, maybe a little roughly?"

Meg nodded. "Normally, I'd protest, but given what we're looking for, be my guest."

Peg took the book and began examining the cover and spine, all the while talking. "When Meg pulled out the bibliography, I was immediately struck by something. Anyone want to guess?"

Kaj said, "It's soft cover. Incredibly expensively worked and ornamented, but soft cover. As far as I could tell from a quick look, all the other books are hard covers."

"You," Peg said, "are doing Ohent proud. I noticed the same thing. Why couldn't Dmen Qeres have had whoever printed up all these other tomes make him the equivalent of a blank journal? The only advantage I could see to this soft-cover version—and I'd bet this was his excuse, too—is that it would be easier to add extra pages. But, face it, that's a flimsy excuse. I think what he wanted was this."

She gave a satisfied sigh and gently pried at the endpaper, pulling it away from the front cover, then turning it so everyone could take a look.

"There's no spell written there," Grunwold said in evident dismay. "It's blank!"

"Ah! Don't give up hope, my boy." Peg perched a pair of drugstore reading glasses on the tip of her nose and inspected the stitching. Then she reached into her knitting bag and pulled out a pair of delicate scissors.

"Wait!" Vereez said. "Do you want to undo the stitching? I think I can pick the stitches apart."

"By all means, my dear," Peg said, pushing back from the table so Vereez could take her place. "You have magnificent fingernails. Mine are sadly blunt. Let's do as little damage as possible to the book."

Vereez bent her head, studied the stitching then said, "Teg, you have a magnifier in your archeologist kit. Can you hold it for me?"

Teg unsnapped the case on her belt that held a compact magnifying glass. "Tell me where you need it."

"There. Perfect!" Vereez's black-tipped claws neatly undid the knot that held the stitching. Then she gently pulled out the heavy waxed thread. As she did so, Peg explained.

"After I removed the endpaper I noticed that a basting stitch had been used, apparently to hem the edges of the cover together. That doesn't make sense. You'd use a running stitch for that. The basting stitch was to hold... Do the honors, Vereez, you have a more delicate touch."

Vereez poked her fingers between the front cover and a false backing that the basting stitch had held closed. With infinite care, she slid out a heavy piece of folded parchment.

"To hold closed what is actually a pocket," Peg continued. "A pocket would have been much more obvious in a hard cover book, but with this soft cover, any irregularities would be excused as a result of burdening the leather with the gems that decorate the front cover."

The parchment was folded in a fashion that enabled a single sheet of paper to become its own envelope. It was stamped with Dmen Qeres's seal, and below that, the altered version of the seal that Xerak suspected linked elements in the bibliography to a spell.

Vereez set the parchment on the table, then looked expectantly at Xerak. He gave a gusty sigh.

"The spell is probably not trapped," he said, "or warded, because Dmen Qeres would not have wanted his future self to be barred from accessing it. Still . . . everyone should step back, just in case. I'm going to take a moment to put up a limited personal ward."

"If you can ward yourself," Teg asked, "why haven't you before this?"

"Because its ability to protect is really limited. I was going to be teaching you, Vereez, and Kaj the spell pretty soon, because it's basically meant to protect apprentices from the consequences of their own stupidity. It seems very appropriate now."

He took a deep swallow from his flask and seated himself in one of the chairs. Teg didn't catch the scent of wine, but even if she had, she wouldn't have said anything. Xerak had confided that his drinking problem was indirectly related to his discovery years before that being a little unfocused made him more magically capable.

And, anyhow, at some point, I've got to trust him to know his limits.

﹛CHAPTER FIFTEEN﹜

The rest of them, knowing that spellcasting took time, took advantage of the break to have a snack. Peg handed around a nuts and dried berries mix. Kaj pulled out one of the chairs and offered it to Meg with a courtly gesture that robbed it of any condescension of youth for age.

"Can I get you something to read?"

"Thank you," Meg said. "When I was looking at the printed parts of the bibliography, I noted there was a collection of autobiographical essays. If you could get me that."

As Kaj nodded, checked the listing, and turned away, Peg said, "Know thy enemy?"

Meg twinkled. "Or maybe I'm just nosey."

Although the small room was fairly crowded, no one left, bound together by an unspoken sense that they were on the edge of something important. Teg considered following Meg's example and reading, but the stir of Petros in her pocket reminded her of something else useful she could do.

"Vereez, Kaj, it would be a good idea for us to make certain our mana reserves are up and we're focused in case Xerak needs us."

Both her fellow apprentices nodded agreement. Teg settled herself on the floor, back against the elevator door, cupped Petros in her hands, and closed her eyes. A moment later, she more felt than heard Vereez then Kaj compose themselves. She heard a slight scrape as the remaining chair was pulled out, followed by the rhythmic click of Peg's knitting needles. No one spoke. Eventually there was a shuffle and rustle as Xerak unfolded the parchment. Teg opened her eyes and saw that Grunwold had moved to read over Xerak's shoulders. Grunwold cleared his throat. When he spoke, the gruffness in his voice didn't quite hide his nervousness.

"I can't read it, but I recognize some of the glyphs. That's written Hekametet, right? So, it's a spell. But is it active or stowed away for later use? I mean, is it the one we're looking for?"

Xerak said, "It's an active spell. I can tell that much right off. As for the rest..."

Teg felt Petros pinch her hand. When she closed her eyes to focus on the amulet, she saw what the sun spider had been trying to draw her attention to. "Xerak, look at it without your eyes. I'm seeing something, but I don't really know what it is."

Silence then Vereez said, hesitantly, "Strings?"

Kaj said, "Tentacles."

"Whatever you want to call it," Xerak shrugged. "That's the spell reaching out for Dmen Qeres's works. I'm having trouble getting a sense of direction, but what's odd is that none of those tentacles terminate in this room."

Peg said, "Well, that makes sense to me. We haven't met Dmen Qeres, but we do know he had a very substantial ego. I expect the spell was set to devour his works but reserved destroying any of the copies in this collection for a last resort. I bet there were duplicates distributed throughout the Library of the Sapphire Wind."

Kaj barked a dry laugh. "Poor Dmen Qeres. He sets up the Library to hide Ba Djed. That plan worked, sort of, but because Uten Kekui didn't remember his past life, he didn't come to claim Ba Djed on schedule. Because of that, the Library was badly damaged so the book wraith spell—which I'd bet was set to take over Dmen Qeres's successor, if that person had too much independence or too little interest—doesn't have a nice rich field to gather from, but instead is picking around through busted up books."

Xerak coughed something that wasn't quite a laugh. "That's quite a theory, and I like it—all but the bit about 'poor Dmen Qeres.' The more I learn, the more I dislike him. Now, everyone, pay attention."

Xerak carefully folded the parchment back into its former configuration. "I think that we can go after the book wraith, but I'm going to need to consult Cerseru Kham-va before we do it. I don't think the book wraith is fully 'here,' yet. However, because of what it being 'here' might do to Uten Kekui-va, I don't think we should wait until it has completely manifested."

"The book wraith is likely to be stronger the more time we give it," Vereez said anxiously, "so that's another reason to go after it. But why do you need to talk to Cerseru Kham?"

"Because going after it is going to mean going into the spell," Xerak said. "Despite my reputation as a great traveler, I'm not at all certain that I know how to plan that particular trip."

If Xerak had hoped that consulting Cerseru Kham would mean they would be able to avoid telling Uten Kekui that his past life was preying on his present, she quickly disillusioned him.

"Uten Kekui has to know," she said, "just as anyone who accompanies you in your effort to save him needs to know the risks."

Xerak only got as far as, "I thought I would go alone," before Vereez and Teg—who had insisted on accompanying him, because the whole group expected him to try something like this—shut him down. They needn't have bothered, because Cerseru Kham shook her head, large okapi ears flapping.

"You can't go alone," she said.

Vereez asked, "Cerseru Kham-va, before you explain why Xerak can't do whatever it is he's going to try alone, could you explain why it has to be done at all? Xerak sort of skipped that. I thought that once we found the spell, we could tear it up or burn it or something. When I was in school, we were always told to handle written spells with care, because they could be easily damaged."

"And that's quite true, for some sorts of stored spells," Cerseru Kham replied. "However, this is an active spell, one with a great deal of mana already in use, more with every article and text that is devoured. As such, it needs to be dismantled, and the only way to do that is to confront the book wraith."

"And unless," Teg said, feeling her way into the idea, "we wait until the book wraith is strong enough to manifest here, by which time Uten Kekui would have been hurt in some way, then we need to go to it."

"Yes. Also because the stronger it becomes, the harder it will be to dismantle," Cerseru Kham added. "Remember, this is a spell created by Dmen Qeres, who also created Sapphire Wind, and found ways to bind natural creatures like dobergoats and abau to the Library's care and protection. He is not a trivial opponent, certainly not one who a very junior wizard, no matter how rawly talented, can be expected to defeat alone."

"But if Uten Kekui enters the spell space," Xerak protested, "it will be easier for the spell to influence him. We might end up with two opponents."

Unspoken, but completely understood was, "One of whom I couldn't bring myself to attack."

"Cerseru Kham-va, are you going to help us then?" Vereez asked hopefully.

"Help, yes. Accompany, no. I have other responsibilities, ones that take precedence even over rescuing my fellow custodian from the machinations of his own soul. For this reason, Kaj also cannot go with you."

"Is this spell space somewhere a nonwizard can go?" Teg asked, thinking of some of the brawnier members of the construction team.

"Sadly, no," came the reply. "I think the three of you and Grunwold will be the most suitable. Peg and Meg, also, because although they have not shown themselves to be wizards, they are otherworldly creatures."

"Grunwold?" Vereez said. "He's not a wizard."

"No, but he is magically gifted, and his gift is tied to transportation. I believe he should be able to take you through on *Slicewind*. The ship has already shown it has the capacity to cross into alternate realities."

"And you," Xerak said resignedly, "have knowledge of the proper spells to make this possible. But why does Uten Kekui need to know?"

"Because he, my dear young wizard, is going to be your doorway. It's the only way we can possibly get you where you need to go with sufficient speed."

Xerak gaped. "But that could kill him!"

"The book wraith almost certainly will, if not terminate Uten Kekui's physical life, then make him into the merest shadow of who he is. I think he will accept the risk." Cerseru Kham's nostrils flared as she emitted a theatrical sigh. "Uten Kekui is capable of self-delusion, egotism, and lack of responsibility, certainly, but one thing is certain: he is not a coward."

Uten Kekui actually seemed relieved to learn there was a reason for his memory lapses. Teg, who had watched as one of her archeological mentors had declined and then vanished as a result of early-onset Alzheimer's, completely understood.

Uten Kekui and Cerseru Kham immediately went to work designing the intricate tangle of spells that would enable the others to pursue the book wraith. Despite the urgency, this could not be rushed, so Teg welcomed Tamildah's announcement that same evening at dinner that she had located the cargo hauler's preferred nesting place.

"I've also found several probable backup locations," Tamildah continued, "so that if we lose it, we can more easily track it down. I've made a rough map, and we can use that to work out tactics."

Although she addressed the group in general, the final comment was clearly intended for Grunwold.

"We'll have a conference after dinner," Peg said. "Huy, will you join us?"

"You couldn't keep me away," the prairie-dog-headed man said, earning a spattering of applause from the rest of Wagh's crew.

The former conference room had included a very nice slate board, which had been carefully removed, then framed by Peynte, the carpenter, in his spare time. He'd also built a sturdy stand for it. By the time the "Capture the Cargo Hauler Committee" met shortly after dinner, Tamildah had sketched a rough map.

She stood next to it, Uah perched on her shoulder, and tried to seem poised. Teg never ceased to be impressed that someone with a white tiger's features could still look so unsure.

Tamildah began, "Huy asked me earlier why it took us so long to locate a creature the size of a mature cargo hauler, so I'm going to start with that." She indicated the map. "This is the area in the forest south of the campus hill."

"That's near the hot springs, isn't it?" Grunwold asked.

Tamildah curled her whiskers in pleasure. "It is. Those hot springs are the reason we took so long to find the cargo hauler's den. We were relying on the xuxu for scouting, and they don't like the odor."

"Stinks!" honked Heru, while Uah blatted agreement.

"However," Tamildah continued, tugging Uah's wingtip in reprimand, "during one of her scouting flights, Pest saw something flying, nearly blending into the tree line. She valiantly braved the stink, and learned that the cargo hauler is using the remnants of one of the pools as a nest. The cargo hauler blends in very well with the surrounding natural colors, which is doubtless why those who have been looking from *Slicewind* didn't spot it."

"Or Horn Head was spending too much time admiring the sky," Vereez quipped, poking Grunwold—who had, predictably, managed to get a seat next to her—in the ribs.

Grunwold held his head high. "They're antlers, not horns. You're just jealous."

Tamildah narrowed her dark amber eyes, clearly less than amused by this bit of childish banter.

And not because it's childish, either, Teg thought, noting that both Meg and Peg were aware of Tamildah's reaction.

Meg asked in her kindest voice, "Tamildah, have you been able to scout more closely?"

"I did," Tamildah said. "I asked Emsehu to go with me, since pretty much everything in these woods is intimidated by him. There's a rise on the trail from which you can get a pretty good view, so we didn't go closer, lest we spook the cargo hauler. This time it might flee into the mountains or even further."

"Good thinking," Meg encouraged. "I assume the different sort of rounded shapes on your map are the various pools. Why have you shaded them differently?"

Tamildah's long tiger tail gave a satisfied flick, indicating that she was pleased that Meg had noticed.

"Those are the pools, pretty much to scale, although I could be off by a few meters, since I didn't go in to actually measure. The ones that are shaded in are completely full of water. The ones that are crosshatched were only partially full. The ones with just scattered dots were empty but steaming, and the ones without markings were empty."

"Excellent!" Peg said, toasting Tamildah with her poffee bowl. "Huy, do you remember if this is how the pools were before the catastrophe?"

"It wasn't," Huy said. "They were all more or less what I'd call 'full.'

Definitely none were empty or just steaming." He pointed to where Tamildah had indicated the cargo hauler was denning. "That was definitely a pool. Full. Since cargo haulers don't habitually den in water, I'd say that one's empty."

Peg gave what Teg was coming to think of as her "commander approves" nod. "We knew the critical magical overload had changed the area, so no surprise that the hot springs are changed as well. The changes might be due to something as simple as debris tumbling in and blocking the water's flow."

Unspoken but understood was, "But it might not be."

"We'll definitely be careful," Vereez said.

"Huy," Peg continued, "other than boathooks, and possibly nets, what do you suggest might be useful for capturing the cargo hauler?"

"Ropes with a weight at the end," Huy said, "if we can sneak up, catch it napping, toss weighted lines across—lines that we'd anchored to trees in advance—we should be able to get a net over it before it can take off. If we could settle for dropping a net from *Slicewind*, I wouldn't suggest this, but the ship's going to need to stay a distance away, maybe as far as down near the lava field, where the cargo hauler is used to seeing the ship patrol."

"Weighted ropes should be easy enough to get," Peg said. "What's the best time of day to go after the cargo hauler? Do they like to sleep in in the morning or are they likely to take an afternoon nap?"

"In nature, they're pretty much diurnal," Huy said, "but if this one has been moving about, it's been by night, so all bets are off. I'd suggest morning, not too early. At least we'll have time to make mistakes and track it down again, if our first effort fails."

"Practical, if somewhat defeatist," Peg said. "*Slicewind* will track it if it gets away. I'll assign myself as crew and backup helm. We may need a couple of strong bodies to handle the sails, since we're likely to need to adjust tack. How about Kaj?"

Kaj nodded.

Peg continued. "I want a wizard aloft, too. How about Xerak? I'd rather not have his fireballs, even toned down, at ground level."

"Makes sense," Xerak said. "Vereez and Teg can handle ground-level magic, if needed.

Vereez looked disappointed, probably because Kaj was going to be sky-side.

I bet Peg did that on purpose, Teg thought. *Xerak has always been in good control of his fire magics, but Vereez showing off for Kaj has been a liability in the past.*

Peg gave a crisp nod. "Then, everyone, get plenty of sleep." If her gaze rested on Meg, Teg didn't blame her. "We'll launch Capture the Cargo Hauler tomorrow morning."

Tamildah took point when the group started the hike down to the hot springs. Huy came behind her, then Teg, and, finally, Vereez. *Slicewind* lifted about the same time. The plan was for Grunwold to take the sky sailer along a more or less usual patrol route, rather than risk disturbing the cargo hauler by sitting at anchor on the southern border. Heru and Uah flew over the ground team. Heru would split off to alert *Slicewind* when Grunwold needed to bring it closer.

Not as easy as using phones, Teg thought, *but not a bad way to coordinate.*

The group on the ground wasn't precisely sneaking, but neither were they making undue noise. Teg felt herself drifting into the detached mindset she used when walking survey, seeing more than thinking. Here and there, she saw evidence of old trails, but she couldn't be certain whether they were left from when the Library had been an active concern, or if they were game trails. She was vaguely wondering what spike wolves and piranha toads ate when they weren't attacking tourists, when Tamildah raised her hand, and motioned them forward.

"We're still a distance away," she said, "but from this rise, you can get a look at the area around the hot springs."

Teg opened the case at her belt and took out a compact set of binoculars. Adjusting the focus, she scanned the area. It reminded her somewhat of photos she'd seen of Japanese *onsen*, almost too perfectly natural, rather than the over-groomed look of many Western resorts. The tangled growth that was so prevalent in the Library grounds crowded up to within a few meters of the pools, but not much grew between them. She wondered if the plants didn't like whatever was in the mineral-rich waters.

Vereez experimentally tested the air, her fox nose tilted back. "I can almost catch the smell of the waters, but it's not as bad as I expected, especially after what you said about the xuxu avoiding the area."

Tamildah gave a noncommittal shrug. Teg had noticed she avoided talking to Vereez as much as possible.

"Is that," Teg pointed, "where you saw the cargo hauler?"

Tamildah nodded. "It is. Can your long-seeing things see it?"

Teg checked. "I think so... That area definitely seems a bit greyish-greenish. Good!"

"I plan to have Uah do a flyover when we're almost there," Tamildah said. "She'll let me know whether or not the cargo hauler is there."

"Shall we continue?" Huy prompted.

They definitely smelled the hot springs before they reached them. Teg heard Vereez muffle a sneeze. Ahead, she could see Tamildah and Huy rubbing their noses.

Once again, it's nice to be reminded that there's an advantage to having a less sensitive sense of smell, Teg thought. To her, the odor was present, but not nearly as strong as she'd encountered at Rotorua in New Zealand, or even a couple of natural hot springs she'd visited in the U.S.

Uah dove down from above, landed on Tamildah's shoulder, nuzzled her ear, then launched again, the signal that the cargo hauler was there. Heru would be alerting *Slicewind* to begin a slow approach. Now things would get more complicated.

Tamildah and Vereez were to creep around to the far side of the cargo hauler's nest, find a place to anchor their weighted ropes, while Huy and Teg did the same on the closer side. In this way, both teams had magical support, if needed. Teg hadn't much liked pairing up the rivals in romance, but there was no logical way to raise an objection without also bringing up Tamildah's undeclared crush on Grunwold.

I'll just have to hope that Vereez will remain clueless or indifferent, whichever she is. Tamildah has the incentive of wanting to look good in Grunwold's eyes to assure she does as well or better than Vereez.

Teg knew Huy from working together on Wagh's crew, so she had no problem taking his lead. By the time Uah rose from the trees across the way, indicating that Vereez and Tamildah were ready, Teg and Huy had their ropes anchored.

To coordinate the two team's throws, they'd agreed on a slow count of ten. When Huy softly said, "Ten!" Teg tossed out her weighted line. She'd practiced the night before, but if there was one thing that helping crew the *Slicewind* had upped her skills in, it was in getting ropes to go where they were needed.

Teg and Huy's lines arched like twin rainbows across where the cargo hauler—unseen below the edge of the empty basin—rested. Vereez and Tamildah's lines came at almost the same time, although not so neatly coordinated. Teg ran out to get one of the other team's lines, grabbing it above the weight, bracing for when the cargo hauler would bolt.

It did, almost immediately, but when it met the obstruction of the four ropes, it couldn't create the rippling, flapping motion it used to fly. A shadow from above announced *Slicewind*'s arrival. Meg waved from the mast as she called orders down to Peg, Xerak, and Kaj, who had the capture net ready to go.

The net dropped neatly over the cargo hauler. Huy grabbed his boathook from where he'd propped it against the trunk of a tree, and ran forward. Cargo haulers were trained to a wide variety of sound commands, but most were accustomed to being steered with tools similar to boat hooks.

Everything was going perfectly until, with an explosion of steam and a sound like train whistles seriously out of key, some thing or things burst from the surrounding pools. Hot water splattered through the air as serpentine shapes fountained forth.

Teg reeled back, trying to figure out if the steam creatures were defending the cargo hauler or merely resenting intrusion on their territory. Huy flung himself down on his face, letting go of the boathook, which rolled to one side.

From across the pool, Teg caught the russet of Vereez's fur as the fox woman leapt back into the cover of the forest. There was no sign of Tamildah. Huy was bellycrawling to cover. Teg rendezvoused with him behind a tree, craning her head to see if *Slicewind* was okay. Grunwold had brought the ship up and was taking her in a wide spiral to catch the wind.

Vereez called. "Teg! Huy! You okay?"

"We're fine. You two?"

"Fine."

Tamildah's voice came from somewhere near Vereez. "The cargo hauler is still there. Hunkered down. But I'm not sure how we'll get it out of there. We can't just leave it! It's trapped by our nets and ropes."

Heru soared down, landing on the arm Teg put out. "Grun say, go back to the rise on the trail. *Slicewind*'s gonna meet you there."

A short while later, they'd assembled at the assigned meeting place. Grunwold had brought *Slicewind* low enough that they could confer without the ship's crew needing to debark. However, within moments, a rope ladder was flung over the side, and Xerak scrambled down.

"Reinforcements," he said. "Vereez, you're going to need to not do any of your pet spells."

Vereez nodded. "Lightning and water are a very bad combination, nearly as bad as fire and forests."

"But I can contribute more than just tossing fireballs around," Xerak said. "For one thing, I know what those things that came out of the hot springs are."

Peg leaned over the siderail. "I don't know what their name is, but from where I was, they looked a lot like the nessies in the lily pond in the bathroom. Bigger and more steamy, but the same shape. Steam snakes."

"There are a lot of similarities," Xerak agreed, "but they're not related. Do you remember the oehen-serit?"

"The lightning shadows," Teg replied. "You said they were creatures associated with storms, sort of storm dragons. Cerseru Kham had a host of them protecting the Roots of the World."

"Them," Xerak nodded. "The creatures in the hot springs are mu-serit, water shadows. You find them more usually near volcanos and in very geothermally active areas. Normally, a hot spring this size wouldn't have any, or if it did, the mu-serit would be small." He held up his little finger, slightly crooked. "They couldn't do more than sting."

Meg joined Peg at the rail. "May I speculate that we owe the critical magical overload for these being attracted to this hot spring?"

"Absolutely," Xerak agreed. "As we can see from what remains of the lava field, there was a time when the area south of here was extremely geothermally active. The mu-serit probably came then, and a few remained."

"I wondered," Teg said, "if they were defending the cargo hauler or defending their territory. So, it's their territory they're defending. I wonder why they didn't mind the cargo hauler?"

"Maybe they did at first," Xerak said with a shrug. "Then when it didn't show any interest in basking in the springs, they let it stay. They don't think the way we do, but whatever it is that makes them territorial is why they make good guardian creatures—if you know how to work with them."

"Do we need to recruit Cerseru Kham?" Teg asked. "I know you don't want to pull her away from her work on the book wraith spells, but I agree with Tamildah. We trapped the cargo hauler. We need to get it out of there."

"But how do we fight something that's made out of steam?" Vereez touched the hilts of her swords in evident frustration. "With the lightning shadows, we were able to lure most of them away. Then I could parry what the few who remained threw at us. Even if I was affiliated with water, I don't think I could parry steam."

Almost everyone inadvertently looked at Kaj, who had joined Peg and Meg hanging over the rail.

"You can look at me all you want," he said, "but I don't think I can do anything. But if Xerak has any ideas, maybe I can support him like I did when we fought the beti-teneh."

Grunwold leaned over the rail on the far side of Meg. "Well, Scraggly Mane. I recognize that curl to your whiskers. You have an idea, don't you?"

"I do," Xerak admitted, "and Kaj's support would help."

"So how do we fight something that is made of steam?" Vereez repeated.

"We don't," Xerak said. "We block it. We distract it. Then, while it's blocked and distracted, the rest of you go after the cargo hauler. Free it if you can. Capturing it would be even better."

"Let me guess," Grunwold said. "*Slicewind* serves as a distraction. Those things really got worked up when we sailed in to drop the net."

"Exactly," Xerak replied. "Not all your brains have gone into the fancy headgear. I figure you bring *Slicewind* in from the east. My job— and Kaj's—will be to put up a variation on a shield spell between the steam snakes and the cargo hauler. After seeing Kitet Un use a shield at the ford, I prepped a spell that I can adapt for this. Vereez, I want you to act as bodyguard, since I'm going to need to put my full concentration into the shield. I think Kaj will have mana enough."

Kaj barked a dry laugh. "All I've been practicing lately is storing mana. I hope I have enough."

"But if I need more," Xerak continued, "Vereez, you weigh in."

Teg waved a hand. "I'm a good battery. Why not me?"

"Because you're going to help with the cargo hauler," Xerak said. "Petros's 'Spidey silk'"—the last two words were spoken in careful English—"could be useful. Also, Huy and Tamildah may need you to sit on it."

Teg thought the last was meant as a joke, but she wasn't sure.

There were a few refinements but, overall, Xerak's plan was adopted without protest. Kaj dropped over the side to join the ground team. Meg went back to the crow's nest, and Peg resumed the role of crew. Once again, Heru and Uah would provide communication between the two teams.

Inspection with various binoculars and telescopes confirmed that the steam snakes were no longer active, and that the cargo hauler remained tangled up in the dry pool.

As *Slicewind* sailed off to (hopefully) calm the steam snakes by resuming a more usual patrol route, the ground team headed back to the hot springs. Teg could definitely feel the amount of hiking she had been doing in her legs, especially since the trail rose and fell with the landscape.

Must make certain to get some muscle rub from Kuvekt tonight. Reserve the tub for a long soak.

But sore muscles were forgotten as they got ready to make their new attempt.

"Best I get the shield up first," Xerak reminded them. "If that doesn't work, we're going to need to cancel anyhow."

Tamildah stood with Uah on her arm, ready to signal *Slicewind*. "The one thing I don't like is that we won't know how well your new spell will work until you get attacked. What if the shield doesn't hold?"

"Then we run," Kaj said, giving her a long-jawed canine grin. "You guys did fine with that the first time. Why shouldn't we?"

"Right," Teg said, putting on her best project-director manner, when, in reality, she was feeling out of her depth. "Xerak, Kaj, and Vereez first. Let's do this!"

❧ CHAPTER SIXTEEN ❧

Xerak in the lead, the three walked out east of where the trapped cargo hauler lay. Except for Vereez holding her twin swords, they were trying for the body language of three hikers who had just happened on the area.

"Won't the steam snakes remember we were just here a short while ago?" Tamildah asked.

"Not necessarily," Xerak reassured her, gently rolling the shaft of his spear staff between his palms. "My master taught us that creatures like the mu-serit and oehen-serit do not perceive either our sort of living creature or time as we do. That's one of the difficulties that arise when someone like Cerseru Kham makes an agreement with them."

Certainly, nothing happened when the trio entered the area between the pools, nor when Xerak went through the series of motions—almost a dance, involving as it did his feet, hands, and swishes of his tail—that would activate the shield spell.

The cargo hauler was another matter entirely. Very much of this world, it began to thrash in its den, but its previous struggles had succeeded in getting it thoroughly tangled in the ropes and net.

"Poor thing," Tamildah said, her ears pinning back. "How long before we can go help it?"

Teg was watching. Xerak had promised her that she would know when the spell was up, but she was far from certain. It turned out that she need not have worried. As Xerak completed his spell, the deeper pools began to agitate: bubbles forming on the surface, and then geysers shooting up, taking the form of serpentine necks topped with heads not unlike—for all that they were made of steaming water—those popularly attributed to the Loch Ness monster.

I wonder, Teg thought, *if all the magic that* Slicewind *must use is what alerted them the last time?*

Beside her, Tamildah flung her arm into the air, launching Uah. "Get *Slicewind*!"

The xuxu probably didn't need any instructions, but she gave a reassuring tootle on her crest as she went up above the tree line. She trumpeted again, and more distantly came Heru's reply.

Teg was aware of this as only one of many things going on simultaneously. Her attention was fixed on Xerak's shield, seeing it catch the greater amount of the steam that flew from the rising bodies of the steam snakes.

"Go!" she ordered Huy and Tamildah. "The shield's working for now, but I don't know how long it will last if the mu-serit start breathing steam at it."

Huy ran full tilt, pausing to scoop up the boathook with an ease that reminded Teg that, even if she thought of him as among the "older" members of the Library community, he was still at least a decade, probably more, younger than she was. Uah had dropped down to join Tamildah, soaring over the younger woman's striped head to land on her shoulder. Tamildah jumped directly onto the cargo hauler. Kneeling, she began to untangle the ropes.

Huy moved to the cargo hauler's front, then tapped the boathook gently but firmly against its upper lip. The cargo hauler made a sound that didn't mean anything to Teg, but it stopped wriggling and puffed out its breath.

"I tried the most usual command for 'wait,'" Huy explained. He knelt and joined Tamildah in untangling the cargo hauler.

"It somehow managed to haul in a couple of the weighted ropes," Tamildah said, holding up one she'd freed, "and they've dropped under it. Let's cut the weights loose, so they can drop the rest of the way. We'll tie the remnant of the ropes to the edges of the net, so it— and the cargo hauler—will be anchored."

Huy made a sound of agreement and started sawing at one of the problem ropes.

Teg went over to help. "How about I deal with that rope?"

"Good," Tamildah said. "I'll get another one loose. I can do that while sitting on our friend here."

As Teg knotted the rope to the net, she kept glancing over to where Xerak, Kaj, and Vereez were doing a good job maintaining the shield, possibly because the steam snakes were attenuating themselves to get a better angle at *Slicewind*. She noticed that with each puff of steam, the level of water in the pool dropped.

The mu-serit are exhausting their ammo faster than whatever spring is feeding the pond can replenish it, Teg thought.

Tamildah stretched out full length to knot another rope into place. She moved around the edges, doing her best to straighten out areas where the net had bunched. As soon as Huy had finished the final line, they'd be ready for the next stage, whatever that would be.

Huy anticipated Teg's query, because he began talking as he sawed through the rope. "Assuming this cargo hauler is the same one that was roosting on the top of the Library, we know it's strong enough to rise with an adult on its back. I want Tamildah to stay in place, near the center. We untie the ropes from the trees, then Teg-lial, you take the two ropes at the back. I'll take the two in front. I'll give Tamildah the boathook and she can tap out the command to lift. After that, we should be able to walk the cargo hauler out of here. The overflow from the hot springs forms a stream that should be open enough for us to get the cargo hauler down it until we meet the Qubhaneb."

"Are you good with that, Tamildah?" Teg asked. "You're the one at the greatest risk."

"No problem," the younger woman replied. "You two are the ones who are going to be hopping along a streambed while managing a really awkward balloon. I'm just going for a ride."

Vereez had taken a few steps back so she could listen. "Sounds like a great plan. When we're clear and Xerak can let the shield down, we'll come help with the lines."

Teg held her breath when the time came for Tamildah to give the cargo hauler the command to rise, but it lifted obediently. With Huy coaching, Tamildah performed the series of commands that brought the cargo hauler around and facing (although it didn't have much in the way of a face, other than its slightly gaping mouth) the overflow water course. Teg kept a firm hold on her own pair of lines, letting Huy set the pace.

They hadn't gotten more than a few steps away when a train whistle-scream announced that the steam snakes had noticed the peculiar new creature that had suddenly encroached upon their territory. Teg swiveled in time to see the numerous snaky necks come together, twist into one topped with a flat, long-jawed head that, despite the lack of obvious eyes, certainly seemed capable of sight.

This single steam snake didn't so much rise as rocket into the air, easily clearing Xerak's shield. *Slicewind* had been dropping back, preparatory to joining them down by the Qubhaneb, so it at least was safe.

Rather than breathing out steam—maybe its ability to maintain the mass needed for this larger form was precarious—the mu-serit darted out its head, targeting the closest moving person. That was Vereez.

Flinging herself to one side, letting her swords go skittering across the ground, Vereez managed to avoid that first strike, but it was evident when she pulled herself up that she'd wrenched something in one of her legs. She tottered, then sunk to one knee, looking up in open-jawed horror as the gigantic steam snake reared back for another strike.

"Take these!" Teg shouted, throwing her lines toward Huy, and fumbling in her pocket for Petros. The Spidey silk would have no effect on something made of water and air, but maybe she could pull Vereez away.

Even as she formulated her plan, Teg knew there wouldn't be enough time. *Slicewind* was racing forward, but for now the steam snake seemed uninterested in the sky sailer.

Whatever gods look out for fox-headed girls, Teg thought inarticulately as she tried to compose herself enough to interact with Petros, *protect Vereez!*

But when help came, it came in the form of a slim tiger-headed girl. Tamildah leapt from the cargo hauler's back and tackled Vereez, using the force of their impact to carry them out of reach of the striking steam snake. She rolled, wrapping herself around the smaller woman, so that when the steam snake breathed out its scalding cloud, most of it hit her in the back.

The steam snake was making so much noise that Teg knew she saw, rather than heard, both of the young women scream. Shoving

Petros into her pocket, she bolted toward them, determined to get them to cover before the mu-serit could breathe again. When the shower of scalding raindrops ebbed, then ceased, she realized that Xerak and Kaj had managed to turn the shield. Kaj was gripping Xerak under his arms, half dragging the lion-headed wizard, but Xerak's grip on his spear staff was firm.

Slicewind had closed the gap at such a speed that Teg suspected some of the precious stored wind had been used to overcome any such minor inconveniences as prevailing air currents. This was confirmed when a powerful blast of air blew the steam snake out of its coherent form. Later, Teg would learn that Meg had taken the helm, allowing Peg and Grunwold to turn the remaining bagged wind into a weapon.

For the moment, Teg's concern was Tamildah, who lay curled on her side, softly whimpering. The back of Tamildah's shirt was soaked, and Uah was circling her and making a sound far too much like keening for Teg's liking. Vereez's fur was matted with water, and she was crying as she tried to pull herself out from under Tamildah, while at the same time trying to support the semiconscious woman.

"She's crying, Teg-toh, and her breathing is really erratic. Help her! Please!"

Teg decided to trust in Xerak's shield, and used her belt knife to cut Tamildah's shirt from her back before the fabric could merge with the blistering skin. The skin surface, lightly striped with tiger markings, but without fur, looked puffy. For good measure, Teg popped the button to loosen Tamildah's belt, then slit the back of Tamildah's drawstring trousers, and pulled away the fabric.

"We've got to cool her skin off," Teg said, reaching for her canteen. "Have you been burned?"

"Only a little," Vereez replied. "Let me pour the water over her. Can you get more?"

A shadow passed over them and Teg looked up to see *Slicewind* overhead. The stretcher they kept in one of the topside lockers was being lowered.

"Won't need to," Teg said with relief. "There's plenty aboard. You've got to be feeling that leg, but if you'd steady Tamildah, we'll get her aboard while she's still out, because she's going to be in a world of hurt when she comes around. You go up after her."

The next short while had the tight focus Teg associated with operating theaters as depicted on television. First Tamildah, then Vereez, then a barely conscious Xerak, then a not much better Kaj were hauled aboard *Slicewind*. Grunwold had the sky sailer up and heading for the Library as soon as his last passenger was aboard. As the ship rose into the sky, Teg could hear Peg calmly giving orders to continue cooling Tamildah's burns, and asking Meg to check if Vereez's leg was broken.

Then Teg turned to where Huy had somehow managed to keep hold of the cargo hauler through all the commotion. She took the rear lines. Pushing back a desire to start weeping from shock, she trudged after him, following the feeder stream down to the Qubhaneb. There they were intercepted by Peynte and Throog, who had been sent to help.

As she turned the ropes over to Peynte and Throog, and lowered her stiff arms, Teg looked up at the remarkably docile cargo hauler.

"I hope you're worth it, pal," she said, then steeled herself for the hike back up to the Library, too tired to even want a smoke.

When Teg walked through the doorways into the Library of the Sapphire Wind, her cats, Thought and Memory, greeted her as if this were her house back in Taima and she'd been gone for a more or less normal day of giving lectures. She bent stiffly to pat them both, paused long enough to grab a bottle of poffee, then walked over to the makeshift medical clinic that Kuvekt and Nefnet had set up near the southern wall of the reception hall. Originally, only screens had set off the space, but Qwahua's crew had used salvaged wood to make solid walls. They also had run pipes from the bathroom area, so there was both hot and cold running water.

The clinic's walls didn't run all the way up to the high ceiling, and assorted xuxu were perched along the upper edge, undoubtedly checking in on their handler. Teg made a mental note to see if Huy or Grunwold could take over Tamildah's work in the xuxu roost while the younger woman was recovering.

The door into the clinic was open, so Teg—doing her best to avoid tripping over cats—walked in. Peynte and Kaj had made proper frames for the clinic's beds, including headboards. Vereez sat up in one bed, leaning back, while Tamildah lay face down on the other. Given how many of the sennutep had snouts, not just noses, the clinic's mattresses were designed with a section that could be pulled out, so that patients could lie prone without having their breathing obstructed.

Peg was sitting next to Tamildah, holding a glass with a straw under the edge of the bed. "Go on, girl. Drink up. Kuvekt-lial says you need to avoid getting dehydrated."

"If I drink," Tamildah replied, her voice slightly muffled, "I'm going to need to pee, and even with the stuff Nefnet put on my back, it hurts to move."

"If you need to pee," Peg said, "we'll draw a curtain and I'll help you. My stepdaughter, Tasha, broke both her legs skiing, and I got to be a real expert on the use of bed pans. I'm sure I can adapt that to people with tails."

Vereez forced a laugh. "What ever would we do without your daughters and stepdaughters and all the rest of your brood, Peg-toh?" She raised her voice slightly, as if Tamildah might not be able to hear her. "I can't believe that the hero who threw herself between me and a steam snake is afraid of anything."

Tamildah's initial response was so soft that even Vereez's sharp fox ears couldn't catch it, then she spoke more loudly.

"I'm not a hero."

"You most certainly are," Vereez retorted indignantly. "If you hadn't done what you did, that blast would have caught me in the face, maybe blinded me, certainly done something awful to my nose leather. I couldn't even turn my head, much less roll. When I twisted my leg, it felt like I had a full-body charley horse. Because of you, when Nefnet finishes brewing something for me, I should be up and at least hopping about."

"Ouch," Teg said, her inadvertent response to the idea of a full-body charley horse alerting the rest to her presence.

"Teg-toh!" Tamildah said. "Is that Teg-toh?"

"It is. And Thought and Memory." Teg sat in one of the straight-backed chairs along the wall and patted her lap. Memory jumped up, while Thought went under her chair.

"Teg-toh, you're *my* hero," Tamildah said, her words tumbling out in a fashion that made Teg suspect she was dopey. "Kuvekt-lial and Nefnet-va both agree that if you hadn't acted so quickly, there would have been fabric all through the burned area which would have needed to be pulled out. I can't believe you charged in in front of a steam snake and started doing burn treatment."

"I trusted that Xerak and Kaj would keep it back," Teg said awkwardly, because the reality was she hadn't done much thinking at all. She'd just been worried about the two younger women. "And I'd noticed it took time for the steam snake to, well, get up steam, so I figured we had at least a little leeway."

"And how," Vereez persisted, turning back to Tamildah, "is what you did any less heroic than what Teg-toh did? You knew that thing was going to spit. You saved me."

Tamildah muttered something, and Peg said gently, "But you did save her. Isn't that something, even if you didn't do it for her?"

"What?" Teg and Vereez said almost simultaneously.

Peg patted Tamildah softly on an area of her leg that had escaped the steam. "She said, 'I didn't do it for her. I did it for him.'"

Tamildah burst out. "I mean, I didn't want Vereez to get hurt, yeah, that's right, but I knew if she got hurt, he'd never forgive himself, and he'd probably devote himself to her memory or to caring for her and I'd never ever have a chance, so I did it for him and for me, and I'm not a hero."

Vereez looked stunned. "Him? Are you in love with Kaj?"

"No!" Tamildah nearly shouted, then dropped back to a softer tone. "Kaj is all right, sure, but I'm in love with Grunwold, and I can't bear how you can't even see how terrific and wonderful he is, what a generous spirit he has, and so kind. Why you moon around after that mommy's boy, who will never be able... I just don't get it."

Tamildah's outburst must have carried outside the clinic walls, because Kuvekt, who had been all the way across in the kitchen brewing something when Teg had grabbed her poffee, now came in at a jog.

He pulled up short, huffing, looking from person to person in a mixture of confusion and annoyance. "Peg-lial, I told you my patients need to rest. What is this?"

Peg bent to give Tamildah the straw, but her voice came clearly. "Just a wound being lanced," she said. "I think Tamildah is going to rest a lot easier after this."

∗∗∗

Given that Vereez was in the clinic as well as Tamildah, it was inevitable that Grunwold would come to visit some hours later, when Kuvekt next gave grudging permission. Teg had come to take a turn sitting with the patients.

Tamildah was sitting up, but definitely not leaning back. Earlier, after Kuvekt had chased them (and the cats) from the clinic, Peg had filled Teg in on how the two younger women were doing.

"They're keeping Vereez mostly for observation. Nothing is broken, but there may be something torn. I think Kuvekt is perfectly aware that our girl tends toward extremes, and the staying in bed is to keep her from injuring herself while the swelling goes down."

"And Tamildah?"

"I've never quite gotten straight what makes a what degree of burn," Peg admitted. "She has some blistering, and, although it's harder to tell because her skin is tinted with white and black, other areas are reddened, and will probably peel. She's right to be grateful. Your getting her shirt off and cold water on the skin probably saved her from a lot worse."

Teg made a dismissive gesture. "How much of Tamildah's surface area was hit?"

"Her upper back took the worst of it. She had on a fairly heavy shirt, and a wide leather tool belt that acted as armor. Kuvekt is taking precautions against infection, and Nefnet has been making various potions that, best as I can tell, taste horrible."

Tamildah was choking down one of those potions when Grunwold came in, Heru on his shoulder. Grunwold was trying for his usual grumpy swagger, but his expression as he looked between the two patients wasn't quite right. Something in how his gaze rested on Tamildah longer than it usually would have done, especially with Vereez right there, made Teg fight to keep her expression neutral.

Someone has told him Tamildah "likes" him. Teg looked to where Heru was softly tootling to Uah and revised that. *And I bet that if it wasn't quite "a little birdy," it was a couple of mini pterodactyls.*

Vereez might be a daughter of privilege, but she knew far too much about problematic love affairs to take Tamildah's situation lightly. Teg thought it probably helped that Vereez herself had not realized her childhood friend was nursing a major crush on her until only a few months before.

And since Vereez doesn't reciprocate the crush, she's not going to feel threatened. She might even welcome playing matchmaker, as a way to feel less guilty. Sort of a "It's not that you're not great. You're just not right for me."

"Sorry I couldn't come by sooner," Grunwold said, addressing the room in general, rather than the two young women of whom he was definitely all too aware. "*Slicewind* tracked Wagh's group as they walked the cargo hauler down the Qubhaneb, around the bluff, and then all the way around to the lakeside meadow. Huy went overland, grabbed Qwahua, and they lashed together the cage Tamildah designed. Huy's busy making friends with the cargo hauler."

"I hope that goes well," Tamildah managed.

Grunwold shrugged in a "We'll just need to see" fashion. "We didn't hang around too long but, from what I gathered, Huy is determined. Maybe he was being sentimental, but he said he thought it might be lonely, and that's why it didn't leave the area entirely. When I left, he was trying out sounds, to see if he could guess what would be a good name. Grace was thrilled and kept echoing him."

Taking a deep breath, Grunwold looked back and forth between Vereez and Tamildah. "You both look a whole lot better than when they brought you aboard *Slicewind*."

Vereez said, her tone teasing, "Don't tell me you were worried about me?"

Tamildah stiffened, and Grunwold replied defensively, "Of course, I was!"

"And what about Tamildah?" The teasing tone was still there, but slightly artificial.

"Absolutely! From everything I heard, she saved you from a world of hurt. I don't know what you've ever done to deserve that from someone who's only known you a couple weeks."

Vereez turned absolutely serious. "I agree. I've done nothing to deserve it. She didn't do it for me."

Tamildah whispered. "Please don't..."

Vereez nodded crisp understanding. "She did it because she's a terrific person. If you're really glad I'm doing so well, then I have a favor to ask you."

Grunwold's ears flapped in agitation. "What?"

"I wouldn't be doing so well if it weren't for Tamildah. But

Kuvekt-lial has told me I'm going to need to do PT on my leg, and she'll be in here all alone. Can you come visit her? Talk about xuxu or something?"

"Uh, sure. I'd be really happy to do that. Really."

Grunwold did look pleased—and more than a little poleaxed. Teg decided to do her bit to help.

"I was thinking someone is going to need to take over the xuxu roost until Tamildah is a bit better. Maybe you could do that. I'm sure Tamildah's going to be worried about her charges."

"Not worried about them." Tamildah managed a completely unstrained smile. "Worried that they're not doing their jobs, more likely. It seems as if far too many are flapping around down here. Who's flying messages? Who's watching the boundaries?"

Uah drew in air through her crest with a sound too like an indignant sniff to be accidental. "Only five are here, and Heru. Seven are working. We would not shame you, Tami. For you, we will help Grunwold."

Vereez said a touch too coyly, "Teg-toh, would you help me to the bathroom? I am supposed to practice with the crutches, but not alone."

"Absolutely," Teg said. She picked up the glass Tamildah had been drinking from and hefted it. "On the way back, I'll stop by Nefnet's lab and find out how the next potion is coming along."

"Thanks, Teg-toh," Tamildah said, but a bit absently. Grunwold had settled in one of the straight-backed chairs, and didn't seem unhappy about the idea of visiting alone with Tamildah.

Maybe something good, other than getting a cargo hauler, will come out of this, Teg thought. From the slightly worried, definitely hopeful, cant of Vereez's ears, Teg knew she wasn't the only one thinking that.

When Uten Kekui and Cerseru Kham emerged from their spellcrafting that evening, Peg consulted them about whether the mu-serit were likely to remain a threat.

"I don't think so," Cerseru Kham said. "It sounds as if your battle with them would have exhausted their mana. Without a critical magical overload to provide them with a surge, they will take a long time to remanifest—if they ever do."

Meg asked, "How is your work going?"

Uten Kekui made a seesaw gesture with the hand that wasn't stirring sweet syrup into his fyari tea. "We're making progress, but not yet ready."

Cerseru Kham saw the worry on Meg's face and hastened to reassure her. "Don't worry, I think we're close."

"Then," Meg said, "I think it's time for another planning session."

"We can do that," Peg agreed. "How about tomorrow morning? Since we don't know whether the wraith can overhear us, why don't we take a jaunt to Yemgar Farmstead for some groceries? The mail should be due, too."

Unspoken was that this would be easier on Vereez's healing leg than hiking around outside. Kuvekt had taken her off the crutches as soon as he'd confirmed there was no break nor any tears to muscles or ligaments, but it was apparent that even if she was "only" badly bruised, Vereez hurt when she had to be on her feet for too long.

The next morning, once *Slicewind* had lifted, Teg took her turn in the bow as scout, her binoculars trained on the mountains below, since these remained the mostly likely way for trespassers to come in. Once they were at the right altitude to catch a following wind, Peg opened the meeting.

"Despite how they're being all scholarly and cautious, I think we can count on Cerseru Kham and Uten Kekui to get us to the book wraith."

Grunwold gave a characteristic snort. "So, any ideas how we fight something like that? It would be super convenient if it really was basically a book. Then Xerak could whomp a fireball at it, and we could turn around and go home."

"It's an appealing idea," Xerak said, "but I doubt that will be a solution—it's just too direct and easy."

"Sadly," Grunwold said, adjusting the elevation to better catch the wind, "I agree. Even wizards wouldn't overlook something that obvious."

Teg spoke without lifting her gaze from the landscape. "As far as I can tell, the worst thing about being a wizard is how difficult it is to store enough mana."

"Our Lady of the Perpetual Faint speaks wisely," Peg said. "Meg, does Zink have any idea where the book wraith might be getting mana?"

"One definite source is from the books it has destroyed," Meg said. "More tomes than those written by Dmen Qeres himself have been ruined."

"So, it's eating the work of other wizards for mana," Vereez said slowly, as if trying on the flavor of the idea. "That technique suits that egotistical creep for sure."

"If lack of mana will weaken the book wraith, just as it would any other wizard," Grunwold said, "then we need to get it to waste some. Maybe we can get it to attack us, but be prepared to deflect those attacks. Any idea what Dmen Qeres had by way of affinities?"

"Too many to . . ." Xerak began, as Meg said, "A great many, I fear," then they both stopped, laughed, and Xerak made a half bow.

"Please, madam librarian, share with us the results of your research."

Meg opened her journal, flipped it to a page marked with a black ribbon, and cleared her throat. "We must never let ourselves forget that Dmen Qeres was the custodian of one of the great artifacts, and had probably been so for several lifetimes. It is easy to forget—given that the custodians currently in place are relative newcomers to their roles—how potent a custodian can be."

"You'd even call Cerseru Kham a novice?" Vereez asked. "I mean, Uten Kekui spent most of his life in denial, and Kaj is definitely a newcomer, but what about her?"

Meg replied, "I'm including Cerseru Kham among the newcomers because—largely due to choices made by Dmen Qeres, which later influenced Uten Kekui, but also because of how Ansi Abzu and his forerunners tied Qes Wen of the Entangled Tree to the role of Grantor of Miracles in the Creator's Visage Isles—when Cerseru Kham inherited the guardianship of Maet Pexer of the Assessor's Wheel from her mentor, Cerseru Kham found herself in the unenviable role of needing to maintain the Roots of the World and the Bridge of Lives all by herself. This means she has had to focus her own skills on those two tasks, and has not been able to diversify as she might have done."

"Also," Xerak added, almost diffidently, "this may be Cerseru Kham-va's first life as a custodian. Not all of the custodianships were cycled through the same people, as Dmen Qeres attempted to do."

"Going back to the question of Dmen Qeres's affinities..." Meg said in her most calmly commanding tone of voice.

"Sorry," Vereez and Xerak muttered, like school kids.

"Interestingly, his elemental affinity is similar to Teg's."

"He was an earth bender?" Teg asked. "I wonder if that's why the Library building dropped into the ground, rather than falling apart like a more sensible structure."

"You're quite possibly correct in that conjecture," Meg said. "Dmen Qeres also, unsurprisingly, had a reputation as a researcher into creating enchanted items. I wouldn't be at all surprised if he wanted to try and figure out what made the great artifacts capable of bridging worlds."

"Sounds like him," Grunwold agreed. "Probably wanted to create his own new world, where he'd be the supreme creator deity."

"Well, we've found no direct evidence of that," Meg said, "but I agree, it fits with his personality, and who better than someone with an earth affiliation to make a world? If I may continue?"

"Sorry..."

"Dmen Qeres had an interest in extremes, especially as related to sacred spaces," Meg continued. "He has written learned pieces about shrines under the sea, including the legend of the formation of the Creator's Visage Isles, but he has also written about sacred spaces in deserts so arid that most could not survive there, or on the tops of mountains where the air is nearly unbreathably thin."

"I don't like the sound of that," Vereez said. "I wonder if book wraiths need to breathe?"

Meg sighed. "I have no idea. I don't think Zink breathes, though. Now, let me finish. I'm almost done."

"Sorry."

"An erratic thread running through Dmen Qeres's publications is that of how to keep people out of places where you don't want them. Early on, he advocated elaborate locking mechanisms, but as these could be circumvented by violence—breaking through a wall if you can't get through a door, is one example—he began to favor guardians."

"Such as Sapphire Wind or even poor Emsehu, who was offered the choice of death or becoming a guardian." Peg held up her knitting to check the gauge. "You know, I think Dmen Qeres screwed himself over on that one."

Xerak was nodding vigorously. "Zink, right? I'd wondered why Zink manifested. Dmen Qeres's obsession combined with the Library's internal safeguards to provide a means of warning whoever was actually caring for the books that there was a threat targeting them."

Meg ran a finger down the left margin of the page she'd been consulting. "As is unsurprising for a wizard scholar of Dmen Qeres's lifespan, there are other areas of interest, but I think I've hit the major ones."

Vereez recited, "Earth magics; research into the creation of magical items; sacred spaces, especially those in nearly unlivable locations; keeping people out of where you don't want them, whether by more usual locks or by guardian creatures. As to that last, let's not forget that he co-opted otherwise 'normal' creatures, like the dobergoats, to serve as guardians, not just Unique Monstrosities."

Peg paused in her knitting. "It sounds as if Dmen Qeres's interests were very suitable for someone who would become a guardian himself. I wonder how long he knew he was in line for the job?"

Teg waved her pipe, which she'd been assiduously cleaning, rather than smoking, out of respect for her companions' almost universal objections to the odor of burning pipe weed. "Let's stay on track. In the book wraith, we're up against the doppelgänger of a solidly grounded, highly creative, quite probably paranoid, individual. Is there any way we can trace along those lines or tentacles that Xerak saw reaching out toward the books, so we can find out what's on the other end?"

"I asked Cerseru Kham-va that," Xerak replied. "She said it wouldn't be a good idea. The book wraith's extensions are closer to tentacles than to lines or ropes. Lines or ropes we might trace back to their source, but tentacles are meant to pull, to squeeze, not to serve as guides."

Peg gave a theatrical shudder. "I think we can do without that."

Grunwold's ears flapped in alarm. "I know I've agreed to sail *Slicewind* in after the book wraith, but are we certain we can get out?"

Xerak gave a shrug that was an intentional mimic of Grunwold's favorite action. "Sure. All we need to do is destroy the book wraith. When we've done that, then the spell pulling in material to create it should cease. When that's done, you sail us out through the portal Cerseru Kham-va and my master are creating at this very moment."

"A portal," Grunwold stated, "that will be anchored in Uten Kekui."

"That's right." Xerak tried to keep his tone light, but it was evident he was very, very worried.

❧CHAPTER SEVENTEEN❧

For the return trip, Teg resumed her place in the bow, promising to keep watch while testing a blend of pipe weed one of the Yemgar had presented her with.

After the residents of Yemgar Farmstead had proven interested in doing business with their neighbors over the mountains, the Rough Diamonds had decided that it would be unwise to conceal the reality of the humans. Rather than manufacturing an explanation, they let the general assumption that Meg, Peg, and Teg were some sort of monstrosities created by the Library go unchallenged. Teg's smoking had attracted a degree of attention. She'd been amused to find out that one of the younger adults had made something like a corncob pipe and was cultivating the habit—which was apparently no more popular with the residents of Yemgar Farmstead than it was among the Library community.

Between puffs on her pipe, Teg scanned the ripples of the mountain that they were flying over, her attention alert for any anomalies. Anyone else might have dismissed the motion below as local wildlife, the glint of light as a chance reflection, but a corner of Teg's brain had already begun to wonder about some irregularities she had spotted in the landscape on the way out.

"Meg, look down, to the north side of the pass. I think there's a camp there, very neatly concealed, including so that it won't be obvious from above."

Upon hearing Teg's words, Grunwold spilled some wind from the sails, so that *Slicewind* slowed, but not enough to attract the attention of whoever—for Teg felt certain the reflection she'd seen had been from a telescope—was watching their progress from below.

Meg directed her own binoculars where Teg indicated. "I can confirm there's something odd. I'm sorry I didn't see it myself."

She sounded miffed. Teg, remembering how Meg had admitted to feeling less than useful, was quick to speak up.

"I'm at a better angle."

"Want me to circle back around?" Grunwold asked.

Heru honked before anyone could reply. "No! No! I go. Me and maybe Uah or Sen. No one notice us. We are very sneaky."

"That's a good idea," Teg said. Heru flapped over to her, and she pointed. "Down there."

"I lead others later, when *Slicewind* gone. We check around. We also check other places. If Tamildah give us more, a little flock, we can spread out, see more, but they just think us wildlife."

"Sounds great," Teg agreed. "If that's the next set of treasure hunters heading in for a try at us, they're smarter than Mennu Behes and her pals, that's for certain."

Peg nodded somberly. "That doesn't exactly reassure me, especially with so many of us Rough Diamonds getting ready to go after the book wraith."

"We can't wait to go after the book wraith," Xerak almost pleaded.

"We won't," Peg reassured him. "Even if we didn't care about the risk to Uten Kekui—which we do—we can't have a book wraith stalking us from inside while treasure hunters and claim jumpers push our borders."

"And treasure hunters and claim jumpers," Meg added, "should be easier for those we're leaving behind to deal with. Better get them in practice."

Xerak forced a laugh. "True. Even after we win through the homesteading terms, we'll probably need to rescue the occasional opportunistic idiots, but let's hope we'll be done with the weird heritage of Dmen Qeres."

When they got in, Grunwold settled *Slicewind* into her docking cradle, then tossed a rope ladder over the side and nearly slid down it in his eagerness to reach the ground.

"Peg-toh, I'll leave it to you to supervise getting the sails furled," he said as he was doing this. "I want to consult with Tamildah about who best to send with Heru to check the pass."

He vanished down into the Library ravine so quickly it wasn't necessary for anyone to hide their grins. Xerak opened his mouth to comment, but at that moment Uten Kekui came loping across the drawbridge, his bison head slightly tucked as if he was about to charge into something. In the last few weeks, he'd lost the softness he'd picked up as Cerseru Kham's prisoner at the Roots of the World, and Teg could definitely see why Xerak—who clearly liked his men on the buff side—had acquired such a serious crush on his master.

"Xerak! Glad you're back. Cerka and I had a breakthrough while you were out, and we want your opinion."

Now it was Xerak's turn to hurry down the ladder. "If you're concerned about discussing this inside, *Slicewind* could go aloft."

"Might be a good idea," Uten Kekui admitted, "but aren't there supplies to unload?"

Wagh's crew had detached from their work and come over.

"We'll have her unloaded by the time you get Cerseru Kham-va," the prairie-dog-headed man said.

"Great!" Uten Kekui vanished back over the drawbridge. "I'll get Cerka and our notes."

Xerak and Teg heaved the steps over the side, while Peg adjusted the sail settings.

"Can you handle the wheel, Teg? I want to go inside, help Leeya get the supplies stowed, then see how lunch is coming along."

Teg's stomach growled. "Sure. Is there anything in the galley?"

As Peg sorted out some eggs, flat bread, cheese, and fruit from their recent purchases, Vereez limped over.

"I'd like to hear what Uten Kekui-va and Cerseru Kham-va have come up with. I'll handle the wheel if Teg-toh will make us some of her wonderful burritos. I think we both should be aboard, so we can both hear."

"Good idea," Peg agreed, adding ysiting, a spicy tuber that worked well as a substitute for onions and green chile.

Wagh was good to his word, and by the time Uten Kekui returned with Cerseru Kham and a daypack stuffed with papers, *Slicewind* had been unloaded and was ready to go aloft. Meg and Peg waved as the ship went up, Peg calling cheerily, "Don't storm the castle without us!"

Teg had listened to enough wizardly consultations by now that she wasn't worried about missing much while she was below making the burritos. When she came up with the lunch basket, Vereez opened her jaws in the foxy equivalent of a grin.

"They've just about started making sense," she said, accepting the cloth napkin in which the burrito was wrapped. "Xerak promised he'd explain more when you got up here. Sounds as if we'll both have parts to play."

Teg listened, and although the discussion was simplified, she had to admit that a great deal of why any of the spells should work went right over her head. However, since her main job seemed to be making sure Xerak didn't run low on mana, while Vereez's would be to make certain *Slicewind* had enough wind to sail where they wanted her to go, Teg figured she didn't need to understand the complicated details.

It's probably going to be like learning a board game, how it sounds really confusing until you actually start playing, and then after a few rounds, everything makes sense.

However, from what Teg could gather, they were going to be playing this game without knowing much about the board—or the rules. When she asked, Cerseru Kham nodded.

"That's one reason we're so glad you and the other mentors will be going along. You've shown you're capable of adapting very quickly to unusual situations."

When it was put that way, how could Teg protest? Nonetheless, she did try to get more clarification, in case this might be one of those situations where everyone assumed the three humans knew more than they did.

"Every spell takes shape in its own little space," Cerseru Kham explained patiently. "When you think about it, that only makes sense, since most magical workings violate at least one, if not more, of the more standard rules of the universe—violating those rules is what magic does."

Teg nodded. It did make sense when put that way.

Cerseru Kham continued, "In most circumstances, the spell space exists for very little time. Even the spaces that hold stored spells, like Vereez's lighting or Xerak's fireballs, collapse once the spell has been readied. Think of these like tight-fitting gloves on a hand."

Vereez said, "Are the areas where the Bridge of Lives was or where the island that held the Roots of the World spell spaces or something different? Am I right that they're different?"

Cerseru Kham made a small pleased noise that Teg recognized. It was the sound one made when a student showed more insight than anticipated.

"They are," Cerseru Kham said. "Peg introduced me to the term 'pocket universe.' Both of those places are closer to being pocket universes than simple spell spaces. However, you could say that a long-term spell, like the one to create a book wraith, creates a pocket containing the new rules needed for the spell. However, once the spell is completed, the pocket returns to normal space."

"Quickly?" Teg asked, visions of books and movies and computer games where the characters had to flee the collapsing ruins of some wizard's creation.

"Pretty much instantly," Cerseru Kham said, "but you needn't look so worried. Those within when the spell is ended will simply find themselves safely back in the consensual universe."

Uten Kekui frowned. "At least that's what usually happens in the cases where a spell has gone awry, so there is a need to go into its spell space and dismantle it. However, Dmen Qeres has shown himself very unpredictable. This is one reason we want you people to venture over on *Slicewind*, because that will give you a reality of your own as a base of operations and a possible platform for escape."

Teg tried not to show how nervous this made her. After all, she'd just been praised for being adaptable. But she had to admit, none of this made her feel any more confident.

When they returned from their aerial conference, Grunwold came aboard to help with furling the sails and settling *Slicewind*. As they all pitched in, he reported that Heru had taken four of the xuxu out to scout the western mountains.

"They'll focus on the pass where Teg-toh spotted those tarps, but check other areas as well. We figured that Heru and his team would need daylight to do their scouting."

"Sounds good," Xerak replied. "By the way, *Slicewind* may have already figured this out, but we're ready to try our new project, probably as early as after breakfast tomorrow."

"I'll tell her," Grunwold said. "It'll be strange sailing for her, so best she knows in advance. Oh, by the way, when we went through the mail, Fardowsi-toh had sent some of the gear we'd asked her to locate for us. She also included a letter for you."

Xerak brightened. He wasn't close to his parents, like Grunwold, but neither was he estranged, as was Vereez. Fardowsi had been helping the Rough Diamonds by selling some of the scavenged materials from the repository to supply much-needed ready money. She'd also been finding deals in "scratch and dent" hard goods. Xerak had said, with apparently no irony, that since Fardowsi was doing the work for him, she was only taking a token commission.

"Thanks!" Xerak said, accepting the scroll tube. "I'm going to help Uten Kekui-va and Cerseru Kham-va with a few finishing touches, then I'll go read Mom's letter."

When Xerak showed up for dinner, his shoulders were tight and his tail was swishing so violently that Teg half expected to hear it snap. Her first thought—that Uten Kekui had said something tactless to his still slightly smitten former student—vanished when, making the excuse of needing to brief them for the next day's expedition, he drew their core team off to one side.

"I need to read you something from my mother's letter," he said, pulling it out. Running a claw tip along the margin, he found his place. "Mom writes, 'When I went to the apothecary to get the materials you had requested, I happened to overhear something. I'll leave it up to you whether or not to pass this along to Vereez, since I know her relationship with her parents is not at its best right now. Anyhow, it seems that both her parents have mange. They're keeping this quiet, since mange is always an embarrassing ailment, but surely their daughter should know.'"

"Mange," Vereez said softly, then repeated it again, like a curse. "Mange!"

"Well," Peg said matter-of-factly, "we all know what that means, don't we?"

"They've broken our contract," Vereez replied, "and we're in a lot of trouble."

That Inehem and Zarrq had broken their contract with the Rough Diamonds made it all the more imperative that the threat of the book wraith be eliminated as quickly as possible, but first Ranpeti, Ohent, Kaj, and Nefnet—the other signatories—needed to be brought up to date.

Ohent thrust her claw-tipped fingers through the fur between her rounded snow leopard ears. "I wish I could say I'm surprised, but I'm not. If we'd been content to settle down, live on Inehem and Zarrq's beneficence, they probably would have felt they'd won. But not only didn't we stay low profile, if we can pull off this homesteading gig, we're going to be high profile."

"You know my parents," Vereez said heavily, "obviously a lot better than I do. How hard do you think they'll push? Is there any way you can think of to make them back off?"

"I don't really know," Ohent replied. "As for making them back off... Ranpeti, Inehem's your sister. What do you think?"

Ranpeti, still damp from having given Brunni her evening bath, looked troubled. "It's possible they could be bought off, but I don't like the price."

"Me," Vereez guessed. "Maybe Brunni, too. I don't like it either, but if that will save the people here from being harmed, I'll do it."

"I won't give them Brunni," Ranpeti stated.

"I wouldn't either." Vereez was trying, and failing, to look brave. "But if I can breed them another grandchild or more, they'll leave her be. I hope."

Over the general rumble of disapproval and dismay, Nefnet said, "I can't speak for certain, of course, but I think that if any of the Unarchived were told that a threat to their safety had been minimized at the price of prostituting a young woman—a woman who has been a friend and protector to all of them—I think they would all be furious. Maybe I'm too idealistic, but I think I'm correct."

Peg added, "'Minimized' is the correct term. The threat won't vanish. As was said earlier, we're probably always going to need to deal with would-be thieves. That's part of owning something valuable."

Meg half raised a hand. "Something I've been wondering about since we dealt with the first treasure hunters. Our charter requires us to hold and improve the Library and environs. How much are we expected to hold against? Could a rival nation send in an army? What if Zisurru University decided to attack in force?"

"I've talked with each of you from Over There about

governments," Xerak said. "We don't have any of the 'global super-powers' that you three seem to take for granted. Instead, the structure is more akin to what Meg-toh called 'city-states,' but those city-states aren't just defined geographically. Zisurru University could be considered a city-state, because of the influence it wields, both in the form of magical knowledge and in the large body of alumni who feel a loyalty to it. Religions and philosophies also have considerable impact, and their adherents can be considered city-states as well."

Meg nodded. "That's why I included Zisurru University among possible threats." She looked at Peg and Teg. "In our own lifetimes, we've seen how faster and more reliable communication and the ability to travel has reshaped political boundaries. Even back as far as the eighteen hundreds, the telegraph and steam-powered ships meant that news travelled much more rapidly. This world has had some form of both quite possibly since its inception, and I'm only just beginning to understand how differently that has shaped societies. We could talk about it for hours, but I think we need to focus on my question. What would happen if someone—"

"Inehem and Zarrq," Peg interrupted.

"—decided to buy an army and attack? Would that be considered 'all's fair' or not?"

"Not," Xerak said bluntly, and heads nodded all around. "The repercussions would destroy the House of Fortune."

"That's a relief," Meg said. "I can't imagine Inehem and Zarrq have become so crazed that they want a Pyrrhic victory. Therefore, they're funding groups, maybe giving advice, but we don't need to worry about armies swarming over our borders."

Kaj grinned a lean, canine smile at Ohent and Ranpeti. "I think you two have just been promoted to chief intelligence officers. Mom, Inehem and Zarrq are going to be thinking less like financiers than like extraction agents. Ranpeti-toh, even if Inehem hid a lot of her past from you, still, you're going to have insights into her character."

"We'll plan how to deal with them," Ohent replied, "while the rest of you go deal with the book wraith. The sooner you're back, the sooner we can prove to my old associates that they can't have everything they want just because they're nasty and rich. That's going to be fun."

***

The next morning found the original six adventurers aboard *Slicewind*. Heru was staying behind to help with the xuxu patrols, and with translating for Grace. The sky sailer seemed a little empty without him soaring about and honking comments.

They took their posts without discussion. Meg up in the crow's nest. Peg at port, ready to handle the lines or substitute for Grunwold at the wheel. Vereez climbed up onto the roof of the wheelhouse and drew one of her twin swords in her right hand, while she grasped her wind fan in the other. Xerak headed for the bow, and Teg followed him.

"Teg," Xerak began, "keep a hand on my shoulder, but don't tune so deeply into my mana flow that you lose track of what's going on around us. You're not just my battery, you're my eyes and ears as well."

"No pressure," she quipped. Once the young wizard had settled in, Teg placed her left hand on his right shoulder, close to his neck, a position which enabled her to swivel and keep track of the action around her.

As Grunwold brought *Slicewind* up out of her docking cradle, Teg was able to see the Library's roof. The drawbridge had been pulled in, and Kaj mounted guard over the stairway from the interior. Cerseru Kham was walking purposefully about, head bent as she checked over an elaborate pattern that had been inscribed over the roof. Uten Kekui sat cross-legged in the center of the drawing, directly over where Dmen Qeres's hidden repository was located below.

As previously instructed, Grunwold angled *Slicewind* so the sky sailer would pass directly over Uten Kekui, although high enough to easily clear the treetops.

"Our spell," Cerseru Kham had explained, "will make the book wraith's trail visible. It will also enable you to follow it into the space where the spell is taking shape."

As Grunwold coasted *Slicewind* over Uten Kekui, the bison-headed man seemed to disintegrate, causing Xerak to lurch to his feet.

"Easy," Teg said, pushing him down. "It's the spell opening to let us sail through, nothing's wrong."

She hoped she was right and strained to see the promised trail. When she found it, it wasn't much of a physical path at all. Instead, the trail was made up of scattered bits, more like Hansel and Gretel's scattered breadcrumbs. That is, it would have been if the bread involved had been mostly blue and black, although sometimes brown, and a bit sepia, and even red or green or purple. Teg focused harder and realized that the "bread crumbs" were words that were not so much floating as being sucked away from the Library of the Sapphire Wind toward some indefinite point. She tried to read the words to learn if they were forming any sort of coherent text. This was too much for the translation spell, which rewarded her effort with a walloping jolt right between the eyes.

"Teg!" Xerak protested.

"Sorry."

Teg guessed she was forgiven, because Xerak's next words were muttered in Hekametet, the never-translated spellcaster's language.

Something not unlike a soap bubble emerged from the tip of his spear staff and expanded until it encased *Slicewind*. Xerak made the process look so easy that, if Teg had not been linked to him, she would not have been aware of how something within him that was neither breath nor body, although inextricably associated with both, began to whine like a violin string turned one twist too tight.

"You okay, kid?"

"Yeah." Xerak breathed the word out on an exhalation, rather than speaking.

"Xerak's concealed us," Vereez reported. "All senses, including magical, but it won't last long. Grunwold, take us in."

Not so long before, Grunwold would probably have grumbled about arrogant wizards or some such, but now all he did was turn the wheel until *Slicewind*'s bow aligned with the trail of words. The sails flapped as they lost the wind, but before Vereez could release a magical wind, something else took over.

"We've caught a current," Grunwold called. When Xerak didn't seem alarmed, Grunwold called to Peg and Vereez to do things to the sails. Teg barely caught the words as she concentrated on what was ahead of them. Even so, she couldn't be perfectly certain when they stopped sailing over the roof of the Library and arrived in a landscape that was less defined by land than by the confusing muffling of fog. In the distance was a structure of some sort.

As *Slicewind* carried them more deeply into the spell space, expectations Teg hadn't realized she held until they were overturned—better call it by "unreality," because this certainly wasn't any sort of reality—were the first thing Teg had to let go of. Perhaps because of the term "wraith," she'd imagined their destination as some sort of haunted castle, maybe even a shadowed parody of the Library itself. She hadn't envisioned a tower built from books and journals. At the tower's top, crenellated battlements hedged round a person being built jigsaw puzzle fashion, from the words and phrases that had made up their trail.

Grunwold spun *Slicewind*'s wheel out of the current before it could carry them into the book wraith. While Teg had been distracted by the weirdness of their surroundings, Vereez had activated the wind spell she'd prepared. Despite its prevalence in myth and fiction, creating a wind was far from easy. However, Vereez's practice paid off. She gently spiraled the fan in her left hand, and *Slicewind*'s sail bellied out. Grunwold grunted wordless approval, then steered them in a circuit to let them get a good look at their target from all sides.

The book wraith was taking form in splendid isolation. Its stance was much like that of the statue of Dmen Qeres that adorned the plaza, although instead of a book it held a staff topped with a chunk of rough crystal encased in a wirework cage. The wraith was creepily incomplete, even in its outline. Gaps appeared in the most unlikely places, leaving holes in the ornamented robe, along the length of the staff, even in the wraith's head and hands. There seemed to be no priority in what had been filled in, nor were any two of the gaps the same size or shape.

"*I guess this means the wraith doesn't have any vulnerable spots,*" Teg thought ruefully. "*It's an image of a person, not in any way a person itself.*"

A faint echo of Xerak's thoughts came to her. "*At least not yet. At least not until it has taken Uten Kekui's soul into itself.*"

The bubble that hid *Slicewind* and her crew must be breaking down, for the book wraith began orienting on them. There were no eyes in the book wraith's head, only gaps that somehow managed to seem like eyes. Nor was the beak that it now opened complete. The tongue that moved within was represented by a fat and fleshy root and a pointed tip, unlinked to each other but creepily moving in unison.

Teg was acutely aware when a soundless incantation flowed forth from the book wraith's mutilated mouth. Despite the lack of sound, the chest with great gaps rose and fell as the book wraith took impossible breaths. Teg tensed, awaiting the impact of the outward flowing mana.

But the spell was not intended for them. Instead, it sprayed forth from the book wraith's outspread palm to target the surrounding battlements. The book wraith slowly pivoted, distributing the spell's power with a practiced ease that made Xerak's perfectly executed workings look clumsy and jejune.

The textual rampart rippled, pages fanning as might books left open on a windy beach. Lines of written text unspooled from the varied tomes. From them, bipedal figures wove into shape, drifting over the battlements. Initially, Teg thought theses were replicas of the Dmen Qeres book wraith but, as additional pieces wove into the shapes and became more defined, she realized that each of the figures had its own distinct style of head and tail: feline, canine, ursine, lupine, and more.

"Those must be the wraiths of other wizards," Meg cried out. "I wonder if Dmen Qeres has borrowed them with their permission?"

"Somehow I doubt it," Peg said. "Doesn't seem like his style."

"Does it matter?" Grunwold said. "We aren't sure we can deal with one book wraith. Now we've got—what?—a dozen?"

"The book wraith is a spell, not a person," Xerak replied with sublime patience, "no matter how it's behaving. I can disrupt it, but I'm going to need to get closer to do that. As for those other figures, I don't think they're full-fledged book wraiths. I think they're a defense Dmen Qeres built into his spell."

Meg had carefully climbed down from the crow's nest and seated herself on one of the stern lockers. "Those new wraiths may answer a question I've had since Zink came to us, begging for aid against the book wraith. Dmen Qeres could have stored mana to power the book wraith, so why did he choose to mine the Library collection? What if it wasn't so much for the mana, but for the source of the mana?"

Vereez's eyes widened. "That way, he could create wraiths to protect his wraith. That makes sense. It also explains why these new wraiths are being woven, not assembled as a puzzle, and are much less detailed. They don't need to be true doppelgängers, only sufficient to provide defense and distraction while the book wraith finishes constructing itself."

"Which," Peg said, lowering her binoculars, "it seems to be doing with greater speed. The storm of puzzle pieces showering onto it has really picked up."

Even without using her binoculars, Teg could see that Peg was right. When they'd originally arrived, the drifting words had seemed like a snow flurry—if snowflakes were shaded in the colors of ink and shaped like words and phrases. Now the flow looked like the patterns of interference she remembered from the television sets of her childhood. The increased amount of text would have occluded the book wraith, except that, as pieces slotted into place, the wraith became more defined. It had eyes now, bright, yet still unfocused, like those of a doll, rather than of a living thing.

"We don't have much time," Xerak said, "which means we're going to need to get this right on our first try. Vereez, Peg ... You're in charge of keeping *Slicewind* on point and unmoving, while I go down there to deal with the book wraith."

"I'm your battery," Teg stated.

"Sorry, your part isn't going to be so easy. You and Petros are going to get me there first. I want you to create a thick line, anchor it to one of the more massive tomes. I'll slide down, then you'll follow me. I want you to save sufficient mana so that you can wrap a cord around the book wraith's beak. Wrap its arms if the head is too well protected. The book wraith's abilities are going to be restricted to those of a real wizard. If it can't speak or make gestures, it may be slowed down."

"And me?" Grunwold asked.

"Defense. Archery. Swordplay if something closes. If you get a chance to do so without hitting me or Teg, shoot at the book wraith. Meg..."

Meg interrupted. "I'm a librarian. These are books. I have a feeling I need to be free to improvise."

Teg realized that Meg must have been planning something all along, which explained why she had come down from the crow's nest.

Xerak twitched his whiskers. "That does feel right, doesn't it? You'll be our wild card, then. I have a feeling we're going to need one."

⁘CHAPTER EIGHTEEN⁙

"All right, me hearties," Peg shouted a few moments later. "Let's stop this pirating book wraith from looting our library!"

From where she stood at the starboard rail, closer to the stern, waiting for Peg to bring the sky sailer around, Teg could hear Vereez muttering in Hekametet. Teg's own magical workings, if you could even call operating a magical item that, were much less mystic and cool.

"Okay, friend, we're going to need a cord"—she envisioned Xerak's request—*"but we're going to need to keep a mana reserve so we can wrap up the wraith, hopefully without landing me on my ass in a faint. Can you do it?"*

Call it an image; call it an impulse. Petros's reply was a bit of both, as if an engineering diagram decided to laugh, but Teg understood.

Teg called out. "Peg! We need to get in closer. Maybe twenty feet out from the rampart, and high enough to give us an angle like this."

She sketched about a forty-five-degree angle with her forearm.

The lesser wraiths were more distinct now, most making the motions of casting a spell, although one had his head bent over a tome, pen in hand, apparently intent on his research.

I wonder if the book wraith had a lot of control over who he called up as reinforcements? Teg thought. Since the scribing wizard seemed a lot less threatening than many of the others, she decided to anchor her rope in a gap near him.

"Near the writing guy, if you please, Peg."

"I can handle that," Peg called.

Xerak had cut short lengths of line that could be put over Petros's Spidey silk cable, then tied large knots in the ends to serve as handholds. He handed one of the sliders to Teg. She, in turn, made sure Petros understood their purpose.

"Petros thinks these should work," she said to Xerak, "but remember to make sure the Spidey silk has set before you try to slide down. Otherwise, you might stick."

Grunwold had climbed up into the crow's next and limbered up his bow. Now he set an arrow to the string. "Peg, start spilling wind from the sails when you bring us alongside. If there's too much momentum, Teg's rope will snap before Xerak and Teg can get down."

"Already thought of that, Captain," Peg called in her best long-suffering mother voice. "Vereez, you can ease off and rest your leg."

Vereez nodded, sheathed her sword, and lowered her fan, then sat heavily on the wheelhouse roof. Xerak was pushing the moveable steps over to the rail so he and Teg could go up and over without needing to climb.

Between grunts of effort, he managed to snark at Grunwold, "Go shoot a book wraith, rather than shooting off your mouth, Many Tines. Maybe you can save us a world of trouble."

In reply, Grunwold snapped off an arrow. His targeting was perfect, but a lesser wraith with a hawk's head intercepted his missile with a cloud of bright tangerine mist.

Peg shouted, "Coming on your mark, Teg!"

Was Petros listening? Or did it feel Teg's mingled apprehension and anticipation and merge action with her "Now!"? Whatever the reason, the Spidey silk shot out nearly instantly, anchoring firmly on the scaley green leather of the massive text she'd chosen. Teg pulled the sun spider amulet toward her, so she could loop the closer end of the rope around the rail. She sealed the hardening rope into place with a press of her thumb. She glanced over at Xerak, who was crouched, waiting, only the twitching of the tuft at the tip of his lion's tail betraying any apprehension on his part.

"Go!" she said.

With an absolute trust that made Teg more nervous than any doubt would have done, Xerak looped his makeshift slider over the

Spidey silk rope and leapt over *Slicewind*'s side. Recalling how he'd fallen when they'd been rescuing Uten Kekui at the Bridge of Lives, Teg thought he was either very brave or very foolhardy.

And what am I? Doing this sort of thing, especially at my age? After everything I've done to my shoulders over the years?

Teg was about to follow when, from up on the mast, where Grunwold had been snapping off arrows, there came a loud bellow of pain and rage. She looked up and saw Grunwold slumped over the edge of the crow's nest. Blood was running down his face, over his eyes, and an arrow was buried near the top of his head.

Teg wasn't aware she was moving until she had reached the crow's nest. Voices rose from below, shouting questions. She took time to assure herself of a few basic facts, then called down.

"Grun's breathing. Unconscious, but breathing. I'll see what I can do."

Carefully, she lowered Grunwold down into the crow's nest. He was the tallest of their group, with broad shoulders. His rack of antlers didn't make her task any easier, but she managed. As she was moving him, the arrow dropped from the wound, causing more blood to flow, but also showing that the arrow had first hit on the left side of his brow, then sliced sideways, cutting through Grunwold's hide, passing over where—on a human—the eyebrows would be, before being halted by the thick bone of his right antler. The wound was ugly, and had bled a lot, but it was relatively minor. He'd probably been knocked out by the arrow impacting his skull.

Teg was about to call down this good news when *Slicewind*—which had been more or less at anchor—surged into motion, snapping Petros's line, then whipping around the ramparts, heading directly for an equine-headed wraith. The wraith held a staff in one hand, a shield in the other, and seemed remarkably placid for someone about to be hit by a sailing ship.

"Vereez! Cut the wind!" cried Peg, the effort of wrestling back control of the unresponsive sky sailer evident in her voice.

"I never started it blowing again!" Vereez called back. "*Slicewind* is doing this without my help!"

Although most of Teg's attention was on Grunwold, she realized that the mainsail beneath her was indeed hanging limp. Too late, Teg realized that the arrow that had dropped from Grunwold's scalp was one of Grunwold's own. The significance of that little bit of information came to her all at once.

"*Slicewind!* Stop!"

But it was too late. The equine-headed book wraith raised its shield, and the force of the sky sailer's attempted ram reverberated through the ship's hull, causing the ship's timbers to groan. The vibration even reached the crow's nest, where Teg attempted to protect Grunwold's bleeding head.

This has ruined my clothes for sure, Teg thought, knowing the thought was displacement for everything else that was going on, including that she'd abandoned Xerak. Crouched as she was up here, she had no idea how he was doing. Then she realized something very weird. Her clothes were, in fact, relatively undamaged, although they should have been soaked with blood. The crow's nest was also preternaturally clean. She glanced wildly around, and found an explanation.

"*Slicewind* is somehow using Grunwold's blood! I'll stanch the wound, but Vereez, if you have anything in your med kit that will stop the bleeding, get it!"

For this expedition, Teg had put on a pair of her cargo pants. She thrust her hand into one of the upper pockets for a bandana.

Vereez's voice was high and thin with panic. "But someone has to help Xerak!"

Meg's reply came, clear and bright. "I'll do that. You and Teg help Grunwold."

Teg had stood to get a better angle on Grunwold's wound. Now she could see that after ramming the shield-bearing wraith, *Slicewind* had more or less stalled with her bow over the edge of the rampart. Meg was in the fore section of the ship, unrolling a rope ladder over the side with remarkable calm.

In the middle of the ramparts, Xerak and the as yet incomplete book wraith were stalemated. Xerak would attempt to get close enough to do his spell, but the book wraith poked at Xerak with his still fragmentary staff whenever the lion-headed wizard got too close. Xerak would counter with his spear staff. For the moment at least, the lesser wraiths seemed uncertain which threat they should focus on, confirming the theory that they were more facsimiles of their originals, rather than true doppelgängers.

A shaking of the mast confirmed that Vereez was climbing up, and Teg, having applied the folded bandana to sop up the blood that was still oozing forth from Grunwold's head, moved to give Vereez room to take her place.

"I'll go help Xerak," she reassured Vereez. "See if you can bring Grunwold around. Get him to reassure *Slicewind* that he's going to be okay."

When Teg reached the main deck, Peg waited in the wheelhouse. "We're stalled for now. I'm hesitant to even try the elevation controls until we're certain how *Slicewind* will react. Is Grunwold still bleeding?"

"Not onto any part of the ship," Teg replied, mounting the steps, noting that Meg had left a ladder in place when she'd gone down. "Even if *Slicewind* wants to do something, it's going to lack the mana. Any idea what Meg has in mind?"

"None, but she had that determined look."

"Let's hope," Teg said, pausing to see what changes had happened in the last few moments, "she has more than a look."

Xerak was still trying to close with the book wraith, and being fended off.

Well, that's one part of our plan going right. Keep it occupied. Let's hope this also is burning some of its reserve. She noticed that the snowstorm of written characters had remained television-static dense, but that the book wraith was not noticeably more complete. *I think it might be doing just that.*

"I don't see Meg," Teg said uneasily.

"She's gone under *Slicewind*'s hull," Peg said, indicating the viewer in the center of the sky sailer's hull that enabled the pilot to see obstacles beneath. "There's no sign of the horse-headed dude with the shield, so I'm guessing that pushing back *Slicewind* banished it."

"Or it's squashed under the bow," Teg said cheerfully, "not able to do much, which is pretty much the same. I'll go down and see if I can help tip the balance in Xerak's favor."

"Do that," Peg said. "I think I'll trust the ship to stay battlemented, and haul my ass topside to see if I can relieve Vereez on nursing duty, so she can bring her magic into play."

"Battlemented?" Teg asked, as she climbed over the rail and onto the rope ladder.

"Well, I can't say 'beached,' can I?" Peg cackled, pleased with her pun. "Not when there's no sign of a beach or even any sand. Have fun storming the castle!"

"Idiot," Teg said fondly as she clambered down.

Reaching the ground, Teg glanced back under the hull and found Meg apparently communing with the wall. "Meg, what . . ." she began, but Meg gave a sharp "Not now!" shake of her head. Frowning, Teg turned her attention to where Xerak and the book wraith remained immersed in their stalemated battle.

No. Not stalemated. Xerak is getting tired. He's probably using more than his staff fighting against that thing, and I haven't been there to help him. Senseless guilt flowed through her, although Teg knew perfectly well that no one—least of all Xerak himself—would have expected her to abandon Grunwold just because her assigned post had been with Xerak. *The book wraith may be consuming its potential, but Xerak has no such option. Worse, the book wraith's actions are probably harming the Library.*

There was nothing Teg could do to slow the shower of words drifting down, so she looked for another way to tilt the balance in Xerak's favor—preferably something she could do from a distance, so she wouldn't attract attention to herself.

Because it's completely possible that the main reason the lesser wraiths haven't gotten into the fray is its too-tight quarters, and they're not able to do anything that might damage the book wraith. I'm not sure that they'd let me cross the distance, but what about Spidey silk?

She wrapped her fingers around Petros, and considered. Xerak had suggested tying up the wraith's beak or arms, but the book wraith didn't seem to be speaking its spells, and there was no way she could wrap the arms without risking tangling Xerak as well.

And it doesn't have any vulnerable spots, and it probably isn't using its eyes to see, so targeting a shot at those isn't going to work. I wonder if I can disarm it, though? Or at least make it harder for it to use that staff?

Teg held up Petros, wordlessly framing her intentions, while reminding the amulet to wait until she gave the command to launch the Spidey silk. The emotion that flowed back to her lacked the usual eagerness she had come to associate with the amulet.

Don't worry, she thought at it. *We can do this. Xerak isn't going to be able to hold out much longer if we don't distract that thing.*

At that very moment, Xerak stumbled, going down on one knee. Teg sent her will into Petros, and a fresh, sticky line of webbing shot forth, landing on the book wraith's staff right where she'd planned. Teg jerked back, successfully stopping the book wraith from walloping Xerak, buying the young wizard time to regain his footing.

Her cry of triumph was cut short by the sensation that her heart was being ripped right out of her chest—no, not her heart, but something as essential, as intimate.

My mana! she thought, and her guess was confirmed as the book wraith grew more distinct: small gaps filling in, the eyes in the raven head gaining a shrewdness they had not possessed before. There was a second surge of pain, somehow muffled by a cushion of sorrow, and Teg realized what was happening.

I've been an idiot! Both Dmen Qeres and I are affiliated with earth, and Petros is meant to be used by someone affiliated with earth. For all I know, the amulet may have originally belonged to Dmen Qeres!

Teg felt a sharp pinch, followed by the distinctly unsettling sensation of the sun spider's legs—to this point stiff and unmoving—wriggling. With a faint cry of surprise, she let go of the amulet. As soon as she did so, the pain of her mana being sucked out of her nearly vanished. A moment later, she felt something tugging at the leg of her cargo pants. Glancing down, she saw Petros clinging there, the little hooks at the end of each leg firmly gripped into the fabric.

Was she imagining that the eyes ringing the sun spider's disk-shaped body were staring pleadingly up at her? Teg unsnapped the top of the sheath that held her belt knife and, drawing out the blade, used it to slice through the Spidey silk cord that connected Petros to the book wraith. Then she held out her hand, and Petros crept into it, moving over the hilt of the knife, and wrapping its legs around her wrist, snuggling its meteorite body close to her skin.

Teg wanted to marvel over Petros's new mobility, but although her intervention had given Xerak an opportunity to get back onto his feet, she had also given the book wraith the mana it needed to solidify itself further, though there were still gaps in its body. When the majority of the lesser book wraiths slowly turned, shifting their orientation from outside the battlements to the sky sailer perched upon them and the struggling figures within, Teg thought she knew why.

The book wraith has spent mana to give them new orders, and, sure as cats make kittens, those orders are to deal with us.

She stood, indecisive, and Meg called. "Help Xerak. We'll deal with the rest of these."

We? Teg thought, glancing around, in case Vereez or Peg or, unlikely as it seemed, Grunwold had come to join them while she had been dealing with the mana drain. She didn't see any of the others, but she realized that the printer's-ink snowflakes had been joined by an additional form of precipitation.

Tiny sparks of sapphire blue were drifting down from above, intermingled with the "snowflakes" but avoiding the book wraith entirely. Instead, operating completely contrary to the concept that what goes down must stay down, the sapphire sparks were separating from the rest, making a platform.

No, not a platform, a conveyor belt.

Teg's already aching head ached a bit more, because it should have been impossible for the sparkling blue belt to occupy space already occupied by *Slicewind*, by the battlements, but it did. Remembering Cerseru Kham's description of spell space as a minireality created to hold whatever was necessary for a spell to work, Teg understood.

Somehow Meg and Sapphire Wind—she looked up at the conveyor belt and saw the paper doll outline that was Zink—*and Zink created a spell that would work inside this spell.* A battered tome flickered along the conveyor belt and was grabbed by Zink, who set it on a shelf just visible in the indigo-lit shadows behind and to one side. Teg spared one more glance and saw that where there had been a book in the wall, there was now a brick.

Somehow, she thought, *Meg has worked out a way to reshelve the works that Dmen Qeres targeted. I bet Sapphire Wind has at least as strong a claim to them, having been created as the genius loci of the Library. Zink has a claim, too. There's almost something sacred about a written work once it's been completed. When an author, any author, becomes more important than the written work, there's something seriously wrong.*

She longed to pursue this thought, to consider all those times when she'd heard writers—of fiction, or nonfiction, it didn't seem to matter—talk about inspiration, about the feeling that some element of the work came from beyond themselves. She'd felt it herself.

Dmen Qeres's spell violates this on so many levels, but it took a librarian to figure that out.

Although Teg felt certain that as the books were replaced by bricks, the lesser wraiths would begin to disperse, this didn't mean the book wraith was no longer a threat. She hurried to join Xerak, wondering what she could do. Then a terribly dangerous idea came to her.

"Trust me," she said to Petros. *"I'm not giving you up, but we've got to use you—and me—as bait to split the book wraith's attention."*

She felt Petros's apprehension, so different from the merry enthusiasm she had grown used to. With a start, she realized that its dread was for her, not for it.

"Don't worry. I don't plan to do anything too *dumb,"* she told it. Then, without further delay, she put her plan into action.

Holding Petros cupped against her palm, Teg made as if about to shoot for the book wraith's staff again, but this time she shot high, so the sticky silken cord would pass in front of the book wraith and anchor to the battlements, right where, thanks to Meg's work, many of the books were now bricks, and the lesser wraith who had stood guard was hardly more than a foggy outline.

Without pausing in its sparring with Xerak, the book wraith snapped at Petros's cord. Gripping the cord in its beak, it shifted its staff to a purely defensive stance, then started backing away from Xerak, its peculiar snowstorm following it. Obviously, it intended to draw mana from Teg before renewing the attack. However, unlike last time, when Teg had not only anchored the cord, but also been concentrating on it, this time Teg had other plans.

"I might not be a great wizard, but then, neither is it. Two can play at this shared-affiliations game, right, Petros?"

Teg had never particularly disliked spiders, although she'd done her share of black-widow stomping when out in the desert. However, she'd never felt a lot of sympathy for Shelob or the spiders in Mirkwood who'd wanted to dine on dwarves and hobbits. Now Teg's point of view shifted as she envisioned using the spidery nature of Petros to suck mana from the book wraith. Maybe it was the shared-affinity thing. Maybe it was to her advantage that she'd spent a lot of her practice time learning how to draw mana from her environment but, for whatever reason, Teg found it astonishingly easy to turn the book wraith's game back on itself. She'd decided it would be very dumb to use the mana herself, but Petros was equipped to store mana, so she funneled her take into it.

The book wraith might not be Dmen Qeres, but it apparently recognized what was happening to it. It tried to let go of the piece of cord it had gripped in its beak, but Teg had visualized Petros creating an extra gooey version, so the book wraith could neither bite through it nor let go. Instead, bits of the cord stuck to its beak, somewhat like bubble gum after a badly shaped bubble had burst. The gum didn't conduct mana nearly as effectively as the cord had done, but some still trickled over.

To deal with the cord, the book wraith was forced to entirely abandon its fencing match with Xerak. It didn't drop the staff, rather the staff was reabsorbed into the main body. Once the book wraith's hands were empty, it reached up to scrub the remnants of the cord away. As it did so, it wasn't exactly falling apart, but it was definitely looking a lot less intact.

Xerak thrust with his spear staff, but it passed right through the book wraith. He regrouped, then thrust again, doubtless remembering that the more mana the book wraith spent on defending itself, the less it would have for creating the doppelgänger that might well draw Uten Kekui's soul from him.

The snowstorm of letters, words, and phrases was growing in intensity.

Meg called out, her voice holding the controlled calm that is worse than any scream, "Zink reports that the book wraith has begun cannibalizing Dmen Qeres's special collection. This is *not* a good thing."

"I'm on it!" shouted Vereez, her voice coming from high above, so she was probably in the crow's nest. "Hang on!"

Teg expected lightning, this being Vereez's preferred way of dealing with threats, but instead a wind burst forth, powerful enough to make even Teg's short hair go wild. Looking up, Teg realized that what she had felt was only the lower edges of the gust. Vereez's blast had been aimed into the heart of the wordflake storm, scattering them so that they fell every which way, many of them drifting onto the battlements, where they were engulfed by Sapphire Wind's sparkle.

At that point, Meg hurried from her shelter beneath *Slicewind's* bow, pulling from the duffle pack she'd been wearing a coil of rope hung with angular folded paper streamers that reminded Teg of the ones used in Shinto shrines. As Meg came closer, Teg saw that the streamers had been folded from the mutilated pages of books. A slow smile spread across her face as she understood.

"Teg, help me wrap the book wraith with this," Meg said, "while Vereez has it distracted. Xerak, get ready to do your thing."

Grabbing the end of the rope Meg extended to her, Teg moved clockwise around the book wraith, while Meg moved counterclockwise. When they'd completed a full circuit, the book wraith's arms were pinned to its sides, and, more importantly, it could no longer move away or defend itself when Xerak approached, his spear staff extended.

The spearpoint was illuminated with a pearlescent glow that held no one color for very long, seeming to reflect the hues of something that was not present. Xerak sang something in Hekametet, the tone one of triumph. If it could have done so, the book wraith would have shrunk away, but bound as it was, it could only shrink into itself. It did so, collapsing inward. As it grew smaller, Teg and Meg gradually tightened their loop, so it could not slip away. Before long, the book wraith was only a handwritten line of text, letter upon letter, word upon word, scrolling away, like pages turned sideways, then pulled into a single long line.

I bet that's the original spell, Teg thought, *and when that's gone...*

She hadn't been able to read the spiraling spell, but she recognized the final characters as they spelled out D-m-e-n-Q-e-r-e-s.

Without anything to wrap around, the rope dropped between Meg and Teg. The streamers of folded text had vanished, and Meg said softly, "They've gone back to their books."

"And we'd better get back aboard *Slicewind*," Xerak said, "before this spell space vanishes."

But the tower of books lasted long enough for Meg, then Teg, then Xerak to scramble up the boarding ladder. Peg was at the wheel. Grunwold, with a long strip of bandaging wrapped around his head, covering the space between his antlers, was trying to lounge insouciantly on the stern bench, but he couldn't quite hide how much pain he was in. Vereez had remained up in the crow's nest, sword and fan in hand. Teg could have sworn she saw lightning sparking around the fox wizard, but maybe it was just the remnants of Sapphire Wind withdrawing with the last of the stolen books.

Teg swayed a little, feeling the effects of the repeated drains on her mana.

I'm not going to pass out again, she thought, but she did.

❦CHAPTER NINETEEN❦

When Teg came to, Meg was holding her head in her lap, and gently stroking her hair.

"Feeling all right? Xerak caught you before your head hit the deck, but he was too beat to pick you up. The spell space has vanished. Peg is bringing *Slicewind* around to her cradle. We should have you inside before long."

Teg struggled to sit up. "I can manage. I feel a lot better than I usually do after one of those bouts. I think Petros gave me back some of the mana we had left."

And, indeed, the little creature—for it was getting increasingly difficult to think of it as merely an amulet—felt as if it were asleep, or at least drowsing. It wasn't exactly purring, but Teg felt something that was like the imitation of a purr.

"*We did really well,*" she told it. "*You rest now.*"

Peg had insisted on helping Grunwold debark. In midstep, Grunwold paused and looked up at the sky. "How long did that take? It seemed like a half hour, maybe as little as fifteen minutes, but the sun seems to have moved a lot more. Or is my head more messed up than I thought?"

"It took two hours, give or take," replied Uten Kekui, walking a bit unsteadily toward them over the drawbridge. "Spell space does not always sync with our own time, so your head isn't to blame for that. It does look as if you were solidly walloped. Come inside and have Kuvekt-lial take a look at that."

He looked up anxiously, obviously missing his former apprentice among the debarking passengers. "Is Xerak all right?"

265

Xerak hauled himself up from the stern bench and looked down over the side rail. "Just letting the really wounded go first. Teg and I are a bit wiped out. Over poffee and one of Leeya-lial's pastries, we'll tell you all about what we found."

They related the book wraith's defeat, while Peg escorted Grunwold to the infirmary. When the basics had been covered, Xerak asked Meg, "Meg-toh, why didn't you tell us about what you, Sapphire Wind, and Zink had put together?"

Meg poured herself more fyari tea. "Because we didn't know if what we had planned would work. None of us are wizards, after all. However, I agreed with Sapphire Wind and Zink that they had a claim on the books Dmen Qeres was destroying to fuel his book wraith. My only contribution was showing them how to fold the streamers then transporting them into the spell space."

"Why those streamers?" Xerak asked.

"Oh." Meg looked surprised. "In Japanese Shinto shrines, ropes hung with *shide* are used to mark something as special, as sacred. I learned to make *shide* when I was a librarian, as part of a cultural awareness project. I felt that by making *shide* from the damaged volumes—we used mostly journals, so as to have a wide representation of authors—we were reclaiming the value of those written works. I folded some, but the majority were made by Zink, assisted by Emsehu."

"Brilliant!" Uten Kekui said, toasting her with his drinking bowl.

Meg's fair skin showed her blush very clearly. "Our makeshift spell was such a long shot that I think you can see why I chose not to tell you in advance. If you had dared hope we could provide an extra edge, you might have done something foolhardy."

Xerak coughed one of his leonine laughs. "*More* foolhardy. I hadn't counted on the book wraith having such elaborate defenses. Although, given Dmen Qeres's personality, I probably should have."

Cerseru Kham patted him as if he was as young as Brunni. "You all did very well. We will check repeatedly over the next few days, but I think the book wraith, as well as the risk it posed, to the Library, and to Uten Kekui, is well and truly gone."

Although Teg basked in a sense of guarded triumph after their return, it didn't last. She half expected that they would find the

Library under attack at any moment. However, the group camped in the mountains had not made a decisive move. Speculation was that they were waiting for something.

Therefore, as soon as she recovered from her mana depletion, Teg returned to working with Wagh's crew, which was excavating the ruins of the laboratory and scriptorium. This area had been given priority over the hotel because there could be sensitive items amid the debris. Huy had made friends with the cargo hauler, and this had sped up the clearing away. Any beams and larger material that Wagh and Qwahua didn't think could be reused were being hauled down to the bank of the Qubhaneb, to provide, if not a barrier, then at least a further impediment.

Teg was screening a bucket of assorted junk when Sefex, one of the xuxu on watch down at the Qubhaneb, came flapping up, speaking as she circled the plaza.

"Two sennutep creeping from the mountains, but not the main trail, a side one. Tuau says they look uncertain and not dangerous. I am not so sure."

Teg set down her bucket. "I'll go!"

"Not by yourself," Wagh protested. He turned from where he was supervising something complicated involving winches and ropes. "We can't leave what we're doing right now, but give us ten minutes, and I'll send a few people with you."

"I'll ask Emsehu to go with me," Teg replied, pointing over to where the guardian was weeding one of the garden beds. "I don't think this should wait either. Sefex, tell the folks inside. Then catch up, and let me know when I can expect backup, okay?"

"Gotcha, Teg-toh!"

Teg felt Emsehu gently bump her leg with his nose. "I'm ready. Don't worry. I'll protect you."

"I know," Teg said, reaching down to tap him on the head. "That's why I wanted you with me. You've got to be the most terrifying groundskeeper this campus has ever had."

The pair walked briskly down the trail, Emsehu jogging alongside Teg, his crocodilian head swinging slightly side to side, alert to any threat before it could close. Once near the Qubhaneb, they stepped to where they would still be hidden from view by the forest, but could get a clear view of the stream. Two people stood on the far side of the ford—one quite tall, the other very short, both somehow familiar. Teg took out her binoculars.

"Nuzt and Kitet Un! I wonder what they want?"

She realized that Nuzt and Kitet Un had found a place behind some boulders where they were hidden from view from anyone coming down from the mountains, while visible from the riverside.

Sefex soared overhead and reported, "Xerak, Vereez, and Kaj are coming. They say, 'Wait up.'"

Teg ignored this. She'd liked Nuzt. Kitet Un had seemed honestly pathetic when they hadn't let her stay.

And then there's got to be a reason they didn't take the main trail, and why they are trying to hide. I don't think it's a great idea to leave them waiting.

"Tell Xerak, Vereez, and Kaj," she said to Sefex, paraphrasing Nero Wolfe's frequent guidelines to Archie Goodwin, "that I will act as dictated by intellect informed by experience."

As Teg moved ahead, she thought of the reasons the pair could be hiding like that. They could be waiting for dark, when they could cross with less chance of being seen—and given where they were waiting, they didn't care if people within the Sapphire Wind homestead saw them. Maybe they were waiting for one of the periodic patrols. They couldn't know for certain that the Rough Diamonds had posted scouts at key crossings, although given their last experience, they probably suspected it. She decided to act.

"Emsehu, you've got good natural armor, and you've met those two. Why don't you go down to the ford, just far enough so that you can invite them to cross without having to shout. Tell them they can take cover in the forest on this side, but not to try anything, that you have backup."

By way of reply, Emsehu waddled from the forest, his heavy tail held so it didn't bump too much across the gravelly shoreline. Out on the ford, he lowered his head as if to get a drink, then presumably delivered his message, because first Kitet Un, then Nuzt covering her, came hurrying across the ford. Emsehu followed them, closely, and Teg thought that if someone was watching, they might be uncertain as to whether he was acting as escort or as captor.

Emsehu herded the pair to where even a xuxu would have difficulty spying, and grunted, "Sit down on this log. The others often use it as a bench. Relax! I'm not going to eat you, not unless you give me good reason. I don't like eating people. Gives me mental indigestion."

This little speech gave Teg enough time to move to where she could emerge from cover without coming into reach. She leaned against a tree trunk and tried to look relaxed and confident. Kitet Un, who had looked worried, even though Emsehu hadn't offered any threat, let her ears rise in relief when she saw Teg.

"Teg-lial, do you remember me?"

"Absolutely. You're Kitet Un-va, part of one of the treasure hunting groups. You asked to stay, and we sent you home. Are you making another try? Are you with the group holed up in the mountains?"

"Yes, but well, yes, but not really, more like, it's not quite that simple."

The young wizard looked up at Nuzt, her large eyes pleading, her hands pulling at one long ear, like a more usual girl might tug at her hair. He took over.

"Kitet Un-va is making another try at joining you, and she hired me to help her. I agreed, since I didn't think she had a chance without a guard, and my conscience wouldn't let me send a kid out to get hurt."

Kitet Un's ears went straight up, horrified at being called a "kid," but she nodded agreement, if not acceptance.

Nuzt continued, "As for our relationship with the group in the mountains, it's complicated. Kitet Un-va was approached by Mennu Behes and Ha Uher to join a new, larger expedition. They figured she'd be eager, and in a way, they were right, but only in a way. Kitet Un-va, you'd better explain yourself."

Kitet Un took a deep breath. "I *am* eager, but I want to be part of the Library community, of rebuilding it, not be part of looting it. I decided to join, because that seemed like a safe way to get this far." Her voice dropped. "And there's no way I had enough allowance left to get me back all this way, even if I was sure I could convince you to let me stay. I needed something to trade, so I figured I could show my good faith by learning what the others planned, then sneaking off and telling you people."

Despite herself, Teg was impressed. If the terms "innocence" and "deviousness" could ever be said to go together, Kitet Un embodied them. She was thinking how to respond when Xerak's voice came from back along the trail.

"That's very interesting. Since the wind was in our favor, we decided to hear you out before coming forward. So, what do you have to tell us that will gain our confidence? Think carefully before you try out a clever lie. We do have other sources of information."

Kitet Un only nodded. "I'm not a liar! Really. And I meant what I said about not wanting to see the Library of the Sapphire Wind looted and divided up. It's just wrong."

Vereez walked forward and carefully knelt so she could look Kitet Un in the eye. "Tell us. You have my word that we'll listen, no more. But we will listen."

"But that's giving up all I have for no promise!"

"You should have thought of that before," Vereez said, as levelly as either of her parents might have done. "But we believe in giving fair value. You must believe that, deep down inside, or you never would have tried this."

Kitet Un folded her ears down, her nose wriggling in such evident consternation that Teg felt a touch of pity for her.

"You'll have guessed from what I said," Kitet Un began, speaking very quickly, "that the group in the mountains has people from Zisurru University. It has other people, too, though. Mercenaries, not just tough guides like Nuzt and his people, but the sort that are used to fighting if they don't get their way. The reason for the delay is that many of the wizards are recovering from the hike in, and the mercenaries won't move without them."

Nuzt clarified. "The mercs won't be looking for a fight, not if they can get what they want without combat, but they've been hired to bleed if necessary, and they'd rather someone else did the bleeding."

Teg's heart sank as she thought of their band of carpenters and plumbers, librarians and cooks. They'd all shown considerable bravery, but they weren't trained fighters. And a lot of the current residents weren't exactly young, either, or—like Brunni and the other little kids—far too young. And several of the young people were recovering from injuries. Vereez had been released from medical supervision, but still had to be careful of her leg. Kuvekt was still limiting what he'd let Tamildah and Grunwold do.

No matter how shorthanded we are, this would not be a good time to risk awakening more of the Archived. We've been very lucky with those we have awakened. We're going to need to solve this with what resources we have in hand.

Teg dragged her attention back to the discussion. Kitet Un, apparently thinking she hadn't offered enough, was chattering on.

"I can tell you something about the wizards. Most are younger, but a handful of faculty advisors came along. They're older, sure, but they have a lot of abilities between them. And then there are the weird people."

"Weird people? How weird?" Vereez asked.

If Vereez's gaze inadvertently skimmed over toward Teg, Teg tried not to be offended.

Kitet Un didn't notice. "They wore long cloaks, with the hoods up, covering everything. Ha Uher got a peep under one of the hoods, and he said they were wearing masks, the fancy sort, with magical enhancements. You couldn't tell anything about them except one was taller and bulkier, and the other on the small side. Neither of them smelled very good, so they were probably wearing some really horrible ointment to hide their scent, or that's what Mennu Behes thought."

Vereez's ears went flat, and Teg swallowed a sigh.

Inehem and Zarrq. The bad smell is probably whatever they're taking for mange, although they might have decided to hide their personal odor as well.

Teg spoke up. "Well, team? I think Kitet Un-va has at least earned the right to be cross-examined by some of the others. If Nuzt will promise to act only as her bodyguard, then I'll take his parole. He was honest with us last time."

"Agreed," Xerak said. He turned to Kitet Un. "One more question. Do you have names for the older wizards? And are any of them, perchance, in their fifties or older?"

"Yes, and I think so. Some are senior faculty. Some are really old, maybe even seventy! But, remember, older wizards are much more dangerous."

Xerak wrinkled his nose in something he meant as a smile, but looked rather too much like a snarl. "Good. Very good. We'll want as many names as you have. Then, well, it's just possible you'll get a chance to assist our senior librarian in her research."

Back at the Library, Kitet Un and Nuzt were taken inside for a more detailed interview. Extra xuxu were assigned to the borders. While this left the Rough Diamonds without internal communication, everyone agreed that the inconvenience was well worth having additional eyes on their borders. Heru was sent to warn Grace to be even more careful than usual.

"After all," Peg said, "we shouldn't count on an incursion coming only on one front, especially now that someone has to have noticed that Kitet Un and Nuzt are missing."

Nuzt nodded. "We did drop hints that Kitet Un was getting nervous, and I did say that I thought it likely she'd want to go home, but that doesn't mean someone might not check."

"Especially," Ohent added, "if those 'weird people' are who we suspect they are."

"I'm worried," Ranpeti added. "I'm not at all certain that dealing with large groups of hired mercenaries is within what those who drew up the homesteading charter had in mind when they said we needed to 'hold' our homestead, but before we can file an official protest, we may have been overrun."

Ohent spat a sound far too cynical to be termed a laugh. "Don't trust the courts, especially when a group of wizards is testifying how they rescued all these valuable texts from our incompetent hands. Who's to say the judges' pockets won't be full of coins or maybe a nice magical tidbit from the repository? You've never been down and out, Ranpeti-toh, so maybe you trust the law. I don't, not when it's us against magical power and wealth."

Vereez inclined her head in resignation. "Ohent-toh is right, Aunt Ranpeti. I've heard my parents talk about buying legal decisions. They've probably planned to do that from the start."

Grunwold gingerly rubbed the edge of the bandage around his head. "And who's to say a decision against us would be wrong? I mean, if we can't protect this place, as powerful and unpredictable as it is, should we really be able to lay claim to it? Maybe it would be wiser to have the collection broken up rather than keep facing this sort of thing. Maybe those insurance people who called the Library an attractive nuisance were right."

An uncomfortable silence followed this speech, then Peg tapped the table, using her fist as a soft gavel. "Assuming we're not going to quit . . . Does anyone believe we can win an all-out fight?"

Meg spoke quickly. "No, I don't. Our resources are limited. Theirs are only limited by how much Inehem and Zarrq are willing to spend. However, I refuse to surrender. Even if the Rough Diamonds decide to disband, I will not leave."

"Whoa!" Peg said. "I didn't say we should surrender. I asked if we could win an all-out fight. Happens that I agree with you on our chances on direct confrontation. That just means we need to be sneaky."

Teg grinned. "We're better at that anyhow."

Xerak put up a hand. "I have an idea for dealing with at least part of the problem. Ever since Kitet Un-va told us what we're up against, I've had a fragment of an idea. Meg, if we could manage to design a version of the spell the book wraith was using when it drained the texts to gain mana and create sub-wraiths, do you think you could find us works by the wizards Kitet Un-va tells us are out there?"

Meg's pale blue eyes glittered. "Oh, I think so, especially among the journals. Kitet Un-va said that some of the wizards might be really ancient, maybe even seventy." Her voice dripped with irony that Kitet Un probably missed, but none of the others did. "That means they would have been in their forties or fifties when the Library was a going concern."

Xerak looked at Uten Kekui and Cerseru Kham. "What do you think? You should already be partway there, since you figured out how to open up Dmen Qeres's book wraith spell. What I want is to adapt the mana draining so it goes through to the author."

"Nasty," Uten Kekui said, but his tone was admiring.

"And useful," Cerseru Kham added, "even if we can only reach a small number of them, the rest will be soundly unsettled. We'll get on it right away."

Kitet Un dug into her pack and came out with a fat textbook and a couple of scroll tubes. "These might help. I brought study materials. The textbook has work by some of the wizards; I can mark which. The scrolls are group assignments, and some of my study group are out there."

Teg found herself remembering that no matter how cute rabbits were, in more than one culture they had the reputation of being tricksters.

Meg rose and extended a hand to the young wizard. "Leave your textbook and scrolls with Uten Kekui and Cerseru Kham. Let's make a list of the wizards you mentioned being part of the incursion group. Then we'll see what Zink can help us find."

Nuzt asked, "May I assist?"

Meg nodded. She offered a tightlipped smile to the rest of them. "While we work on hobbling the wizards, the rest of you figure out how to deal with the rest of the problem."

Kitet Un paused. "Um, I have a small request."

"What?" Meg's voice was taut, clearly expecting something unpleasant.

"I noticed you call the storied Xerafu Akeru by a short name. May I ask you to drop the -va and just call me Kitun?"

Meg relaxed and smiled warmly. "Absolutely. Come along, Kitun. We have work to do."

"My parents," Vereez said, her voice hardly more than a whisper. Then she squared her shoulders and spoke more firmly. "I guess I could act as bait. Maybe set up a kidnapping or something? That would get me close to them, and maybe I could do something..."

"Charming of you to offer to put yourself at risk," Ohent said, "but unless you can think of a trap they'd walk into, bait isn't enough."

Nefnet's voice cut in, unexpected. Although as a charter member of the Rough Diamonds she sat in on as many strategy sessions as her other duties would permit, she rarely had much to say.

"While you were gone, Ohent and Ranpeti came to me with a possible plan," she said. "But I have an important question first. We believe Inehem and Zarrq have contracted mange, correct?"

"Yes," Xerak replied. "My mother wrote that in her recent letter. Kitun and Nuzt's report seems to confirm that."

Nefnet looked first at Vereez, then at Ranpeti. "I realize this is a very personal question, but does mange run in your family? It's caused by a sensitivity to a common skin parasite, not a disease or infection. My assumption is that the curse creates the sensitivity."

"I've never had it," Vereez replied.

"Nor I," Ranpeti added. "As I said earlier, I don't recall any of our family having it, either."

Nefnet steepled her fingers. "Then I feel I can make this suggestion without violating my ethical code, since what you've said raises the likelihood that their mange is due to their breaking the terms of the contract they signed as a condition for our releasing them.

"Why don't I offer Inehem and Zarrq a treatment for mange? When they were our captives after they attempted to kidnap Brunni from the Visage Isles, I interacted with them, since I was the closest to a doctor we had, and several members of their group needed medical treatment. I suggest that I send a message indicating that rumor has reached me that they have mange, that I have a treatment, and that I wouldn't at all mind padding my bank account."

"But how would a rumor have reached you?" Grunwold asked, clearly torn between a plan that would keep Vereez from needing to risk herself and wanting to make sure there were no holes in Nefnet's plan.

"They must know we're watching them," Nefnet replied, "and, as has been mentioned, the expedition certainly has missed Nuzt and Kitun by now. Certainly, Inehem and Zarrq would wonder what Nuzt and Kitun might have said about the expedition's mysterious cloaked and masked patrons. One thing I've noticed about people: if they're hiding something, then they tend to believe people will guess."

Peg nodded. "Even simpler. If they have broken the contract, then they will have activated the mange curse. If we're accusing Inehem and Zarrq unfairly . . ."

"But I bet we're not," Vereez muttered.

". . . then we don't need to deal with them, do we?" Peg concluded brightly. "Kitun's 'weird people' won't take this bait."

Nefnet looked very pleased at the group's reception of her plan. "Remember what Ohent-toh said when Vereez offered to be the bait, how bait wasn't enough, that we needed a trap?"

Peg nodded. "From the gleam in your eyes, you have a suggestion."

"Yes! My message will tell them they need to come to the hot springs. That will get them inside our borders, and in an area where the odor of the minerals in the water will mask the scent of those who go to capture them."

"The hot springs!" Grunwold did not look thrilled. "Are we certain the steam snakes are really gone?"

Xerak made a rocking gesture with one hand. "Fairly high chance that if not gone, too weak to be a threat. Kaj?"

"I've hiked down there to check," Kaj replied. "The mana is slowly rebuilding, but I don't think we need to worry about giant mu-serit for a long while, possibly ever again—unless there's another critical magical overload, that is."

Peg rubbed her hands together briskly. "Nefnet, is there anything in your plan that might create a critical magical overload?"

"I don't think so. It mostly involves convincing them to strip down and take a soak. That should leave even them vulnerable to capture."

Vereez spoke very carefully, as if the words hurt. "What do we do with them after we have them? We already know they'll break any agreement if they think the gain is great enough."

Ohent leaned across the table to pat her hand. "Sweetling, we won't kill them, if that's what you're worried about. I don't think any of us have the stomach for murder or executions in cold blood. Our homesteading charter is perfectly legal, and so we'll let the law do its part. I trust it for that—especially if we can defeat Inehem and Zarrq first."

Peg grinned. "We'll need to be careful not to violate our own nondisclosure contract, but I think we can hint that this isn't the first time Inehem and Zarrq have behaved in a vindictive manner toward both their daughter and Inehem's sister. I suspect we can get something like a restraining order issued to prevent them from further interference with our homesteading effort, either directly or through agents."

"I like it," Teg said. "It won't necessarily stop other treasure hunters, but it will stop them from operating on a grand scale. While I don't think we can fight off armies, we've shown we're up to smaller groups."

Grunwold added, "The names of the lawyers my parents consulted on the original homesteading charter are on that document. We can appeal to them."

"Good thought," Peg said. "We can also request that Inehem and Zarrq be fined to cover our costs, maybe even for excessive interference. Might not work, but it wouldn't hurt to ask. If we get more than we need to pay the lawyers, then we can use it to set up bonus accounts for the Unarchived, so if and when they decide to rejoin the modern world, they'll be in better financial shape."

"And something for Leeya and Septi," Teg put in.

"But the first step is to trap Inehem and Zarrq." Nefnet rose from the table. "I'm going to go research mange treatments."

"Seriously?" Vereez asked, her eyes wide. "Even with knowing why they have mange?"

Nefnet wrinkled her nose in an otter smile. "I never said I'd give the treatment to them for free, and Peg just reminded me how much nicer it is to be well-off than not. Besides, if we offer aid to those who have wronged us, we're going to look really good when it comes time for a review of our charter."

She trotted off, humming softly.

"We've been rotating which xuxu are spying on the camp," Grunwold said. "Tamildah probably knows which one to ask to find out who knows where these mysterious patrons are staying. Heru is used to flying at night, so he can drop the message. When do you think we should start this?"

Xerak leaned forward, his eyes shining. "Let's time it for when we're ready to set the adapted wraith spell on the wizards. I wish Inehem was old enough that she was likely to have been published, but she'd hardly have been older than I am when the Library went down."

"Worth checking," Teg said. "It's amazing how many professors use student research, then think they're being generous when they credit it in the small print. From what we saw in the vision in the Font, Inehem was quite talented, at least in certain types of magic."

Xerak pushed himself back from the table. "I'll go tell Meg and her research team to add Inehem to the list, then see if I can help. Sometimes I forget, but I was a bit of a scholar myself, once upon a time."

"Let me come with you," Kaj said. "I'm not a scholar, and it's time I learned at least a little about research. At the very least, I can haul books."

Grunwold was already up and heading off to consult with Tamildah. Ranpeti excused herself to look in on Brunni, Mwetor, and Sweks, who were "helping" Leeya in the kitchen.

That left Peg, Teg, and Vereez sitting at the long table, each lost in their own thoughts.

Vereez said softly, "I feel so very strange about this. Even after we learned how our parents had been 'extraction agents,' they seemed, I don't know, more adventurous than evil. Dynamic, not villains."

Peg squeezed her around the shoulders. "Honey, very few people think of themselves as villains. I'm sure Inehem and Zarrq convinced themselves they are being virtuous, even."

"Virtuous?"

"Peg's right," Teg said. "You won't believe the number of pot hunters who explain they were 'saving' valuable artifacts, not looting. The Library of the Sapphire Wind is a dangerous place, full of dangerous things. Looked at from the outside, having a small group of people—many of whom don't know much about magic—decide they can take care of it probably looks insane. I wouldn't be surprised if the Zisurru University group has convinced themselves they're being responsible. I mean, even Grunwold had doubts. Why shouldn't people who don't know us?"

Friba flapped over and landed on her accustomed perch. Teg had no doubt that Sapphire Wind had been listening to the other Rough Diamonds' discussion, even if its duties had taken its mouthpiece elsewhere. Now the spokes-parrot made a very good imitation of a throat-clearing sound to get their attention.

"Thank all of you for not abandoning the Library at this new crisis. No matter what anyone else thinks, I think we Rough Diamonds are the caretakers who can rebuild this Library . . . and I will support our fight in every way I can."

Teg knew she should feel encouraged by this, but there was a fierceness to how the words were spoken that made her very aware that one of the reasons the Library and its grounds were so dangerous was because of Sapphire Wind.

For now, we're all Rough Diamonds together. I'm glad. I'm really, really glad.

❧CHAPTER TWENTY❧

Cerseru Kham and Uten Kekui worked miracles in redesigning the book wraith's spell, but even so, the not quite two days that were needed to adapt the spell and to search the stacks for appropriate reference material seemed simultaneously to race by and to drag on forever. Even Grunwold and Vereez, who were coordinating border patrols, dropped in to help whenever they could. Xerak had been assigned to help his master and Cerseru Kham.

Teg joined those searching through the battered and damaged tomes, as did Peg. The translation spell which gave them fluency in all the languages—as long as the material wasn't overly stylized— made them of incalculable value. The wizards, Septi, Kuvekt, Nefnet, Ranpeti, and several others were all multilingual, but only the three mentors were what Peg cheerfully dubbed "omnilingual."

Kaj and Ohent were only fluent in the local language, but their work in various necropoli had given them immense patience when it came to rooting through dirty and otherwise unappealing areas. Thus, they had rapidly become among the most valuable members of the triage team. Ohent's particular coup was dredging her memory for who had been Inehem's teachers and tutors when they'd been in college together, then checking with methodical vindictiveness through which of their works were available until she found one where Inehem was listed among those thanked as research assistants.

"If Ohent thinks I'm going to let her go back to helping in the kitchen and grandmothering Brunni after this," Meg commented after Ohent nosed out yet another the journal they needed, "she's got another think coming."

The awareness that time was running out was so intense that Nefnet was even convinced to brew up bottle of baheh, a stimulant stronger than poffee or fyari tea, although the regularity with which either she or Kuvekt "just happened" by in the midst of their own duties showed they were concerned about the effect of no sleep and lots of drugs on their elder associates.

Teg didn't mind. She worried about how hard Meg was pushing herself, but knew better than to say anything. Despite how her creativity had been key to defeating the book wraith, Meg still seemed to have something to prove, to herself, if to no one else. Still, when Meg reached for the bottle of baheh and caught Teg looking at her, then at her watch, Meg spoke softly.

"Teg, stop it. What do I really have to save myself for? I told you I wanted to move Over Where eventually, and if I can figure out how to do it without hurting my family, I still want to. But I can't if there is no Library."

Teg snorted. "And what good would you be to the Library if you have a stroke? You're not the only one working on this. Be reasonable."

Meg looked around the reading room where tattered works were being reviewed. "You have a point." And she reached for the carafe of water instead.

When Uten Kekui and Cerseru Kham, trailed by Xerak, emerged up the stairs from the repository, which they'd co-opted as their research lab, carrying the stack of paper upon which they had written the details of their spell, works by many of those Kitun and Nuzt had identified as being part of the expeditionary force had been located.

"I'm sorry," Meg said, "that we couldn't find works by all of them, and in some they're only listed as research aides, and that might not be enough."

"You've all done wonders," Cerseru Kham said, scanning the list Ohent handed to her. "We didn't think you'd find so many, and so we adapted an aspect of the wraith spell to make certain our warning would be clear."

Uten Kekui gestured to Grunwold. "The manner of your injury, while regrettable, gave us an idea. We found a work by the wizard whose shield reflected the force of your arrow back onto you. We adapted his methods, and now whatever spell is used against us will instead be reflected into a doppelgänger of the caster. The doppelgänger will appear in the immediate vicinity of the caster, leaving no doubt of the consequences of using magic against us. We're calling these 'mirror wraiths.'"

Grunwold had dispensed with the bulk of his bandaging the day before, but still wore one of Teg's bandanas to cover the remainder of the wound. It gave him a rakish, piratical look.

"I can't say I'm glad I got conked out," he said, "but I'm glad you found a good use for that spell."

"How long before you have the spells activated?" Vereez asked. "We've a letter ready to be dropped on the 'mysterious patrons,' and can do it as soon as tonight."

Xerak grinned. "The great thing is that we have five wizards right here to set up the spell, since you, me, and Kitun can also cast it, while Teg and Kaj can stand by to provide mana. The mirror wraith spell will stay dormant unless someone attacks us. Then, as in the book wraith spell, the majority of the mana will come from the attackers via their written works."

"And if no one attacks us," Peg said, cheerfully, pushing back from the table, and brushing herself off, "no one gets hurt. It's really very elegant indeed."

For a note that ran only a few lines, a lot of people contributed details. Since Inehem and Zarrq would surely suspect that the fords and trails were being watched, a route to the hot springs had to be suggested. Remembering the hike down to the Qubhaneb with the cargo hauler, Teg suggested that the narrow overflow creek would be a good option.

"Since we didn't want to risk flooding, it's only lightly blocked by the stuff we've cleared from the plaza. They can get through, but they'll need to sneak, so they won't feel it's too easy."

"Yeah," Vereez said. "Let them figure out how to get across the Qubhaneb. We might learn a thing of two about their invasion plans that way."

The time for the meeting was set for the equivalent of about 2:00 a.m., which had the virtue of allowing plenty of after dark sneak-around time. They didn't bother writing anything like "come alone," but they did include "This is a one-time offer, because I can't be certain of getting away unseen at another time, especially since the situation is likely to escalate."

Heru and Uah airdropped the message as soon as evening had darkened sufficiently to provide cover. After Heru reported the drop-off completed, the Rough Diamonds and their allies began slipping away in small groups to take up their posts.

"We can't be absolutely certain Inehem and Zarrq don't have their own spies here," Peg said, "but since ours include xuxu, I think we'd be alerted to any critters hanging out around here."

"I think we're probably unobserved," Ohent said. "Remote viewing is far harder than the stories say. It's possible, but not for long periods of time."

"And," Xerak reminded, "if any of the wizards tries anything against us, they'll be facing the consequences. Quite literally 'facing,' if our mirror wraith spell works."

There had been some concern that the mirror wraith spell might manifest early and cause enough concern that Inehem and Zarrq wouldn't take the bait. Ohent countered with her own theory, which was the reason that Nefnet and her backup weren't going to be the only ones out and about that night.

"What better way for them to arrange cover than to have an attack arranged for that same night? That would give them an excuse for going off on their own, and directing attention away from where they're meeting with Nefnet."

The three mentors were stationed in different areas that night. Meg was remaining at the Library. Peg was with Grunwold on *Slicewind*, which was assigned to go wherever the ship would be most needed. Tamildah was aboard as well, serving as xuxu coordinator.

That left Teg to join the group protecting Nefnet—and hopefully dealing with Inehem and Zarrq. Xerak, Vereez, Ohent, and Kaj were on that team as well. Peynte had been assigned the role of Nefnet's visible bodyguard, since no one would expect Nefnet to go through the forests at night unaccompanied.

If Teg had had her way, Vereez and Ohent, both of whom had far too much baggage where Inehem and Zarrq were concerned, would have been elsewhere, but neither would be persuaded to stay away. Where Ohent went, so did her son.

Uten Kekui was providing wizardly support to the riverside team, while Cerseru Kham and Kitun stayed at the Library. Sapphire Wind's various guardian creatures, most of which usually went about their business unseen and largely overlooked, had been called forth in force, and Teg rather pitied any trespasser who got within their range. The dobergoats in particular were extremely territorial, but the lizard parrots who were lurking on the rooftop would be an unpleasant surprise for anyone thinking to get in that way.

Peg had reported that the piranha toads, which these days were usually only glimpsed when they emerged from the lake to hunt around the lakeshore, were out in force tonight, so Sapphire Wind had probably extended her influence to them as well.

When Teg left with Vereez, Kaj, Ohent, and Xerak, Peg called over *Slicewind*'s siderail, "Remember to bring 'em back alive."

Teg didn't think the reminder was as joking as Peg made it sound. Vereez was particularly grim that night. When they arrived at the hot springs, they took up hiding places near a pool not much larger than the sort of hot tub meant to seat six or so. Xerak suggested that Ohent and the xuxu Sass keep watch while the rest of them meditated. Teg honestly tried but, even with Petros's help, she was pretty restless. From what she could feel, Vereez wasn't doing much better.

Near 1:30 a.m., Heru glided in and whispered, "Attack near th' north ford. Spell workin'. All goin' real good."

Teg strained her ears, but, of course, didn't hear anything. At about 1:45, the four sennuteps' ears all twitched, but as no one moved, Teg was not surprised when Nefnet and Peynte emerged from the forest trail. Nefnet headed directly for the designated pool, placing it between herself and where Inehem and Zarrq could be expected to emerge. She set a few lanterns with their mantles angled to illuminate the pool just a little, and started laying out items from her pack. Peynte, looking suitably fierce in some of the armor Fardowsi had scrounged, holding a hammer chosen for its similarity to the construction tools he routinely used, knives and hatchets bristling on his belt, hovered nearby. If he looked edgy, well, that only made sense.

Shortly before 2:00, the appointed hour, there was the sound of splashing from the direction of the creek. Teg was surprised that Inehem and Zarrq weren't trying harder to conceal their approach. She saw her companions, all of whom had better night vision than she did, looking suspiciously about, as if expecting a trick, but as no one broke cover, she guessed they didn't see anything.

She decided to keep her eyes on where Nefnet was, since the lantern light did help her see what was going on. When the two cloaked figures emerged from the vicinity of the creek, Teg had another surprise. She'd expected Inehem and Zarrq to come with retainers, but there were only the two of them.

Maybe it's not them. Maybe it's a couple of their retainers, disguised, coming to scout.

But, when the taller of the two cloaked figures pushed back the hood of his cloak, it was—even with his head horribly disfigured by mange—definitely Vereez's father. He was a far cry from the ferociously elegant person they had fought two months before. There were bald patches and scabs, but also areas where the fur looked so puffy that the lines of his head were distorted. His shiny black nose leather was bright pink in places, and his small round ears were bumpy with sores.

With the memory still fresh of how he had nearly taken Vereez's arm off during their last encounter, Teg would never have thought she could have felt pity for Zarrq, but she did. Glancing over at Vereez, she was relieved to see her jaws agape in evident horror.

Thank heavens. I don't know what I would have thought of Vereez if she'd still looked so grim or, worse, glad.

When Inehem dropped her own hood, the destruction of her once gorgeous Artic fox head was, if anything more extensive. Teg looked away, her gorge rising.

"What made you risk this?" Vereez asked, rising from cover, the others following her lead.

Inehem raised her hood and spoke from its shadow. "Tell them, Zarrq. You've told me what I did wrong often enough."

Zarrq did not raise his own hood. "Inehem has great skill in magics associated with healing. She thought she could use those to prepare a fail-safe treatment for mange. As you can see, it didn't work. Once we had nothing to lose"—he gave a loose-limbed shrug—"we decided to go after the Library."

Inehem laughed in a fashion that reminded Teg of Ohent before she had relinquished custody of the Bird of Ba Djed and begun to regain her sanity.

"There is great power, great knowledge, both hidden in the Library of the Sapphire Wind. With them I am certain I could reverse the mange, maybe even drive the curse back upon its caster."

Xerak said softly, "That would be your first error, for you yourself are the caster of the curse. That is what happens when you break a curse-protected contract with full knowledge of what you have done."

"So wise, for someone whose mane has barely grown in," Inehem retorted with a shrill laugh. "Just wise enough to be a fool. We may take the Library yet."

Zarrq shook his head. "I think not. Wizards are chancy allies, much more difficult to coordinate than I ever imagined. Moreover, knowing they would be vulnerable when they started casting their magics, they insisted on delay after delay as they tried to prepare for every eventuality."

Inehem pealed laughter. "I never made that mistake at least, hey, my darling? I trusted you to keep me safe and did whatever was needed. Now you have trusted me and I have failed, and you are itching your way into hatred. One error! One error!"

She fell to cackling softly to herself.

"I don't hate you," Zarrq said. He directed his gaze at Nefnet. "Was this all a trap or can you truly cure our mange?"

"I could not live with myself if I did not at least try," Nefnet said. "I had no idea how terrible the affliction would be."

Xerak said, "I suspect the repeated breaking of the contract has made the little creatures you said cause the mange more ferocious." He looked unflinchingly at Zarrq's mutilated features. "If you take an oath to surrender, it is more likely whatever Nefnet does will ameliorate the mange. The mange mites are guardians of the contract you violated. They will know if you intend to turn on us as soon as opportunity arises, and will react accordingly."

Zarrq raised a hand as if to rub a battered ear, then forced it to drop. "I would surrender not only my ambition to take the Library, but also even help you take it into your custody. My first step would be to tell those we have stood as patrons to that I withdraw my support. I can only hope Inehem will do the same. She did not attack out of malice, only because she thought she had found the loophole in the penalty clause. We have spent much of our lives exploiting loopholes and profiting from doing so."

Inehem snuffled what might have been a sob. "I really thought I was skilled enough, powerful enough. I was wrong. Now I am deformed and miserable and can hardly sleep more than an hour at a time. I am done with trying to find loopholes in this contract. It is stronger than I am."

"If you are sincere," Nefnet said, "then we can try. I remind you again: Do not think you can be healed and then return to your ways. Even if I were to give you my formula in every detail, the mange is attuned to truth, and the mange is without pity."

"There are other games to play, other loopholes to exploit, none of which involve the House of Rough Diamonds," Inehem replied. "If I find the need rising, there is no shortage of opportunities."

"Maybe," Ohent said, "you should remember what we all dreamed of years and years ago, when we were even younger than my son, than your daughter. We helped as much as exploited in those days."

Nefnet motioned toward the steaming pool. "We will begin there."

Teg definitely did not want to stay to watch. She knew herself a coward, shying from illness and disfigurement, so she framed her retreat in a nobility of spirit she did not feel.

"Nefnet, how many assistants do you need? I'm worried about the others, even if there hasn't been a call for backup. At least some of us should get to the Qubhaneb."

"If Ohent would stay, along with one of the xuxu, in case we need something"—assistance in case of treachery went unspoken, but a thin stream of laughter came out from under Inehem's hood—"I think we can handle matters. Much of the treatment involves soaking in the waters of the pool while I add a variety of concoctions."

"I'll stay," Ohent replied promptly. "Give me a chance to catch up with my former associates, discuss plans for the future."

Teg didn't think she was the only one to be relieved, but Kaj's ears pinned back in a frown.

"Are you certain, Mother? I could stay."

"They'll need both your muscles and your magic if the wizards won't see sense," Ohent said. "Xerak may need you to bolster his mana. Go along. I don't expect any trouble. First though, perhaps Zarrq could write a note in his guise as patron? It may be of use."

Zarrq did not protest. Once Vereez had the note in hand, they left, using the route via the feeder stream to the Qubhaneb.

Unspoken was that, this way, they could check if Inehem and Zarrq had left any backup.

Sass flying above them, Vereez and Peynte hurried ahead. Vereez was now as eager to get away from her parents as she had been to confront them a short while before. Xerak and Kaj hung back to escort Teg, since her night vision was not as good as theirs. As Teg picked her way along by flashlight, trying not to wrench an ankle or twist a knee on the uneven footing, she heard Xerak speak to Kaj.

"I'm not saying don't worry about your mom, because I'm seriously good at worrying about people I care about, but remember, Ohent-toh is one seriously tough lady."

"She is," Kaj replied, his voice full of pride, "but I've spent just about all of my life looking out for her, one way or another. It's hard to get over that in just a few months, especially since every so often, she still breaks down."

"She won't today." Xerak's tone held no doubt. "Not with Inehem to show up. Those two were never friends—associates, sure, but not buddies."

"Inehem always had Zarrq to back her up," Kaj said. "It made her both stronger and weaker. She could do her magics without worrying about the consequences, but, well, worrying about consequences is important."

"Warning me?" Xerak chuckled.

"Sure. And Teg-toh, who keeps draining herself and falling over," Kaj said. He glanced over at Teg, panting a canine smile. "Peg-toh told me that 'break a leg' is a charm against bad luck in your culture, but, seriously, don't risk it. You won't be any good to anyone if you do."

Teg paused to catch her breath and rub her right knee, which had started to throb after an unwise jump between a couple of rocks, one of which had wobbled. "Promise. No risks."

The trio reached the Qubhaneb without undue injury, and also without finding any trace that Zarrq and Inehem had brought backup.

Really, the sharper sense of smell so many of the sennutep have is a great advantage in such things.

Downstream, near the northern ford, where they had fought the spike wolves, something that wasn't a battle was going on. The wizards had supplied artificial illumination, so the scene had something of the unreality of a stage seen from the darkened seats in the audience.

A large group of elaborately robed people were clustered on the far bank, the Rough Diamonds' much smaller group on the near. *Slicewind* hung, bow pointing west, in the air directly over the Qubhaneb, on the north side of the ford. The ship wasn't floating on the water, but near enough to get splashed. Teg pulled out her binoculars and took a closer look.

Peg stood at *Slicewind's* portside rail, looking down at a coyote-headed wizard robed in a dark blue that went very well with his golden-brown fur. He stood on the widest of the stones that made up the ford, hands clasped around a staff of highly polished, golden-brown wood inlaid with gems in a variety of blues and topped with a long crystal of purplish smokey quartz. Peg's expression was one of impish satisfaction. The wizard spokesperson was pretending to ignore her, his gaze fixed on the eastern bank, specifically on the trail that led back toward the Library.

"Everyone seems to be waiting, I'm not sure for what." Teg shifted her angle of vision. The treasure hunters on the far bank seemed less than confident, this despite the fact that they outnumbered the defenders at least three to one. "Several of the wizardy sorts are sitting down, looking not too well."

"I recognize the wizard out on the ford," Xerak said, "Sepa Khesbedji. Let's hurry. There seems to be a truce of some sort, but who knows how long it will last? We three could tip the balance in our side's favor."

"Go on ahead," Teg said. "I'll catch up."

The young men loped off. Teg picked her way along the riverbank, arriving just as a small group emerged from the forest trail. Meg led the way, followed by little Kitun, walking with a stiff formality that did not quite hide that she was very nervous. They were escorted by Nuzt and Emsehu.

From *Slicewind*, Peg spoke in her best "mom" voice, which managed to be far more intimidating than any other sort could be. "Some of you people justified your earlier intrusion by saying we had taken one of your own captive, although I think at least Mennu Behes and Ha Uher could have provided another perspective. Still, we won't be able to move ahead until that issue is settled. Kitet Un-va, would you like to speak for yourself?"

Kitun walked out onto the first of the stepping-stones. "I wasn't taken captive. I wanted to stay here last time, but the Rough Diamonds wouldn't let me, but they were kind, so I decided to take a risk, especially since I thought what you people were doing stank."

"'Stank'?" boomed Sepa Khesbedji. "Nay! To leave a place rife with uncontrolled magic in the hands of amateurs is unconscionable."

Meg called from the riverbank, "Who are you calling an amateur? I have been a librarian for over fifty years, and I volunteered in libraries before that. What do you know about libraries?"

"Me, specifically," Sepa Khesbedji gave a self-deprecatory chuckle, "how to use one, how to appreciate one, but there are those in our number who are librarians."

He made as if to motion someone forward from the group still on the western bank, but Meg cut him off with an imperious gesture of her own. "Do any of those have even close to my years of experience?" She paused and scanned the group. Teg knew how intimidating that pale blue-eyed gaze could be. She suspected that it was far more so to people unaccustomed to the human face. "I thought not."

"You may be a librarian," Sepa Khesbedji countered, "but are you skilled in the magical arts? Can you deal with the undoubted myriads of cataclysmic effects that will be uncovered?"

"We've done fine thus far," Meg said, stilling an abortive gesture to where the acid bat had burned her. "And even if I have no magic, several members of our company are quite skilled. Perhaps you do not recognize the great Uten Kekui-va? He is a charter member of the House of Rough Diamonds, as is his former apprentice, Xerafu Akeru. And others in our company have great talent, but we will not make your next assault easier by revealing their names to you."

Peg took over. "We are neither kidnappers nor incompetents. Shall we move to what you're risking if you keep annoying us? From up here, I can see that many of your number have been injured or are clearly suffering from mana depletion. Did you think this is pure coincidence?"

Even from her place away from the action, Teg could see the

ripple of unease that went through the gathering. From her slightly elevated post, Peg smiled at something Teg couldn't see.

"I think every culture," Peg said, "has some variation on the Golden Rule. How did you feel as what you were prepared to do unto others was done unto you? Not much fun, really, seeing yourself as your opponent would see you?"

Sepa Khesbedji dodged a direct reply, asking instead, "Your reach extends so far beyond your borders?"

"As to all places where knowledge, not wealth or weapons rule." Peg half sang the words, the voice that had once (so she claimed) nearly beaten out Grace Slick for a place in Jefferson Airplane, reverberating loud and strong. "And you would be well put to remember that, lest you be taken for a fool. The Library of the Sapphire Wind is not abandoned any more, we and we alone are welcome beyond its doors!"

Peg returned to her more normal fashion of speech. "Although, we may accept applications for visiting researchers once we have a new hotel built. Look for brochures to be delivered to all institutions of learning that don't piss us off."

After that, as Peg put it afterward, it was a matter of mopping up the mess. Vereez came forward with Zarrq's letter, and insisted on sharing it not only with Sepa Khesbedji, but with an eagle-headed woman Nuzt identified as the leader of the mercenaries. Since most of the would-be treasure hunters had not cast attack spells, and since even those spells they had cast had been bounced back by the mirror wraiths on their casters with diminished effect, there were no severe injuries.

As a gesture of goodwill, Kuvekt shared some ointments from Nefnet's pharmacological lab. This, along with a great deal of thoughtful uncertainty regarding what other tricks the Rough Diamonds had in waiting, started off the negotiations quite well. When, a few hours later, the mysterious patrons, reeking even to Teg's human nose of sulfur and strange ointments, appeared and publicly confirmed that they would no longer support any trespass—even hinted that they would in fact work against such—what resistance remained melted.

"It probably didn't hurt," Peg said, when Teg joined her aboard *Slicewind* for the short sail back to the Library campus, "that Inehem and Zarrq made clear their prior promise to supply transport back to Zisurru University was only good for those who were prepared to depart more or less immediately."

Meg, who had also come aboard, rather than hiking back, sighed contentedly and sipped from her bowl of fyari. "Nor did it hurt that once the threat of violence was ended, Cerseru Kham and Uten Kekui took point on the negotiations. You, dear Peg, did a brilliant job playing the role of monstrous guardian, but it saved face for the wizards to negotiate with their own."

"No curse to back up the agreement this time," Teg said. "I don't know if I should worry about that or not."

"Don't," Grunwold said from where he stood at the wheel. "I may not be my mom's equal when it comes to reading a customer, but I know enough to read that sort. They were thrilled to challenge us when they felt they had both moral justification and all the good cards. Once they had neither, all they wanted to do was go home and figure out how to make it sound as if we hadn't trounced them."

"And," Meg said, "while we didn't lay any curses, we did promise to withdraw the mirror wraiths only if we were not troubled again. The threat of finding their own magics turned on them will make them behave."

"I'm glad," Teg said. "I'd much rather get back to excavation and analysis than deal with a possible pitched battle."

"We're not done with opportunists," Peg said, "but I think we're done with the sort who think we can be bulldozed."

Grunwold snorted. "Great . . . Now we just need to worry about the sneaky sort, like my parents were."

"Well, we have Ohent, Konnel, and Fardowsi, and maybe even, someday, Inehem and Zarrq, to advise us," Teg said.

"And," Peg said with a grin, "some of us could teach them a thing or two about being sneaky."

But the wizards of Zisurru University had one more surprise for them. Not quite a week after the confrontation, Konnel and Sefit sailed in on *Cloud Cleaver* with a small contingent of what Peg immediately dubbed "suits," even though they were clad in somber versions of the common tunic and trousers, which looked nothing at all like suits.

"These are members of the review board in charge of your homesteading charter," Sefit said. "At the request of Zisurru University, supported by the House of Fortune, they have come to make an inspection of your progress."

At the sound of her parents' business identity, Vereez emitted a low growl, but otherwise everyone who'd gathered to welcome the new arrivals simply stood stunned.

After introducing her colleagues, the spokesperson for the board, a pert leopard-headed woman named Damdahr, said, almost apologetically, "We did not send notification in advance, because this way we could honestly say that you of the House of Rough Diamonds and your retainers had not prepared a show for us. Those who approached us suggested that it would be best for the Library, and the potential danger it represents, if your charter was confirmed sooner rather than later. In that way, treasure hunters or the ambitious and idealistic would no longer feel they had a claim on the area, and you would be better supported by the law of the surrounding governing bodies against such incursions."

"Oh," said Peg, who had clearly been preparing to give the review board a piece of her mind. "Oh. Really? Well, where would you like to start?"

The inspection lasted for many hours. The board turned out to have specialist groups trained to inspect everything from the condition of the structures to the well-being of the residents. Zink, Emsehu, and others of the more outré guardians made a definite impression. Sapphire Wind manifested as a larger than usual sparkling blue tornado and spoke eloquently through Friba about the Library's condition, rehabilitation, and, without quite threatening, about how the Library's *genius loci* was very content with its role as a charter member of the Rough Diamonds, and would not welcome other caretakers.

Their case was not hurt when Uten Kekui revealed that he believed himself to be the reincarnation of Dmen Qeres, and that he was completely unwilling to challenge the Rough Diamonds' claim to the library he had founded in a past life. Kitun spoke with intensity about how well she'd been treated, even when she'd been a trespasser, and of her hope to become a librarian under Meg. Meg hadn't told her "no" this time, only, "We'll need to speak with your family."

When the review board left two days later, Uten Kekui went with them, as did Nefnet and Ranpeti, to represent the Rough Diamonds at the official transferring of the property. When *Cloud Cleaver* lifted, everyone, from Unarchived to Zink and Friba, came out to see them off.

"It really was to our favor that they showed up unannounced," Peg said, patting Grunwold, who remained somewhat miffed that his parents hadn't sneaked some sort of advanced warning to them. "Seeing that we're still practically camping, with just one partially useful building, didn't hurt at all."

Tamildah nodded agreement and reached to take Grunwold's hand. She'd talked with the board at great length about how she'd been injured by the steam snake, and her still livid skin had been testimony to the dangers they had faced. Vereez only looked pleased at Tamildah's proprietary attitude, and Xerak gave a satisfied sigh. If his gaze slid toward Kaj, who was standing next to Ohent, watching *Cloud Cleaver* sail into the distance, well, that was a matter for another day.

"Really, Grun, your dad's so sneaky that he knows when not to be sneaky," Tamildah said. "I liked him and your mom a lot. We had some wonderful talks."

Teg suspected that Grunwold would have blushed at Tamildah's public claiming of him, if he'd been capable, but he didn't pull his hand away either.

Teg started to reach for a celebratory cigarette, then reconsidered, and slid the pack back into a pocket in her cargo pants and picked up her dig kit instead.

We've won and this is a time for new beginnings. Maybe I'll even quit smoking.